Giants, Trolls, Witches, Beasts

Ten Tales from the Deep, Dark Woods

Craig Phillips

ALLEN & UNWIN
SYDNEY · MELBOURNE · AUCKLAND · LONDON

Australian Government

This project has been assisted by the Australia Council for the Arts Children's Picture Book Illustrators' Initiative, managed by the Australian Society of Authors.

First published by Allen & Unwin in 2017

Allen & Unwin
83 Alexander Street
Crows Nest NSW 2065
Australia
Phone: (61 2) 8425 0100
Email: info@allenandunwin.com
Web: www.allenandunwin.com

A Cataloguing-in-Publication entry is available
from the National Library of Australia
www.trove.nla.gov.au

ISBN 978 1 76011 326 1

'Vasilisa the Brave' on p1 retold from 'Vasilissa the Fair' by Alexander Afanasyev, translated by William Ralston Shedden Ralston in *Russian Folk-tales*, published by R Worthington, New York, 1880, pp158–166

'Thor and the Frost Giants' on p25 retold from 'Thor's Visit to Hymir' by Peter Andreas Munch in the revision of Magnus Olsen, translated by Sigurd Bernhard Hustvedt in *Norse Mythology: Legends of Gods and Heroes*, published by the American-Scandinavian Foundation, New York, 1926, pp 65–69

'The Nixie in the Well' on p47 retold from 'The Water Nixie' by Jacob & Wilhelm Grimm, translated by Margaret Hunt in *Household Tales*, published by George Bell, London in 2 volumes, 1884 & 1892

'Snow White and Rose Red' on p67 retold from story by Jacob & Wilhelm Grimm, translated by Margaret Hunt in *Household Tales*, published by George Bell, London in 2 volumes, 1884 & 1892

'Momotaro' on p83 retold from 'Momotaro, or the story of the Son of a Peach', translated by YT Ozaki in *Japanese Fairy Tales*, published by AL Burt Company, New York, 1905

'The King of the Polar Bears' on p107 retold from story by L Frank Baum in *American Fairy Tales*, published by George M Hill Company, Chicago, 1901

'The Boy Who Was Never Afraid' on p123 retold from story by Alfred Smeberg, published in Swedish in the *Among Gnomes and Trolls* anthology no. 6, 1912

'The Devil Bridegroom' on p139 retold from 'Miscellaneous Stories of the Devil', compiled and translated by WF Kirby in *The Hero of Esthonia, and Other Studies in the Romantic Literature of That Country*, published by John C Nimmo, London, 1905, pp186–187

'Finn McCool' on p159 retold from the story from the Fenian Cycle of Gaelic mythology

'The Wawel Dragon' on p173 retold from 'The Dragon of Wawel Hill' by Wincenty Kadłubek, Bishop of Kraków, published in Polish in *Chronicles of the Kings and Princes of Poland*, 1190–1208

Early versions of these Craig Phillips retellings of 'Thor and the Frost Giants' (© 2013), 'Snow White and Rose Red' (© 2012) and 'The Boy Who Was Never Afraid' (© 2011) first appeared in *The School Magazine*, NSW Department of Education, Australia.

Inks for 'Momotaro', 'The Devil Bridegroom' and 'Finn McCool' by Latifah Cornelius
Cover and text design by Sandra Nobes
Set in Komika by Sandra Nobes
This book was printed in March 2018 at Everbest Printing Co Ltd in Guangdong, China.

3 5 7 9 10 8 6 4 2

www.craigphillips.com.au

Contents

For Maria, Eli and Latifah

Introduction

People have always loved scary stories full of evil ogres, spiteful witches and monstrous creatures that are up to no good. Many of these myths and folktales were created hundreds of years ago as oral tales – stories that were spoken aloud by storytellers. People young and old would gather to listen spellbound to the terrifying tales. They'd gasp when it seemed like the monster would win, and cheer when the hero, often an innocent boy or girl, was finally victorious.

Stories from different places have their own local heroes and villains. They also have their own distinctive details – a house with chicken legs, a witch with green hair, an exploding dragon.

At first, people listened to the storyteller's words and then created images of giants, witches and magic mountains in their heads. Later, the stories were written down and published in books containing, perhaps, one or two drawings to illustrate each story.

Craig Phillips has joined that long line of storytellers and has chosen his favourite tales to retell. Like storytellers of old, Craig uses his own words to describe the magical places, the strange and scary monsters and the simple heroes who save the day. He has added a dash of humour. But, more excitingly, Craig has brought these ancient stories to life in graphic novel style. They are illustrated by glorious pictures, not just a few, but hundreds of them.

Giants, Trolls, Witches, Beasts is not only a collection of terrific tales from around the world; it is also a feast for the eyes.

CAROLE WILKINSON
bestselling author of the Dragonkeeper series

Vasilisa the Brave

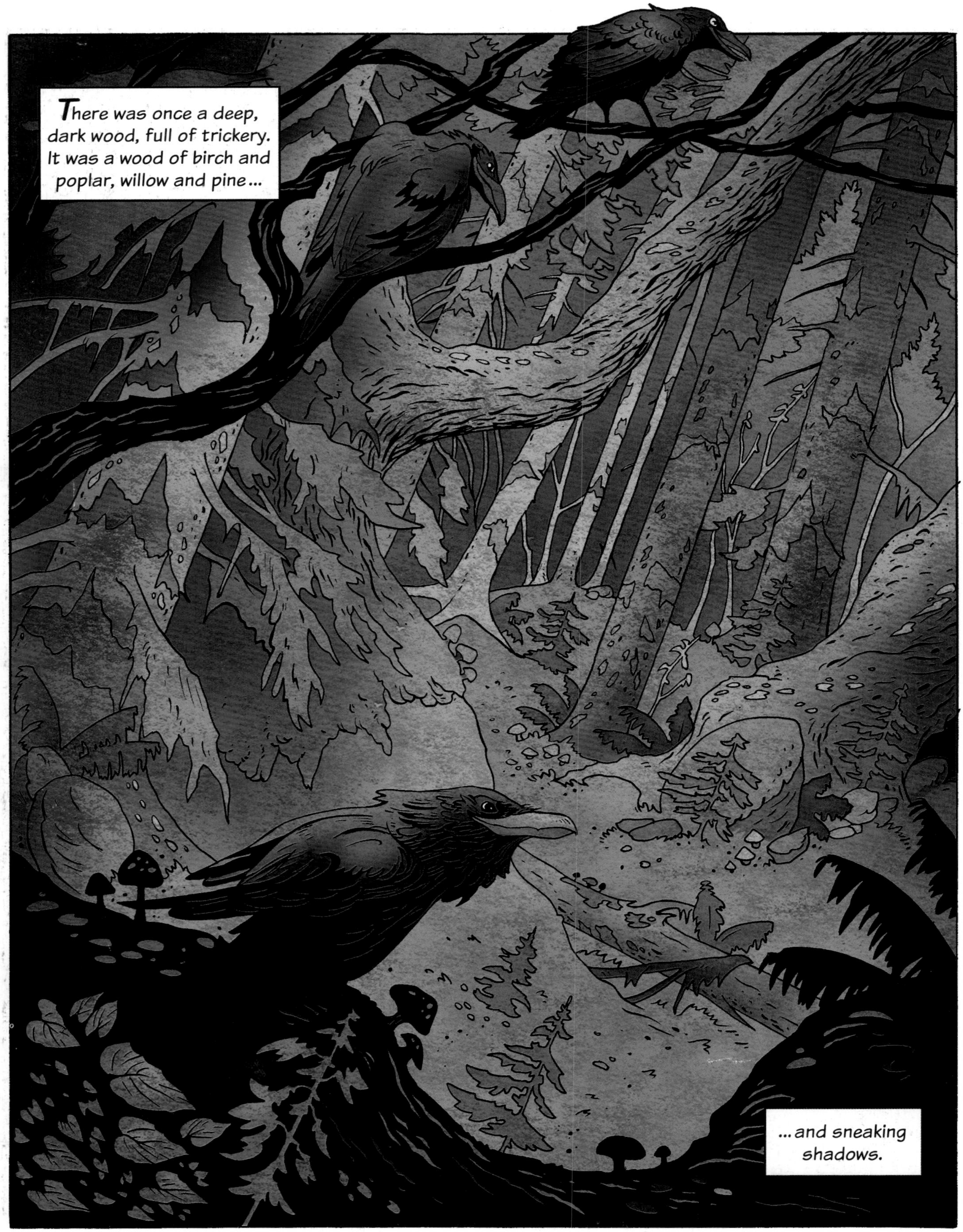
There was once a deep, dark wood, full of trickery. It was a wood of birch and poplar, willow and pine...
...and sneaking shadows.

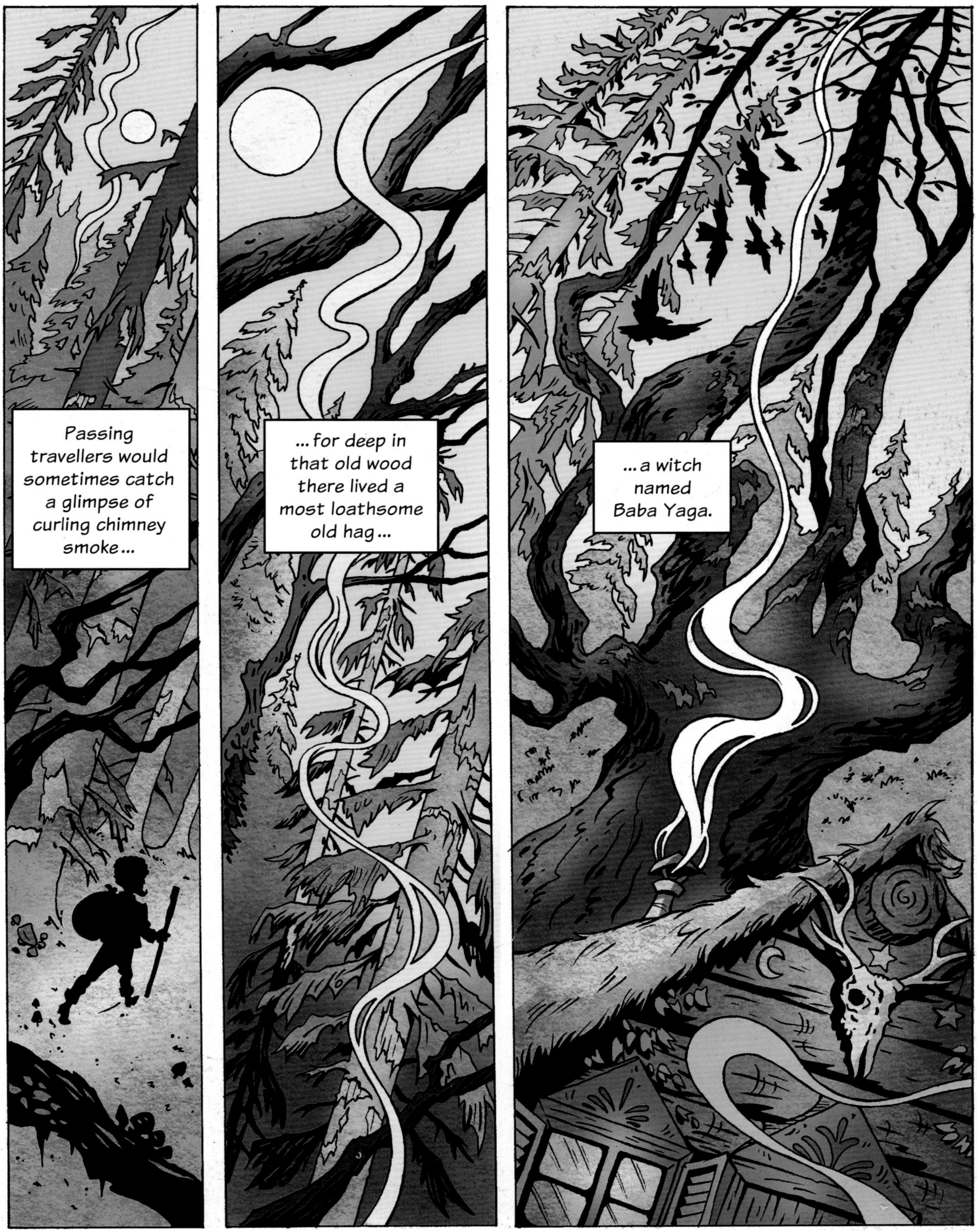
Passing travellers would sometimes catch a glimpse of curling chimney smoke...
...for deep in that old wood there lived a most loathsome old hag...
...a witch named Baba Yaga.

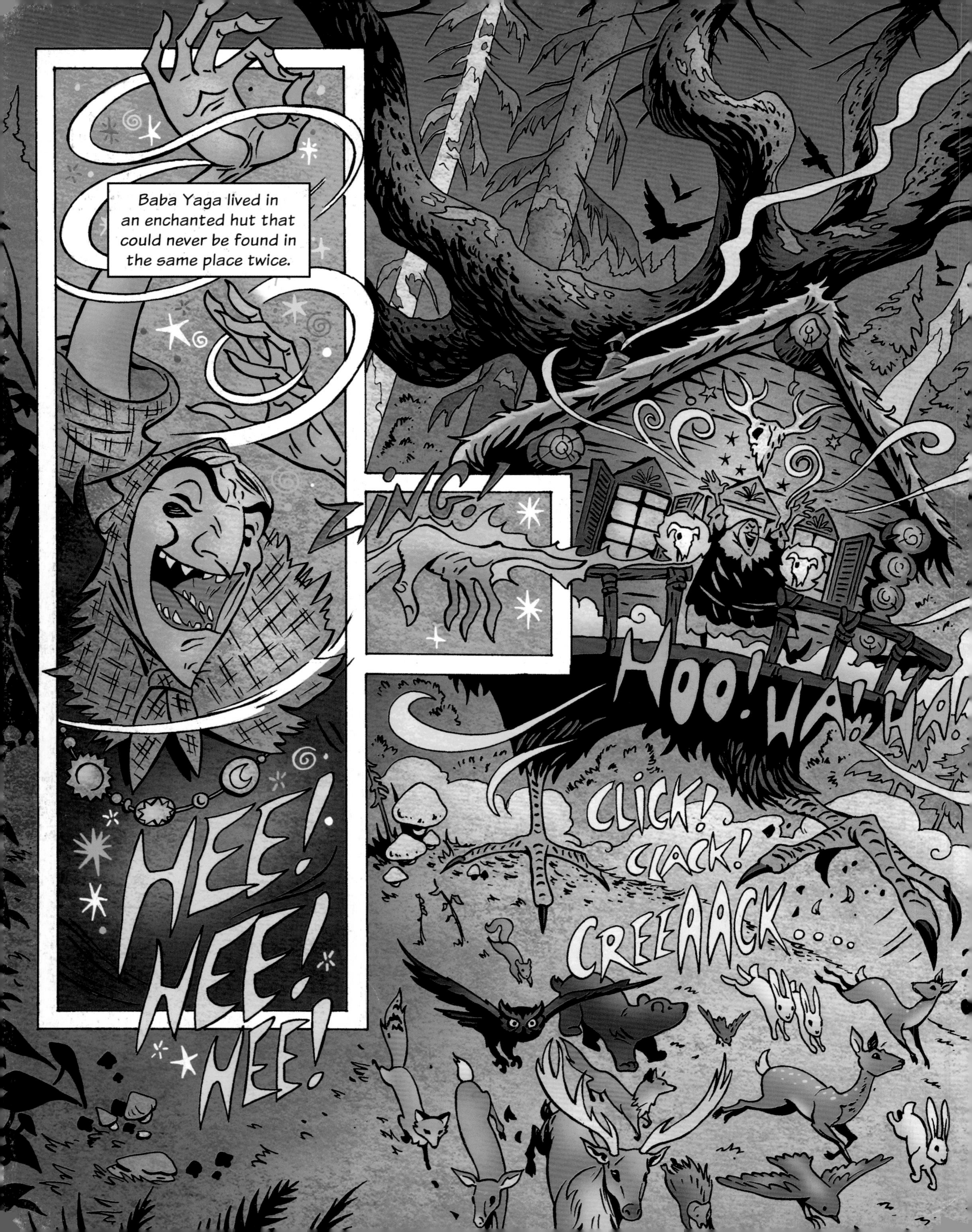
Baba Yaga lived in an enchanted hut that could never be found in the same place twice.
ZING!
HEE! HEE! HEE!
HOO! HA! HA!
CLICK! CLACK!
CREEAACK....

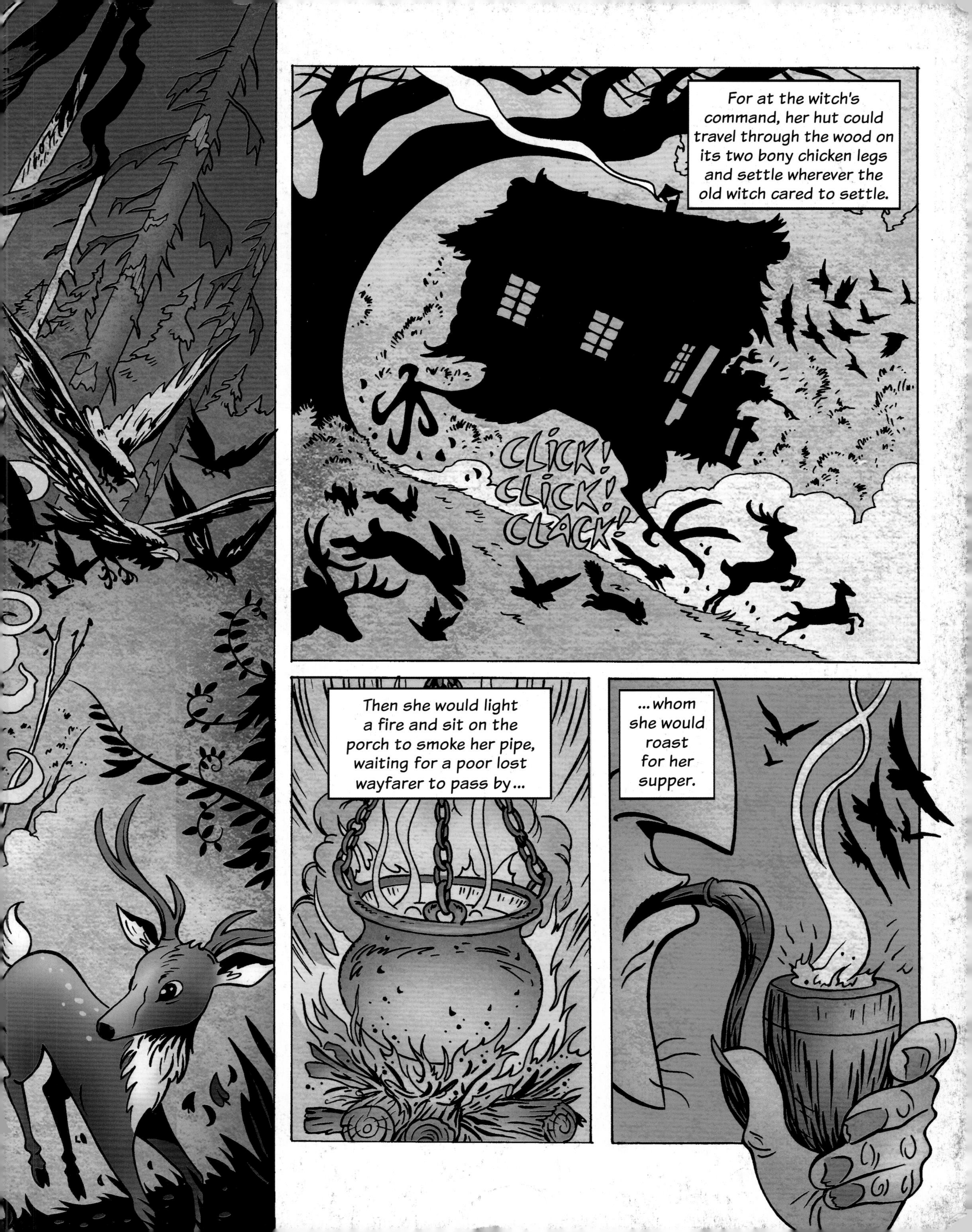
For at the witch's command, her hut could travel through the wood on its two bony chicken legs and settle wherever the old witch cared to settle.
CLICK! CLICK! CLACK!
Then she would light a fire and sit on the porch to smoke her pipe, waiting for a poor lost wayfarer to pass by...
...whom she would roast for her supper.

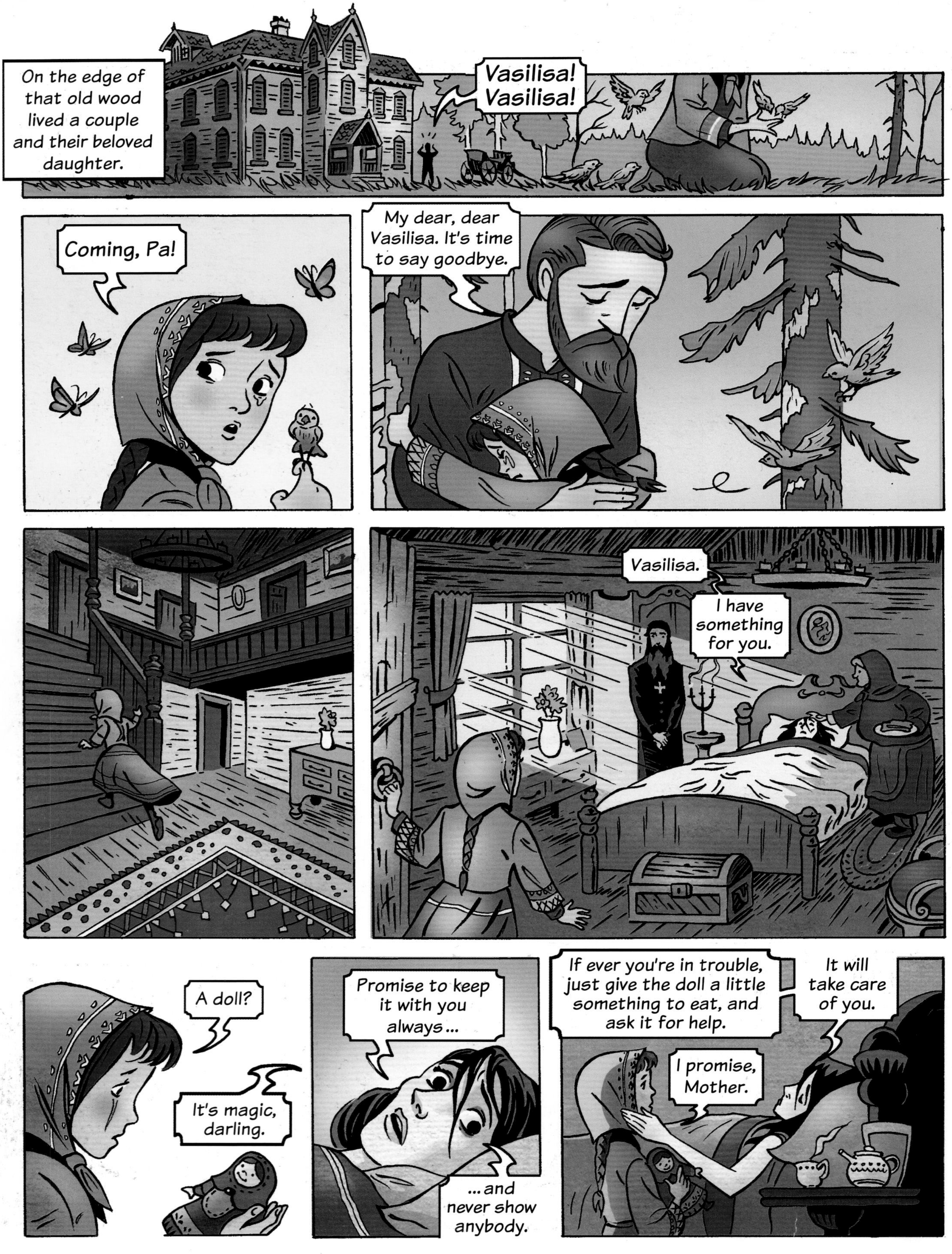
On the edge of that old wood lived a couple and their beloved daughter.
Vasilisa! Vasilisa!
Coming, Pa!
My dear, dear Vasilisa. It's time to say goodbye.
Vasilisa.
I have something for you.
A doll?
It's magic, darling.
Promise to keep it with you always ...
... and never show anybody.
If ever you're in trouble, just give the doll a little something to eat, and ask it for help.
It will take care of you.
I promise, Mother.

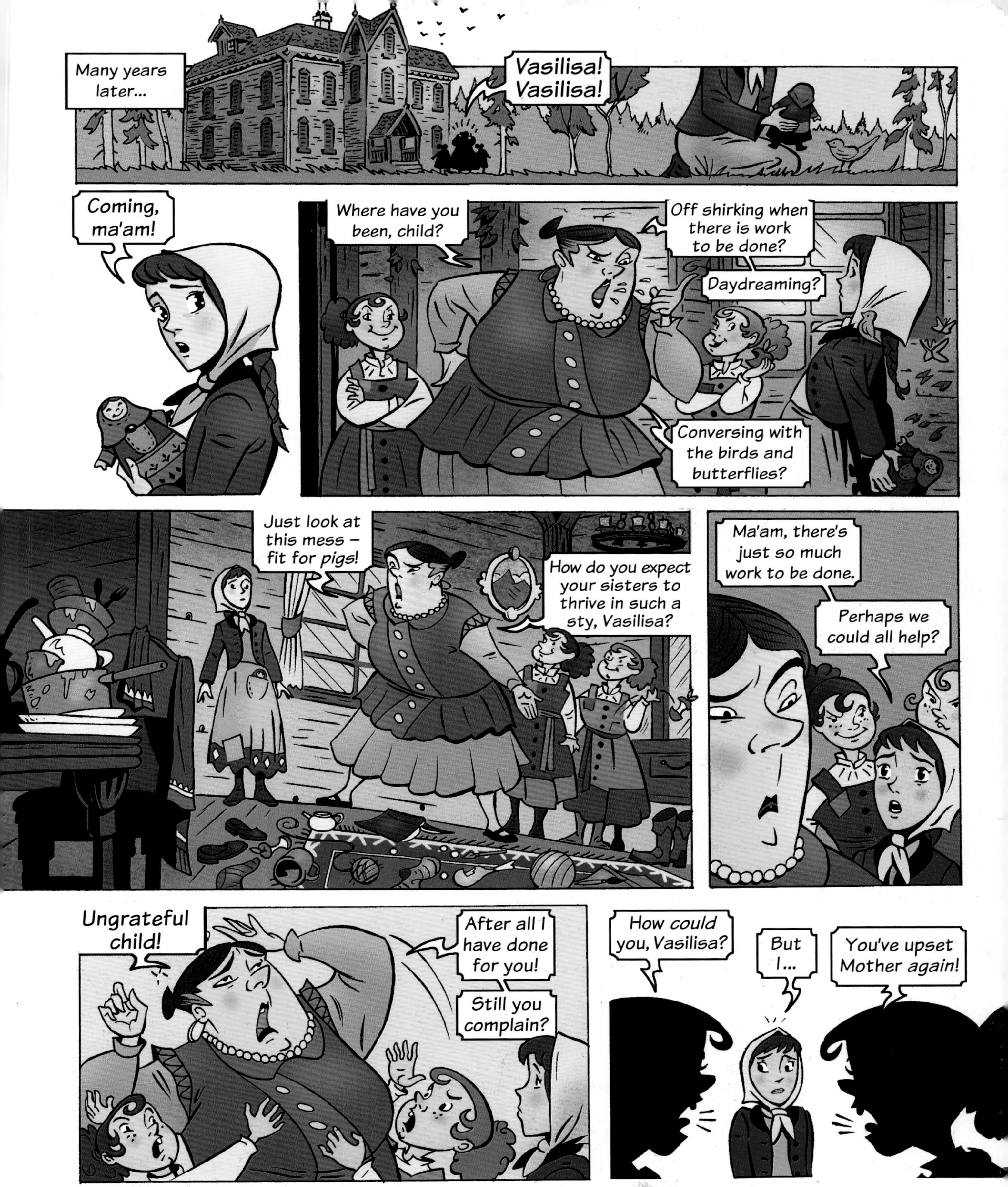

Many years later...
Vasilisa! Vasilisa!
Coming, ma'am!
Where have you been, child?
Off shirking when there is work to be done?
Daydreaming?
Conversing with the birds and butterflies?
Just look at this mess – fit for *pigs*!
How do you expect your sisters to thrive in such a sty, Vasilisa?
Ma'am, there's just so much work to be done.
Perhaps we could all help?
Ungrateful child!
After all I have done for you!
Still you complain?
How *could* you, Vasilisa?
But I...
You've upset Mother *again*!

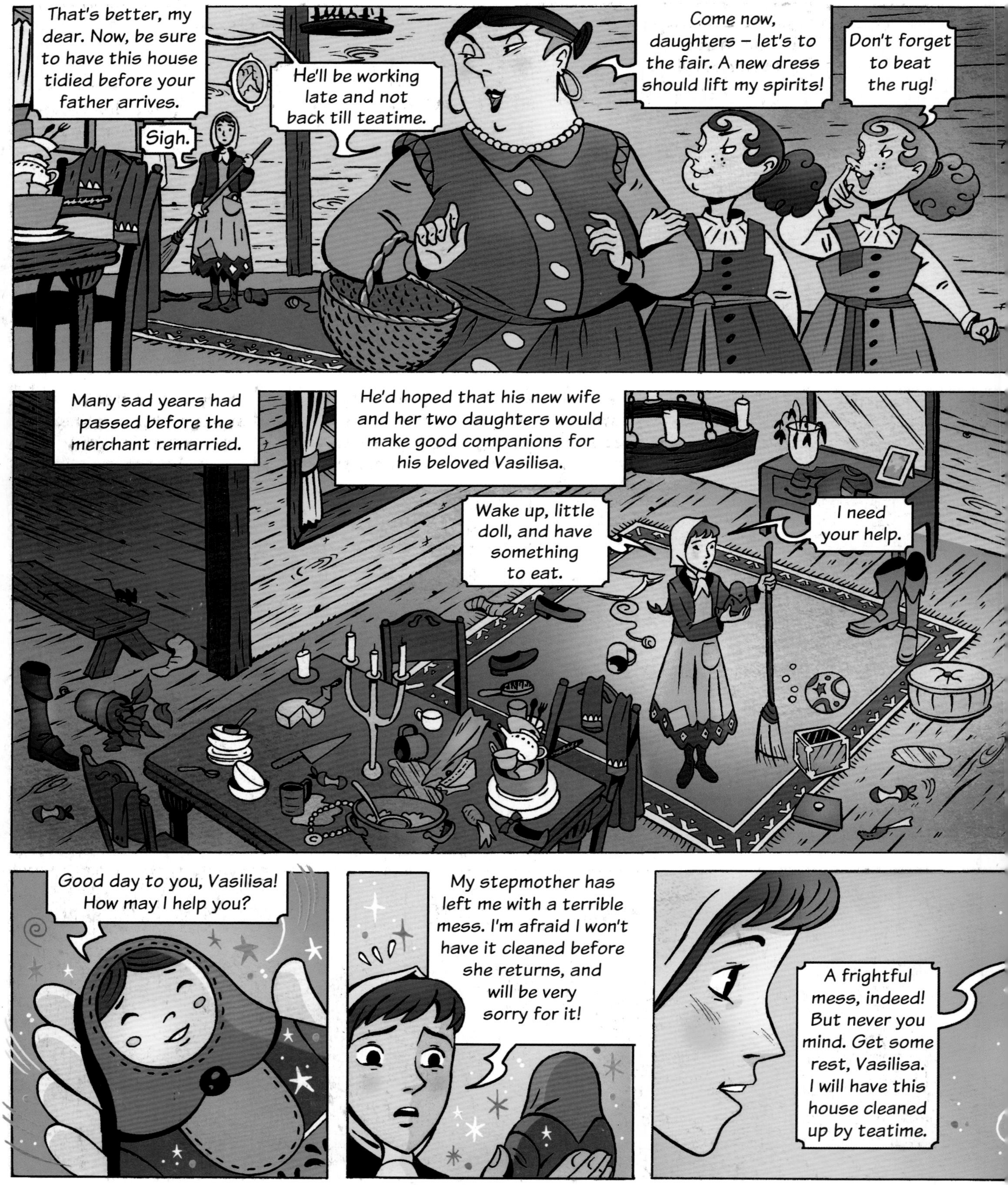

That's better, my dear. Now, be sure to have this house tidied before your father arrives.
Sigh.
He'll be working late and not back till teatime.
Come now, daughters – let's to the fair. A new dress should lift my spirits!
Don't forget to beat the rug!
Many sad years had passed before the merchant remarried.
He'd hoped that his new wife and her two daughters would make good companions for his beloved Vasilisa.
Wake up, little doll, and have something to eat.
I need your help.
Good day to you, Vasilisa! How may I help you?
My stepmother has left me with a terrible mess. I'm afraid I won't have it cleaned before she returns, and will be very sorry for it!
A frightful mess, indeed! But never you mind. Get some rest, Vasilisa. I will have this house cleaned up by teatime.

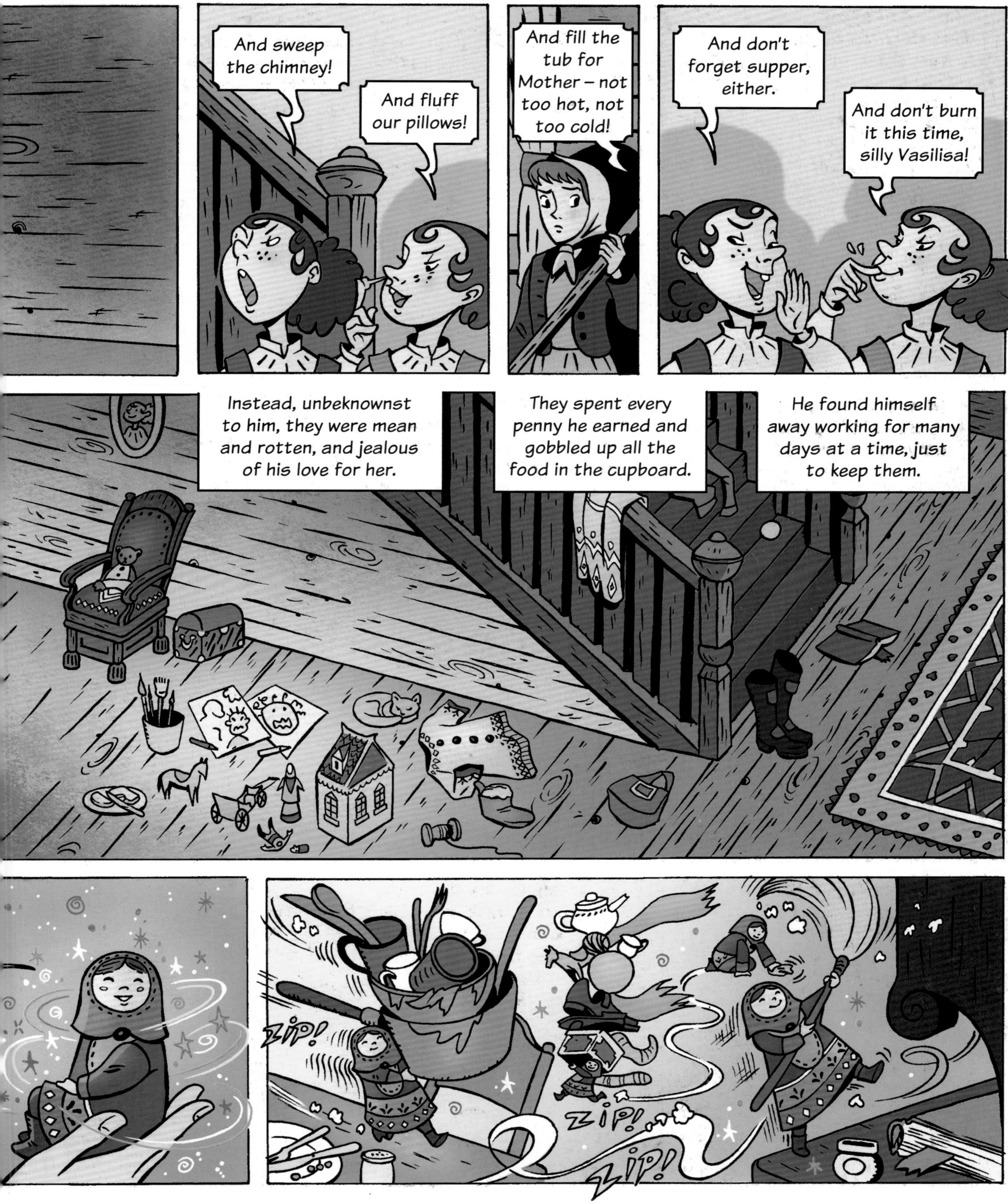

And sweep the chimney!
And fluff our pillows!
And fill the tub for Mother – not too hot, not too cold!
And don't forget supper, either.
And don't burn it this time, silly Vasilisa!
Instead, unbeknownst to him, they were mean and rotten, and jealous of his love for her.
They spent every penny he earned and gobbled up all the food in the cupboard.
He found himself away working for many days at a time, just to keep them.
ZIP!
ZIP!
ZIP!

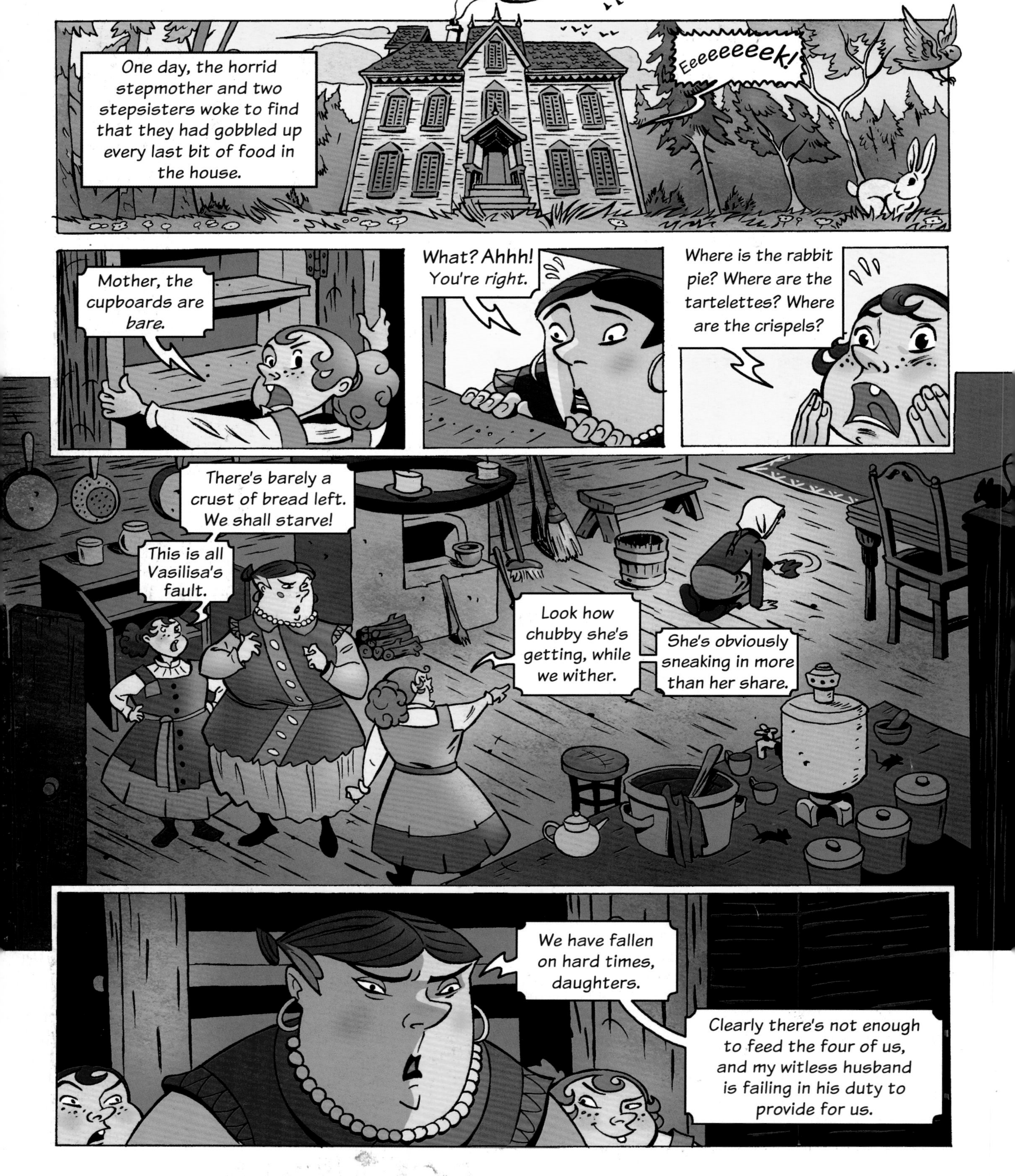
One day, the horrid stepmother and two stepsisters woke to find that they had gobbled up every last bit of food in the house.
Eeeeeeeek!
Mother, the cupboards are *bare.*
What? Ahhh! You're *right.*
Where is the rabbit pie? Where are the tartelettes? Where are the crispels?
There's barely a crust of bread left. We shall starve!
This is all Vasilisa's fault.
Look how chubby she's getting, while we wither.
She's obviously sneaking in more than her share.
We have fallen on hard times, daughters.
Clearly there's not enough to feed the four of us, and my witless husband is failing in his duty to provide for us.

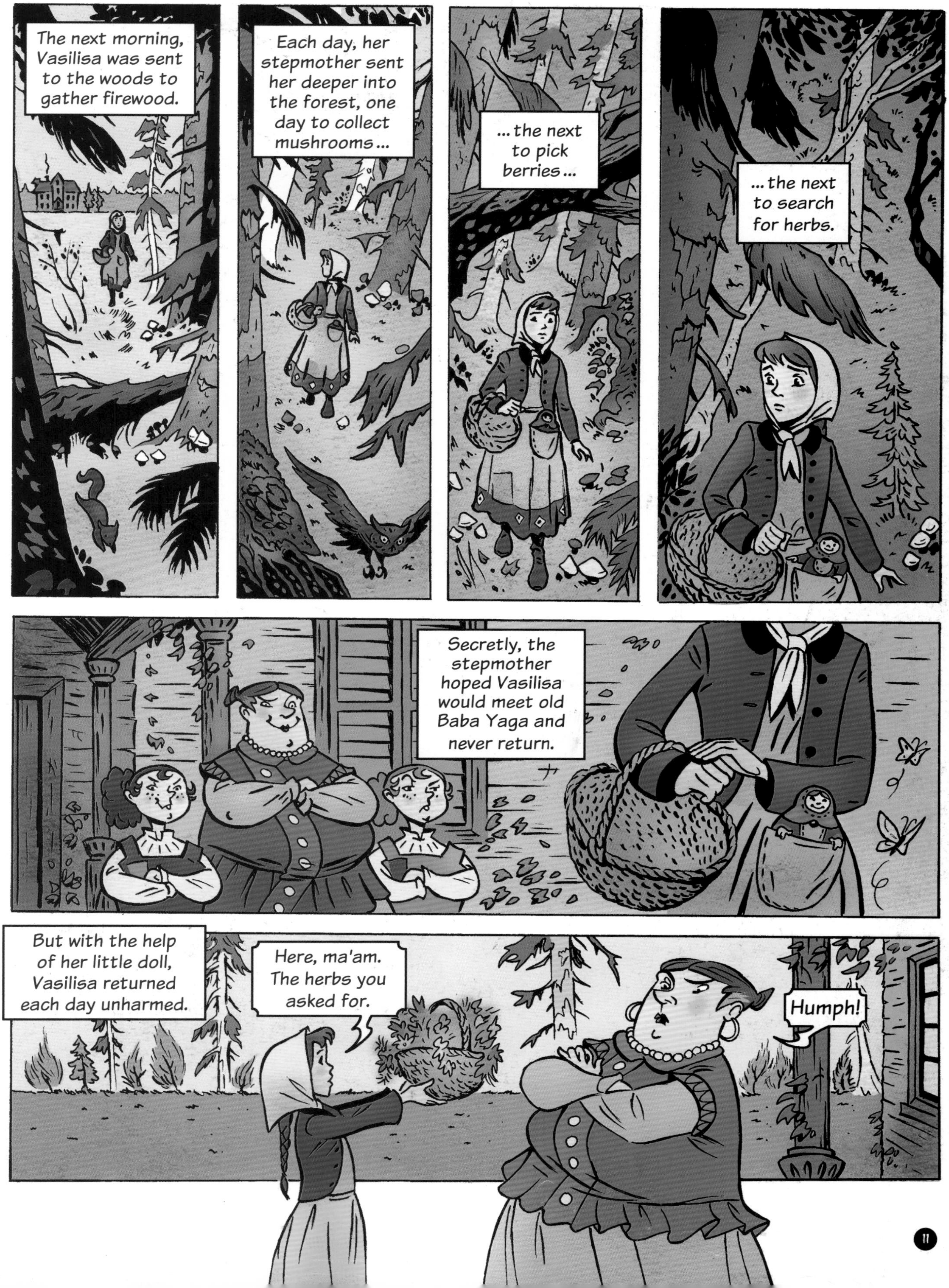
The next morning, Vasilisa was sent to the woods to gather firewood.
Each day, her stepmother sent her deeper into the forest, one day to collect mushrooms...
...the next to pick berries...
...the next to search for herbs.
Secretly, the stepmother hoped Vasilisa would meet old Baba Yaga and never return.
But with the help of her little doll, Vasilisa returned each day unharmed.
Here, ma'am. The herbs you asked for.
Humph!

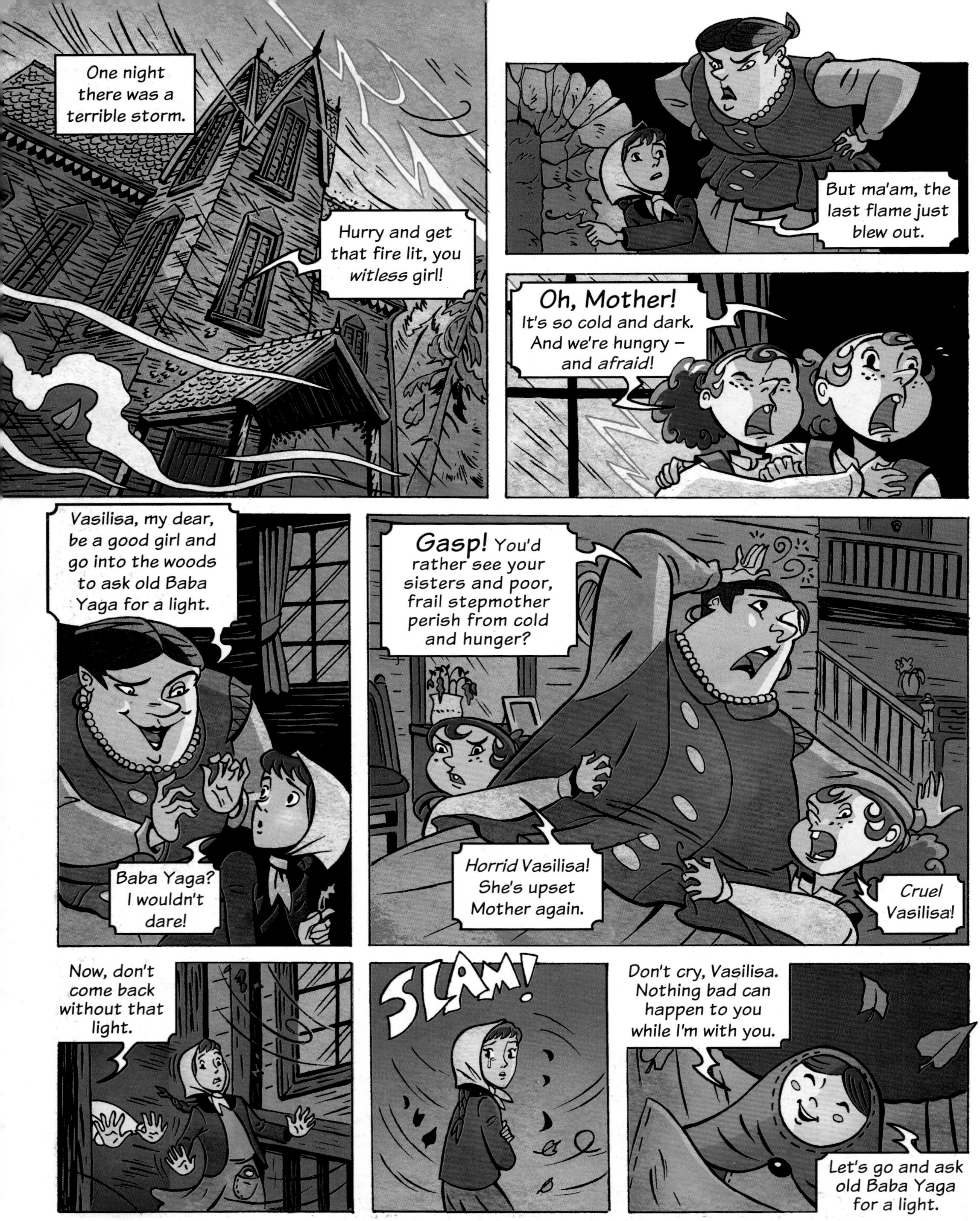
One night there was a terrible storm.
Hurry and get that fire lit, you *witless* girl!
But ma'am, the last flame just blew out.
Oh, Mother! It's so cold and dark. And we're hungry – and *afraid*!
Vasilisa, my dear, be a good girl and go into the woods to ask old Baba Yaga for a light.
Baba Yaga? I wouldn't dare!
Gasp! You'd rather see your sisters and poor, frail stepmother perish from cold and hunger?
Horrid Vasilisa! She's upset Mother again.
Cruel Vasilisa!
Now, don't come back without that light.
SLAM!
Don't cry, Vasilisa. Nothing bad can happen to you while I'm with you.
Let's go and ask old Baba Yaga for a light.

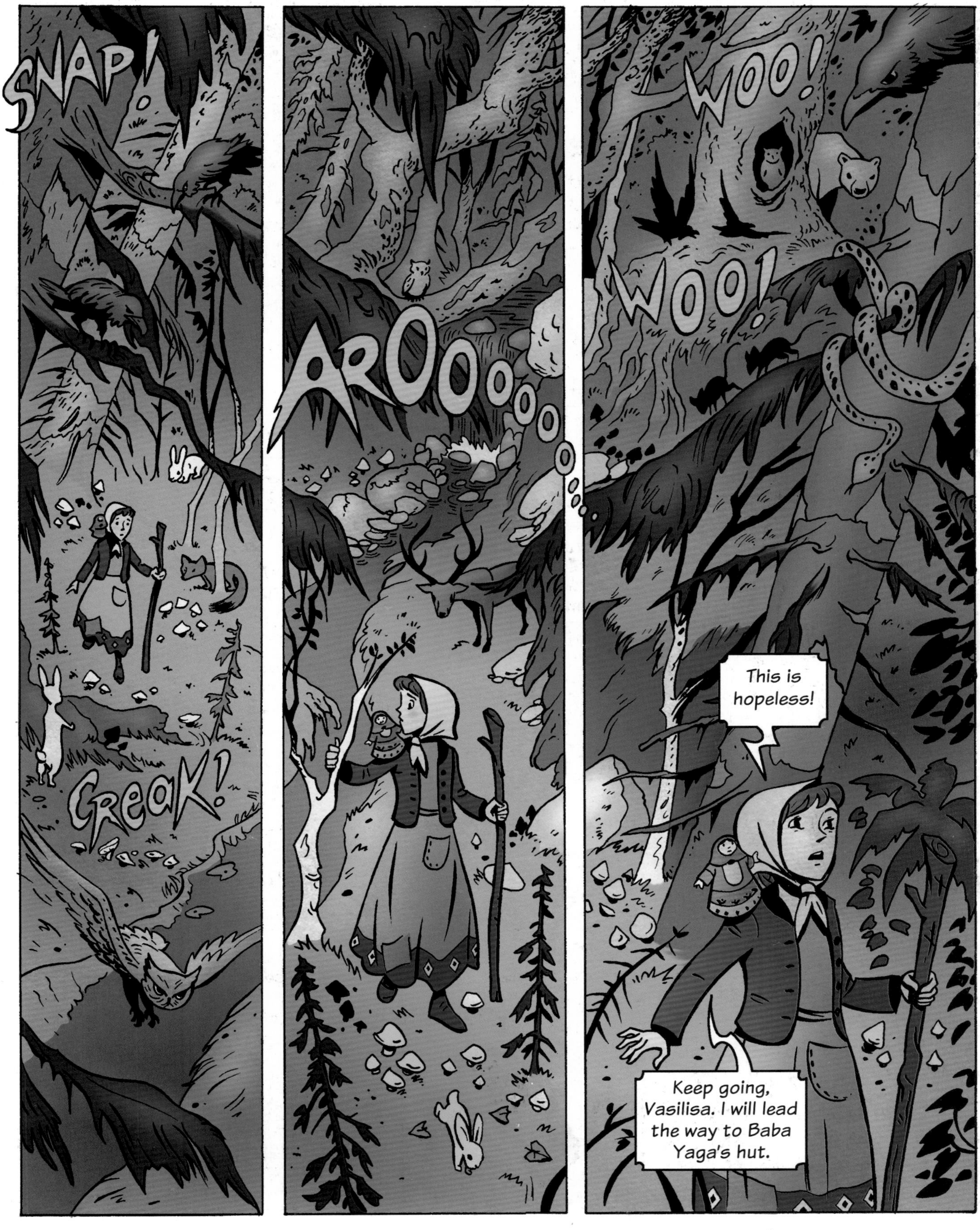
SNAP!
CREAK!
AROOOOOOO
WOO!
WOO!
This is hopeless!
Keep going, Vasilisa. I will lead the way to Baba Yaga's hut.

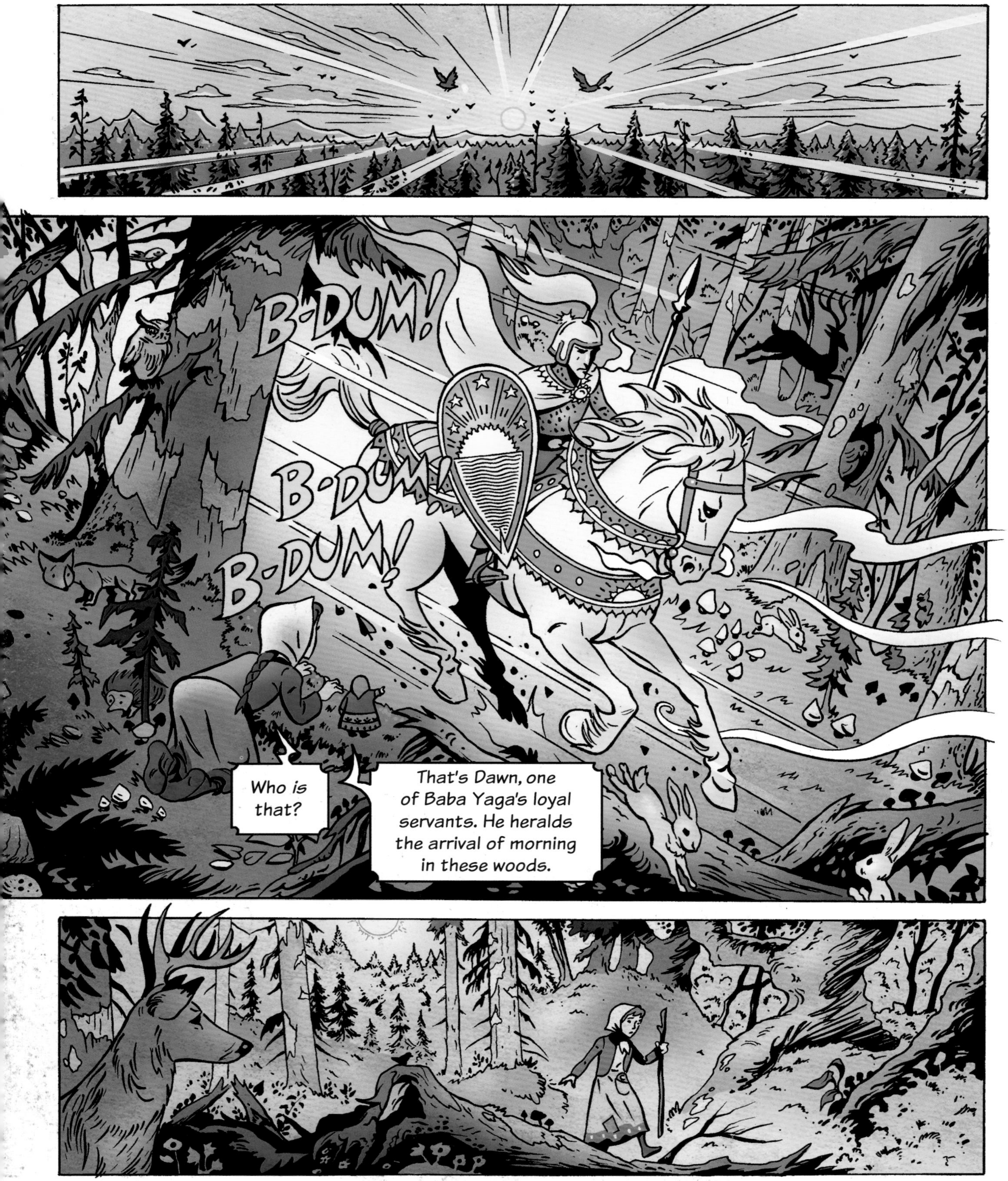
B-DUM!
B-DUM!
B-DUM!
Who is that?
That's Dawn, one of Baba Yaga's loyal servants. He heralds the arrival of morning in these woods.

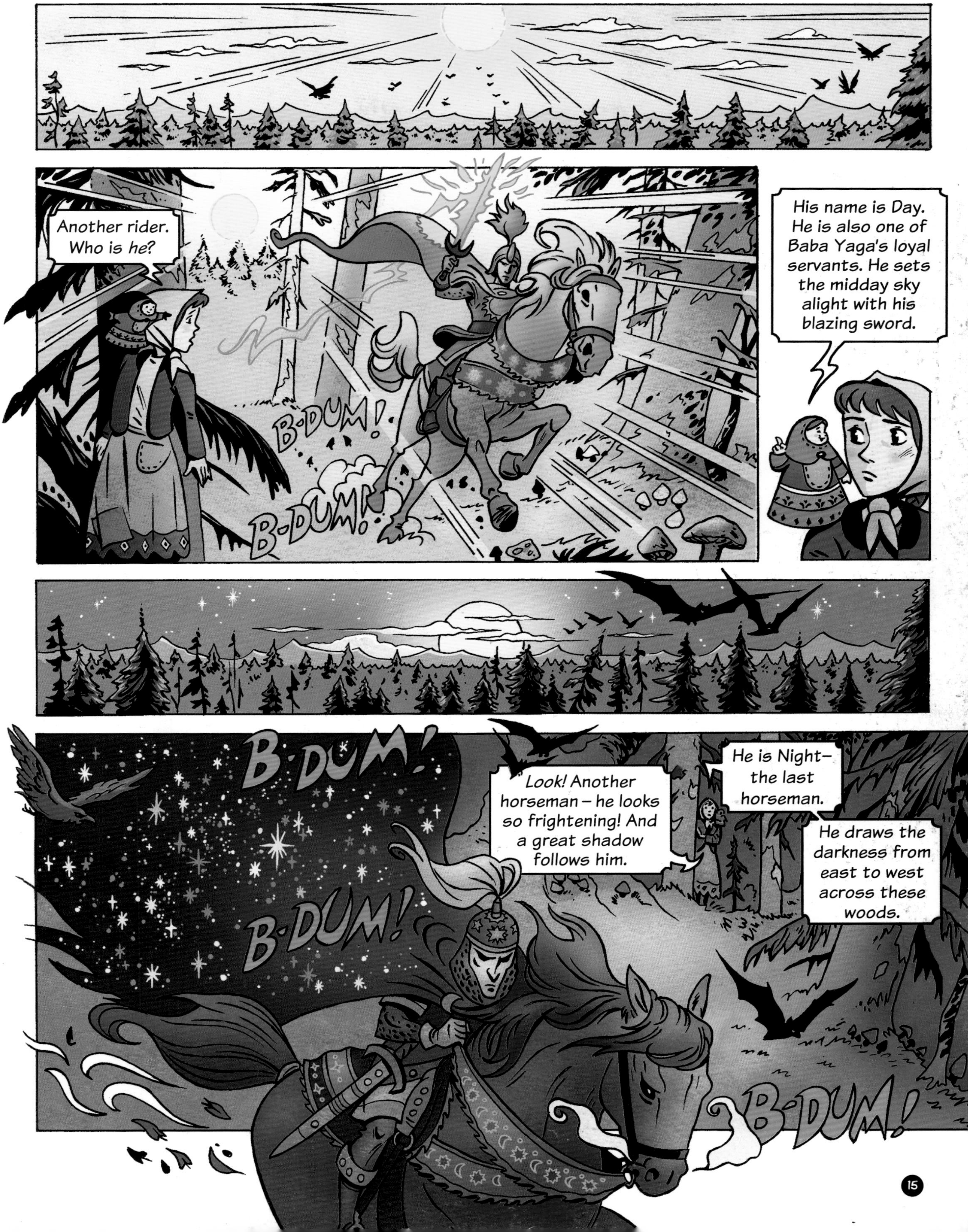
Another rider. Who is *he*?
His name is Day. He is also one of Baba Yaga's loyal servants. He sets the midday sky alight with his blazing sword.
B-DUM!
B-DUM!
B-DUM!
B-DUM!
Look! Another horseman – he looks so frightening! And a great shadow follows him.
He is Night– the last horseman.
He draws the darkness from east to west across these woods.
B-DUM!

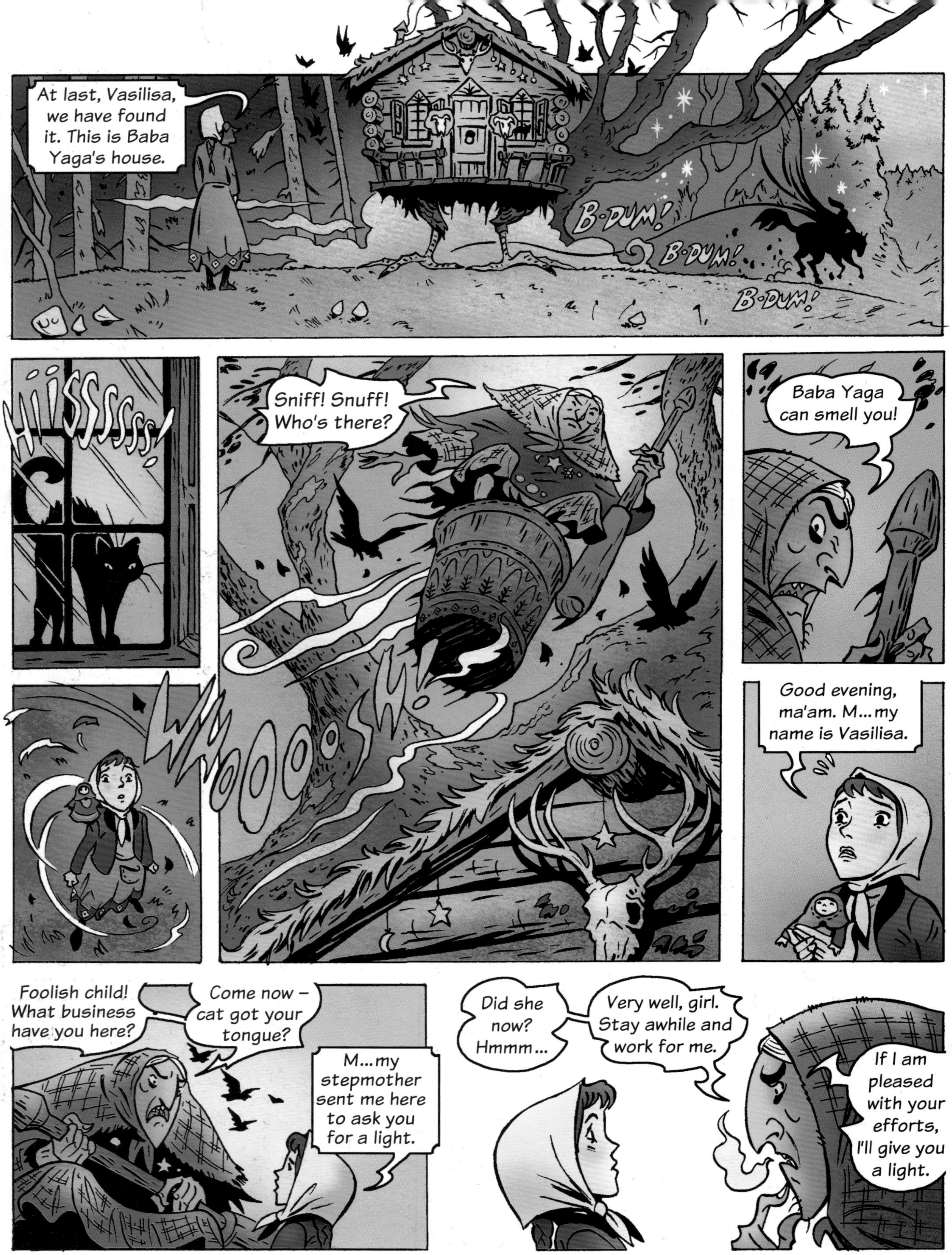
At last, Vasilisa, we have found it. This is Baba Yaga's house.
B-DUM!
B-DUM!
B-DUM!
HISSSSSS!
Sniff! Snuff! Who's there?
Baba Yaga can smell you!
WHOOOOSH!
Good evening, ma'am. M...my name is Vasilisa.
Foolish child! What business have you here?
Come now – cat got your tongue?
M...my stepmother sent me here to ask you for a light.
Did she now? Hmmm...
Very well, girl. Stay awhile and work for me.
If I am pleased with your efforts, I'll give you a light.

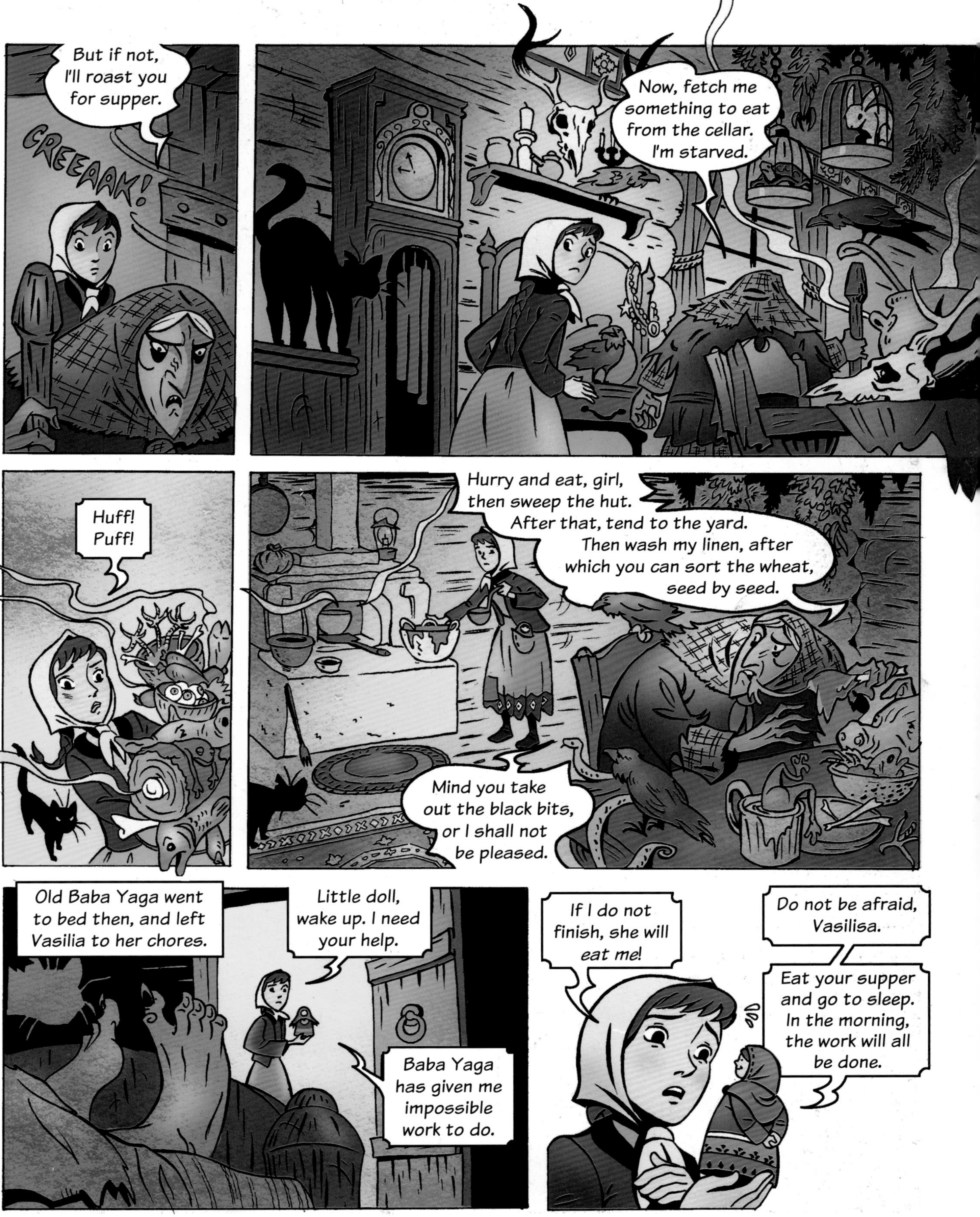
But if not, I'll roast you for supper.
CREEAAK!
Now, fetch me something to eat from the cellar. I'm starved.
Huff! Puff!
Hurry and eat, girl, then sweep the hut. After that, tend to the yard. Then wash my linen, after which you can sort the wheat, seed by seed.
Mind you take out the black bits, or I shall not be pleased.
Old Baba Yaga went to bed then, and left Vasilia to her chores.
Little doll, wake up. I need your help.
Baba Yaga has given me impossible work to do.
If I do not finish, she will *eat me!*
Do not be afraid, Vasilisa.
Eat your supper and go to sleep. In the morning, the work will all be done.

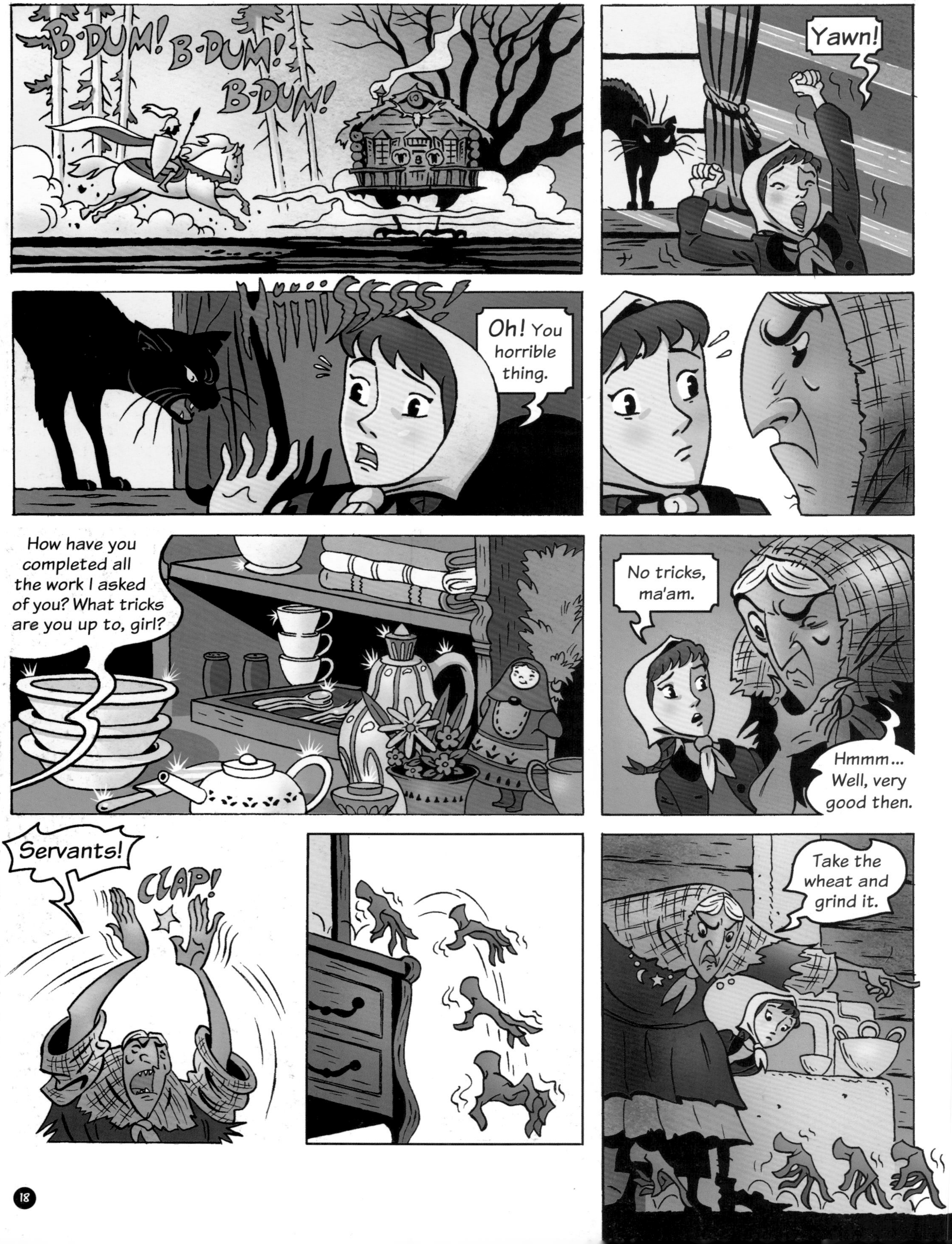
B-DUM! B-DUM! B-DUM!
Yawn!
HHHISSSSS!
Oh! You horrible thing.
How have you completed all the work I asked of you? What tricks are you up to, girl?
No tricks, ma'am.
Hmmm... Well, very good then.
Servants!
CLAP!
Take the wheat and grind it.

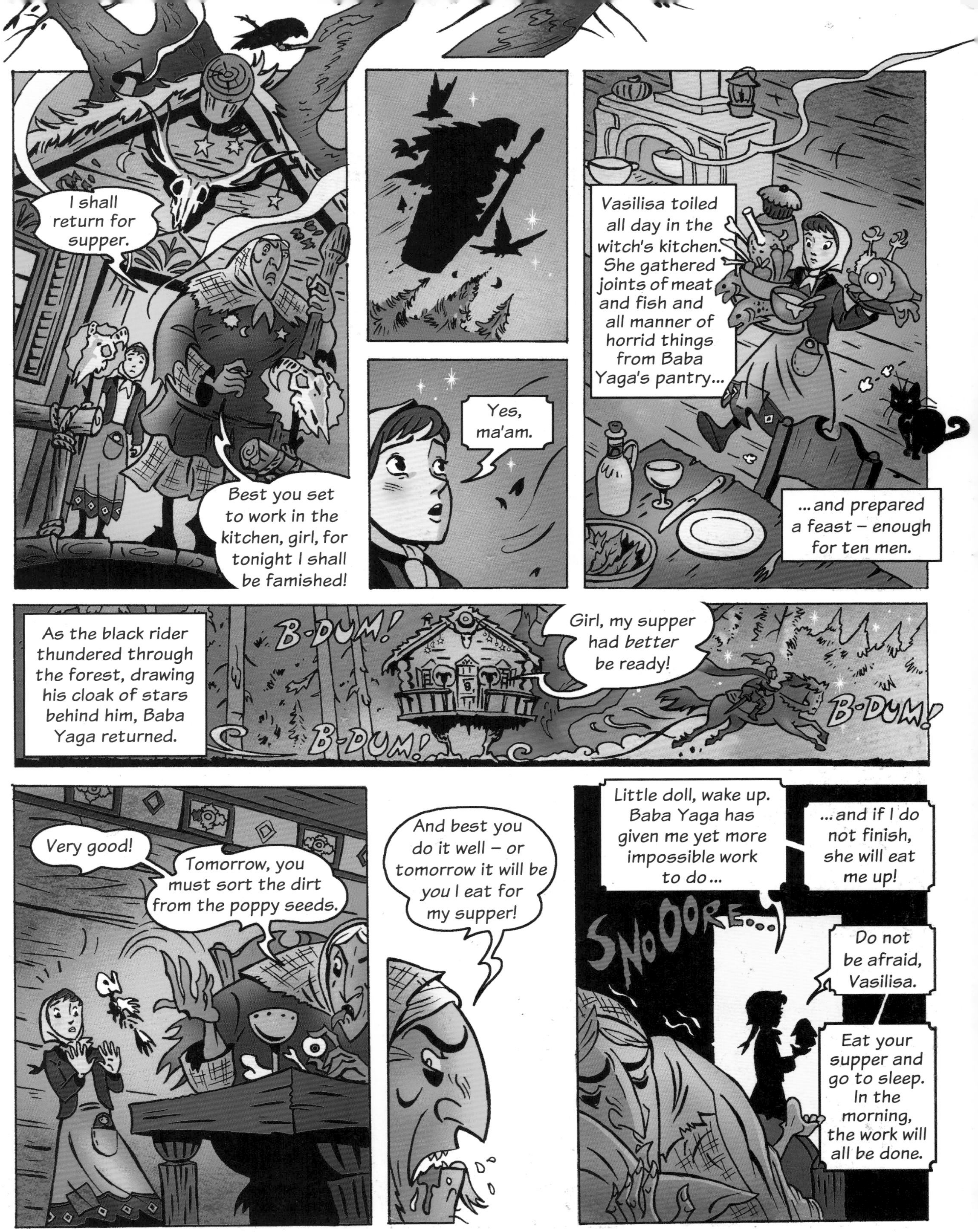
I shall return for supper.
Best you set to work in the kitchen, girl, for tonight I shall be famished!
Yes, ma'am.
Vasilisa toiled all day in the witch's kitchen. She gathered joints of meat and fish and all manner of horrid things from Baba Yaga's pantry...
...and prepared a feast – enough for ten men.
As the black rider thundered through the forest, drawing his cloak of stars behind him, Baba Yaga returned.
B-DUM!
Girl, my supper had better be ready!
B-DUM!
B-DUM!
Very good!
Tomorrow, you must sort the dirt from the poppy seeds.
And best you do it well – or tomorrow it will be you I eat for my supper!
Little doll, wake up. Baba Yaga has given me yet more impossible work to do...
...and if I do not finish, she will eat me up!
SNOOORE...
Do not be afraid, Vasilisa.
Eat your supper and go to sleep. In the morning, the work will all be done.

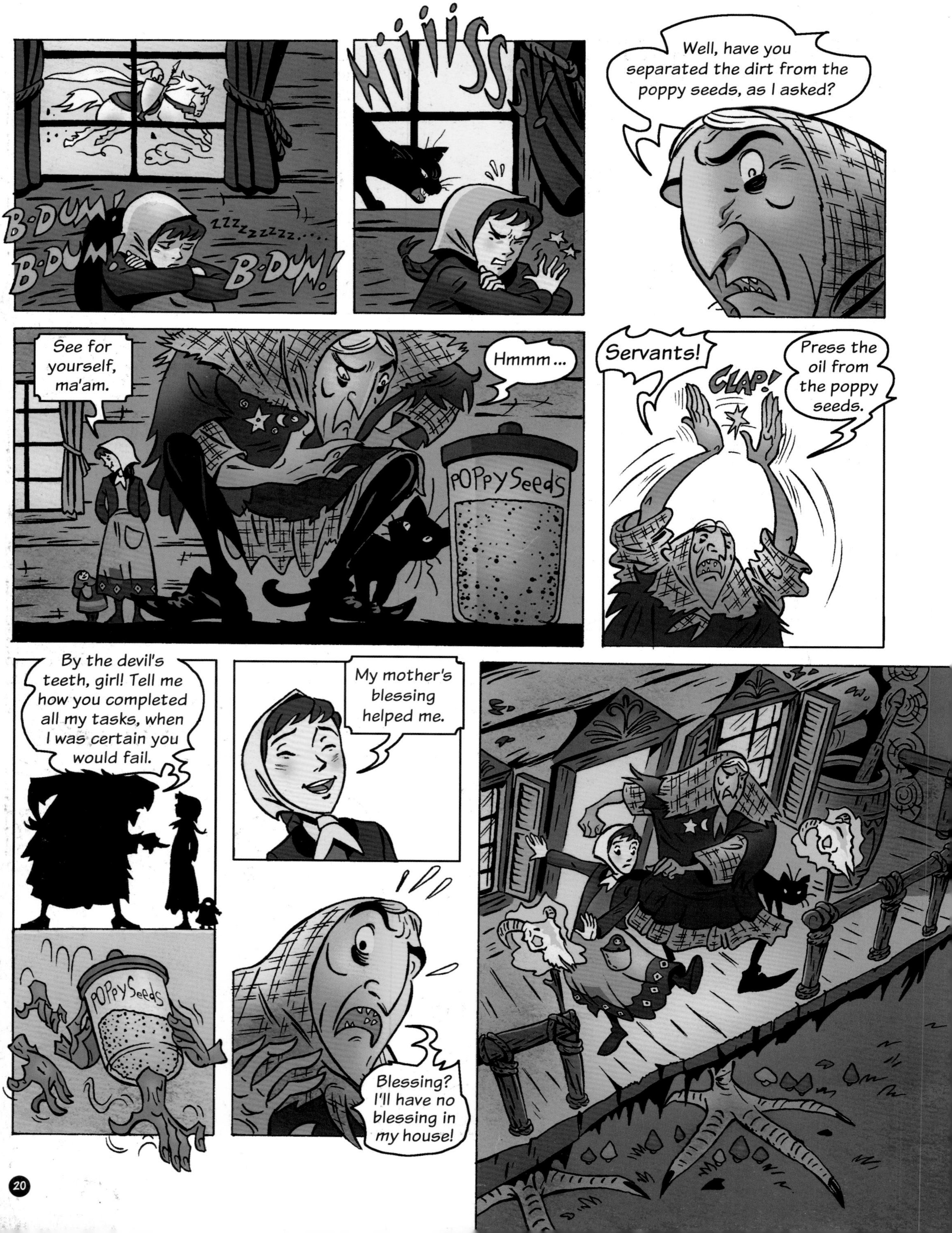
B-DUM!
B-DUM!
ZZZZZZZZZ.....
B-DUM!
HISSS
Well, have you separated the dirt from the poppy seeds, as I asked?
See for yourself, ma'am.
Hmmm...
POPPY Seeds
Servants!
CLAP!
Press the oil from the poppy seeds.
By the devil's teeth, girl! Tell me how you completed all my tasks, when I was certain you would fail.
My mother's blessing helped me.
POPPY Seeds
Blessing? I'll have no blessing in my house!

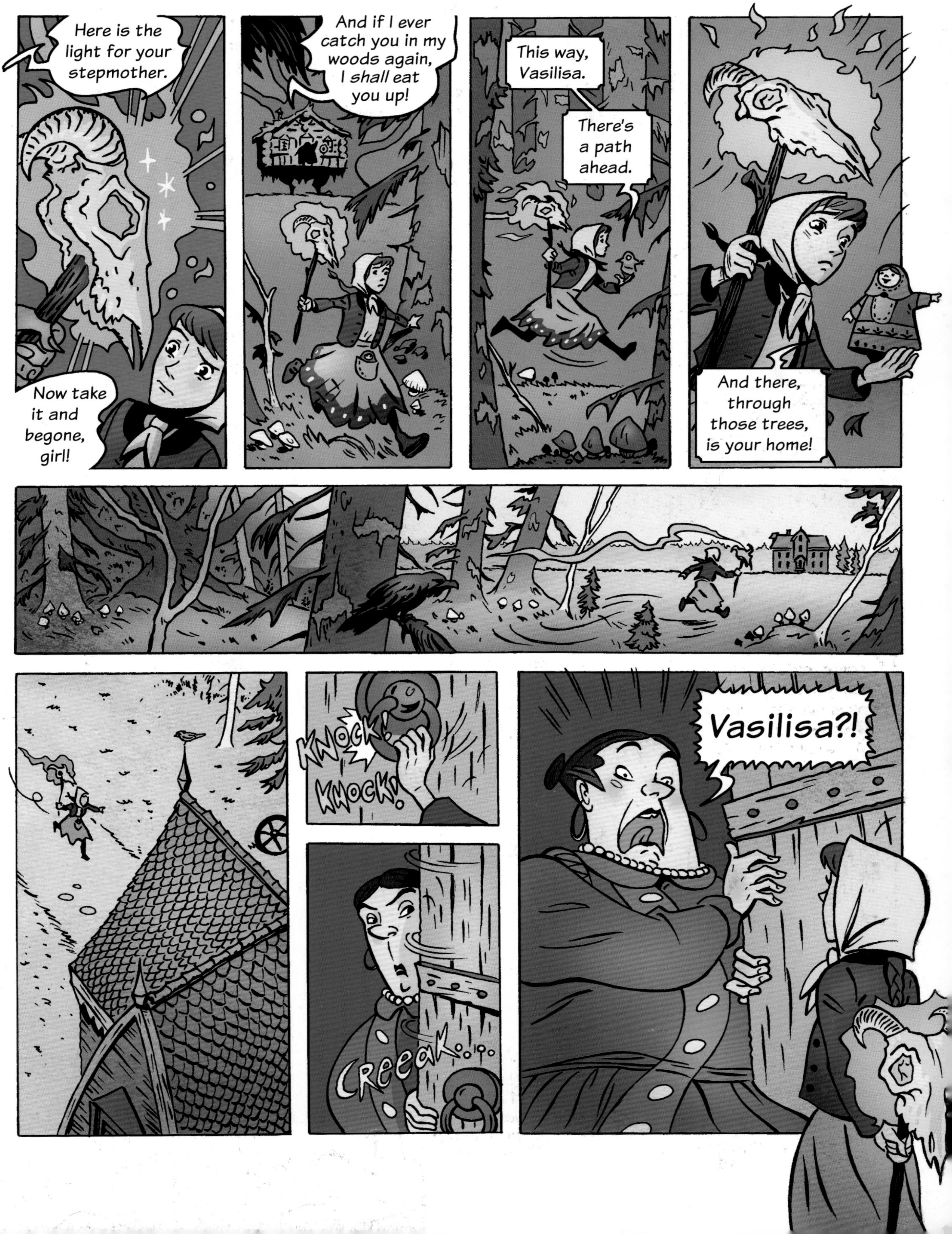
Here is the light for your stepmother.
Now take it and begone, girl!
And if I ever catch you in my woods again, I shall eat you up!
This way, Vasilisa.
There's a path ahead.
And there, through those trees, is your home!
KNOCK
KNOCK!
CREEAK
Vasilisa?!

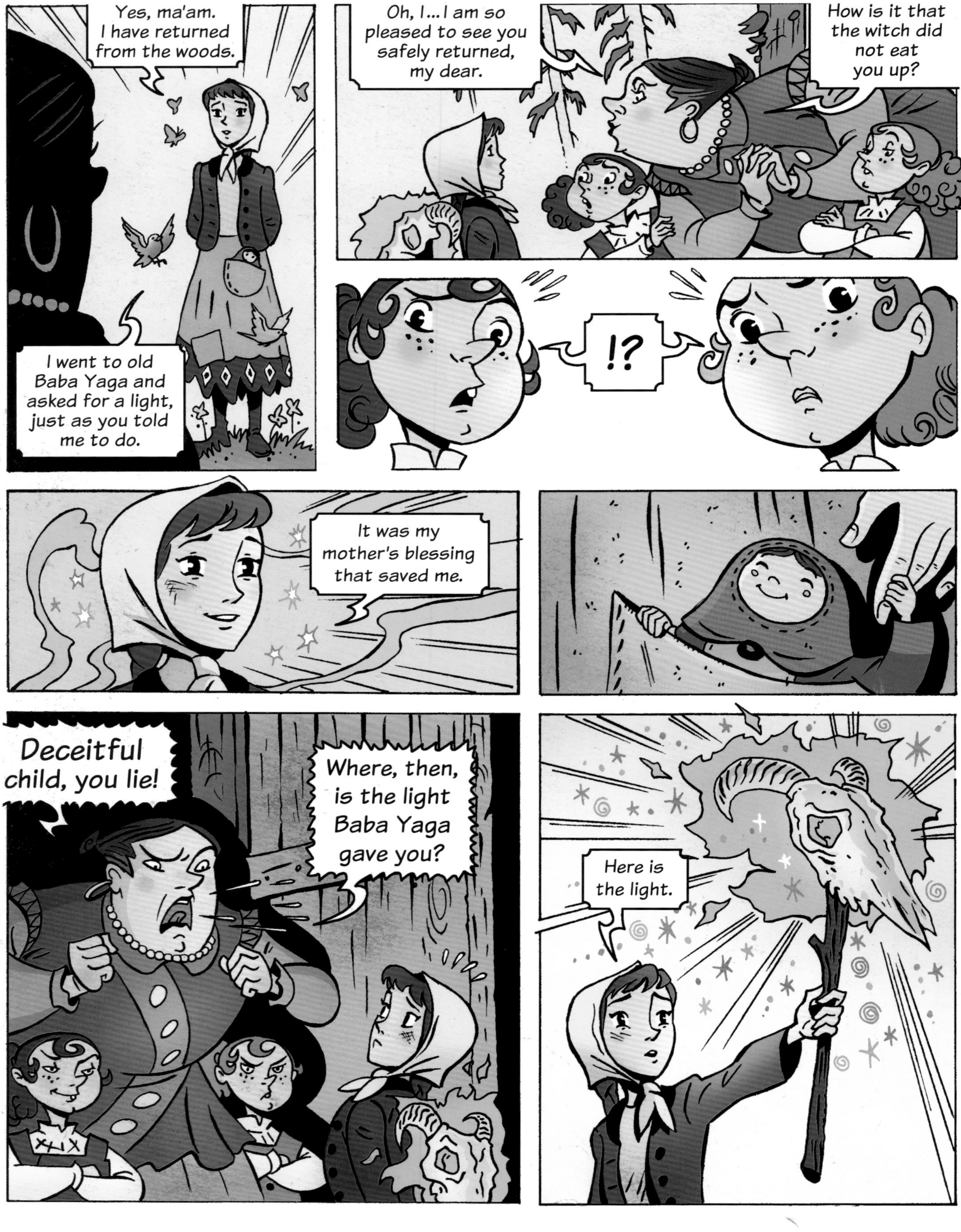
Yes, ma'am. I have returned from the woods.
I went to old Baba Yaga and asked for a light, just as you told me to do.
Oh, I... I am so pleased to see you safely returned, my dear.
How is it that the witch did not eat you up?
!?
It was my mother's blessing that saved me.
Deceitful child, you lie!
Where, then, is the light Baba Yaga gave you?
Here is the light.

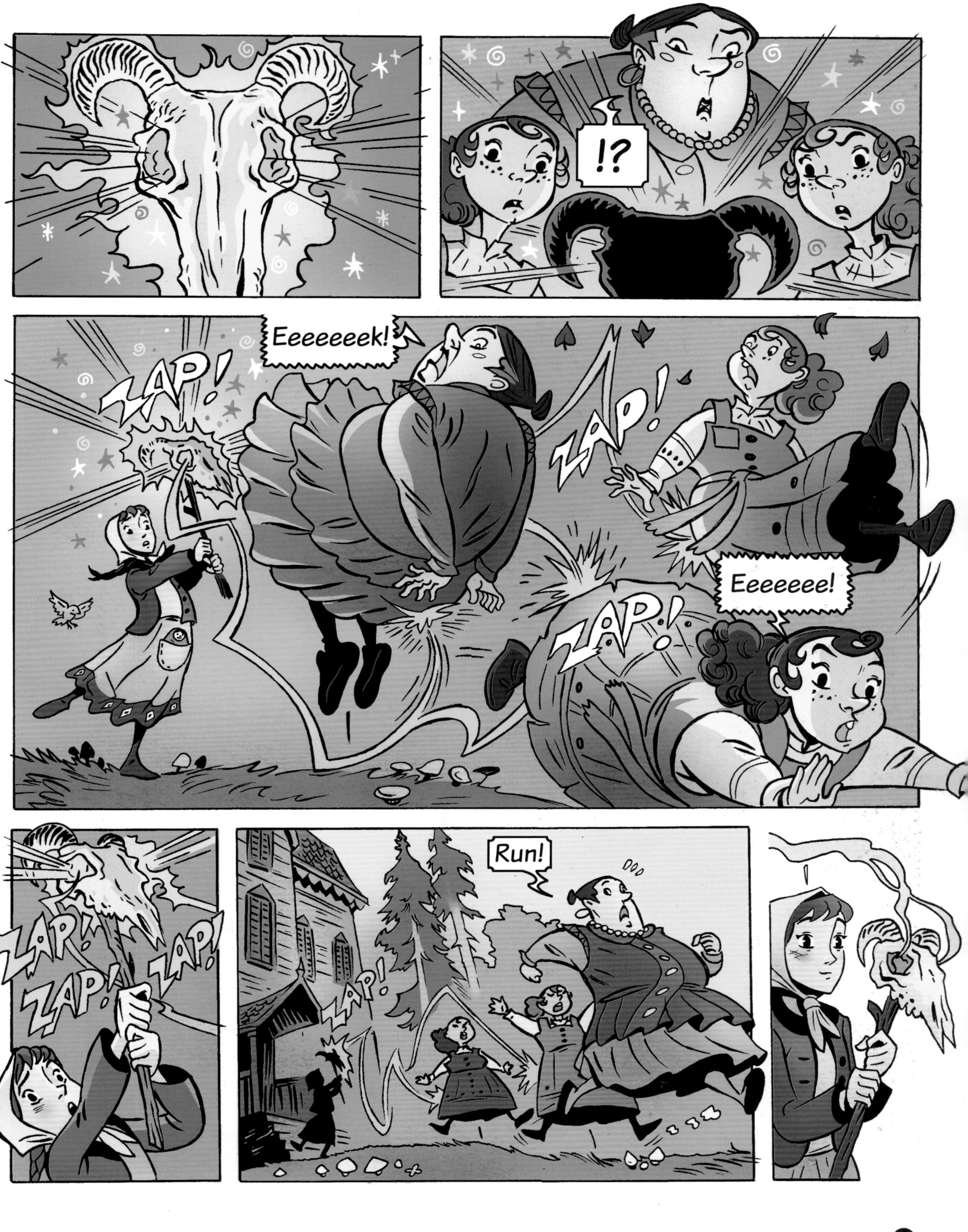
!?
ZAP!
Eeeeeeek!
ZAP!
Eeeeeee!
ZAP!
ZAP!
ZAP!
ZAP!
Run!
ZAP!

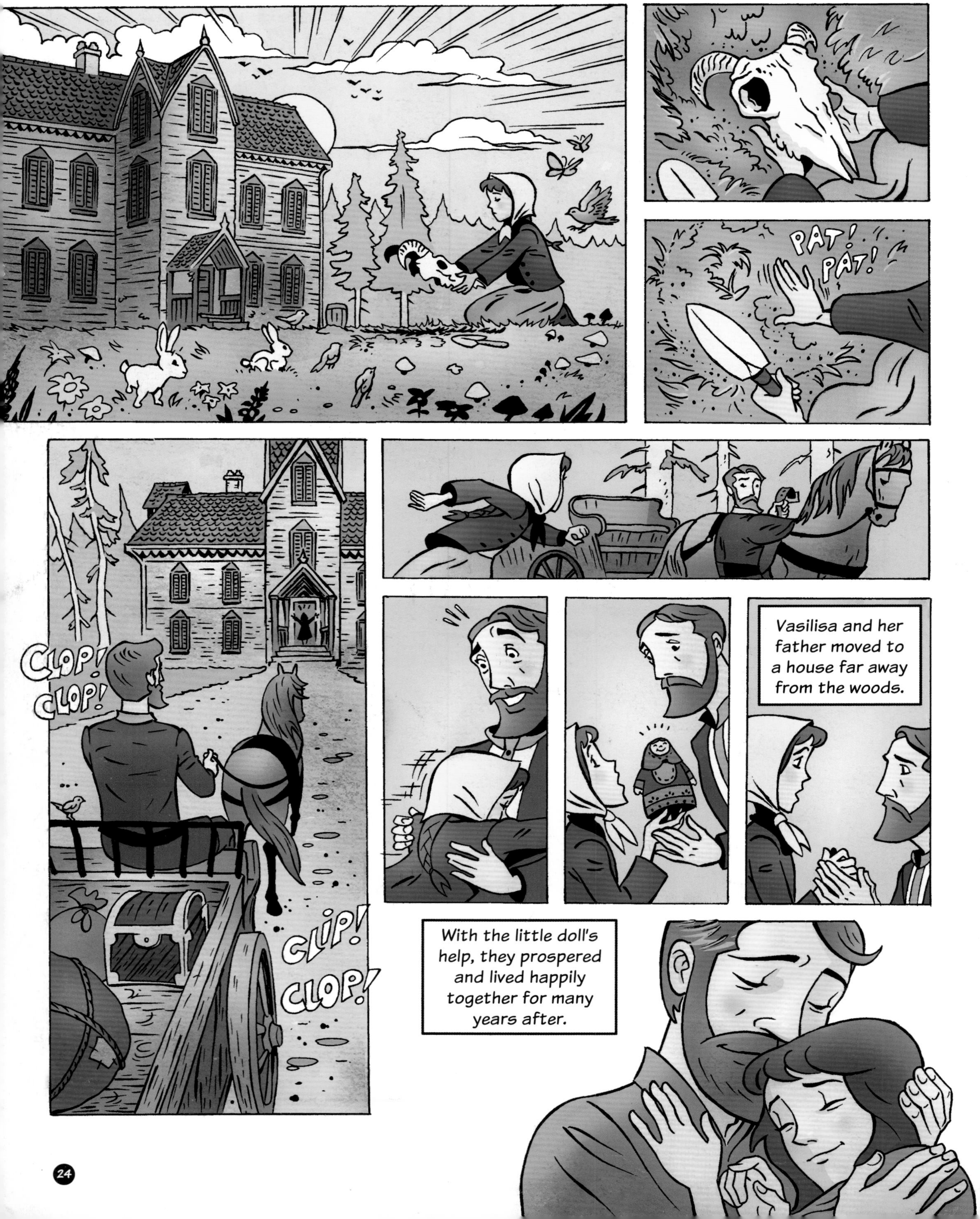
PAT! PAT!
CLOP! CLOP!
CLIP! CLOP!
Vasilisa and her father moved to a house far away from the woods.
With the little doll's help, they prospered and lived happily together for many years after.

Thor and the Frost Giants

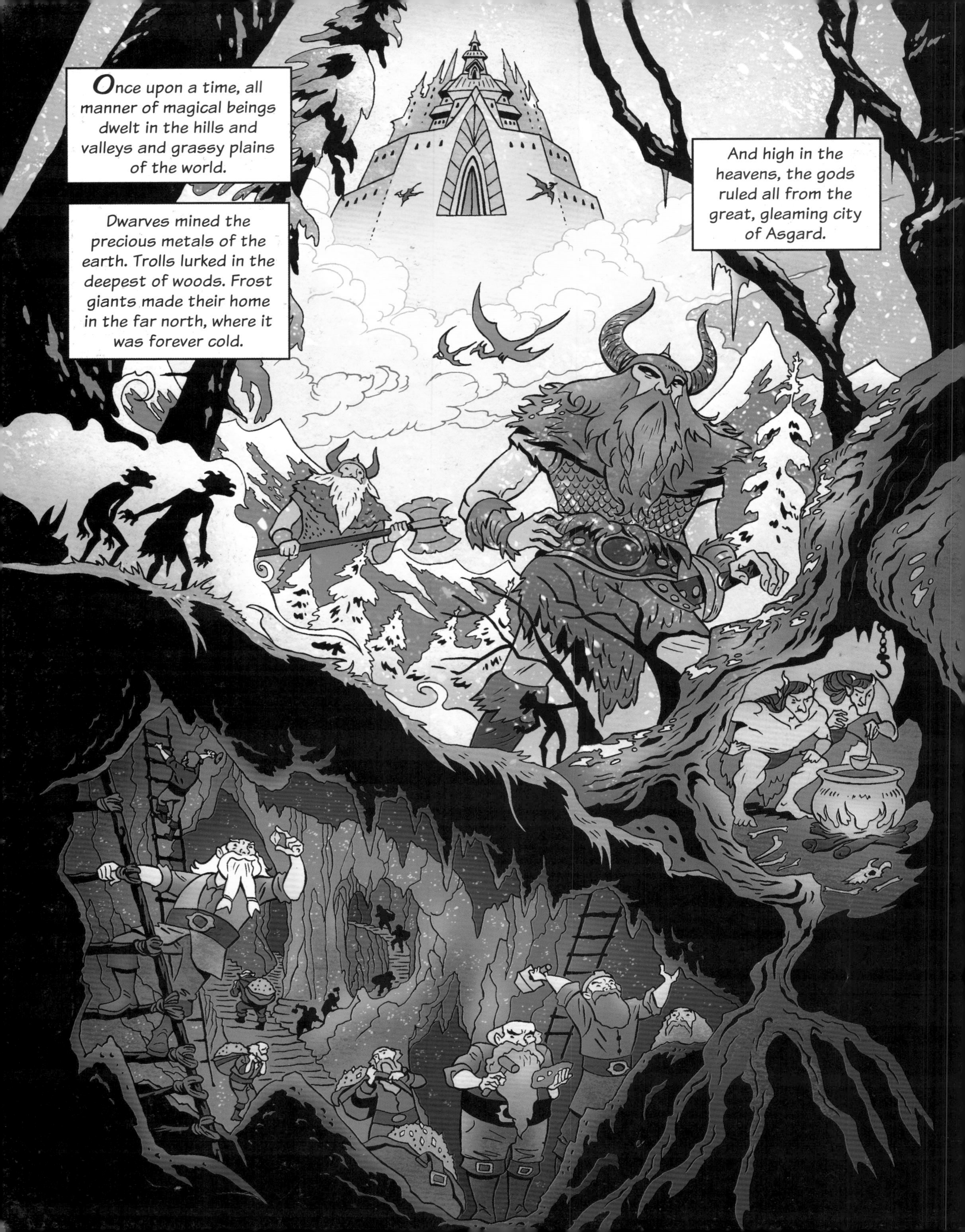
Once upon a time, all manner of magical beings dwelt in the hills and valleys and grassy plains of the world.
Dwarves mined the precious metals of the earth. Trolls lurked in the deepest of woods. Frost giants made their home in the far north, where it was forever cold.
And high in the heavens, the gods ruled all from the great, gleaming city of Asgard.

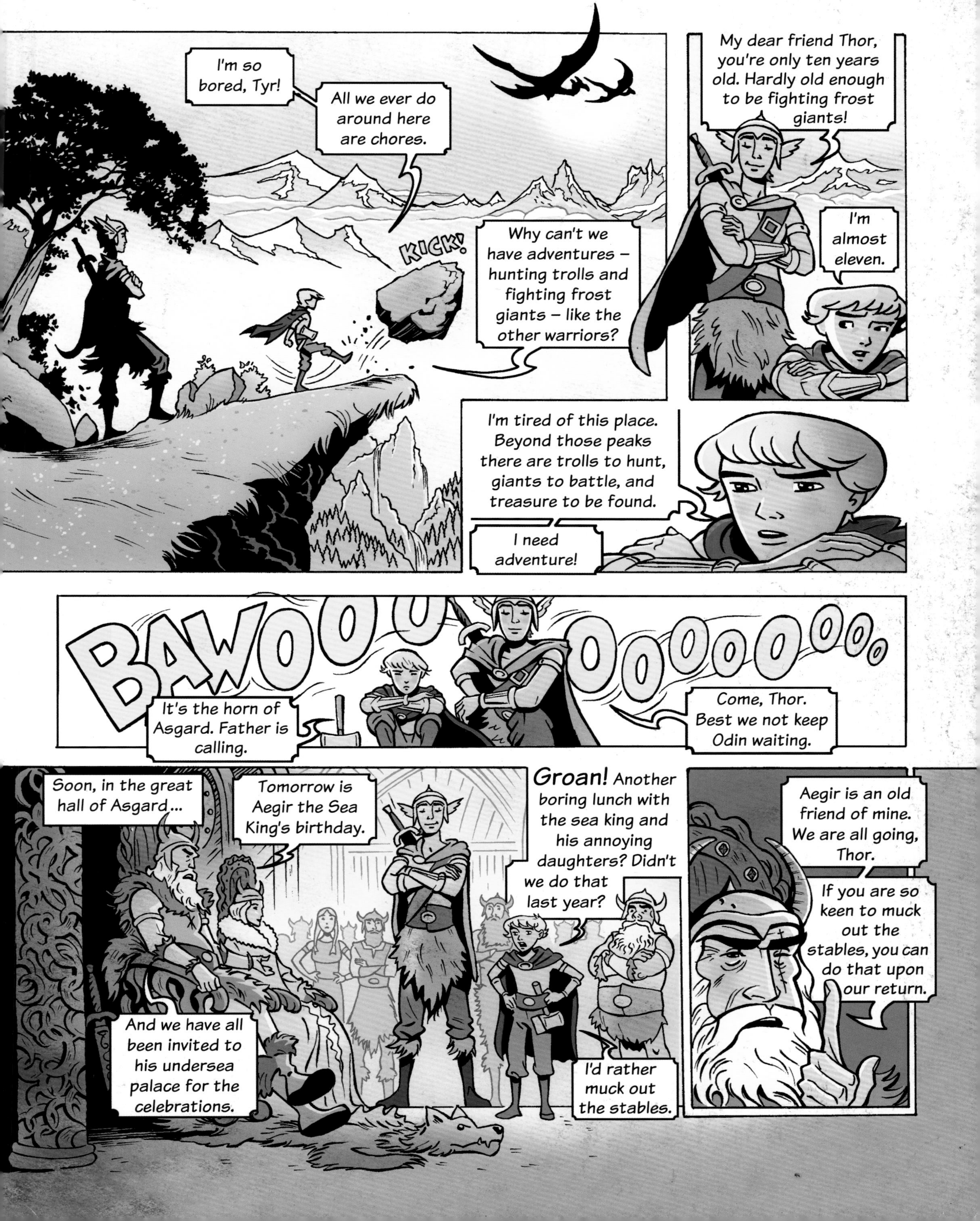
I'm so bored, Tyr!
All we ever do around here are chores.
KICK!
Why can't we have adventures – hunting trolls and fighting frost giants – like the other warriors?
My dear friend Thor, you're only ten years old. Hardly old enough to be fighting frost giants!
I'm almost eleven.
I'm tired of this place. Beyond those peaks there are trolls to hunt, giants to battle, and treasure to be found.
I need adventure!
BAWOOOOOOOOOOOo
It's the horn of Asgard. Father is calling.
Come, Thor. Best we not keep Odin waiting.
Soon, in the great hall of Asgard...
Tomorrow is Aegir the Sea King's birthday.
And we have all been invited to his undersea palace for the celebrations.
Groan! Another boring lunch with the sea king and his annoying daughters? Didn't we do that last year?
I'd rather muck out the stables.
Aegir is an old friend of mine. We are all going, Thor.
If you are so keen to muck out the stables, you can do that upon our return.

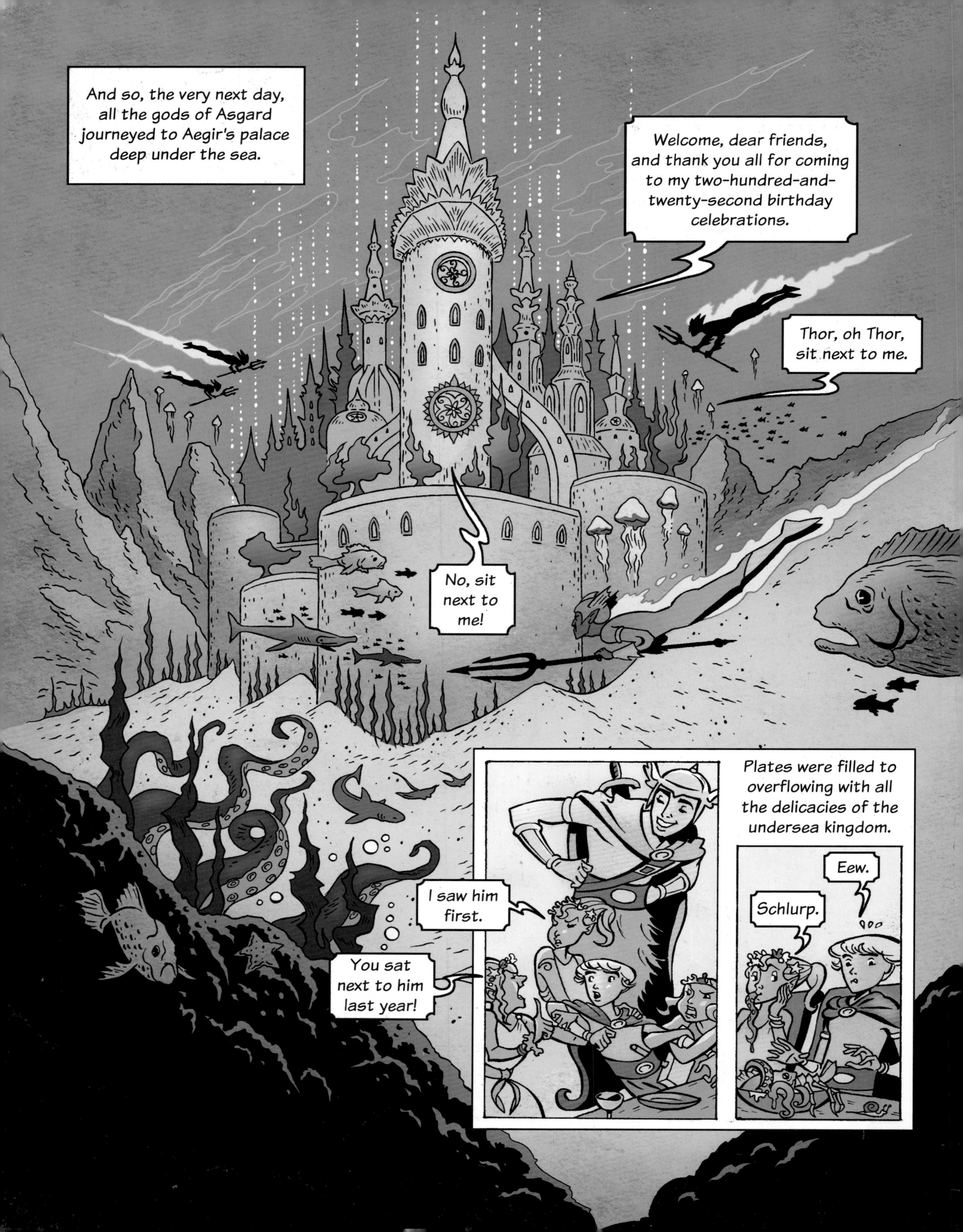
And so, the very next day, all the gods of Asgard journeyed to Aegir's palace deep under the sea.
Welcome, dear friends, and thank you all for coming to my two-hundred-and-twenty-second birthday celebrations.
Thor, oh Thor, sit next to me.
No, sit next to me!
Plates were filled to overflowing with all the delicacies of the undersea kingdom.
I saw him first.
You sat next to him last year!
Schlurp.
Eew.

Now, we have a slight problem in the kitchen.

You see, we don't have a pot large enough to brew mead for all the gods of Asgard.

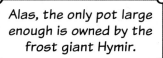

Alas, the only pot large enough is owned by the frost giant Hymir.

And there isn't anyone brave enough to venture to Hymir's castle and borrow it from him.

Hymir is my father. I'll persuade him to lend us his mead pot.

Hymir is still furious with you. That giant fears only me. Perhaps I should go.

Father, you are far too busy! Let me journey to the land of the frost giants with Tyr and fetch Hymir's mead pot.

Absolutely not, Thor. You're much too young.

Your duties are in Asgard, for now.

But I'm old enough now!

CRACK

I'll show you! I'll fetch the mead pot on my own.

Thor!

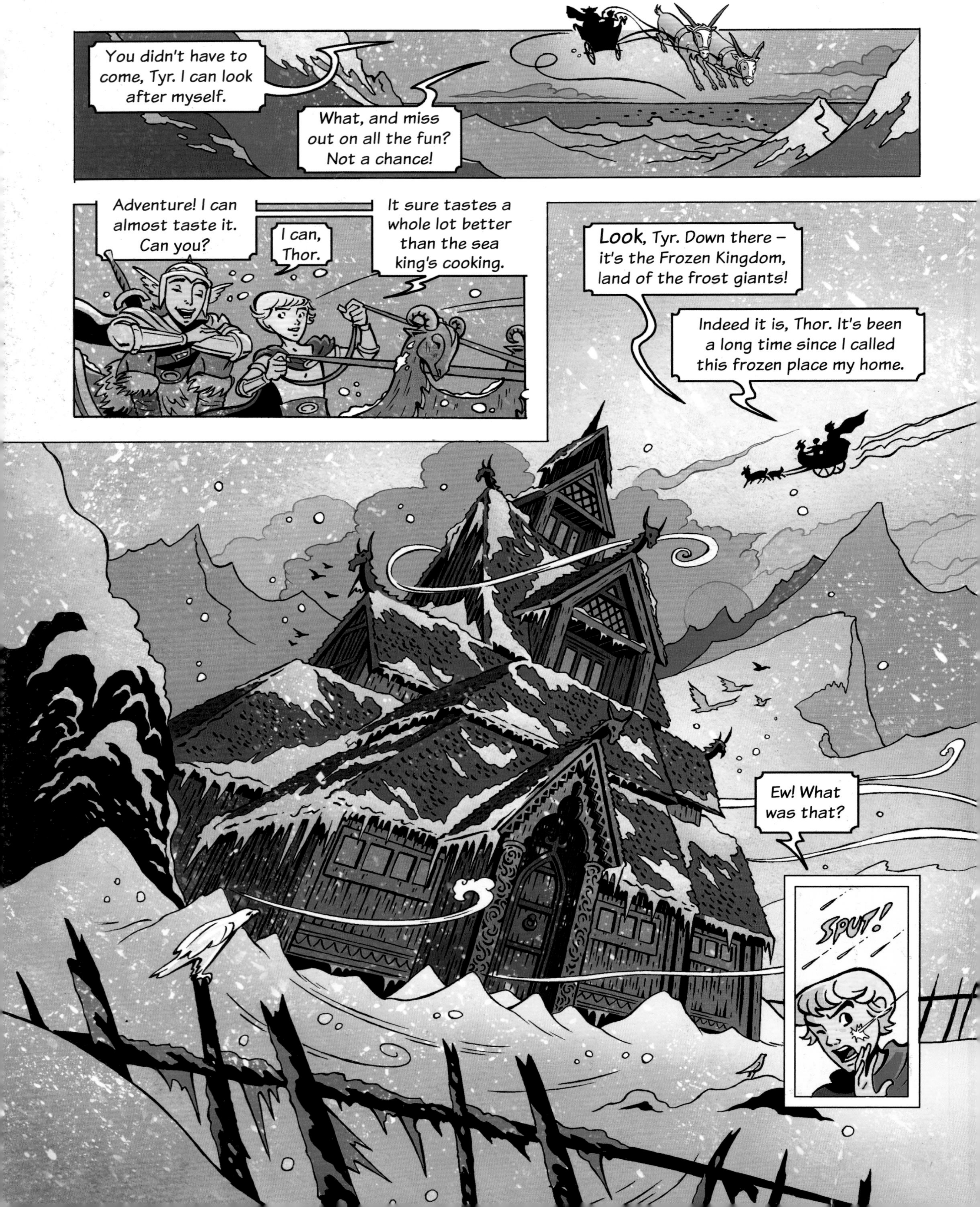
You didn't have to come, Tyr. I can look after myself.
What, and miss out on all the fun? Not a chance!
Adventure! I can almost taste it. Can you?
I can, Thor.
It sure tastes a whole lot better than the sea king's cooking.
Look, Tyr. Down there – it's the Frozen Kingdom, land of the frost giants!
Indeed it is, Thor. It's been a long time since I called this frozen place my home.
Ew! What was that?
SPUT!

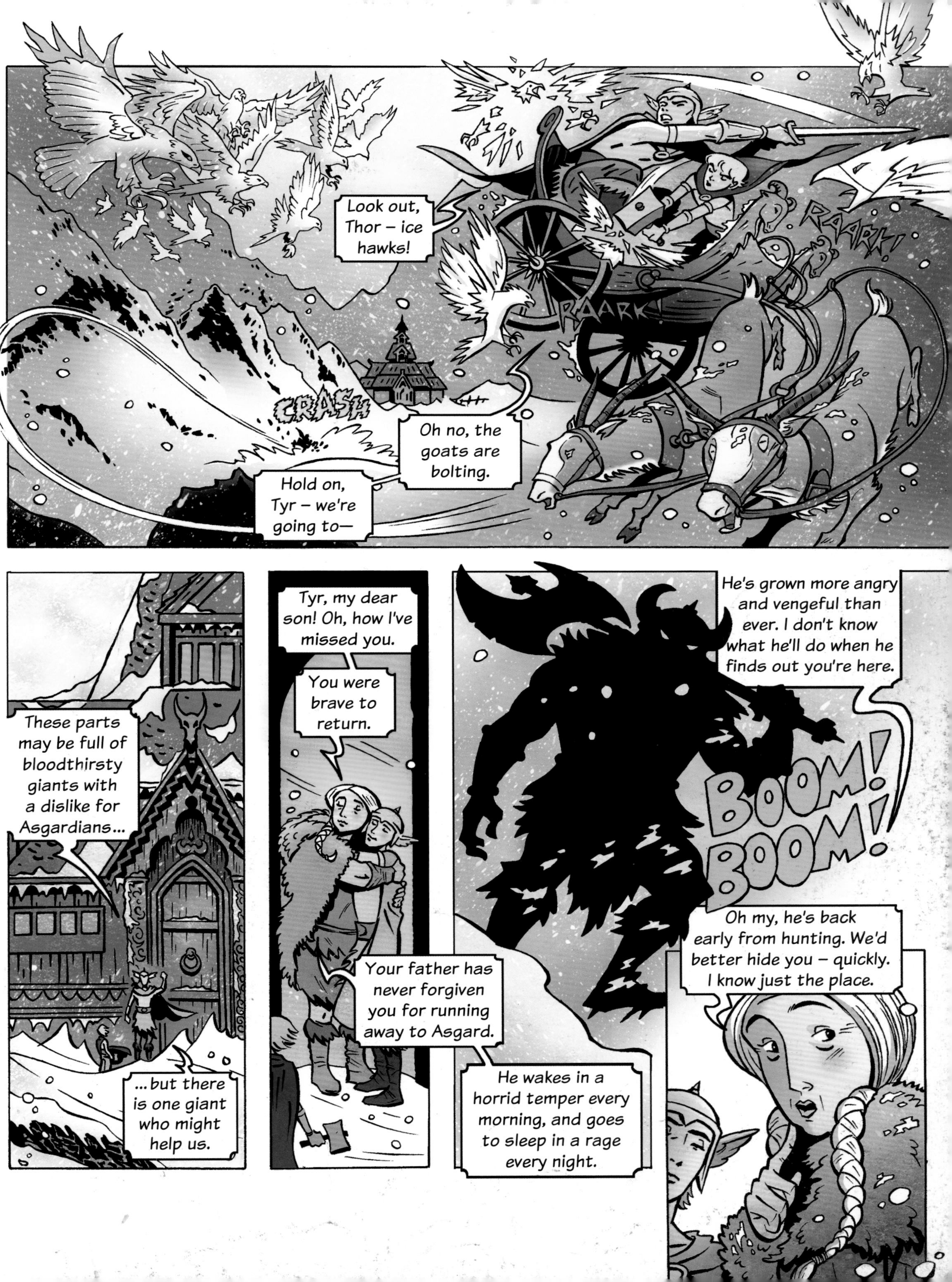
Look out, Thor – ice hawks!
RAARK!
RAARK
CRASH
Oh no, the goats are bolting.
Hold on, Tyr – we're going to—
These parts may be full of bloodthirsty giants with a dislike for Asgardians...
...but there is one giant who might help us.
Tyr, my dear son! Oh, how I've missed you.
You were brave to return.
Your father has never forgiven you for running away to Asgard.
He wakes in a horrid temper every morning, and goes to sleep in a rage every night.
He's grown more angry and vengeful than ever. I don't know what he'll do when he finds out you're here.
BOOM! BOOM!
Oh my, he's back early from hunting. We'd better hide you – quickly. I know just the place.

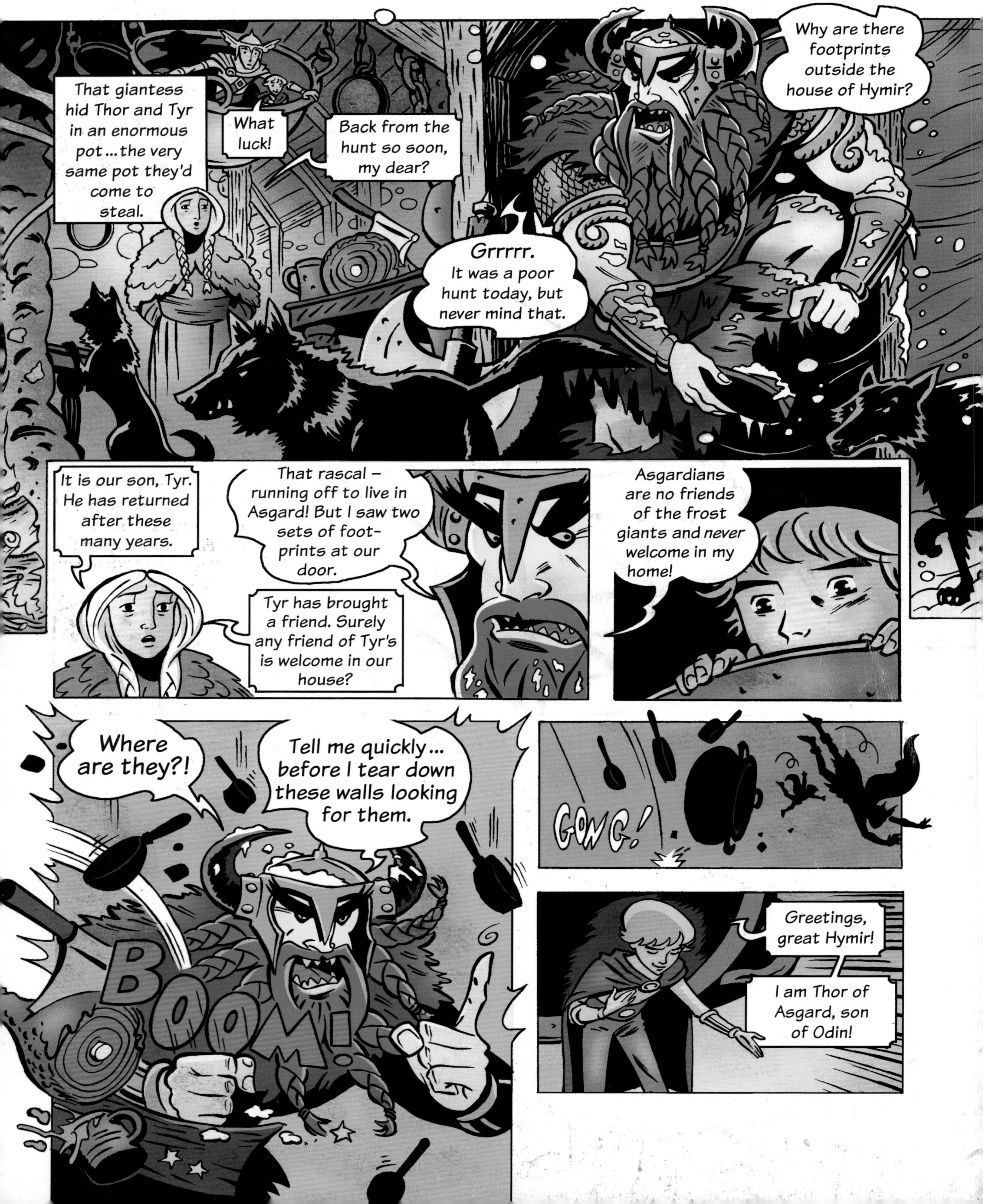

That giantess hid Thor and Tyr in an enormous pot ... the very same pot they'd come to steal.
What luck!
Back from the hunt so soon, my dear?
Why are there footprints outside the house of Hymir?
Grrrrr. It was a poor hunt today, but never mind that.
It is our son, Tyr. He has returned after these many years.
That rascal – running off to live in Asgard! But I saw two sets of footprints at our door.
Tyr has brought a friend. Surely any friend of Tyr's is welcome in our house?
Asgardians are no friends of the frost giants and *never* welcome in my home!
Where are they?!
Tell me quickly... before I tear down these walls looking for them.
BOOM!
GONG!
Greetings, great Hymir!
I am Thor of Asgard, son of Odin!

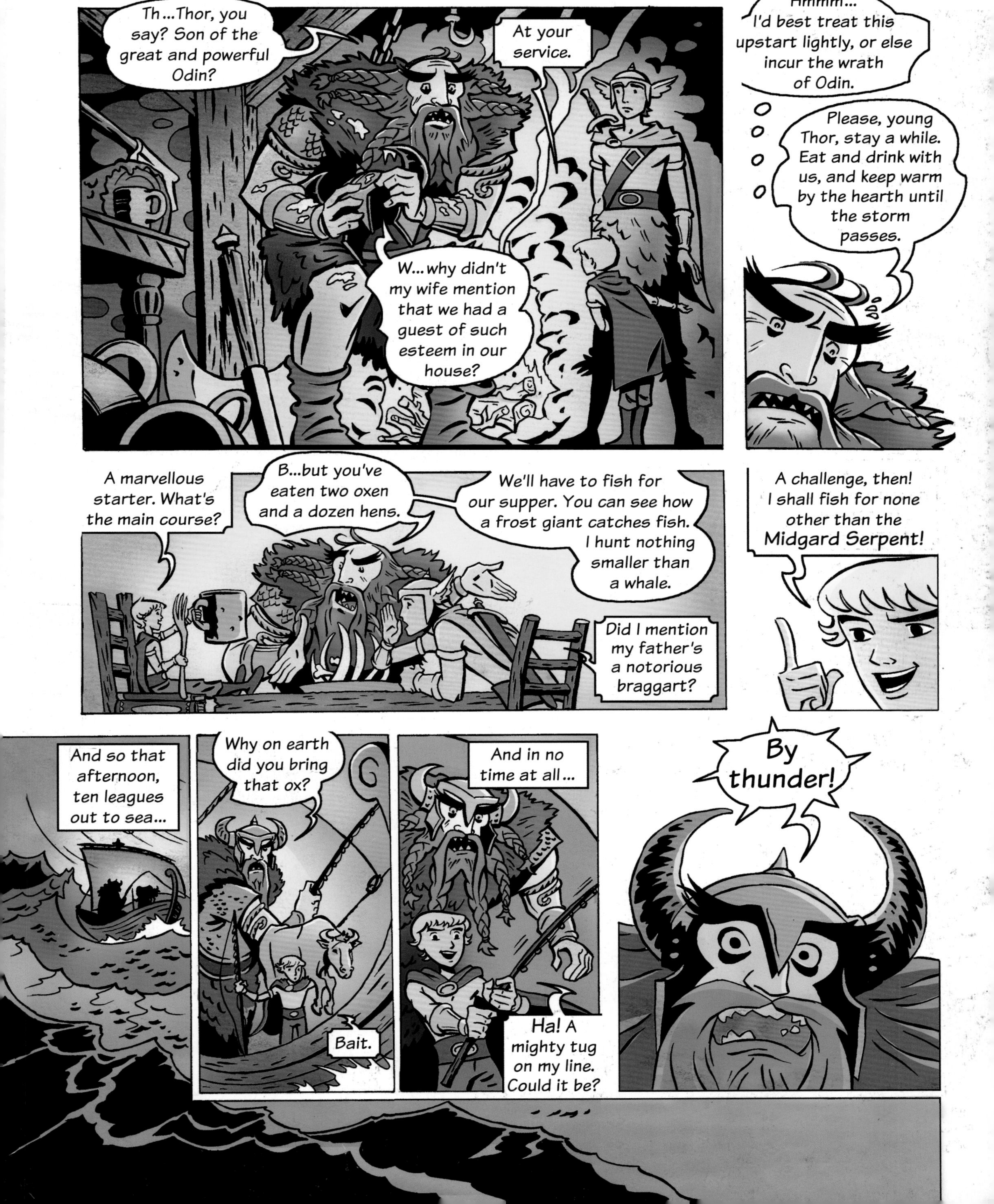
Th...Thor, you say? Son of the great and powerful Odin?
At your service.
W...why didn't my wife mention that we had a guest of such esteem in our house?
Hmmm... I'd best treat this upstart lightly, or else incur the wrath of Odin.
Please, young Thor, stay a while. Eat and drink with us, and keep warm by the hearth until the storm passes.
A marvellous starter. What's the main course?
B...but you've eaten two oxen and a dozen hens.
We'll have to fish for our supper. You can see how a frost giant catches fish. I hunt nothing smaller than a whale.
Did I mention my father's a notorious braggart?
A challenge, then! I shall fish for none other than the Midgard Serpent!
And so that afternoon, ten leagues out to sea...
Why on earth did you bring that ox?
Bait.
And in no time at all...
Ha! A mighty tug on my line. Could it be?
By thunder!

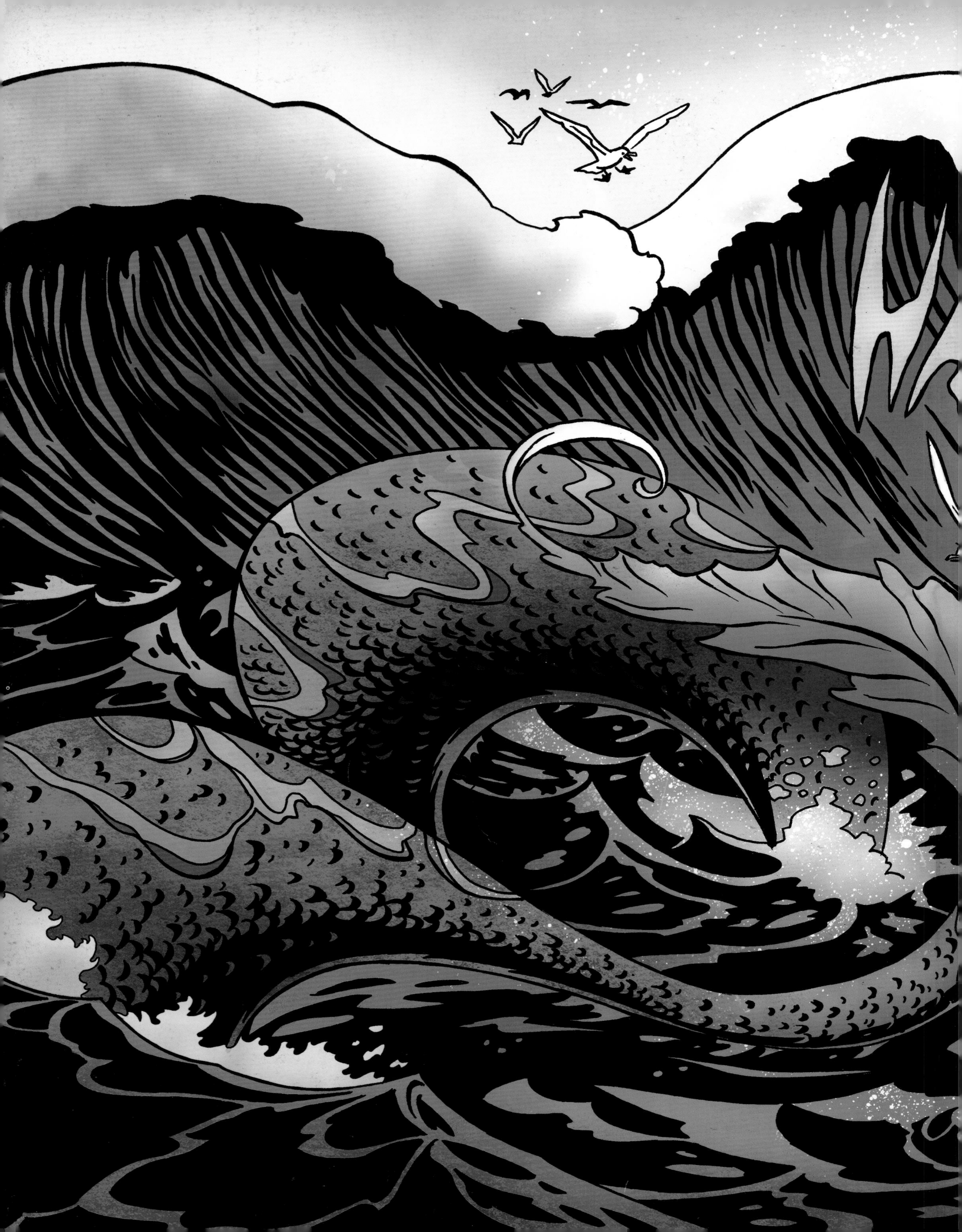

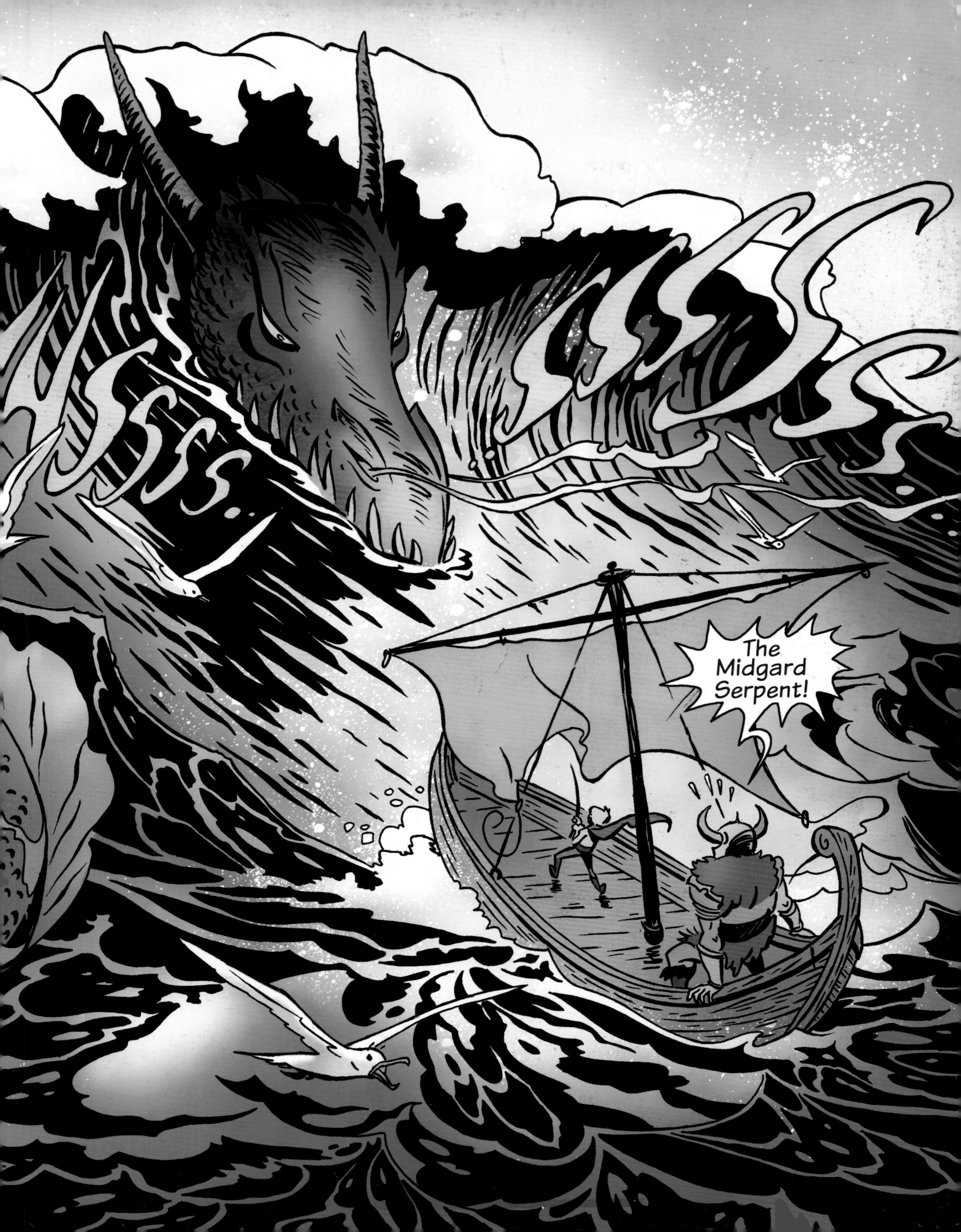
The Midgard Serpent!

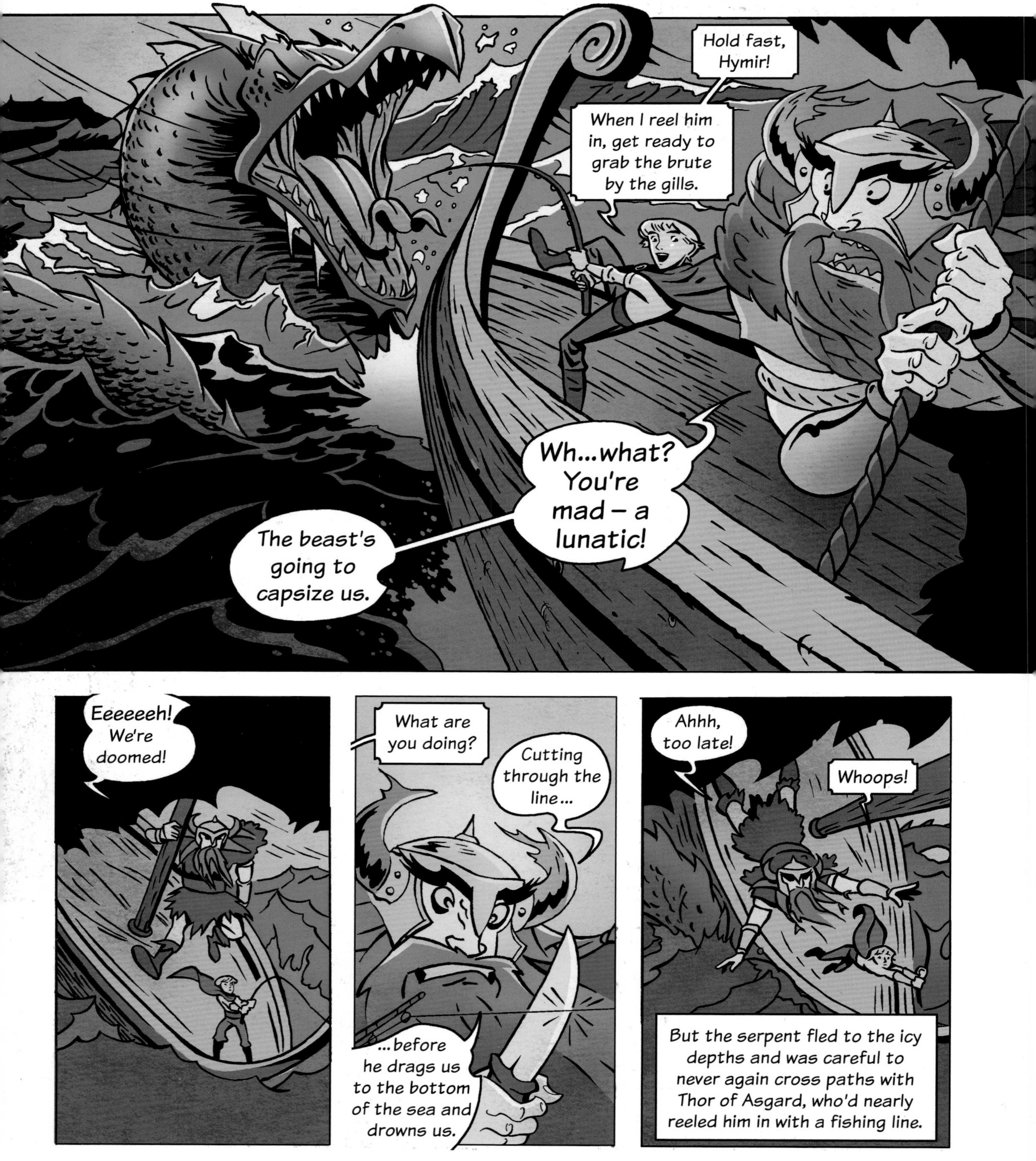
Hold fast, Hymir!
When I reel him in, get ready to grab the brute by the gills.
Wh...what? You're mad – a lunatic!
The beast's going to capsize us.
Eeeeeeh! We're doomed!
What are you doing?
Cutting through the line...
...before he drags us to the bottom of the sea and drowns us.
Ahhh, too late!
Whoops!
But the serpent fled to the icy depths and was careful to never again cross paths with Thor of Asgard, who'd nearly reeled him in with a fishing line.

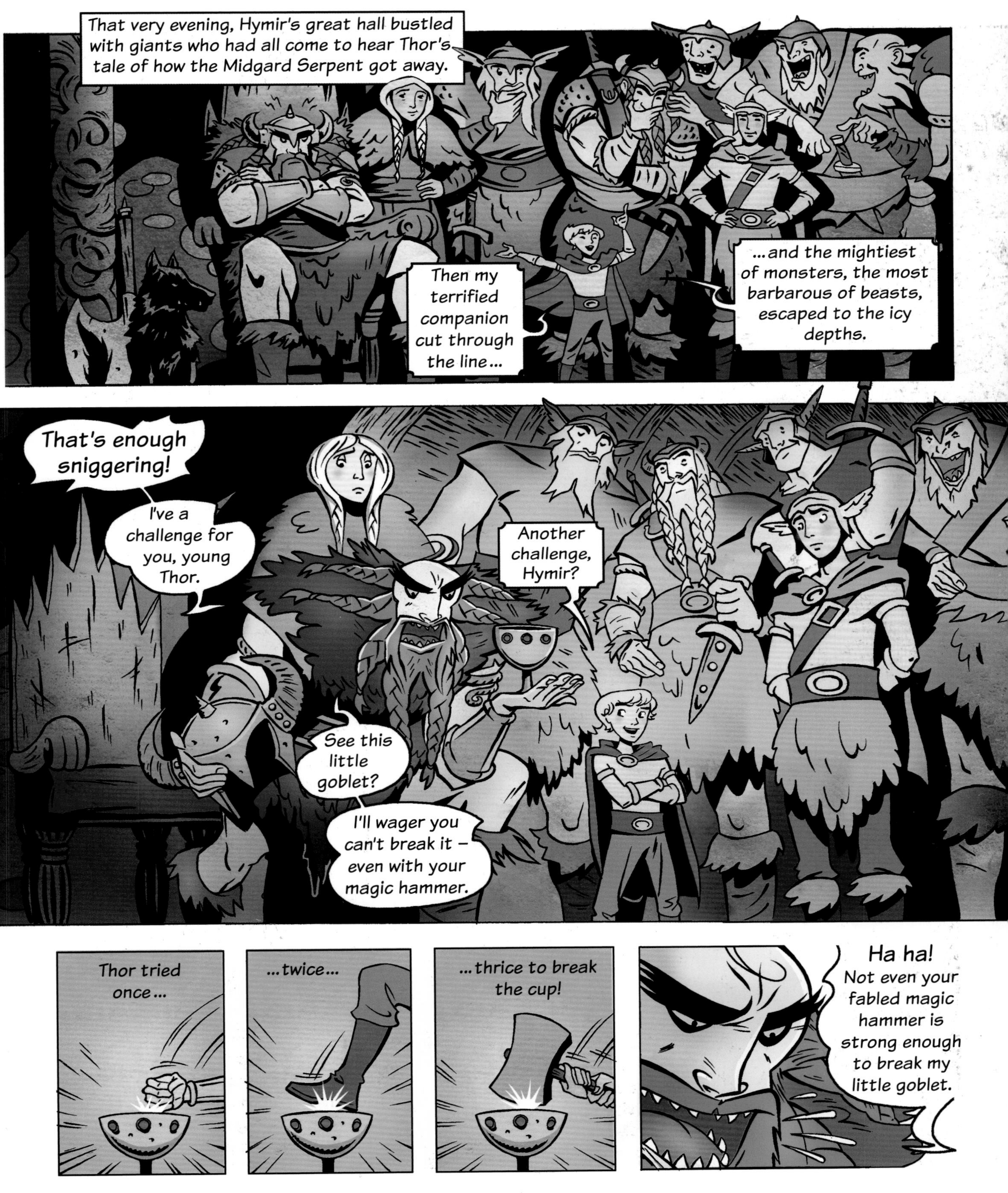

That very evening, Hymir's great hall bustled with giants who had all come to hear Thor's tale of how the Midgard Serpent got away.
Then my terrified companion cut through the line...
...and the mightiest of monsters, the most barbarous of beasts, escaped to the icy depths.
That's enough sniggering!
I've a challenge for you, young Thor.
Another challenge, Hymir?
See this little goblet?
I'll wager you can't break it – even with your magic hammer.
Thor tried once...
...twice...
...thrice to break the cup!
Ha ha! Not even your fabled magic hammer is strong enough to break my little goblet.

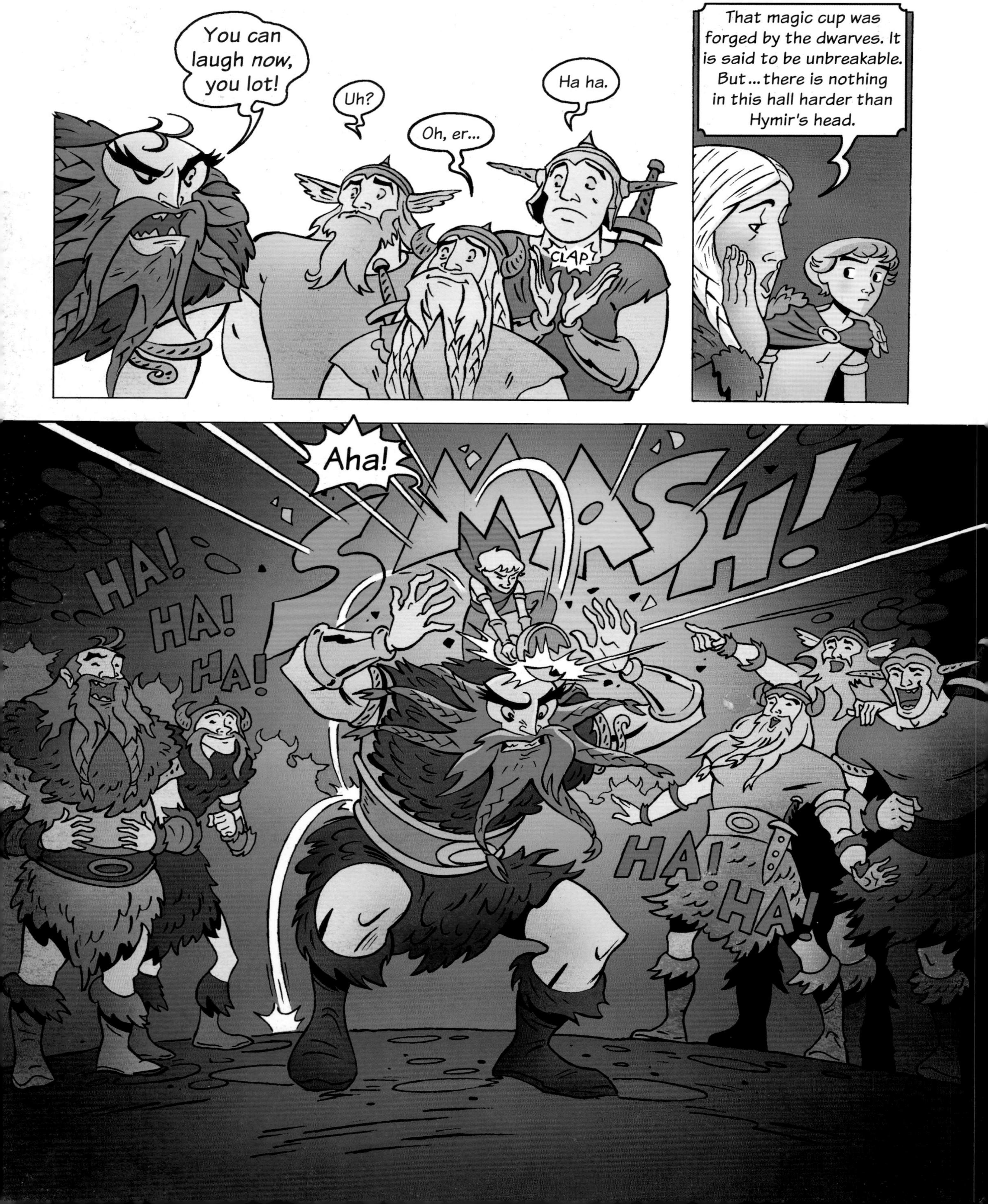
You can laugh now, you lot!
Uh?
Oh, er...
Ha ha.
CLAP!
That magic cup was forged by the dwarves. It is said to be unbreakable. But...there is nothing in this hall harder than Hymir's head.
Aha!
MASH!
HA! HA! HA!
HA! HA!

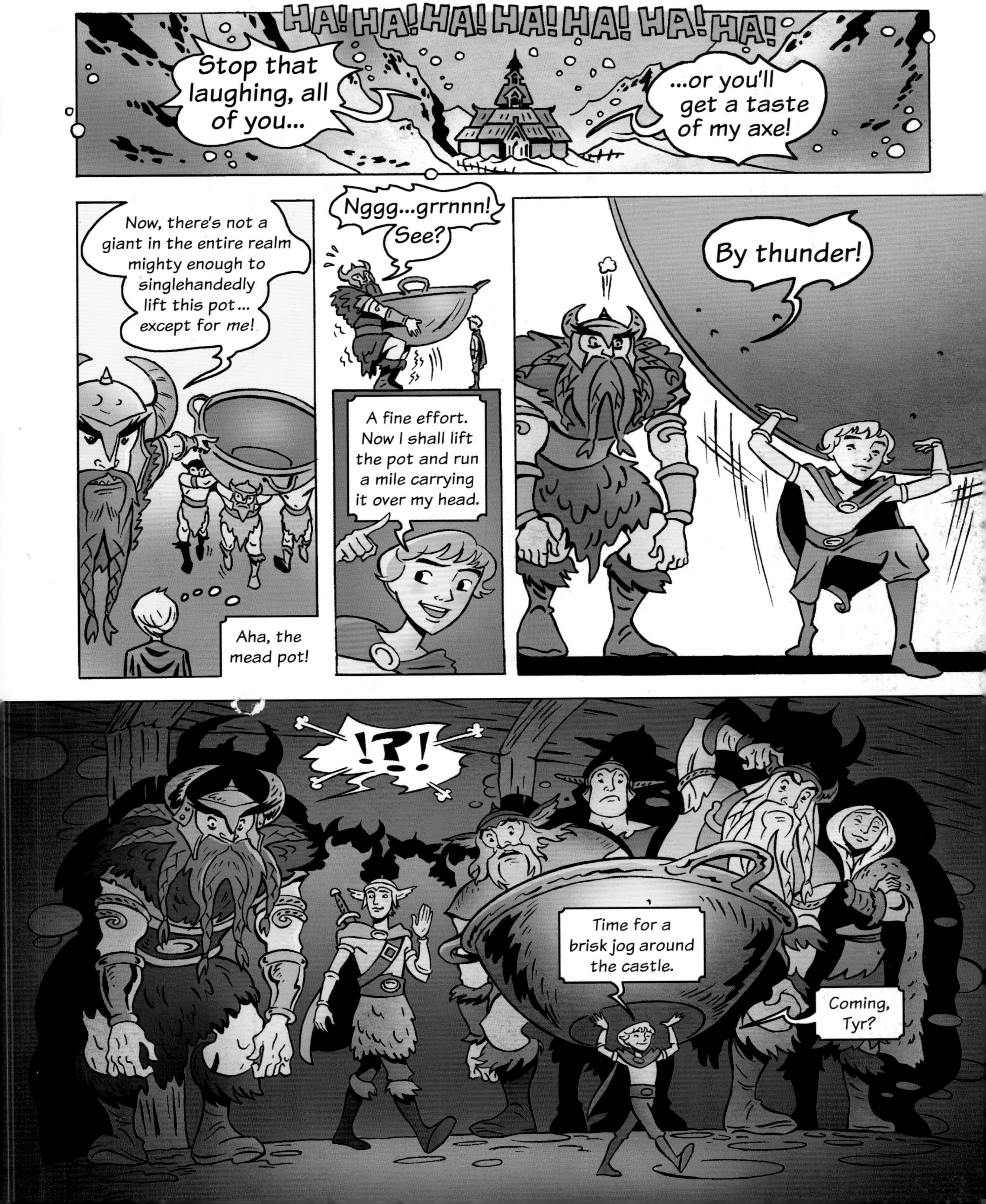
HA! HA! HA! HA! HA! HA! HA!
Stop that laughing, all of you...
...or you'll get a taste of my axe!
Now, there's not a giant in the entire realm mighty enough to singlehandedly lift this pot... except for me!
Aha, the mead pot!
Nggg...grrnnn! See?
A fine effort. Now I shall lift the pot and run a mile carrying it over my head.
By thunder!
!?!
Time for a brisk jog around the castle.
Coming, Tyr?

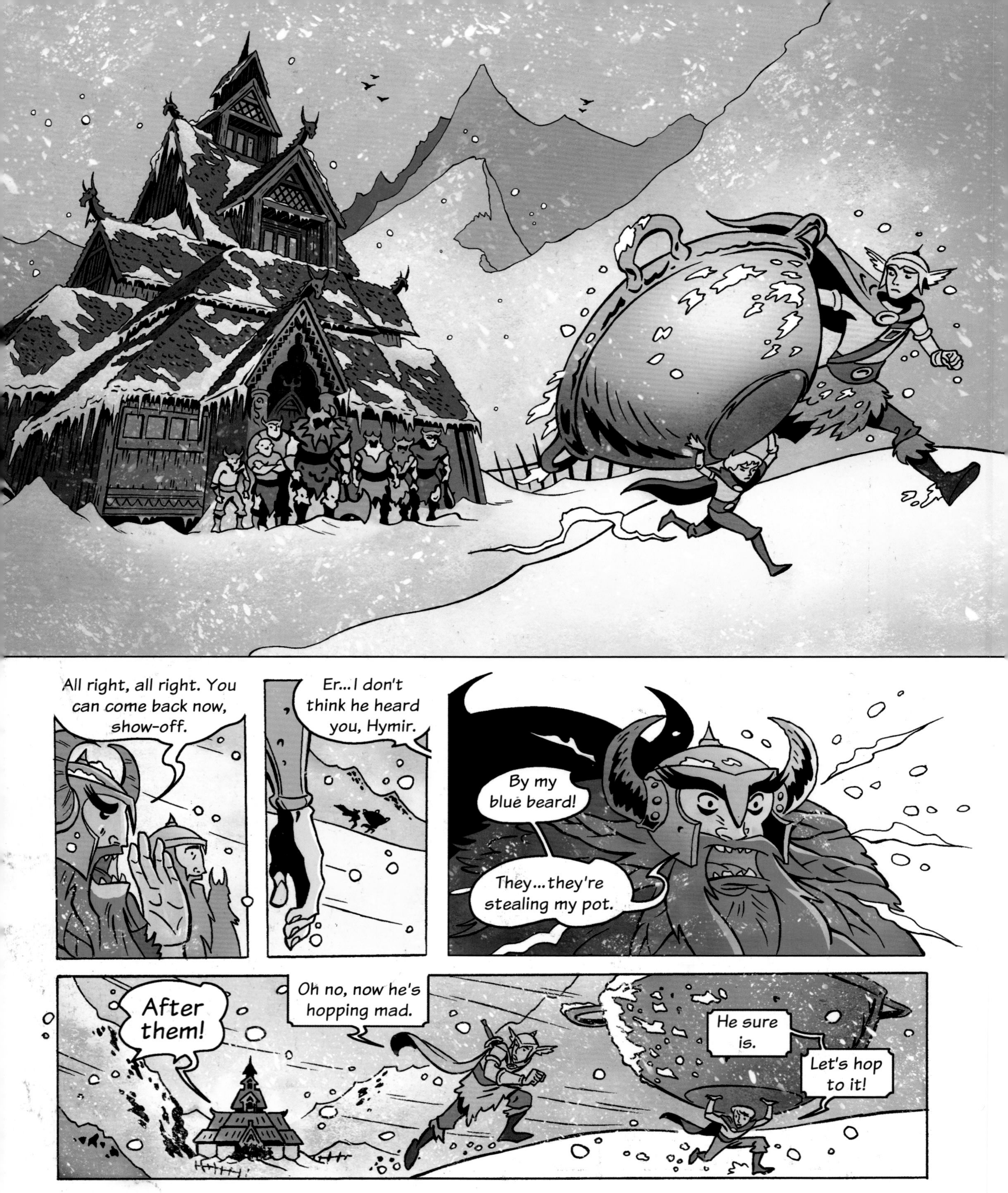
All right, all right. You can come back now, show-off.
Er...I don't think he heard you, Hymir.
By my blue beard!
They...they're stealing my pot.
After them!
Oh no, now he's hopping mad.
He sure is.
Let's hop to it!

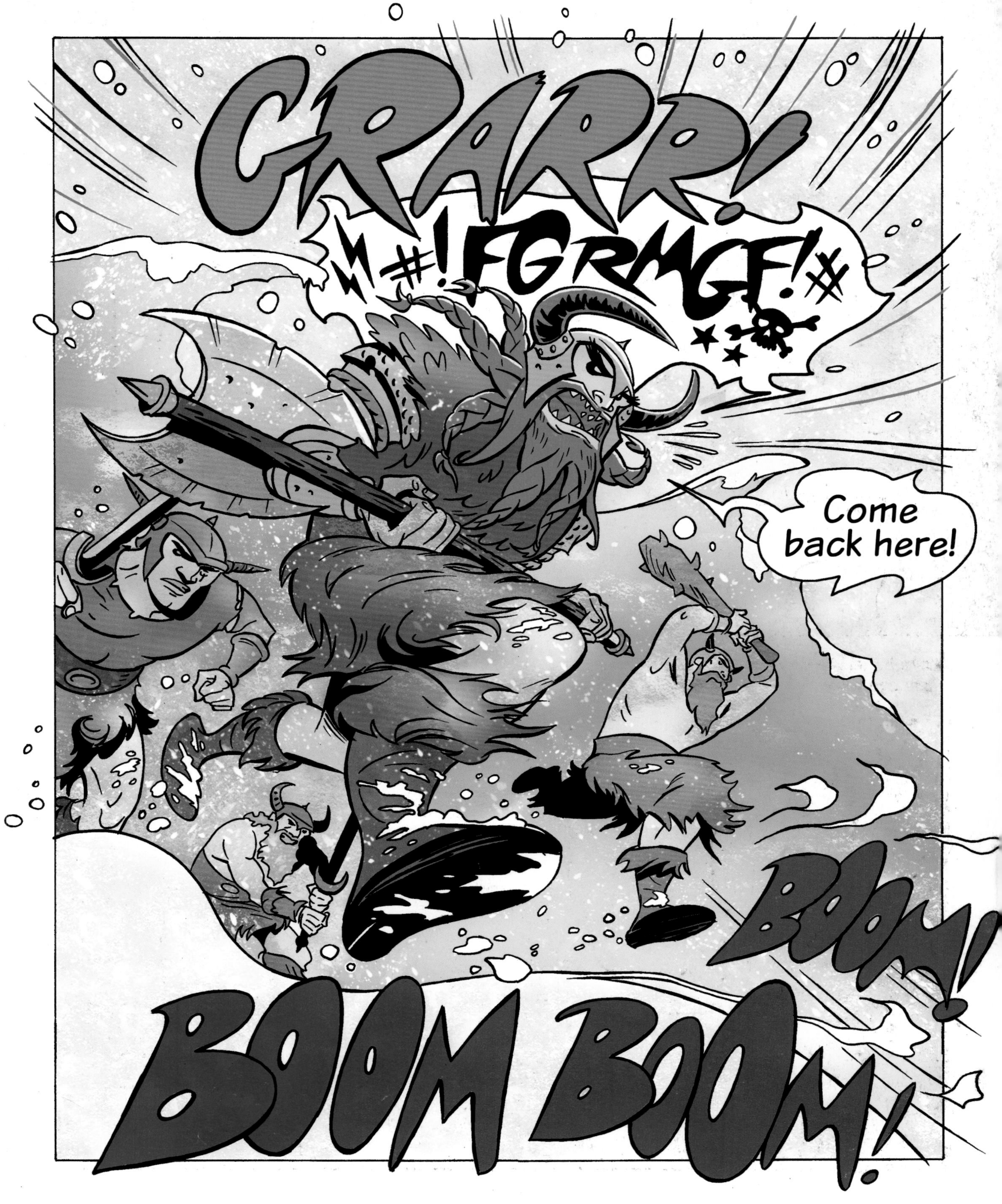
CRARR!
#!FGRMGF!#
Come back here!
BOOM!
BOOM BOOM!

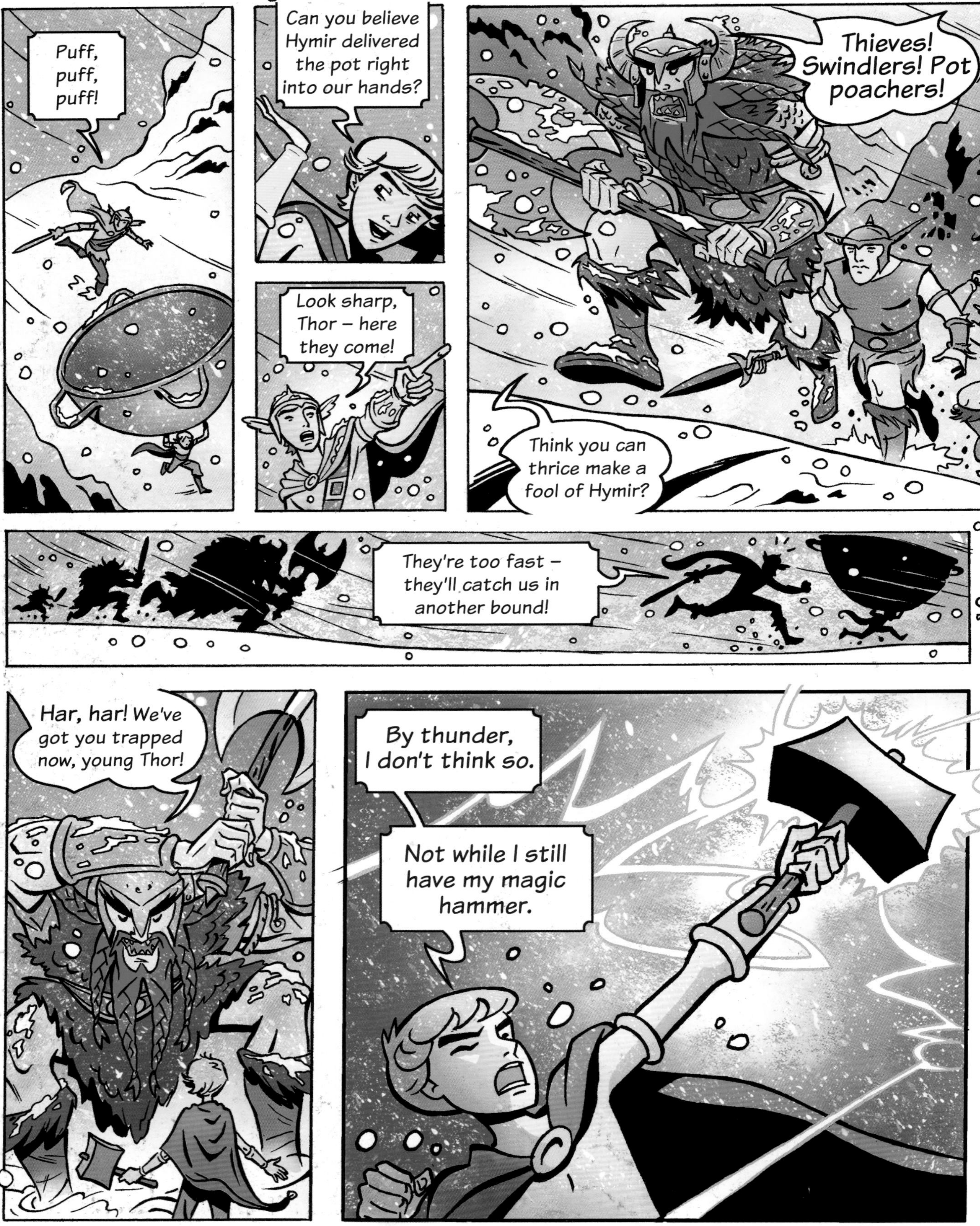
Puff, puff, puff!
Can you believe Hymir delivered the pot right into our hands?
Look sharp, Thor – here they come!
Thieves! Swindlers! Pot poachers!
Think you can thrice make a fool of Hymir?
They're too fast – they'll catch us in another bound!
Har, har! We've got you trapped now, young Thor!
By thunder, I don't think so.
Not while I still have my magic hammer.

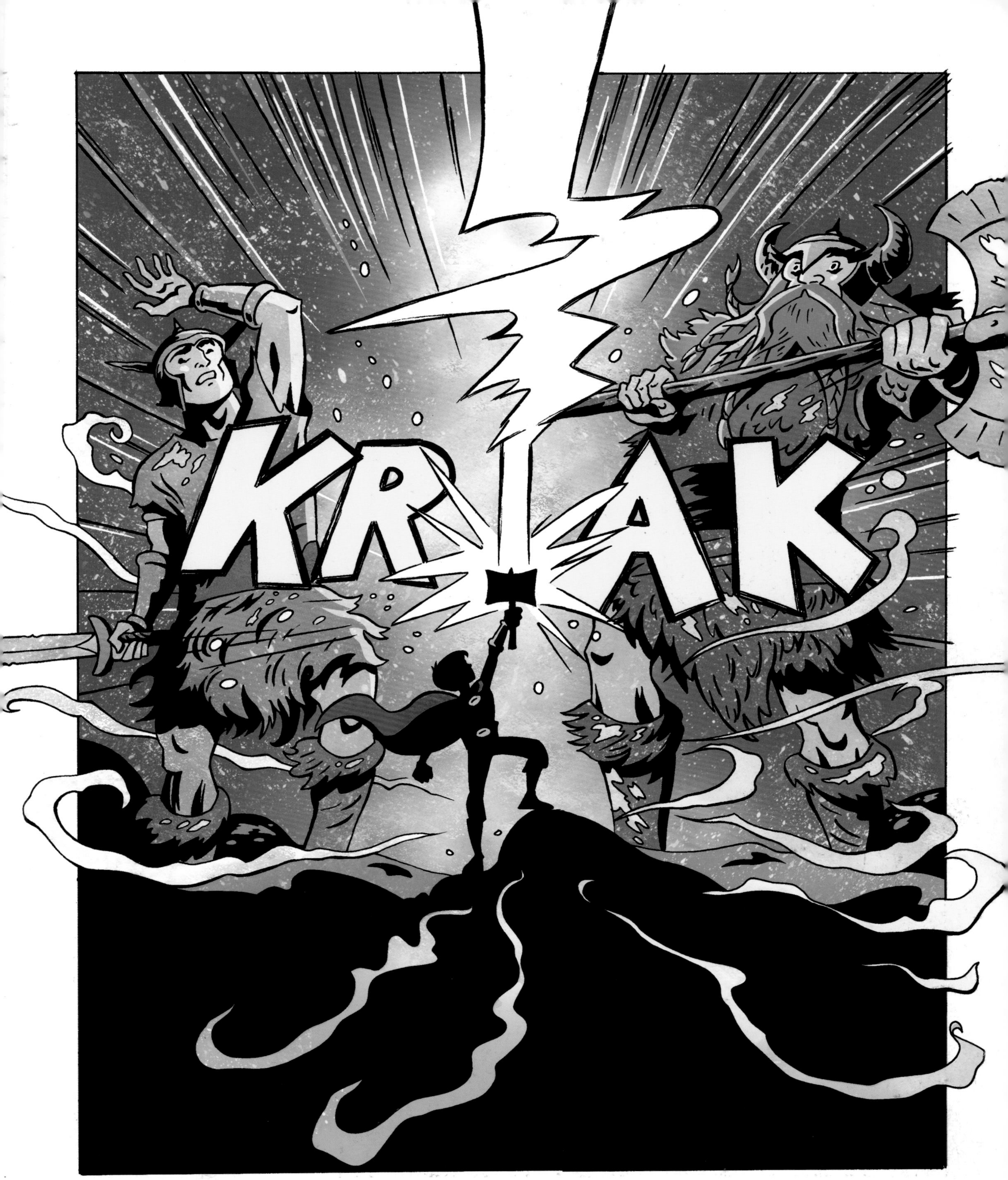
KR AK

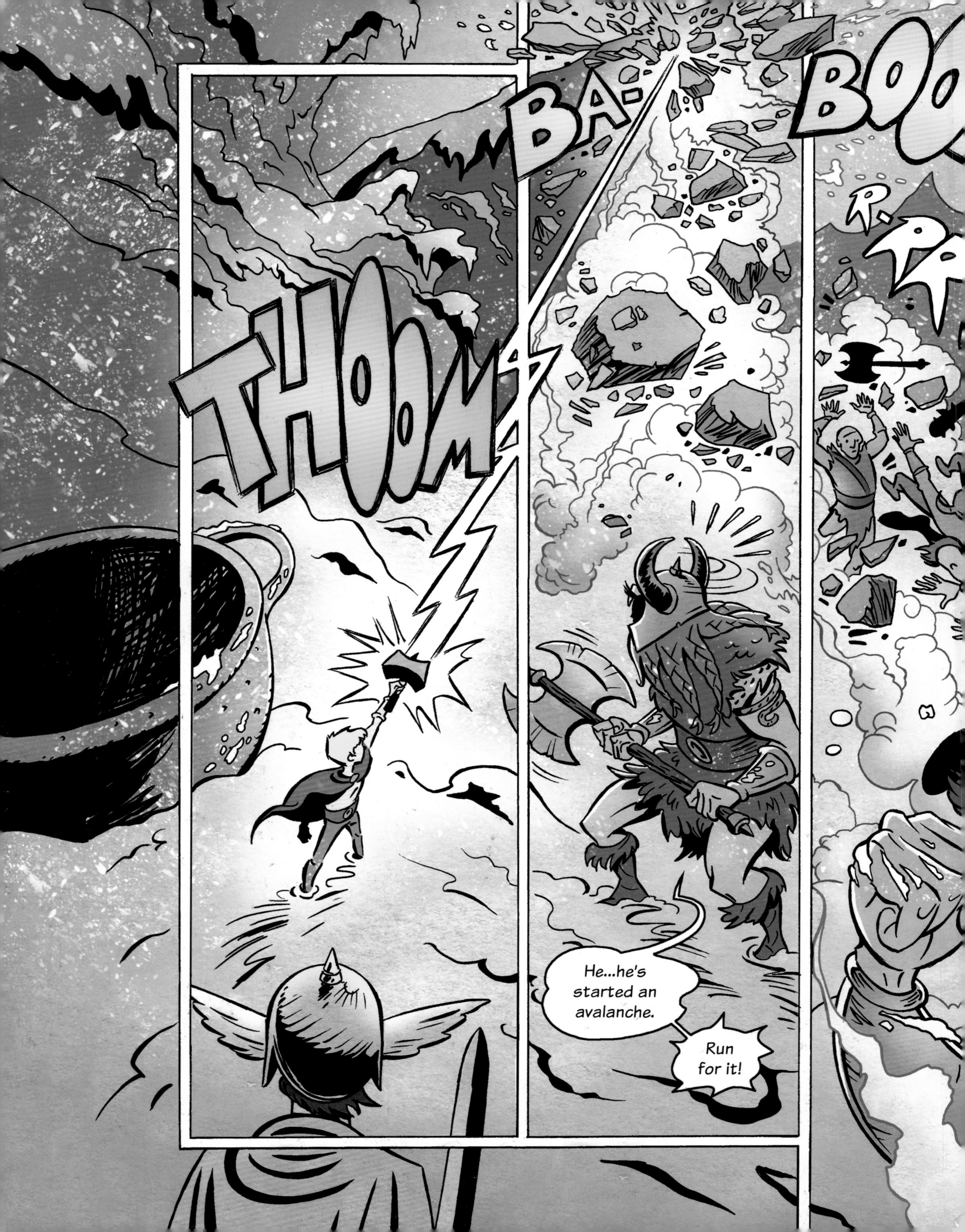
THOOM
BA-
BOO
He...he's started an avalanche.
Run for it!

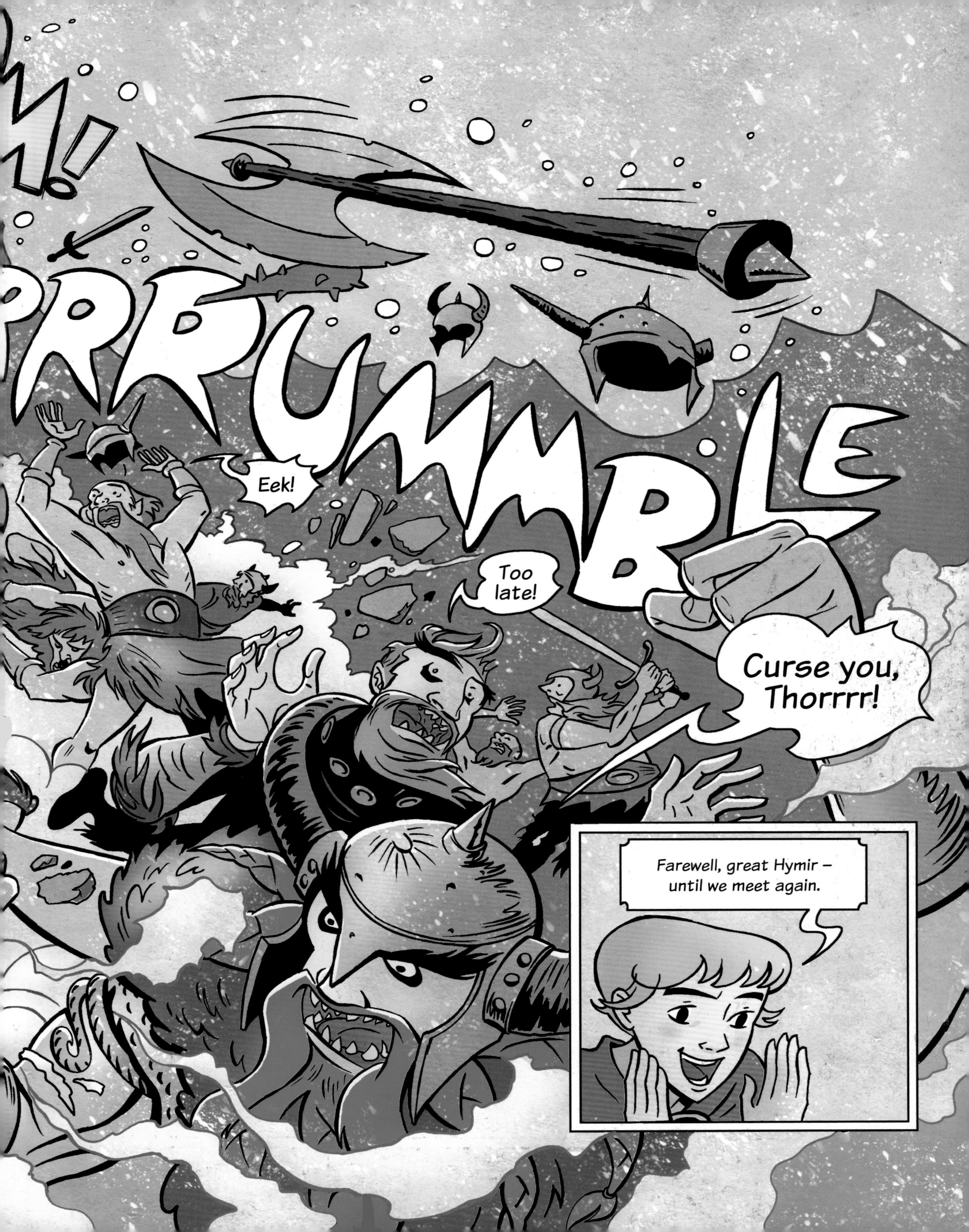
PRRUMMBLE
Eek!
Too late!
Curse you, Thorrrr!
Farewell, great Hymir – until we meet again.

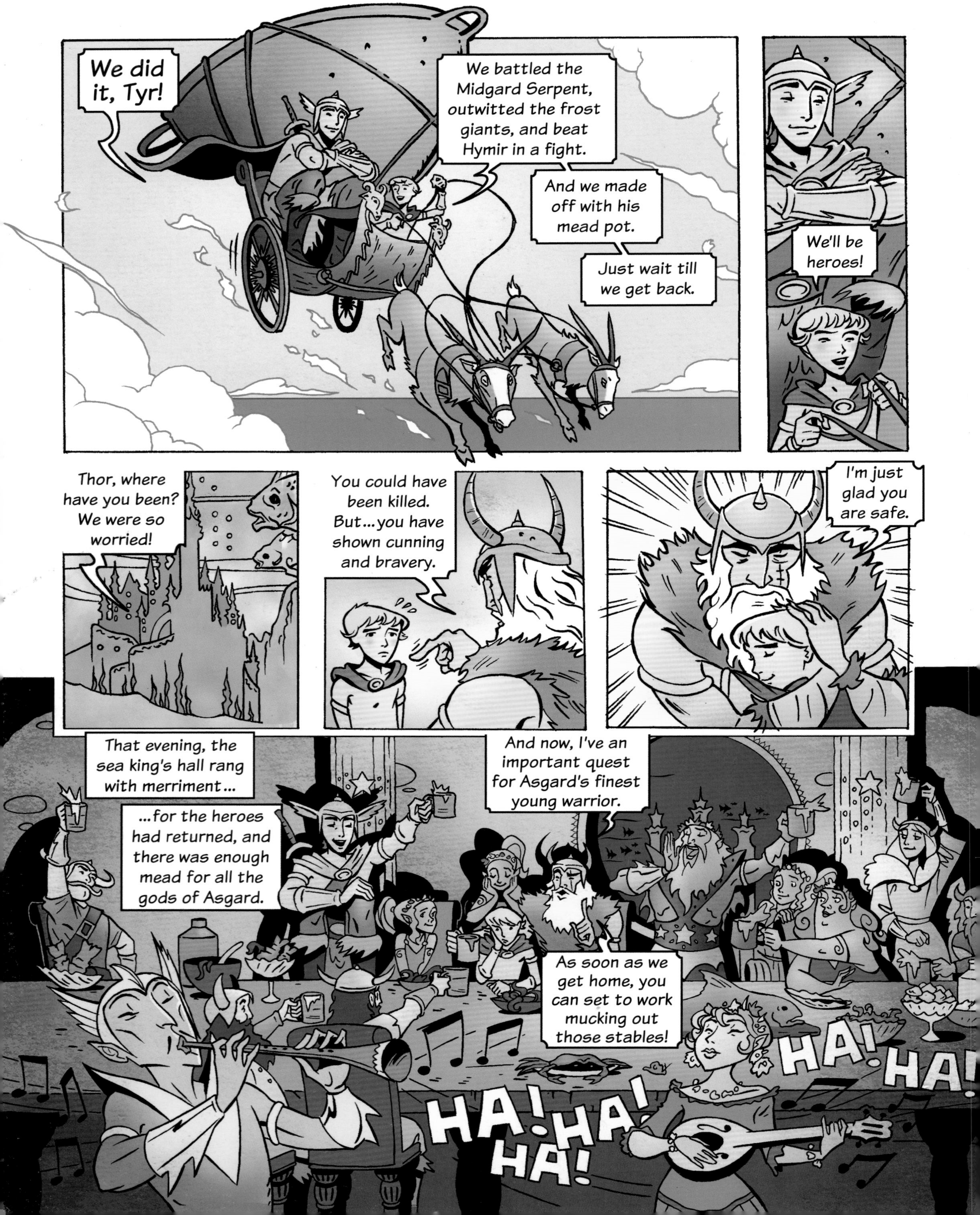

We did it, Tyr!
We battled the Midgard Serpent, outwitted the frost giants, and beat Hymir in a fight.
And we made off with his mead pot.
Just wait till we get back.
We'll be heroes!
Thor, where have you been? We were so worried!
You could have been killed. But...you have shown cunning and bravery.
I'm just glad you are safe.
That evening, the sea king's hall rang with merriment...
...for the heroes had returned, and there was enough mead for all the gods of Asgard.
And now, I've an important quest for Asgard's finest young warrior.
As soon as we get home, you can set to work mucking out those stables!
HA! HA! HA! HA! HA!

The Nixie in the Well

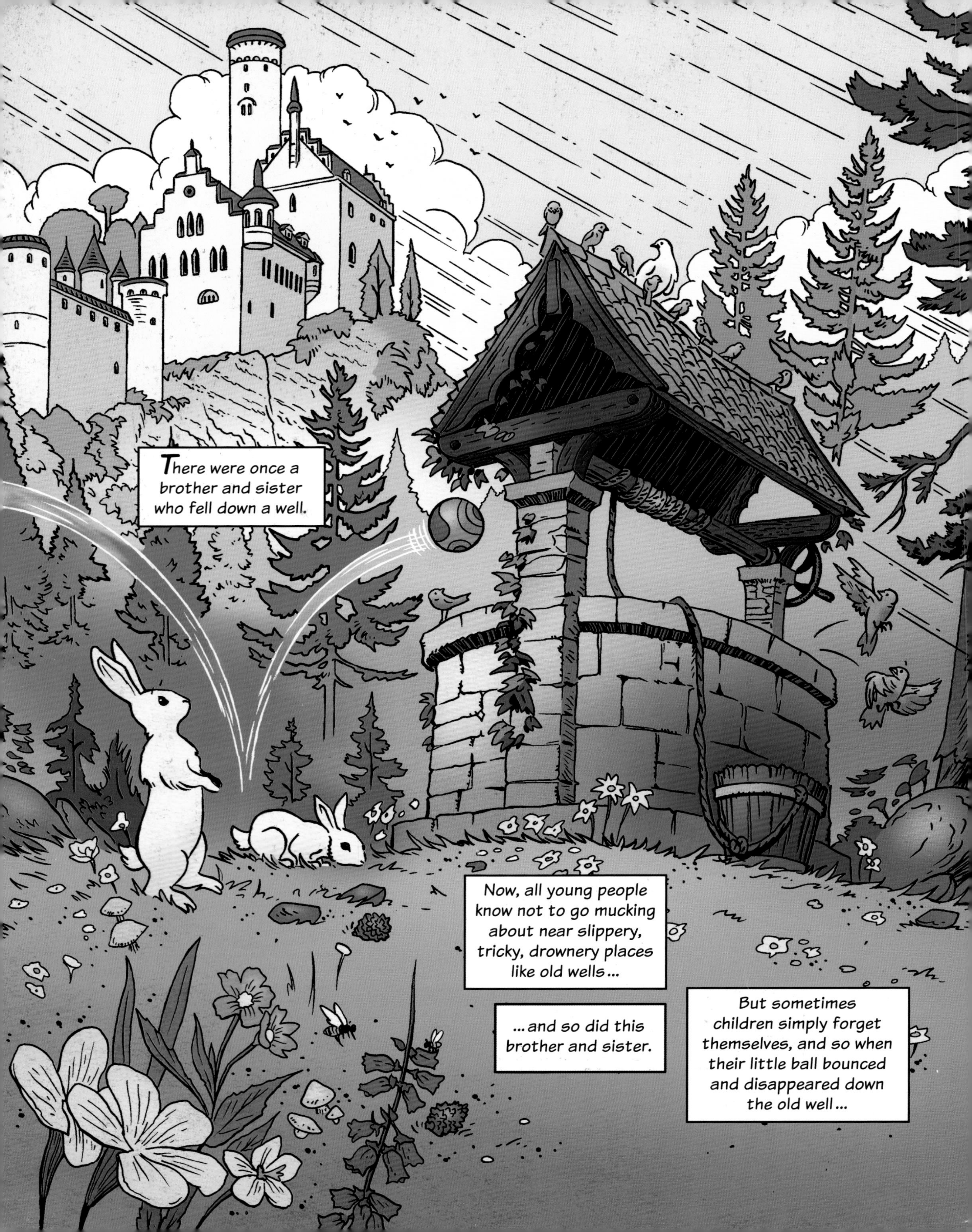
There were once a brother and sister who fell down a well.
Now, all young people know not to go mucking about near slippery, tricky, drownery places like old wells...
...and so did this brother and sister.
But sometimes children simply forget themselves, and so when their little ball bounced and disappeared down the old well...

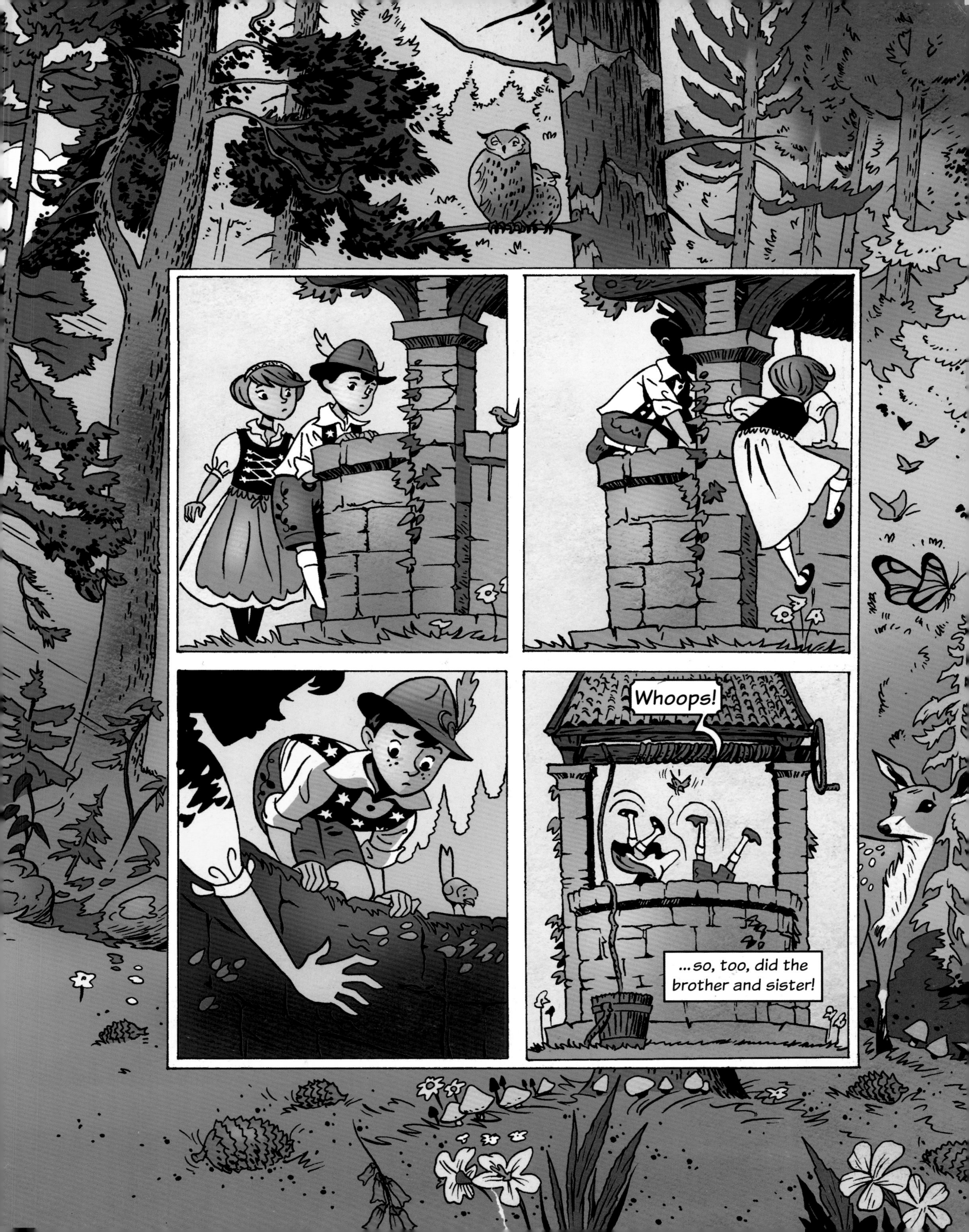
Whoops!
...so, too, did the brother and sister!

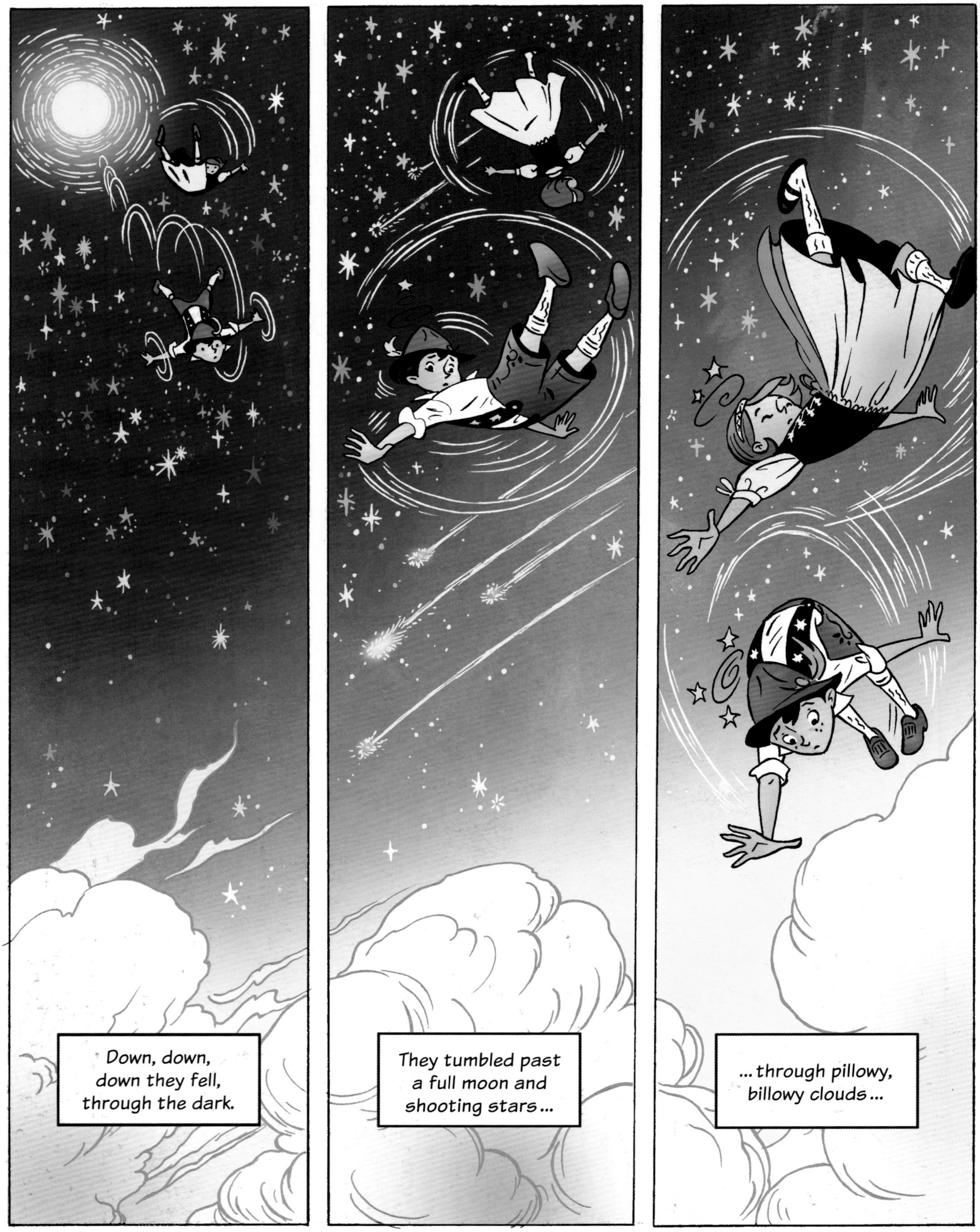
Down, down, down they fell, through the dark.
They tumbled past a full moon and shooting stars...
...through pillowy, billowy clouds...

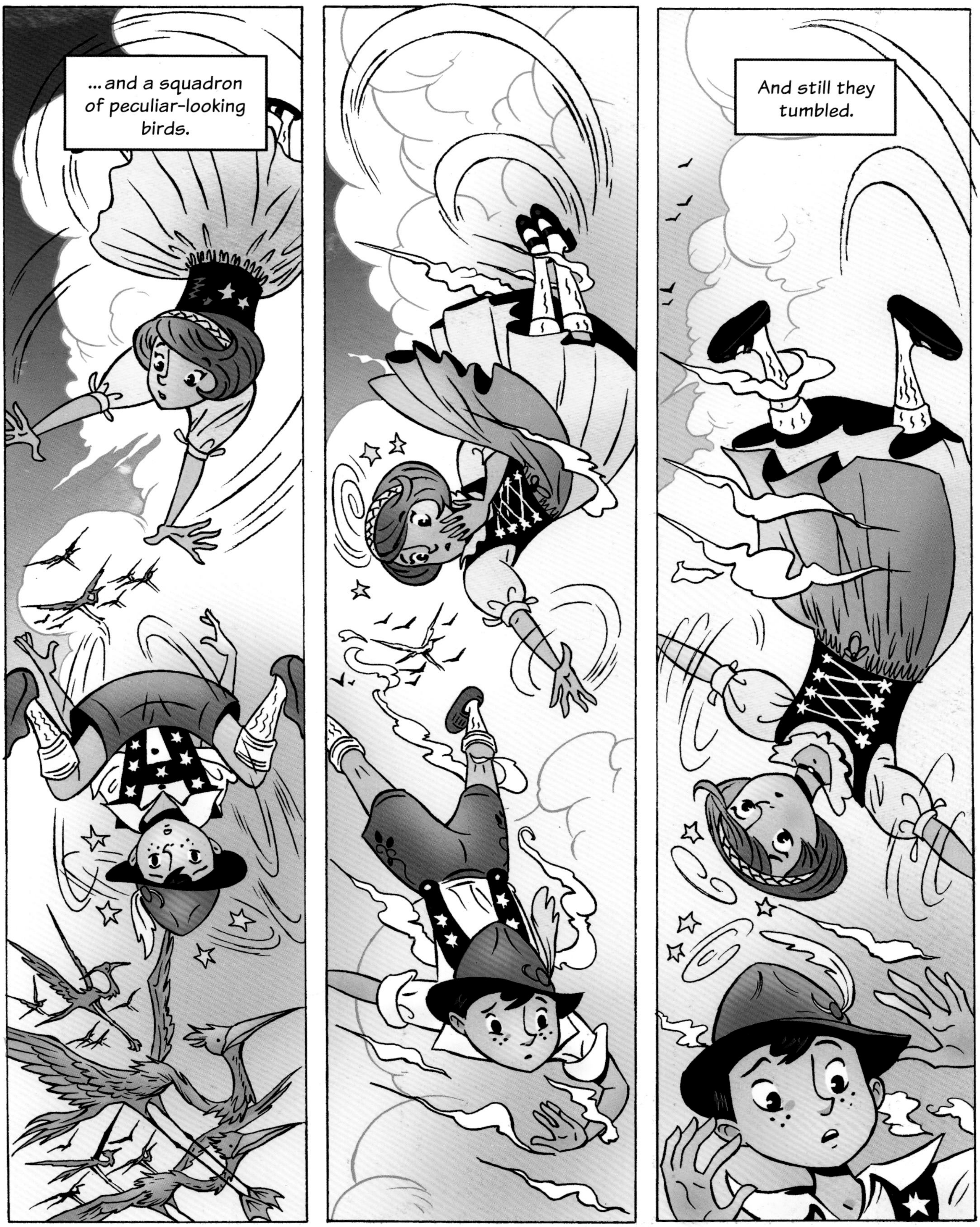
...and a squadron of peculiar-looking birds.
And still they tumbled.

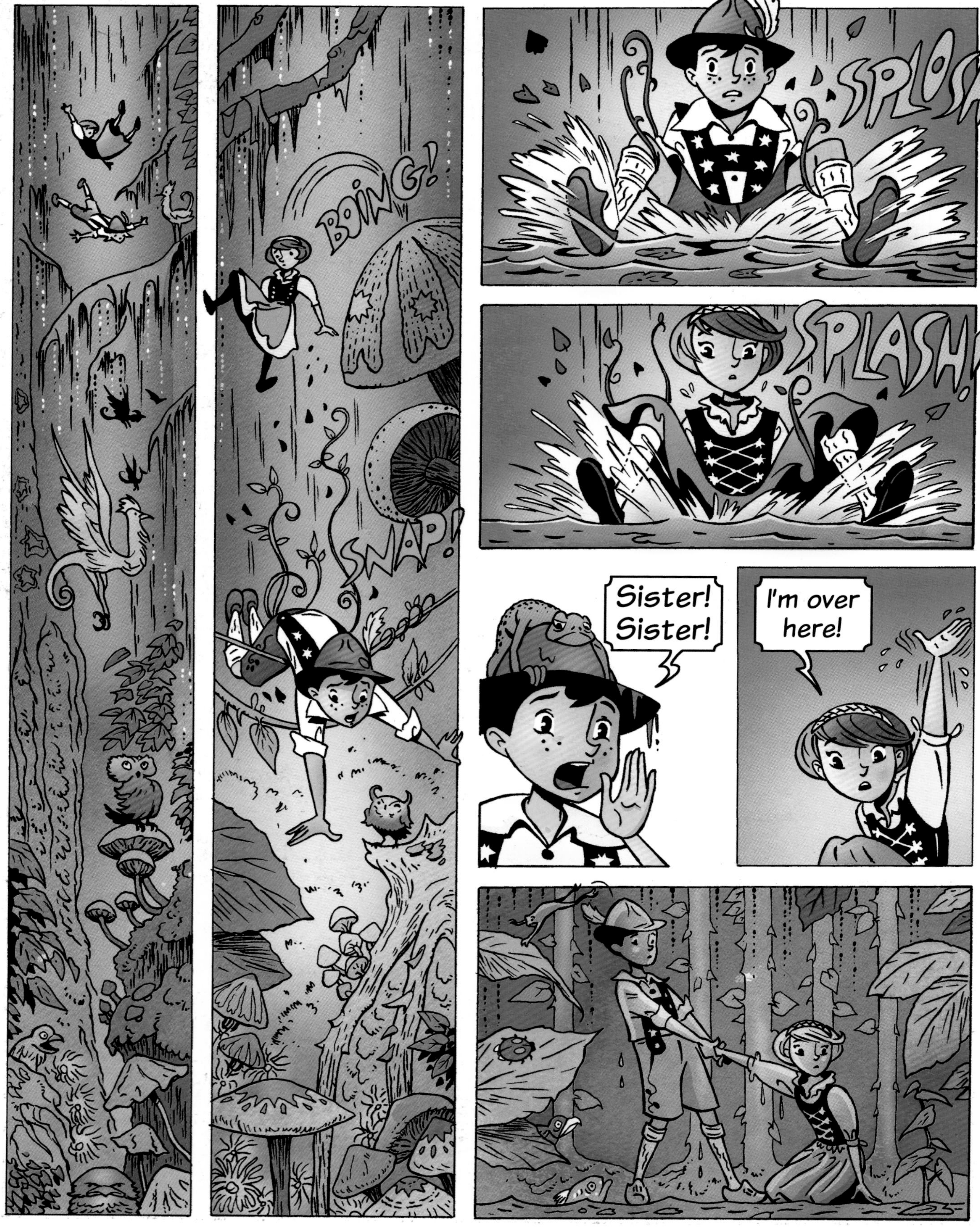
BOING!
SNAP!
SPLOSH!
SPLASH!
Sister! Sister!
I'm over here!

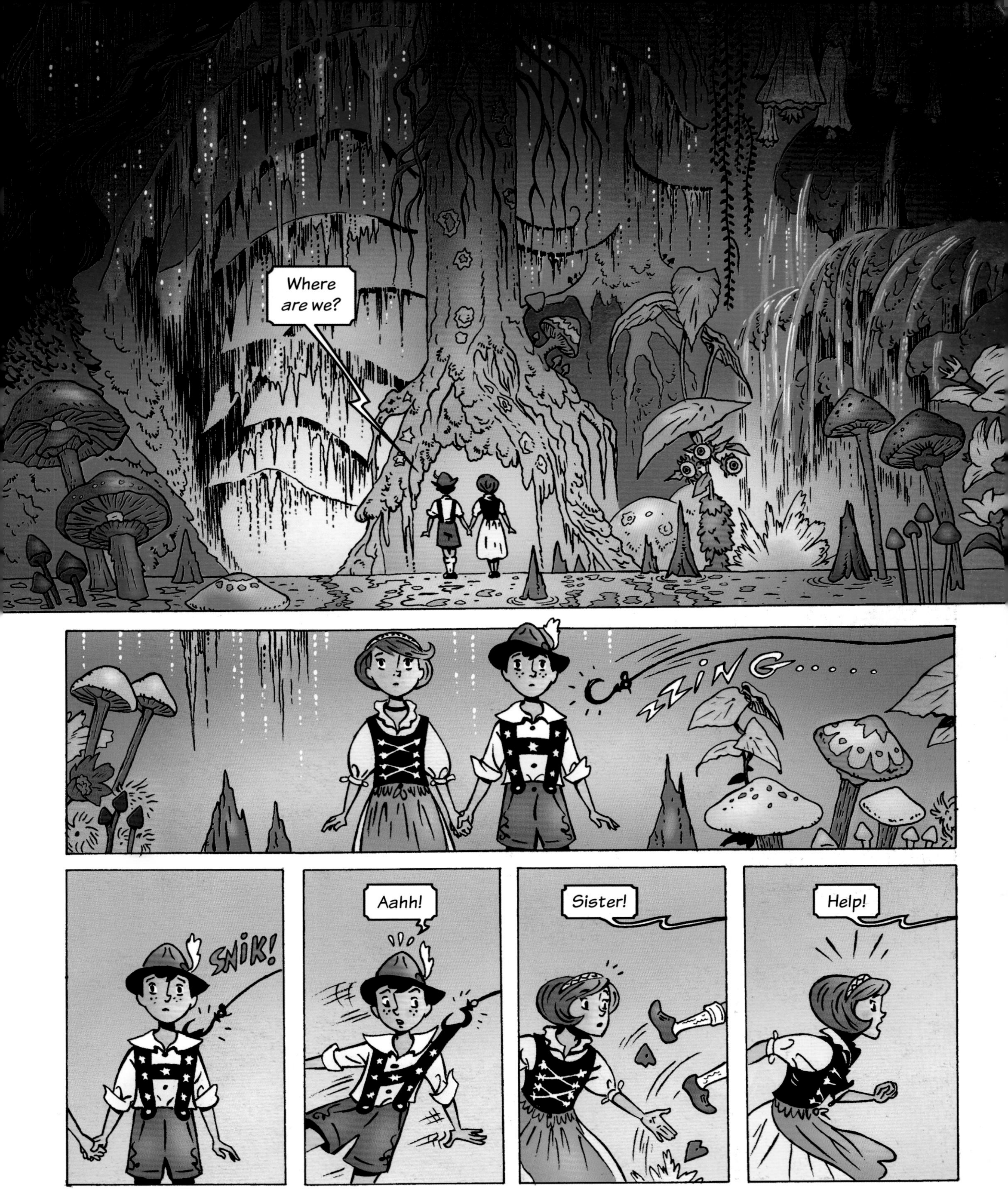
Where are we?
ZZING.....
SNIK!
Aahh!
Sister!
Help!

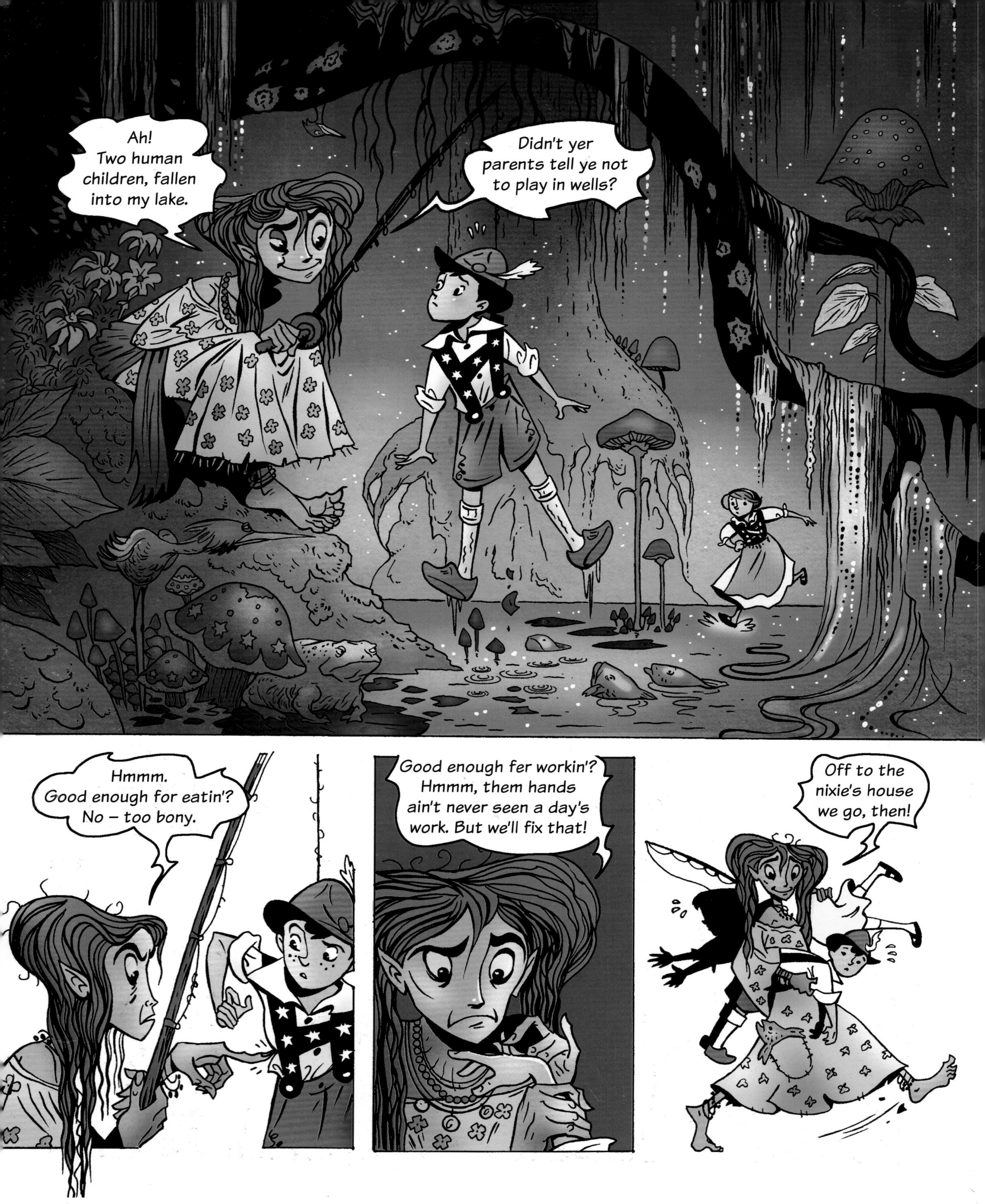
Ah! Two human children, fallen into my lake.
Didn't yer parents tell ye not to play in wells?
Hmmm. Good enough for eatin'? No – too bony.
Good enough fer workin'? Hmmm, them hands ain't never seen a day's work. But we'll fix that!
Off to the nixie's house we go, then!

CLUCK! CLUCK! CLUCK!

CLANK!

In ye go! Ye'll sleep with the chickens.

And best ye get straight to sleep. Plenty of chores fer ye to do tomorrow.

Don't cry, little sister. Let's cuddle with the chickens and stay warm.

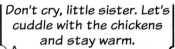

But the little boy and little girl didn't get a wink of sleep that night, so scared were they of the nixie in the well.

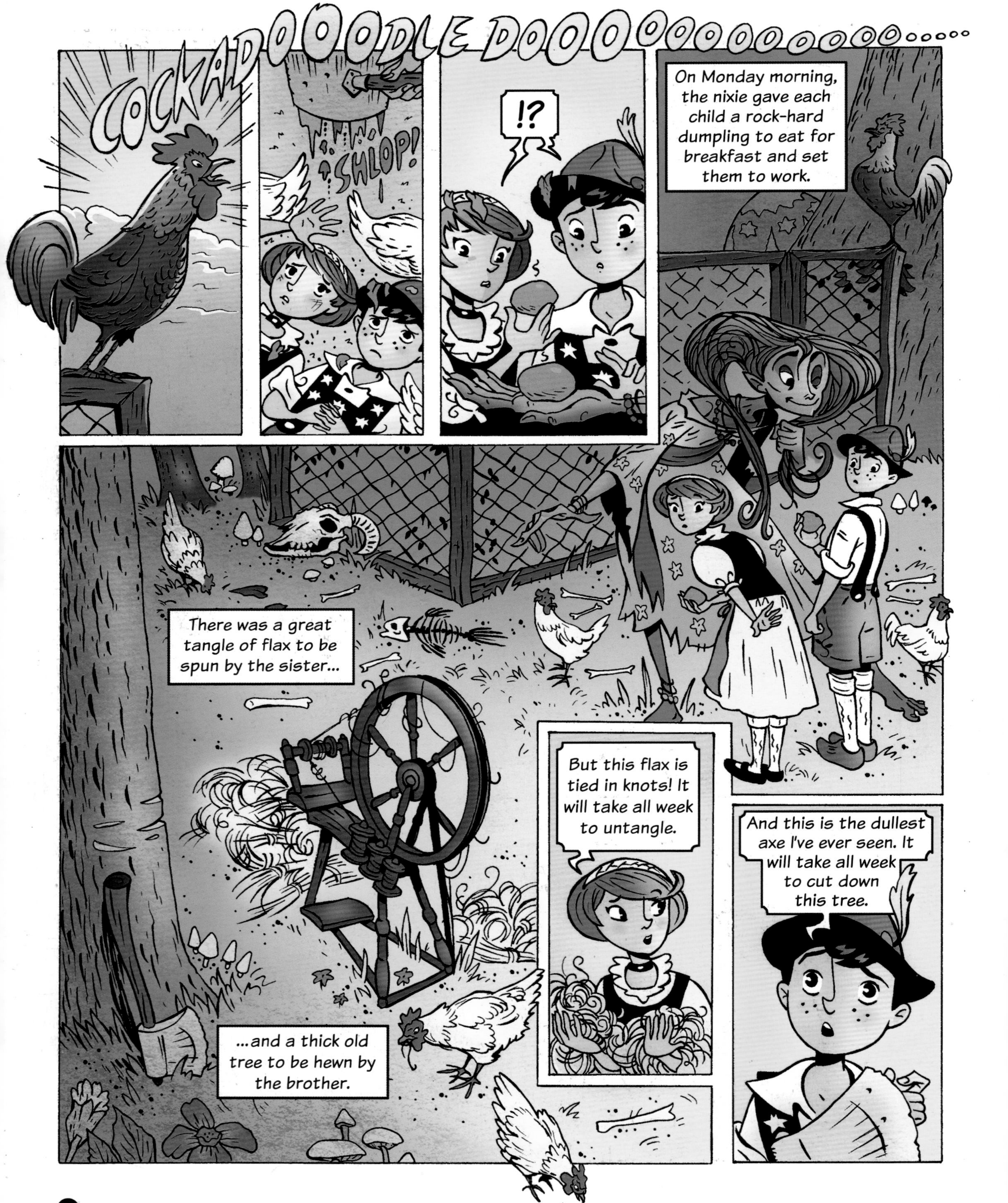
COCKADOOOODLE DOOOOOOOOOOOOO...
SHLOP!
!?
On Monday morning, the nixie gave each child a rock-hard dumpling to eat for breakfast and set them to work.
There was a great tangle of flax to be spun by the sister...
...and a thick old tree to be hewn by the brother.
But this flax is tied in knots! It will take all week to untangle.
And this is the dullest axe I've ever seen. It will take all week to cut down this tree.

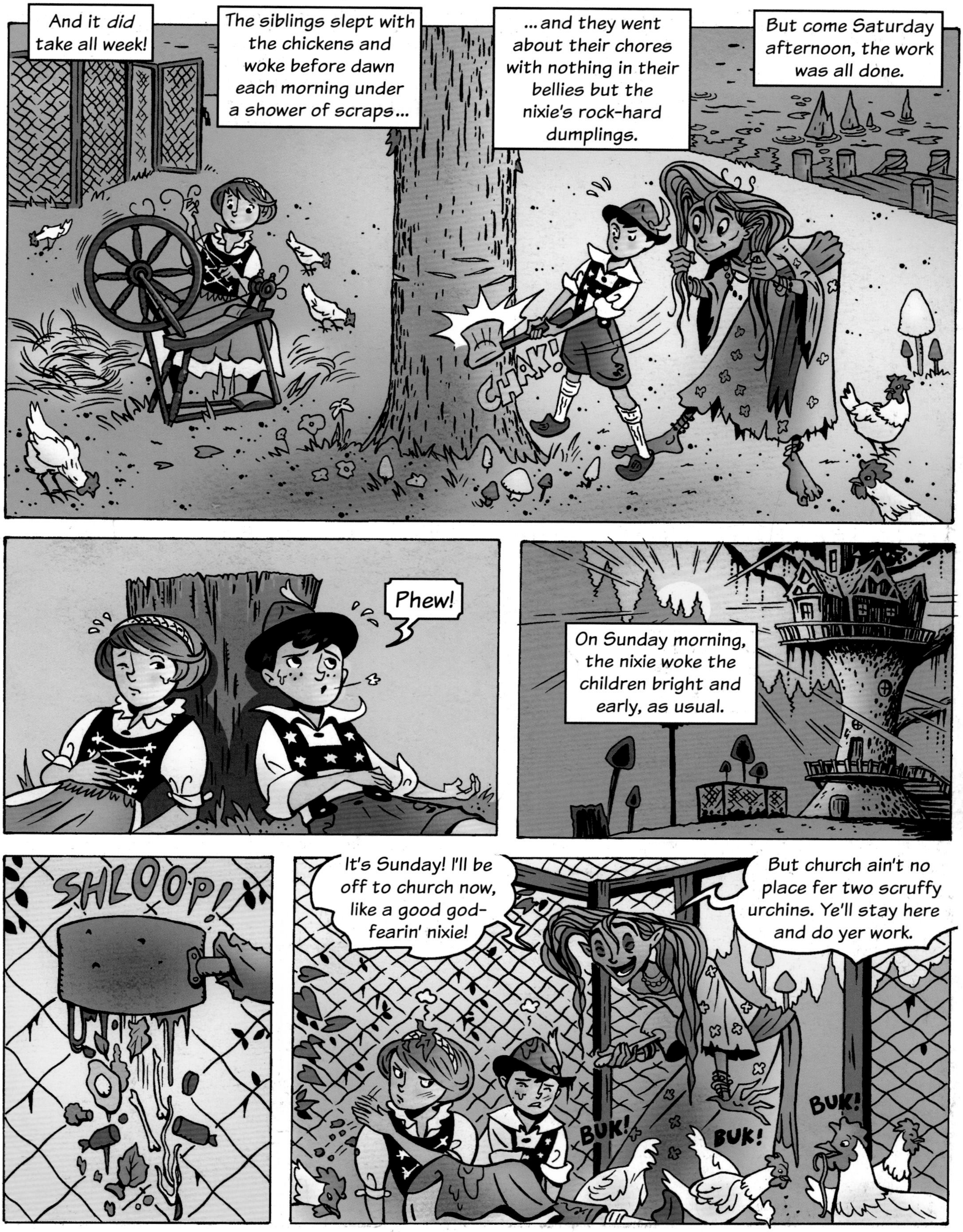
And it *did* take all week!
The siblings slept with the chickens and woke before dawn each morning under a shower of scraps...
...and they went about their chores with nothing in their bellies but the nixie's rock-hard dumplings.
But come Saturday afternoon, the work was all done.
CHAK!
Phew!
On Sunday morning, the nixie woke the children bright and early, as usual.
SHLOOP!
It's Sunday! I'll be off to church now, like a good god-fearin' nixie!
But church ain't no place fer two scruffy urchins. Ye'll stay here and do yer work.
BUK!
BUK!
BUK!

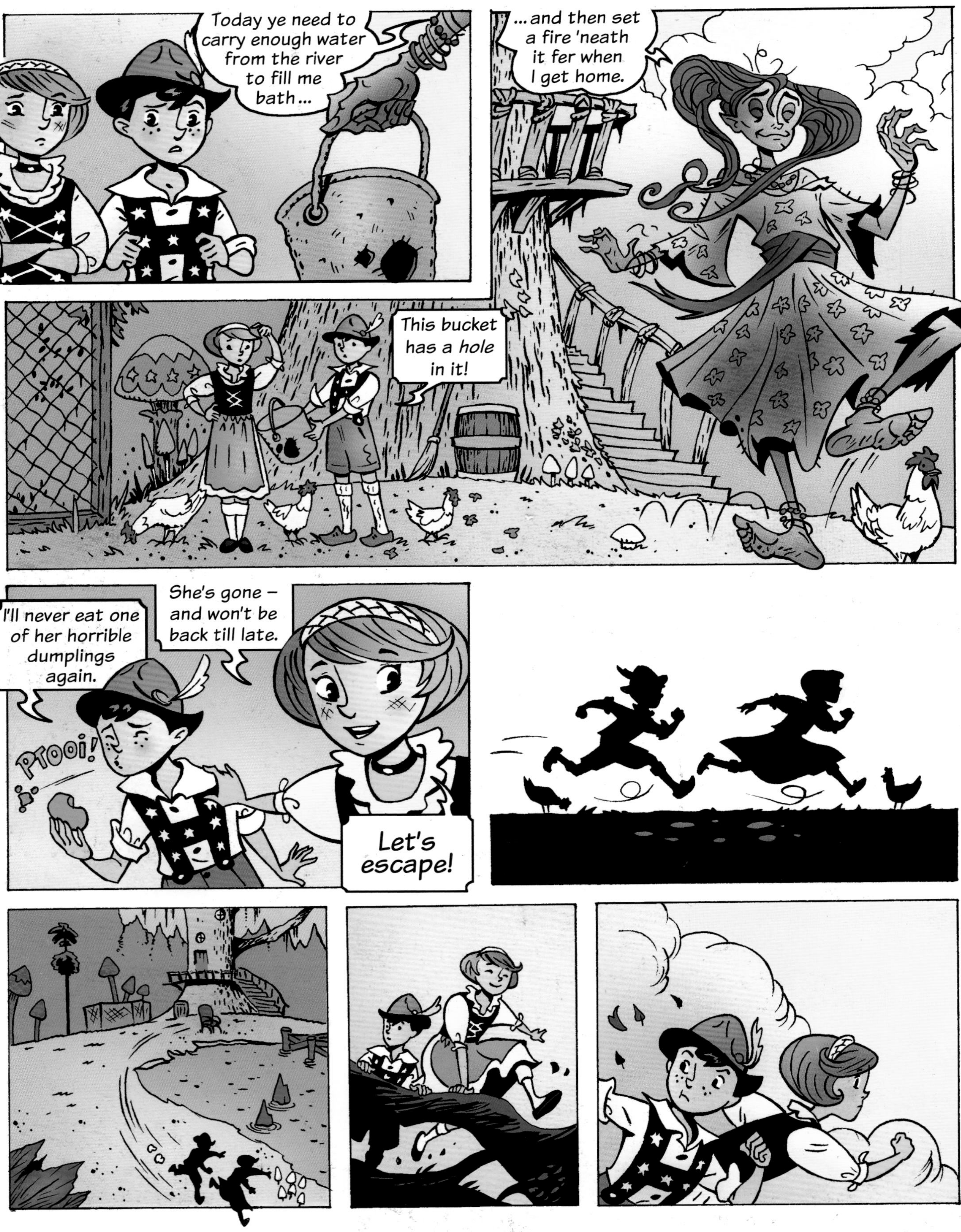
Today ye need to carry enough water from the river to fill me bath...
...and then set a fire 'neath it fer when I get home.
This bucket has a hole in it!
I'll never eat one of her horrible dumplings again.
PTOOI!
She's gone – and won't be back till late.
Let's escape!

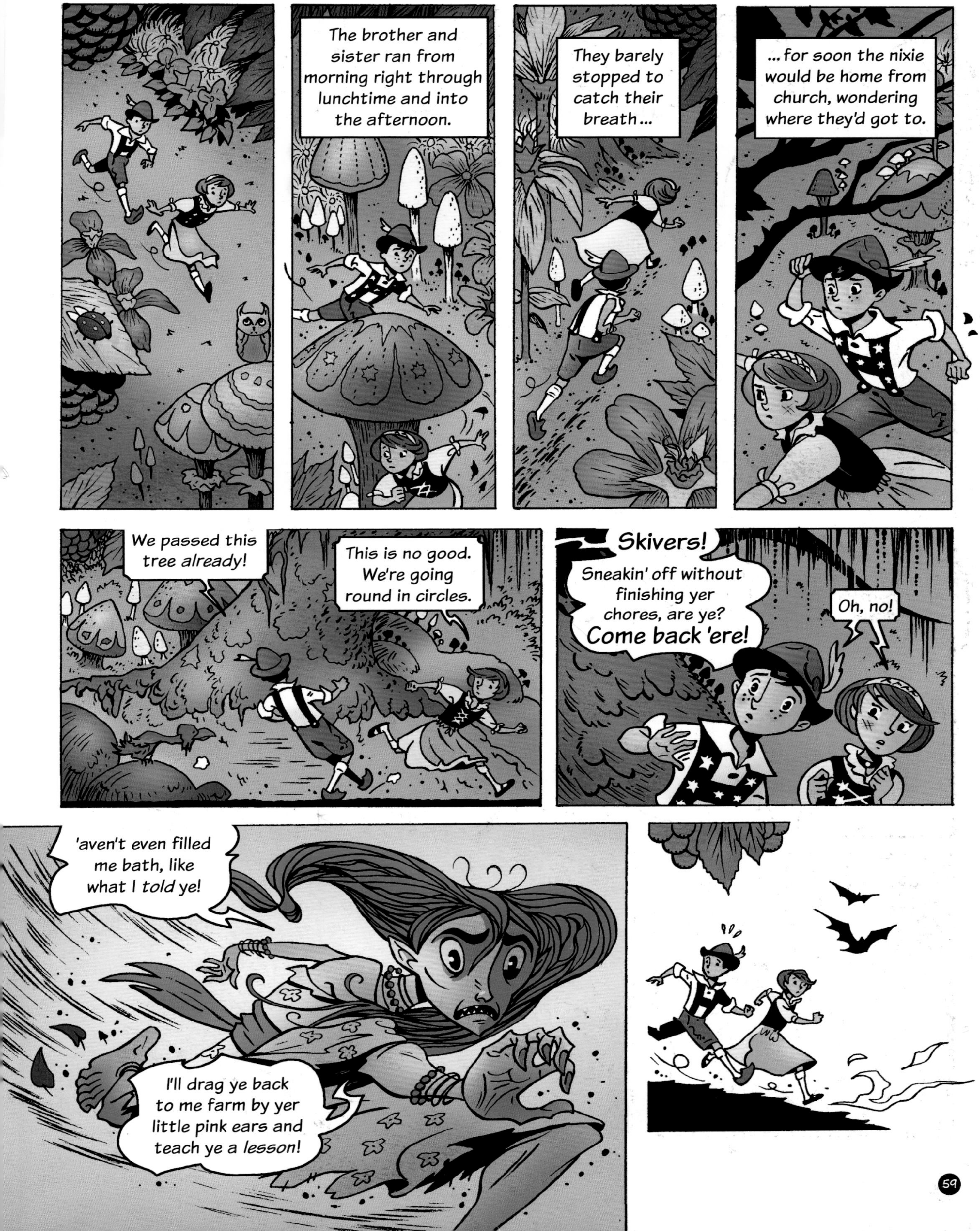

The brother and sister ran from morning right through lunchtime and into the afternoon.
They barely stopped to catch their breath...
...for soon the nixie would be home from church, wondering where they'd got to.
We passed this tree *already*!
This is no good. We're going round in circles.
Skivers!
Sneakin' off without finishing yer chores, are ye? Come back 'ere!
Oh, no!
'aven't even filled me bath, like what I *told* ye!
I'll drag ye back to me farm by yer little pink ears and teach ye a *lesson*!

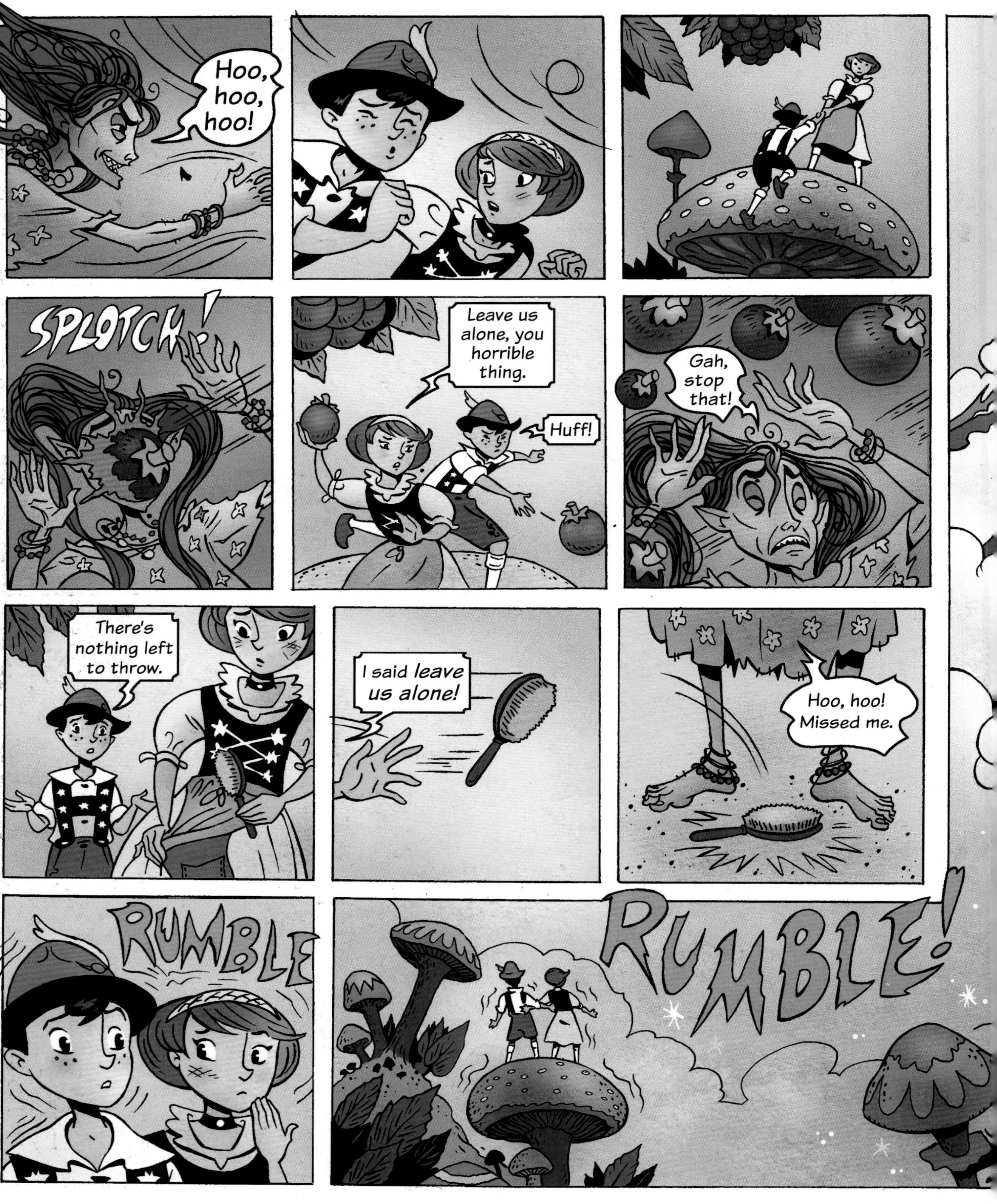
Hoo, hoo, hoo!
SPLOTCH!
Leave us alone, you horrible thing.
Huff!
Gah, stop that!
There's nothing left to throw.
I said *leave us alone!*
Hoo, hoo! Missed me.
RUMBLE
RUMBLE!

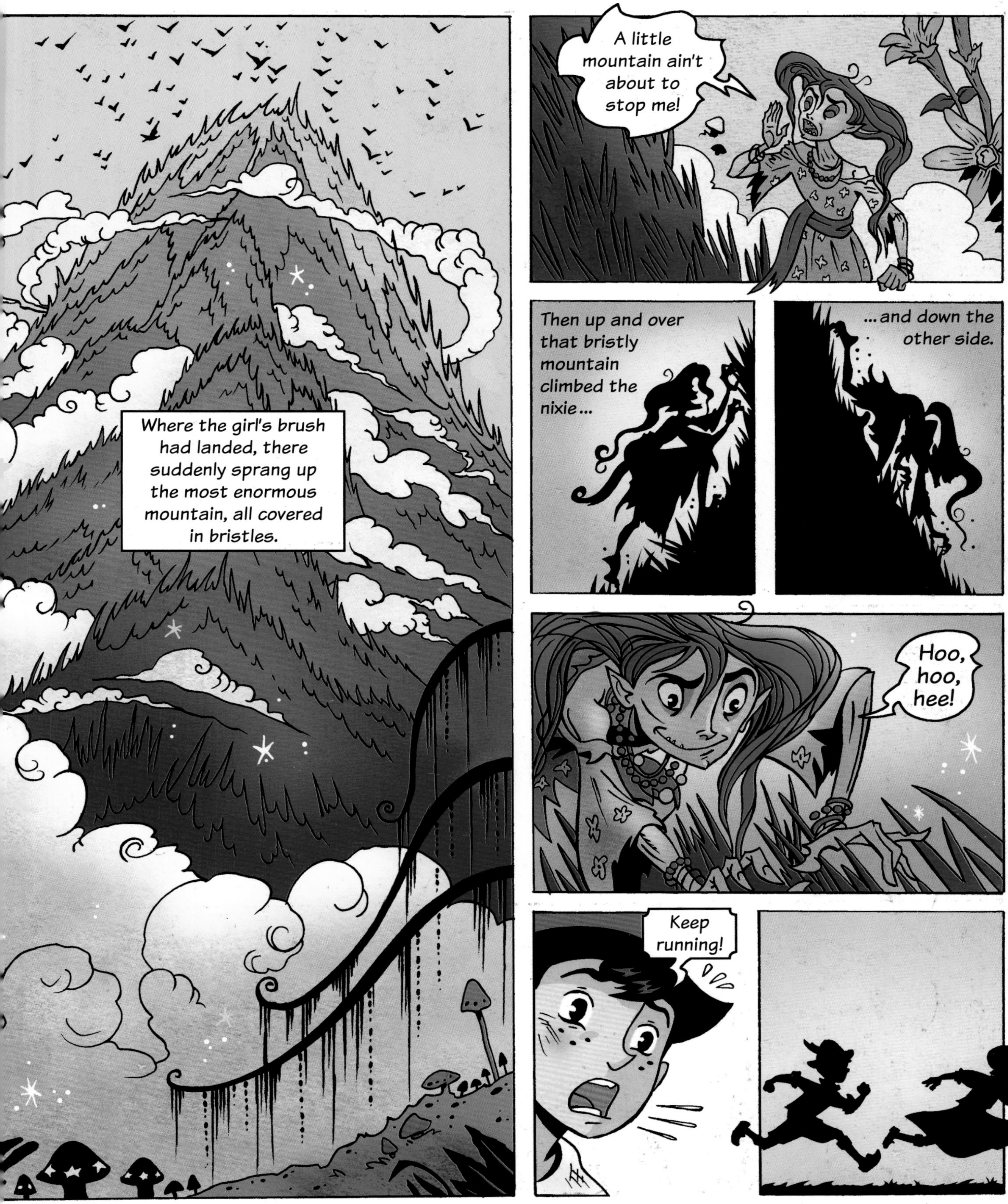

Where the girl's brush had landed, there suddenly sprang up the most enormous mountain, all covered in bristles.
A little mountain ain't about to stop me!
Then up and over that bristly mountain climbed the nixie...
...and down the other side.
Hoo, hoo, hee!
Keep running!

Through a wild and scratchy wood they tumbled, with the wild-haired nixie of the well barrelling after them.

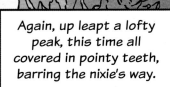

Hoo, hoo! Missed again.

Again, up leapt a lofty peak, this time all covered in pointy teeth, barring the nixie's way.

RUUMMBLE!

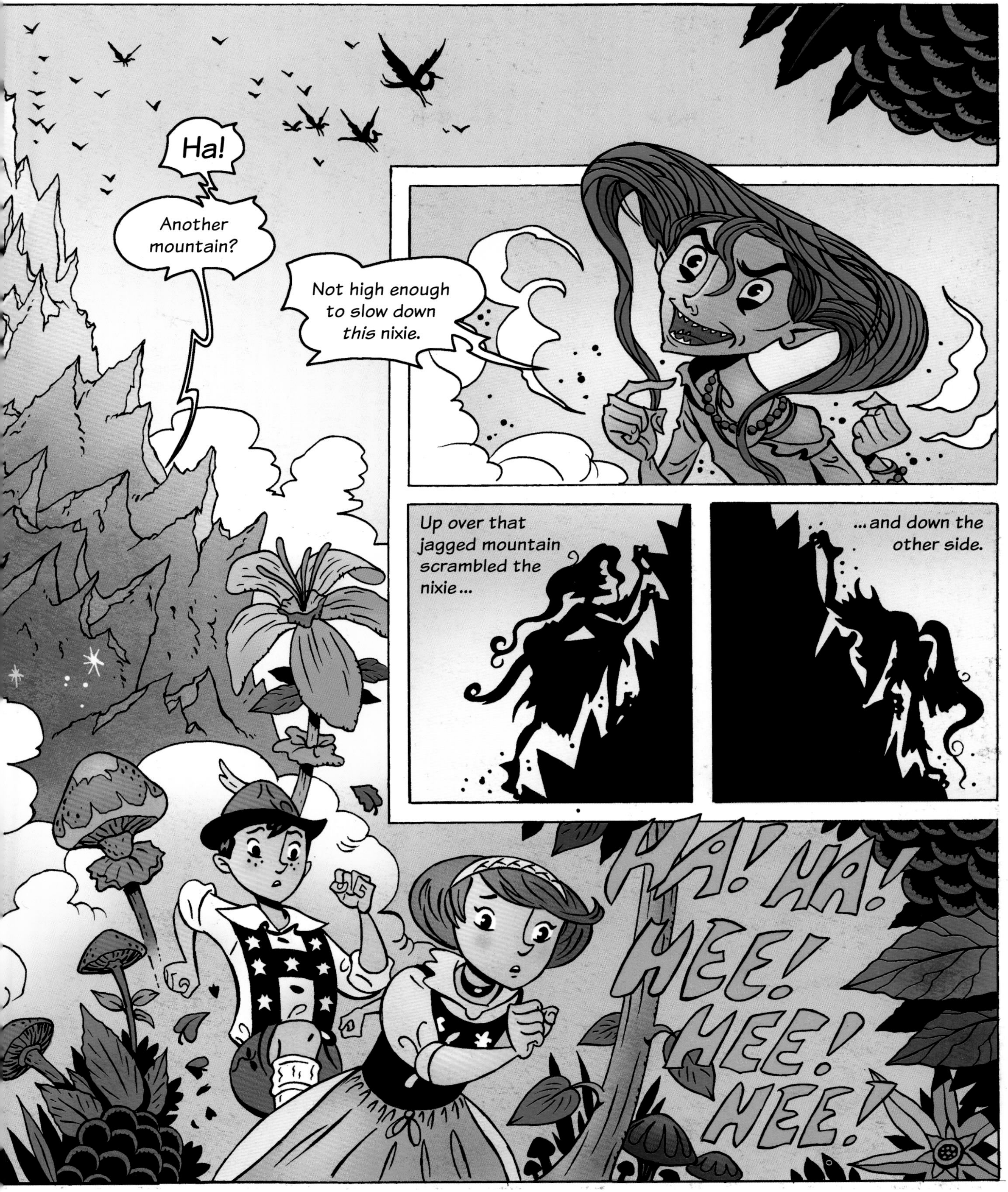

Ha!
Another mountain?
Not high enough to slow down *this* nixie.
Up over that jagged mountain scrambled the nixie...
...and down the other side.
HA! HA! HEE! HEE! HEE!

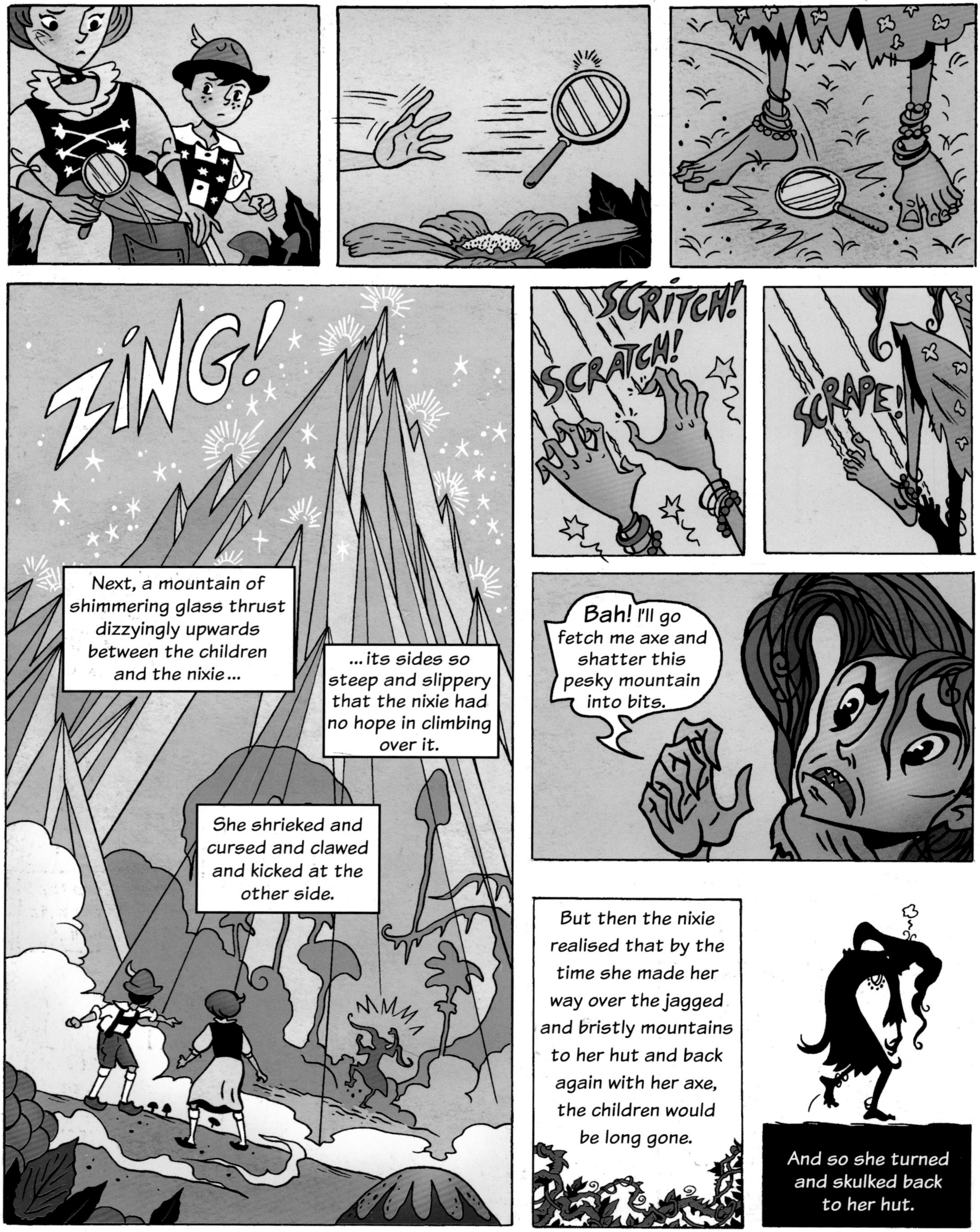
ZING!
Next, a mountain of shimmering glass thrust dizzyingly upwards between the children and the nixie...
...its sides so steep and slippery that the nixie had no hope in climbing over it.
She shrieked and cursed and clawed and kicked at the other side.
SCRITCH!
SCRATCH!
SCRAPE!
Bah! I'll go fetch me axe and shatter this pesky mountain into bits.
But then the nixie realised that by the time she made her way over the jagged and bristly mountains to her hut and back again with her axe, the children would be long gone.
And so she turned and skulked back to her hut.

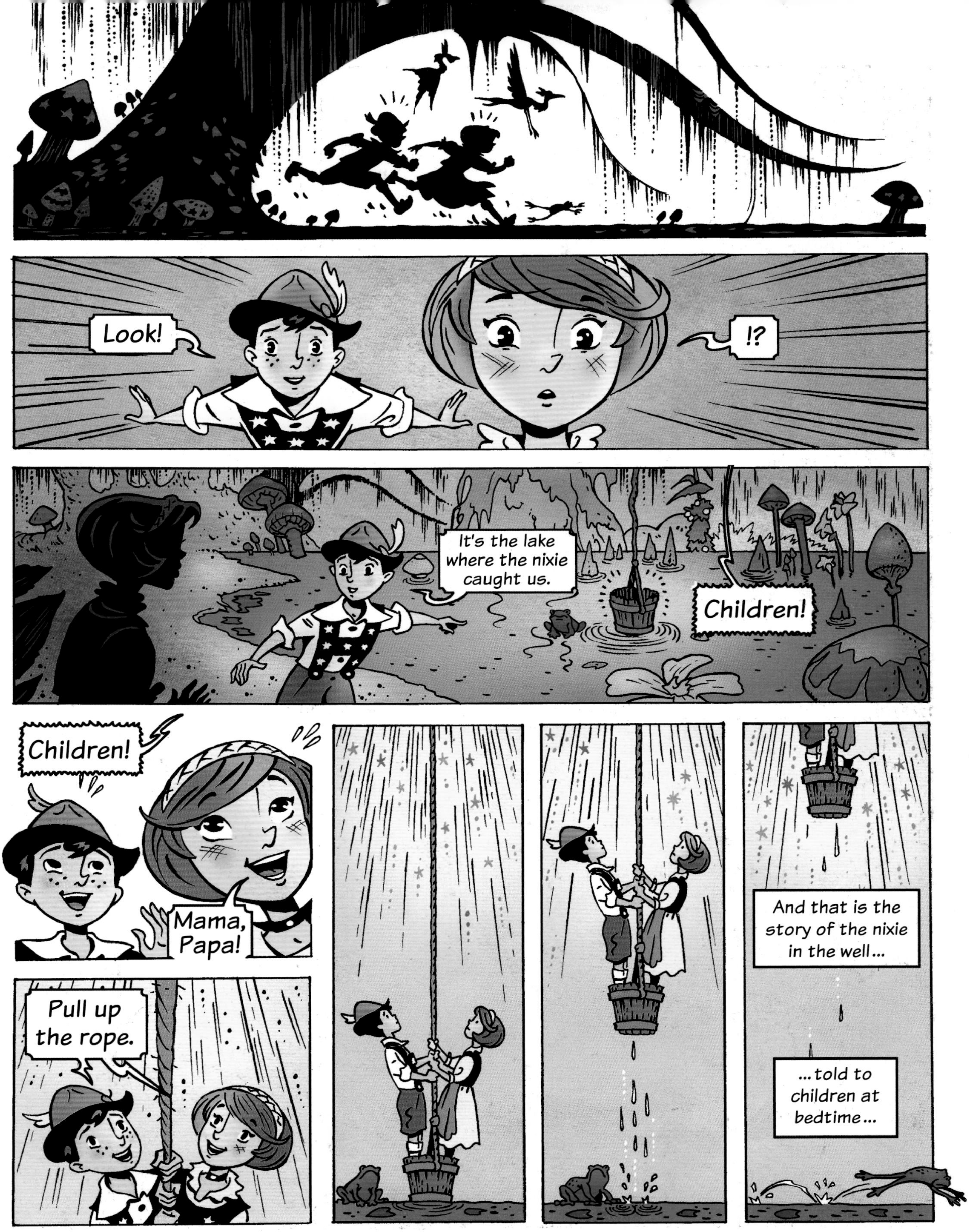
Look!
!?
It's the lake where the nixie caught us.
Children!
Children!
Mama, Papa!
Pull up the rope.
And that is the story of the nixie in the well...
...told to children at bedtime...

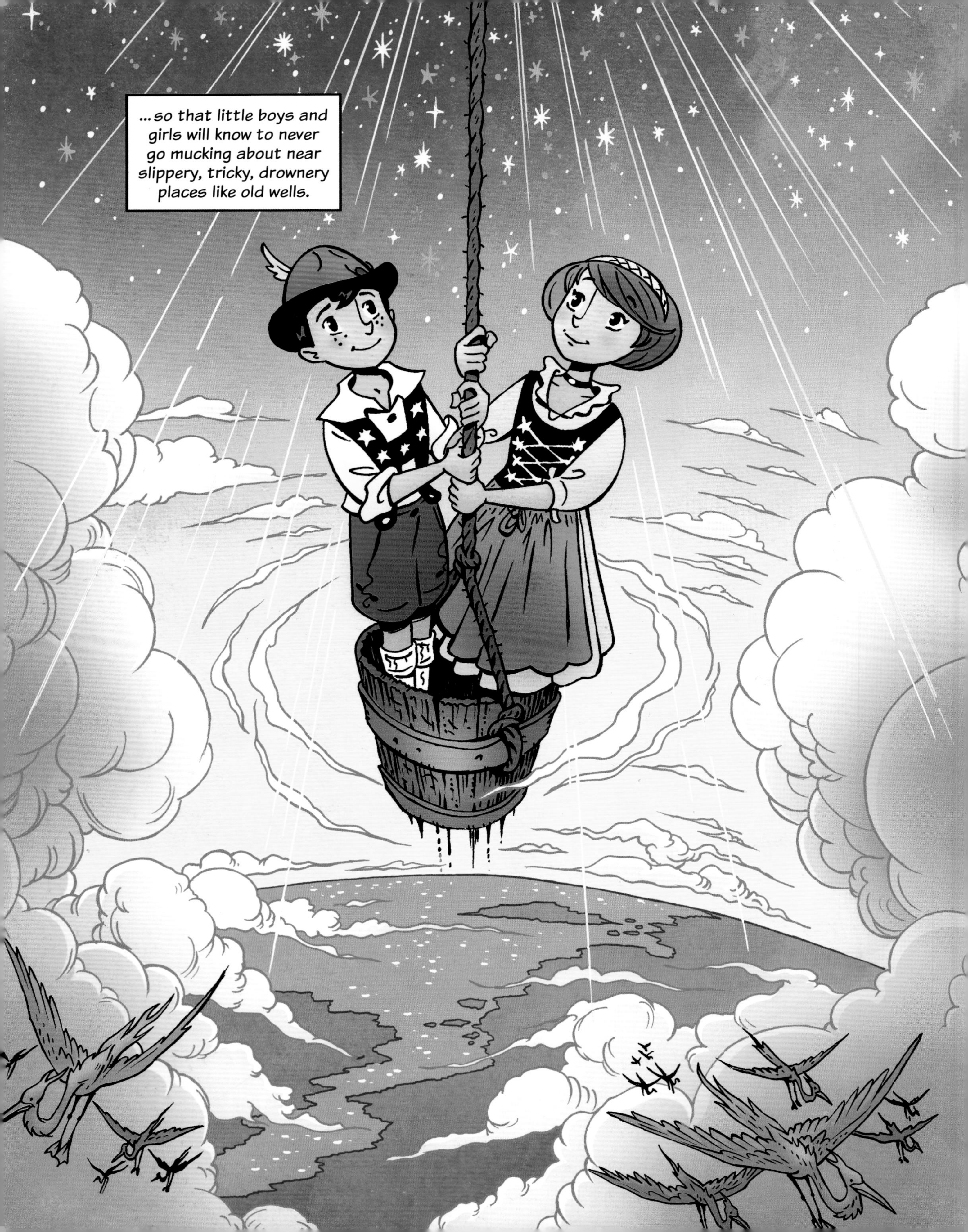
...so that little boys and girls will know to never go mucking about near slippery, tricky, drownery places like old wells.

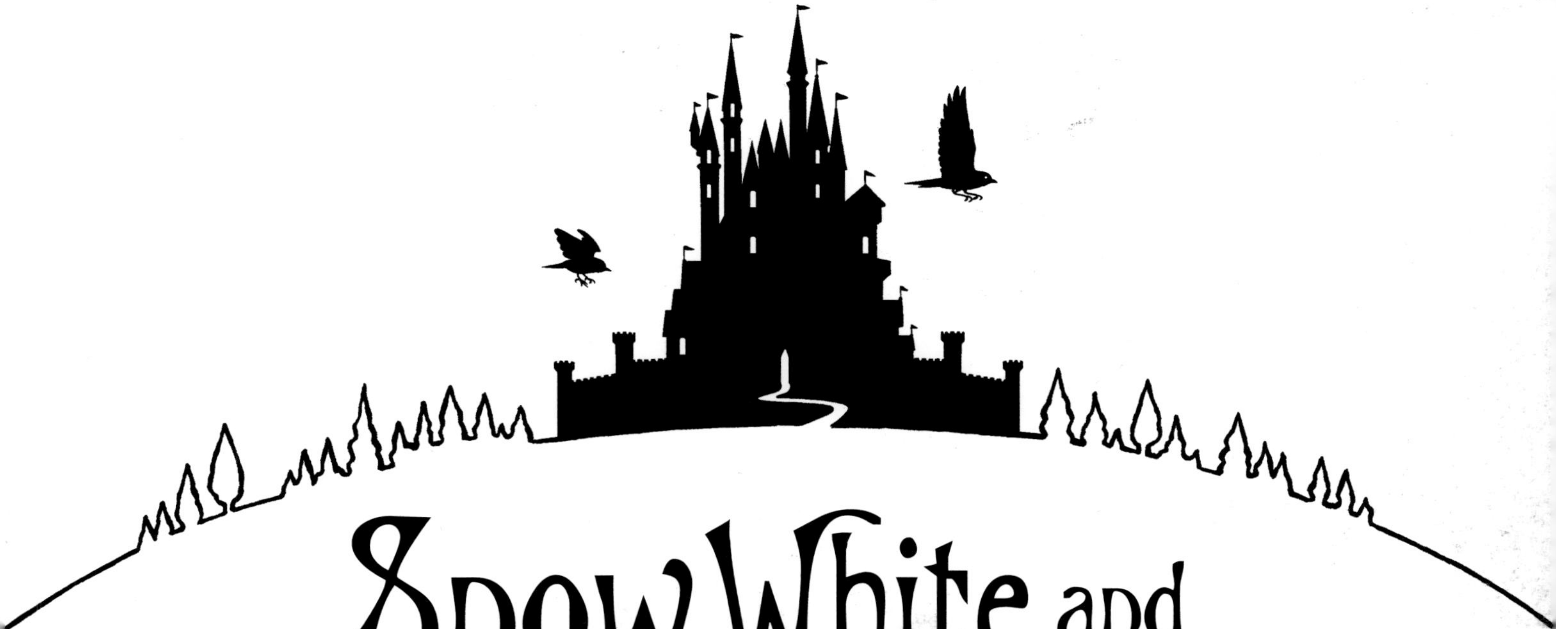

Snow White and Rose Red

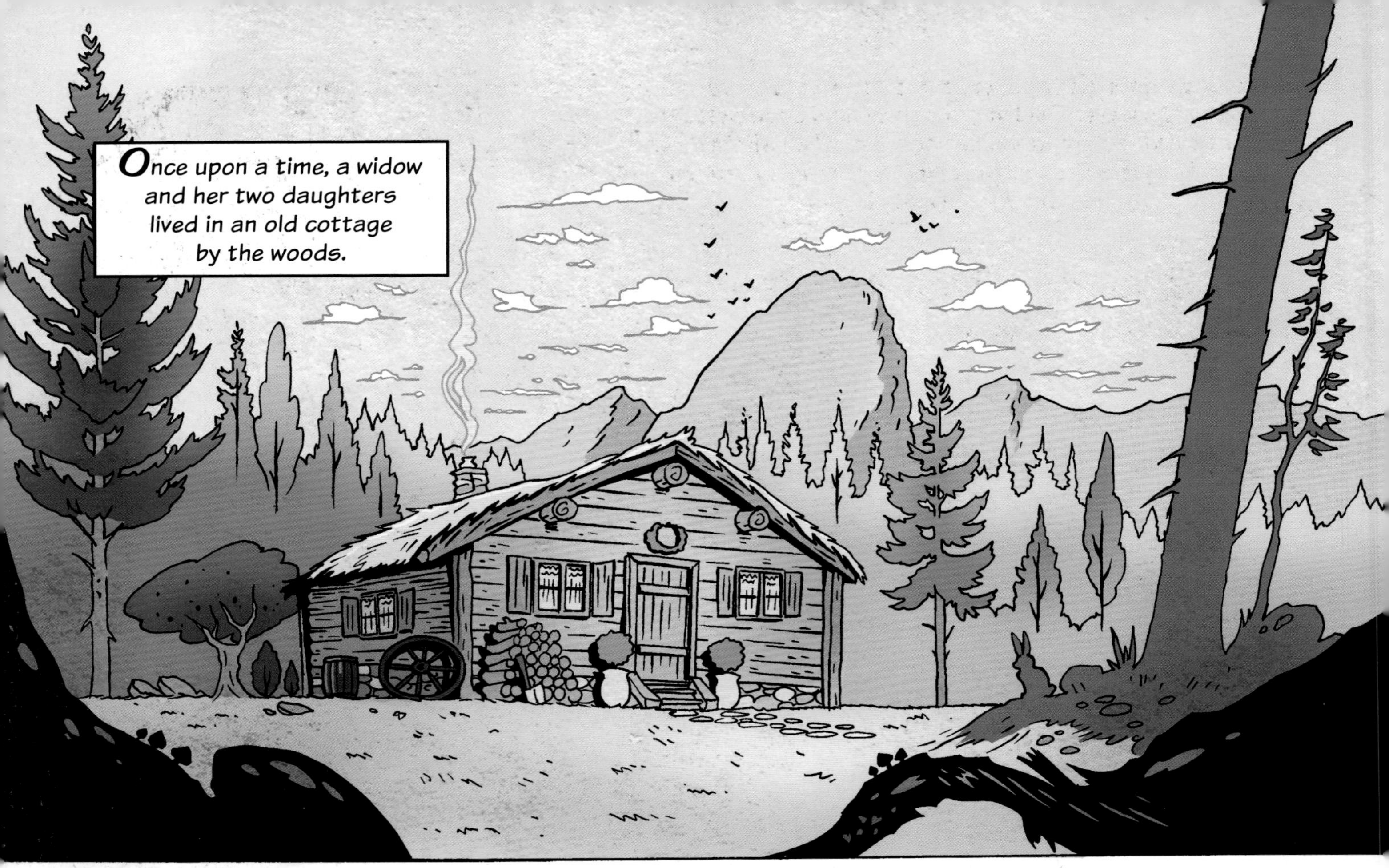
Once upon a time, a widow
and her two daughters
lived in an old cottage
by the woods.

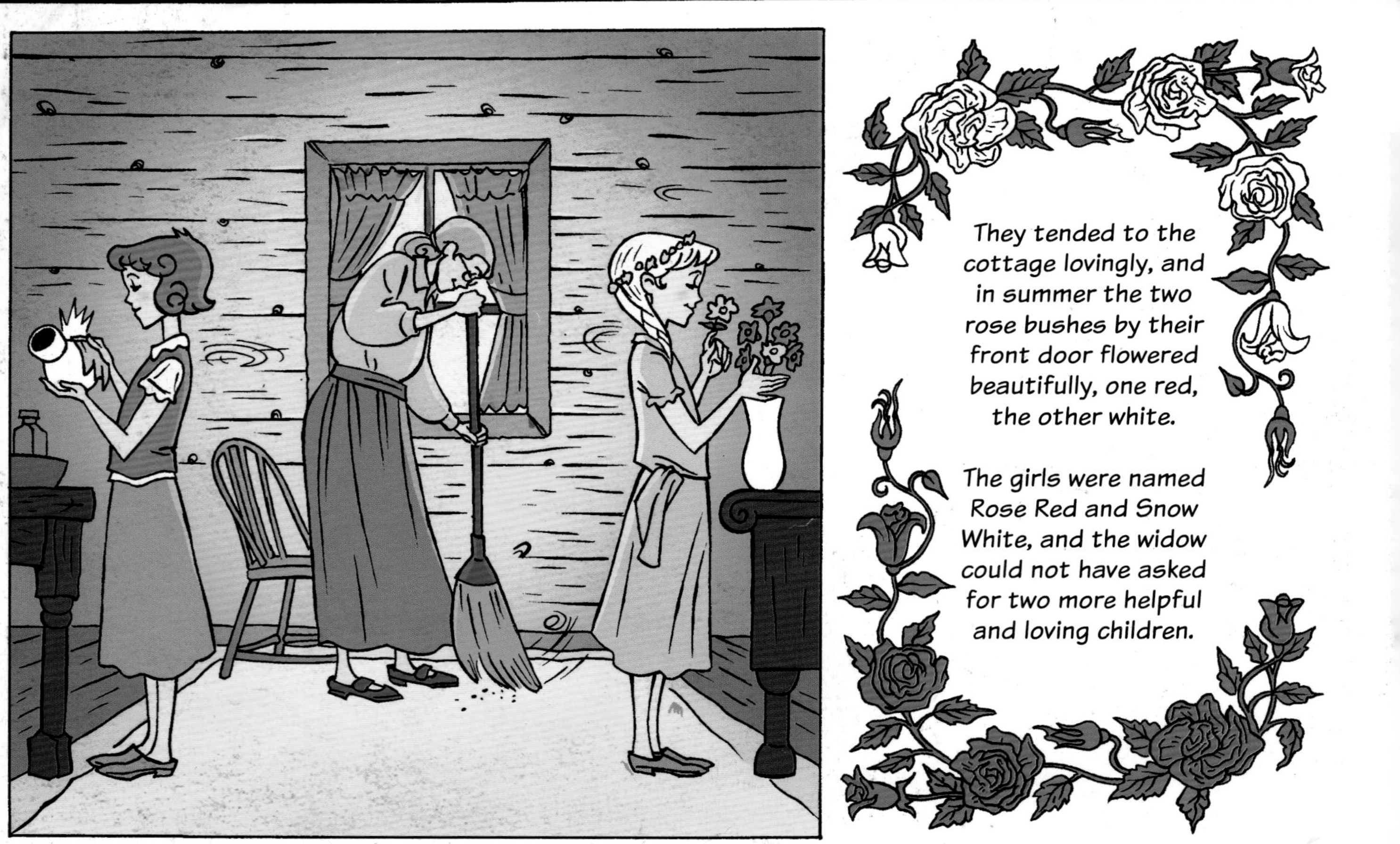

They tended to the cottage lovingly, and in summer the two rose bushes by their front door flowered beautifully, one red, the other white.

The girls were named Rose Red and Snow White, and the widow could not have asked for two more helpful and loving children.

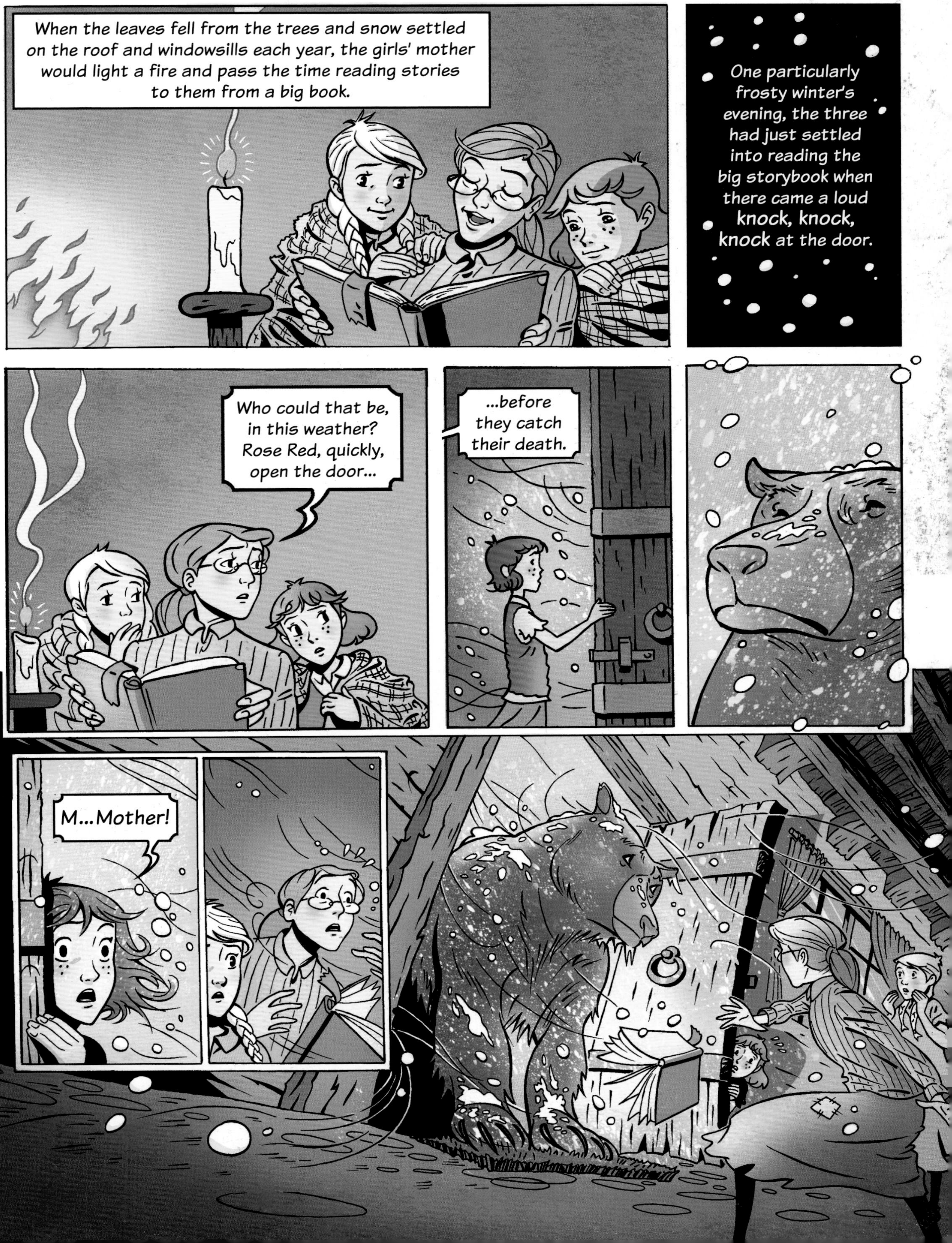
When the leaves fell from the trees and snow settled on the roof and windowsills each year, the girls' mother would light a fire and pass the time reading stories to them from a big book.
One particularly frosty winter's evening, the three had just settled into reading the big storybook when there came a loud knock, knock, knock at the door.
Who could that be, in this weather? Rose Red, quickly, open the door...
...before they catch their death.
M...Mother!

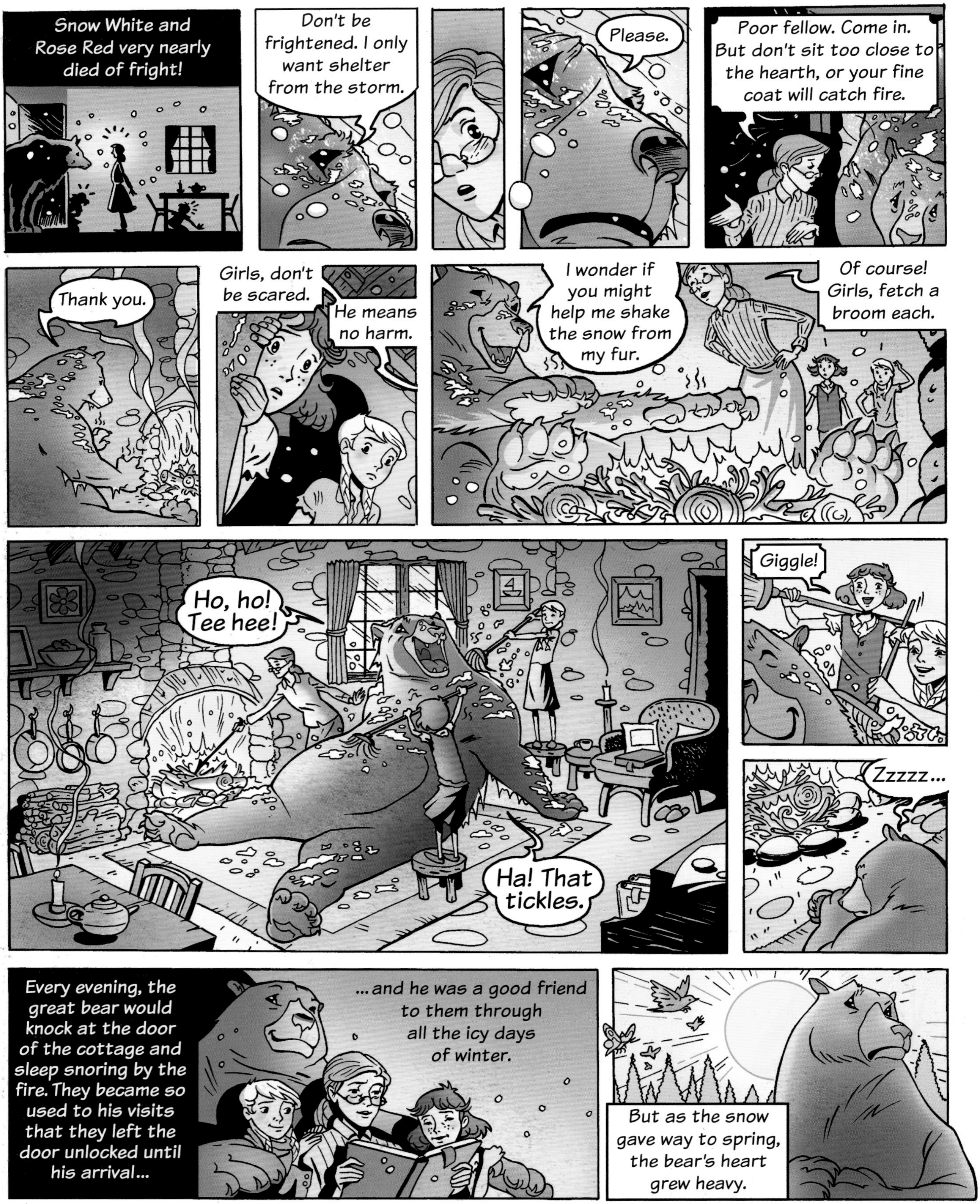
Snow White and Rose Red very nearly died of fright!
Don't be frightened. I only want shelter from the storm.
Please.
Poor fellow. Come in. But don't sit too close to the hearth, or your fine coat will catch fire.
Thank you.
Girls, don't be scared.
He means no harm.
I wonder if you might help me shake the snow from my fur.
Of course! Girls, fetch a broom each.
Ho, ho! Tee hee!
Ha! That tickles.
Giggle!
Zzzzz...
Every evening, the great bear would knock at the door of the cottage and sleep snoring by the fire. They became so used to his visits that they left the door unlocked until his arrival...
...and he was a good friend to them through all the icy days of winter.
But as the snow gave way to spring, the bear's heart grew heavy.

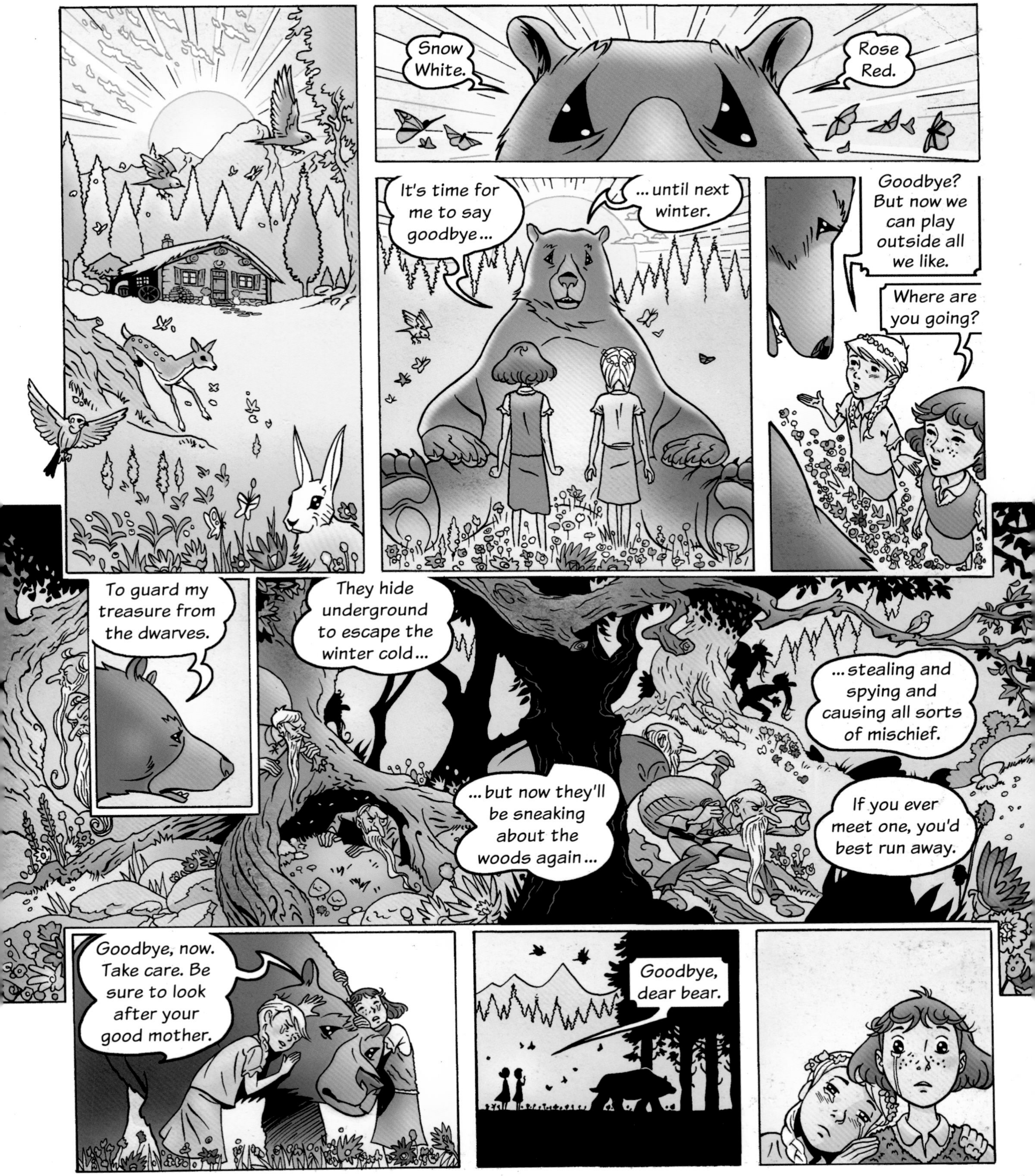
Snow White.
Rose Red.
It's time for me to say goodbye...
...until next winter.
Goodbye? But now we can play outside all we like.
Where are you going?
To guard my treasure from the dwarves.
They hide underground to escape the winter cold...
...but now they'll be sneaking about the woods again...
...stealing and spying and causing all sorts of mischief.
If you ever meet one, you'd best run away.
Goodbye, now. Take care. Be sure to look after your good mother.
Goodbye, dear bear.

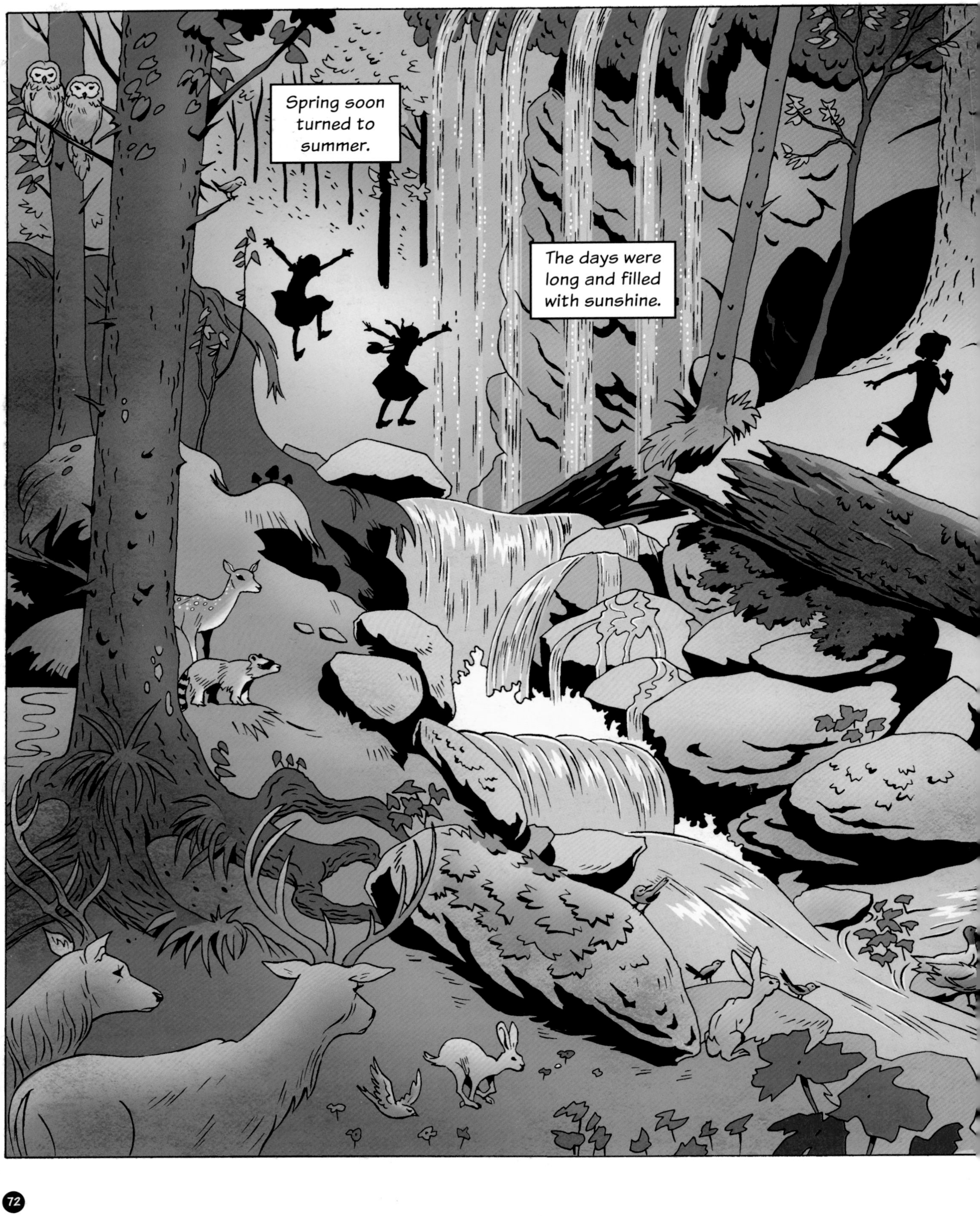
Spring soon turned to summer.
The days were long and filled with sunshine.

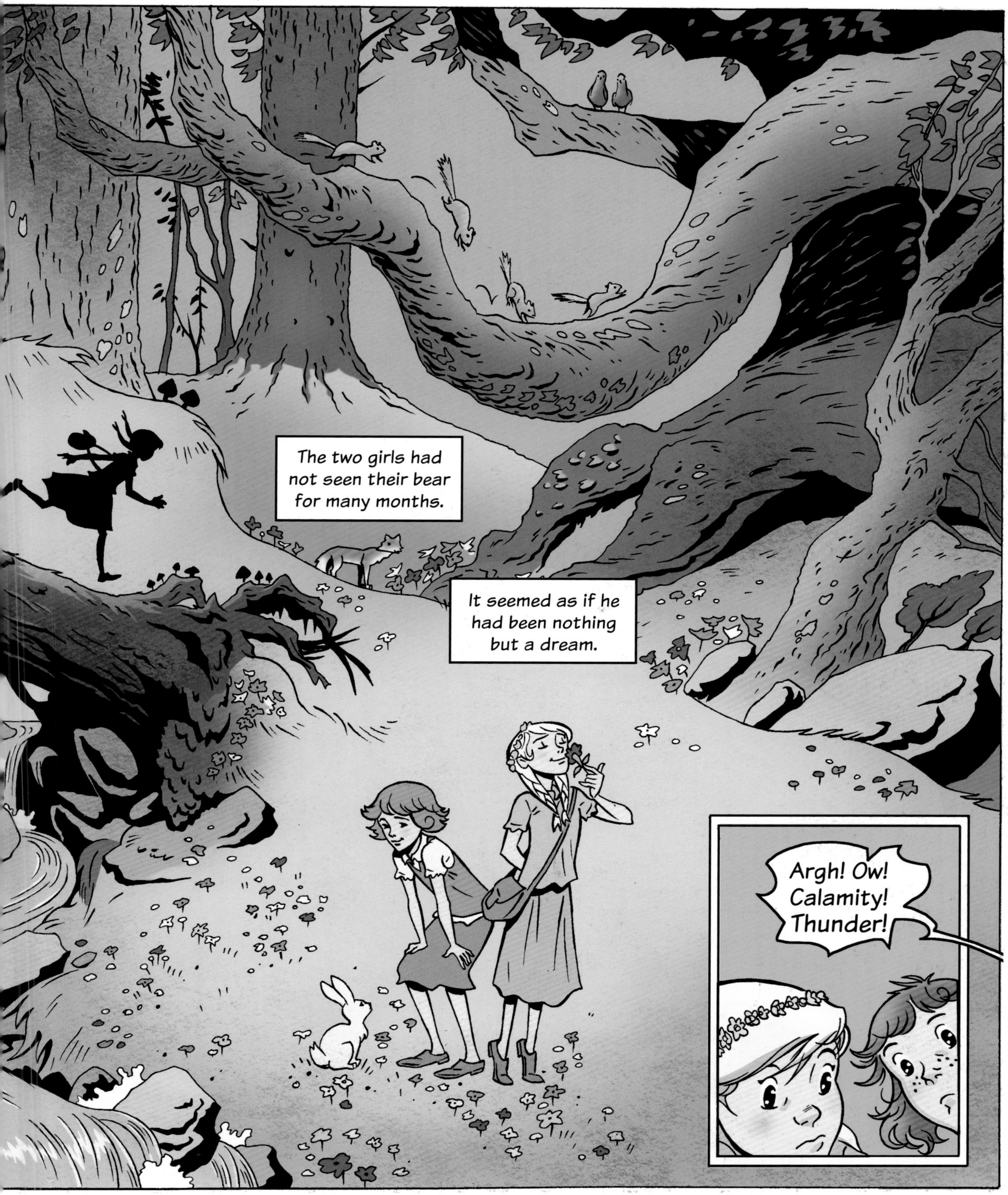
The two girls had not seen their bear for many months.
It seemed as if he had been nothing but a dream.
Argh! Ow! Calamity! Thunder!

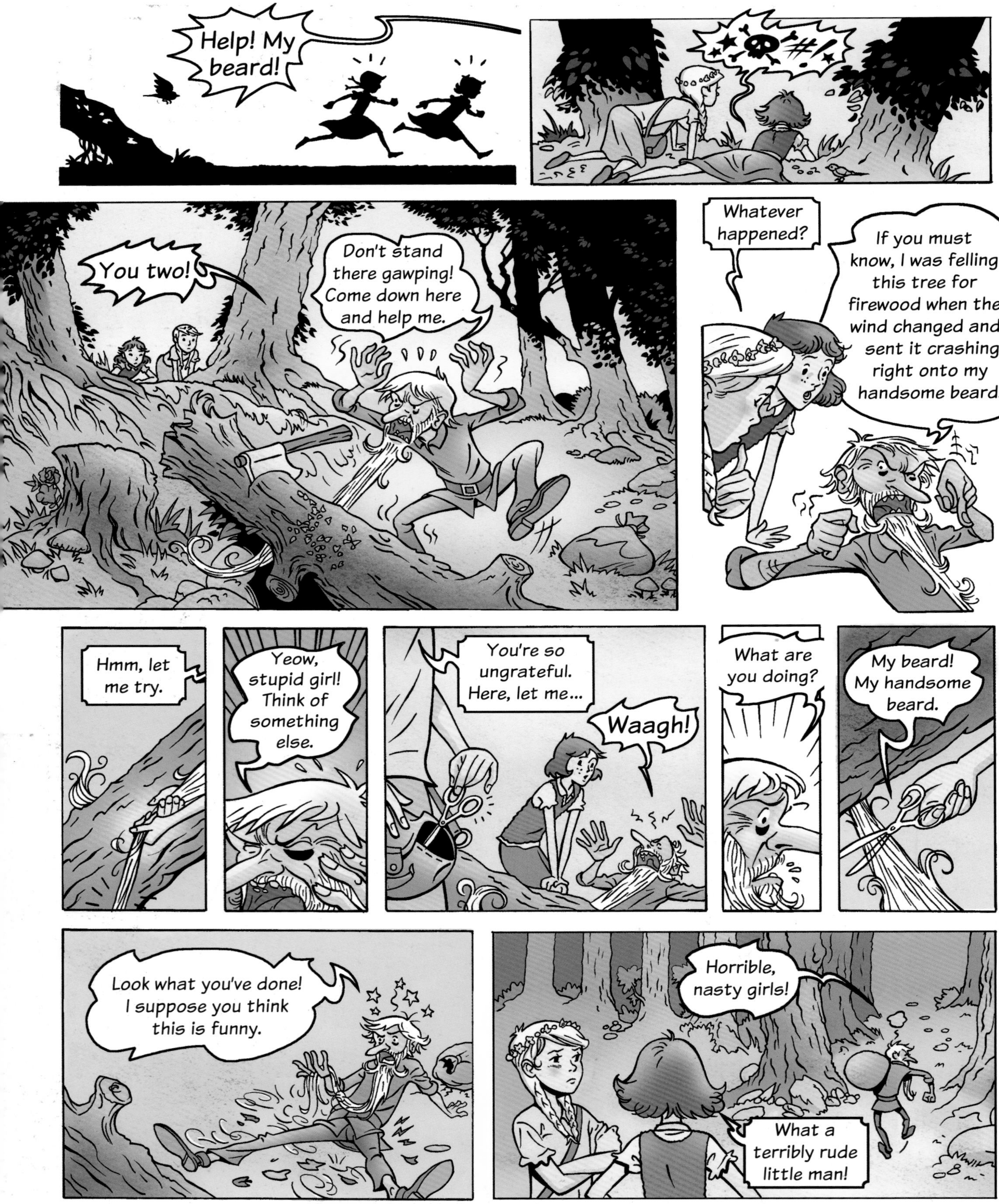
Help! My beard!
You two!
Don't stand there gawping! Come down here and help me.
Whatever happened?
If you must know, I was felling this tree for firewood when the wind changed and sent it crashing right onto my handsome beard.
Hmm, let me try.
Yeow, stupid girl! Think of something else.
You're so ungrateful. Here, let me...
Waagh!
What are you doing?
My beard! My handsome beard.
Look what you've done! I suppose you think this is funny.
Horrible, nasty girls!
What a terribly rude little man!

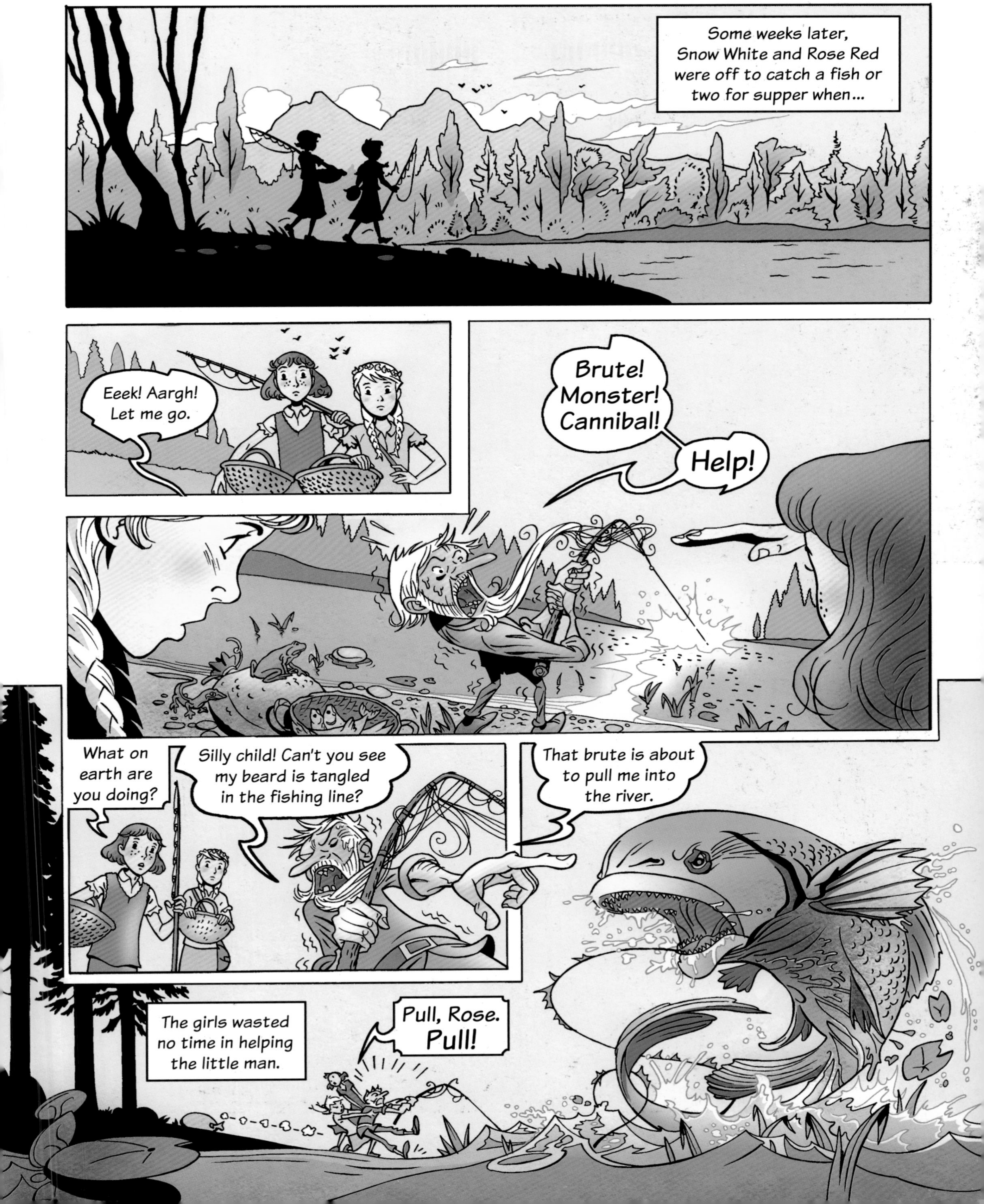
Some weeks later, Snow White and Rose Red were off to catch a fish or two for supper when...
Eeek! Aargh! Let me go.
Brute! Monster! Cannibal!
Help!
What on earth are you doing?
Silly child! Can't you see my beard is tangled in the fishing line?
That brute is about to pull me into the river.
The girls wasted no time in helping the little man.
Pull, Rose. Pull!

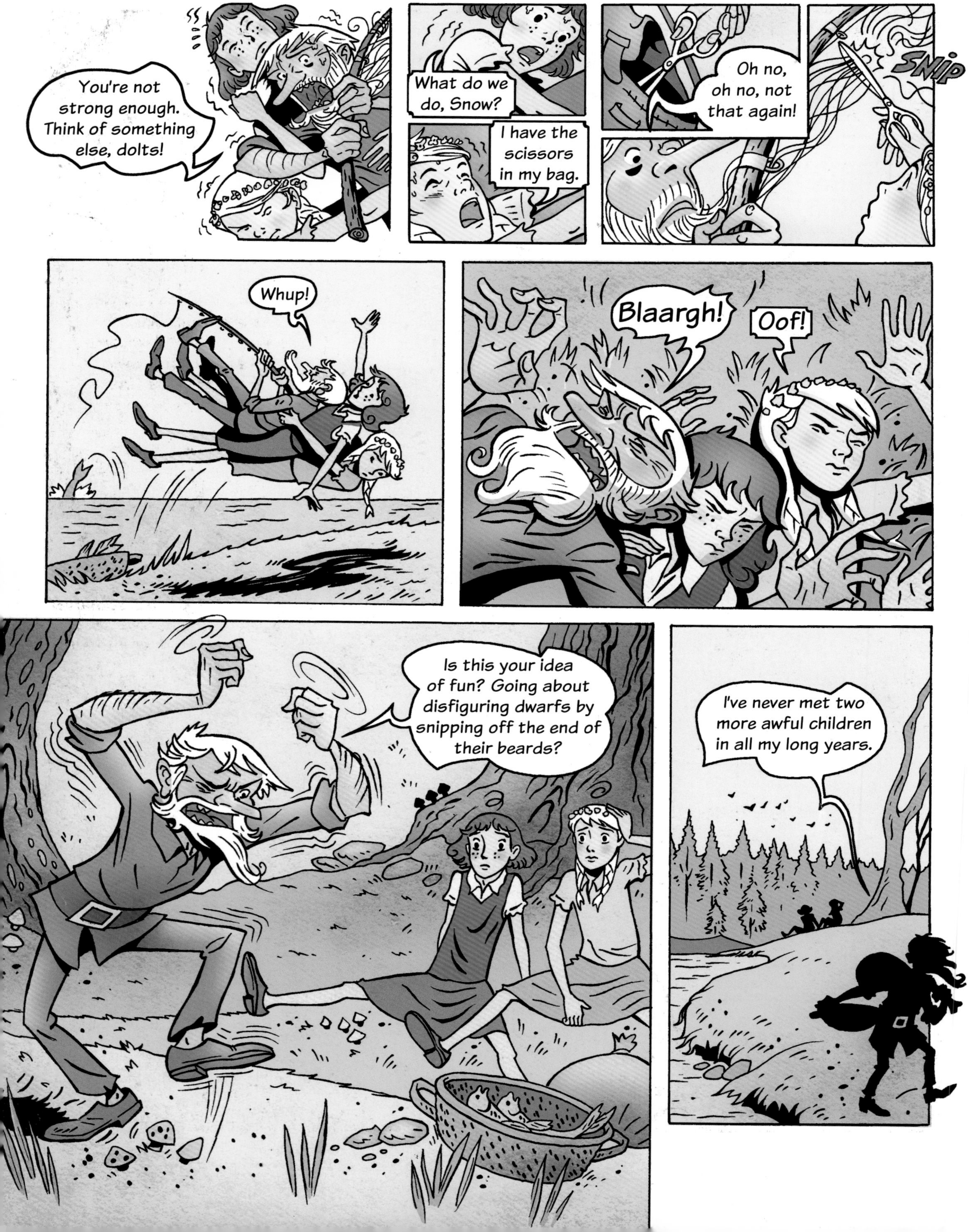

You're not strong enough. Think of something else, dolts!
What do we do, Snow?
I have the scissors in my bag.
Oh no, oh no, not that again!
SNIP
Whup!
Blaargh!
Oof!
Is this your idea of fun? Going about disfiguring dwarfs by snipping off the end of their beards?
I've never met two more awful children in all my long years.

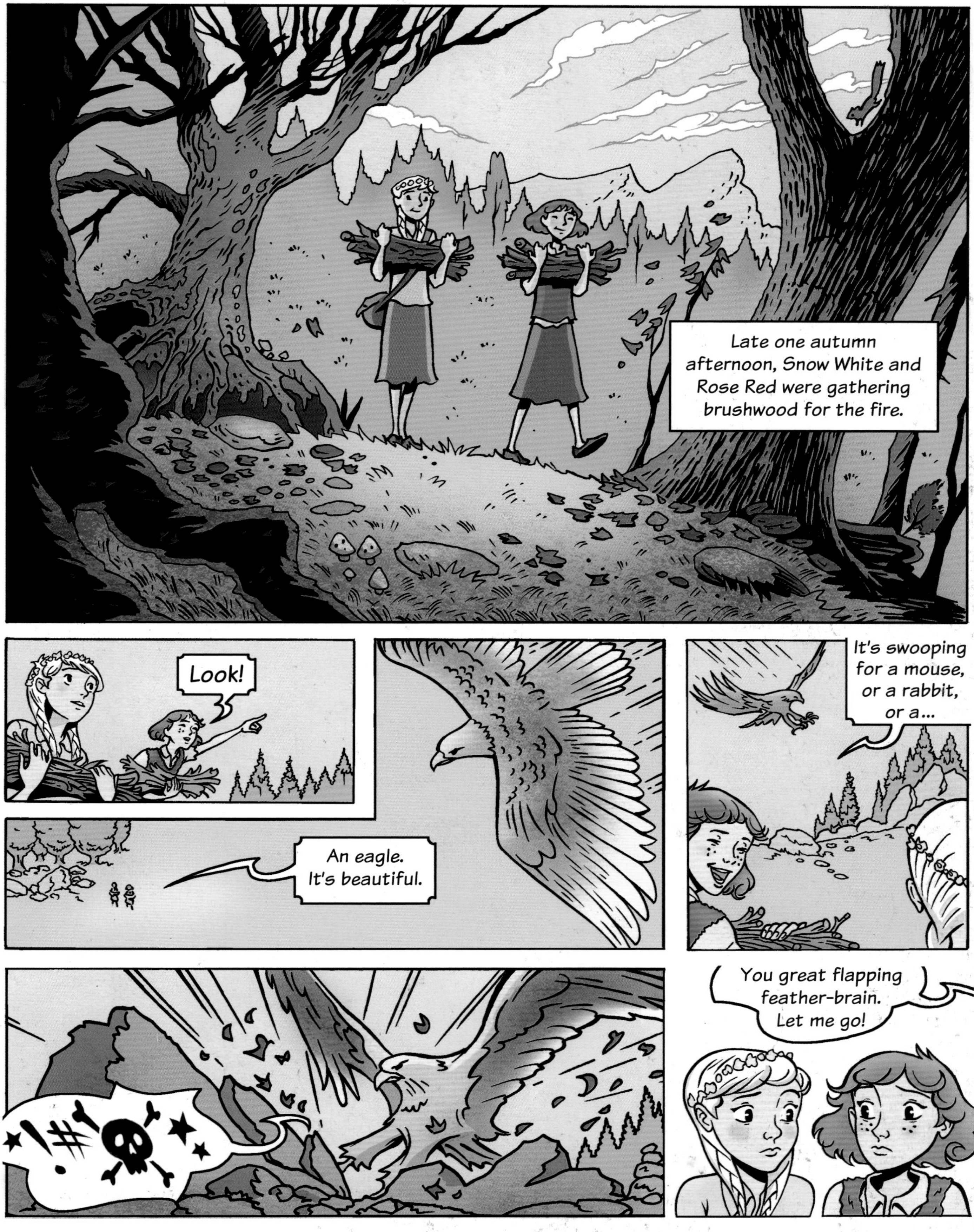
Late one autumn afternoon, Snow White and Rose Red were gathering brushwood for the fire.
Look!
An eagle. It's beautiful.
It's swooping for a mouse, or a rabbit, or a...
!#!
You great flapping feather-brain. Let me go!

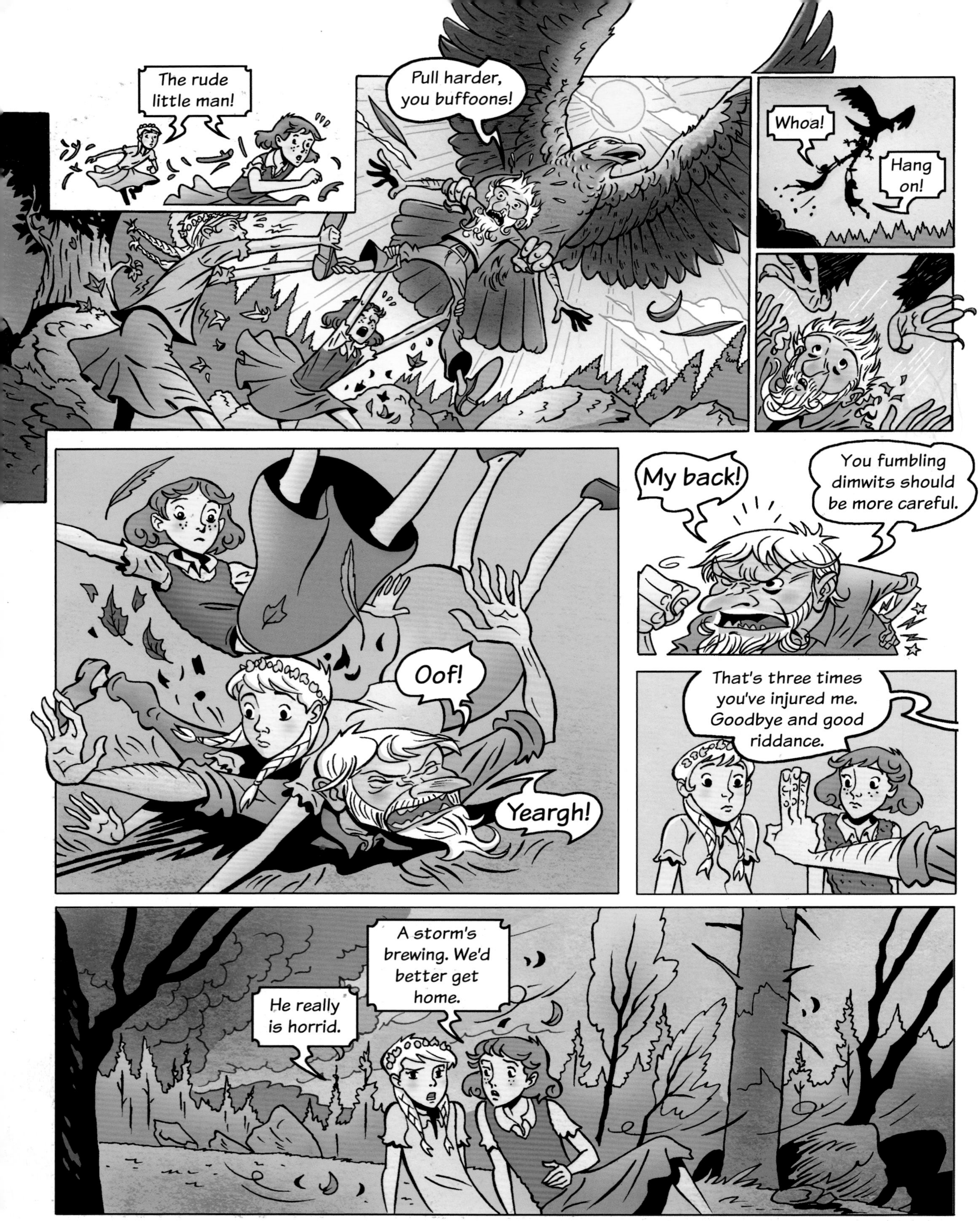
The rude little man!
Pull harder, you buffoons!
Whoa!
Hang on!
My back!
You fumbling dimwits should be more careful.
Oof!
Yeargh!
That's three times you've injured me. Goodbye and good riddance.
He really is horrid.
A storm's brewing. We'd better get home.

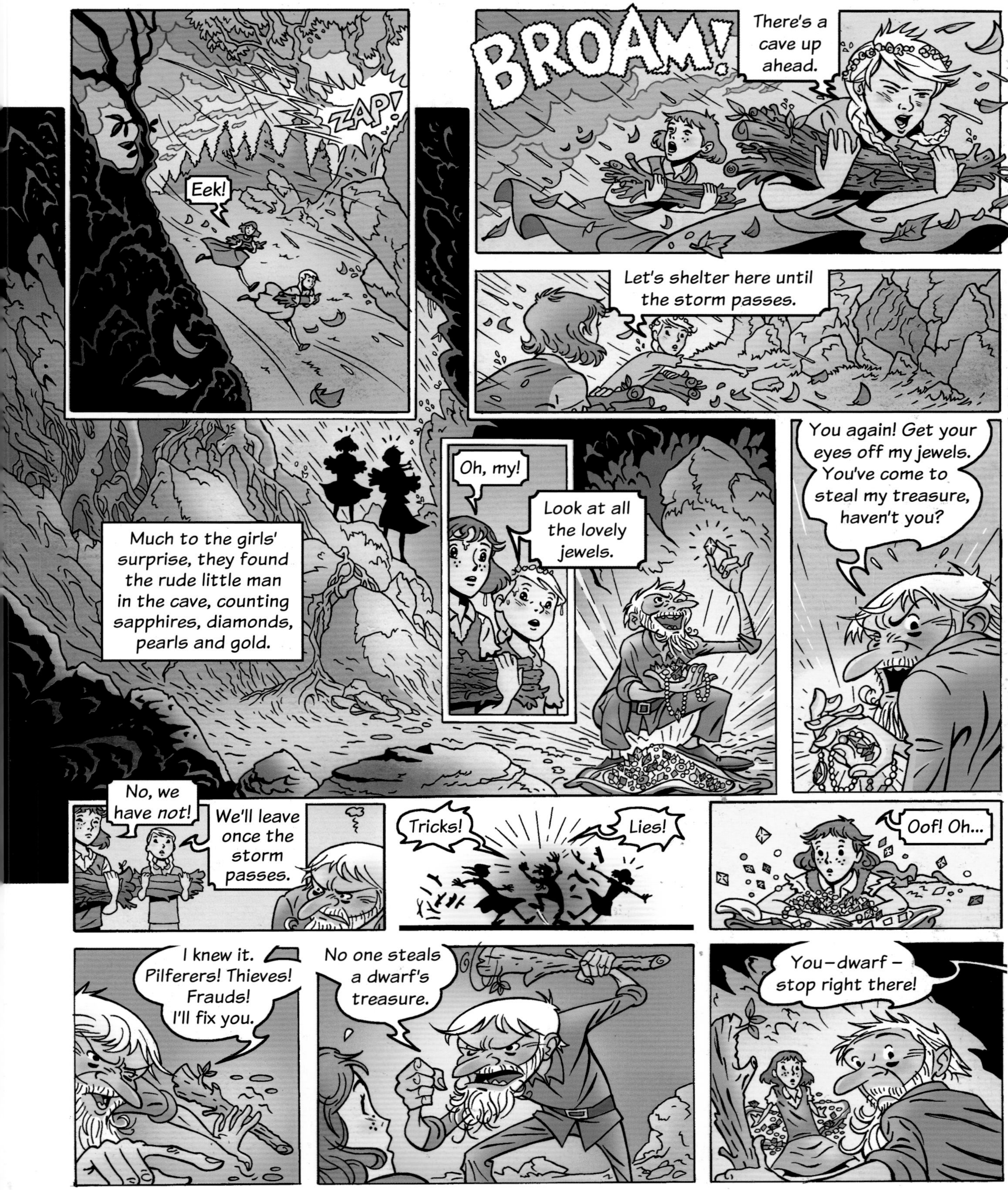
ZAP!
Eek!
BROAM!
There's a cave up ahead.
Let's shelter here until the storm passes.
Much to the girls' surprise, they found the rude little man in the cave, counting sapphires, diamonds, pearls and gold.
Oh, my!
Look at all the lovely jewels.
You again! Get your eyes off my jewels. You've come to steal my treasure, haven't you?
No, we have not!
We'll leave once the storm passes.
Tricks!
Lies!
Oof! Oh...
I knew it. Pilferers! Thieves! Frauds! I'll fix you.
No one steals a dwarf's treasure.
You—dwarf—stop right there!

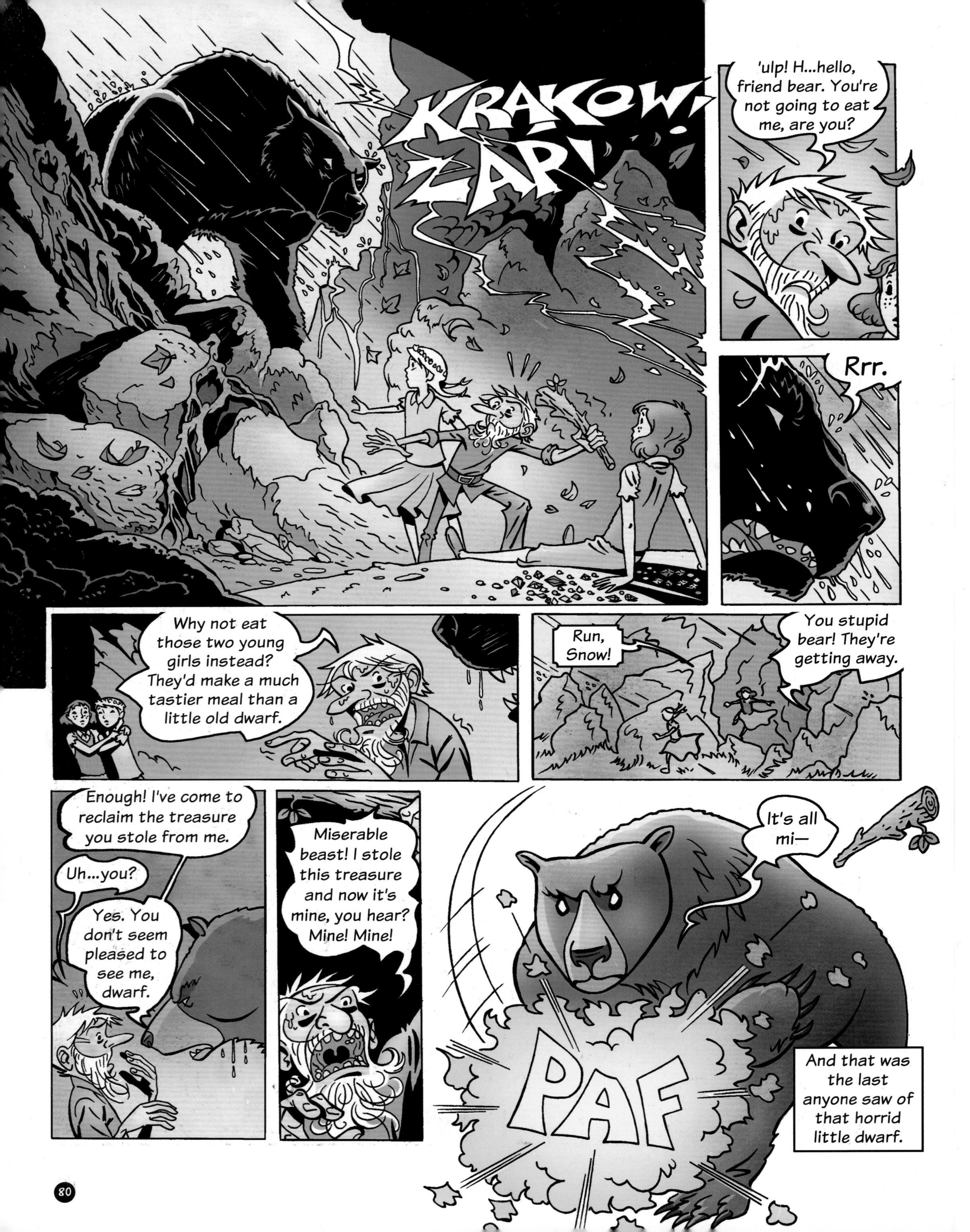
KRAKOW! ZAP!
'ulp! H...hello, friend bear. You're not going to eat me, are you?
Rrr.
Why not eat those two young girls instead? They'd make a much tastier meal than a little old dwarf.
Run, Snow!
You stupid bear! They're getting away.
Enough! I've come to reclaim the treasure you stole from me.
Uh...you?
Yes. You don't seem pleased to see me, dwarf.
Miserable beast! I stole this treasure and now it's mine, you hear? Mine! Mine!
It's all mi—
PAF
And that was the last anyone saw of that horrid little dwarf.

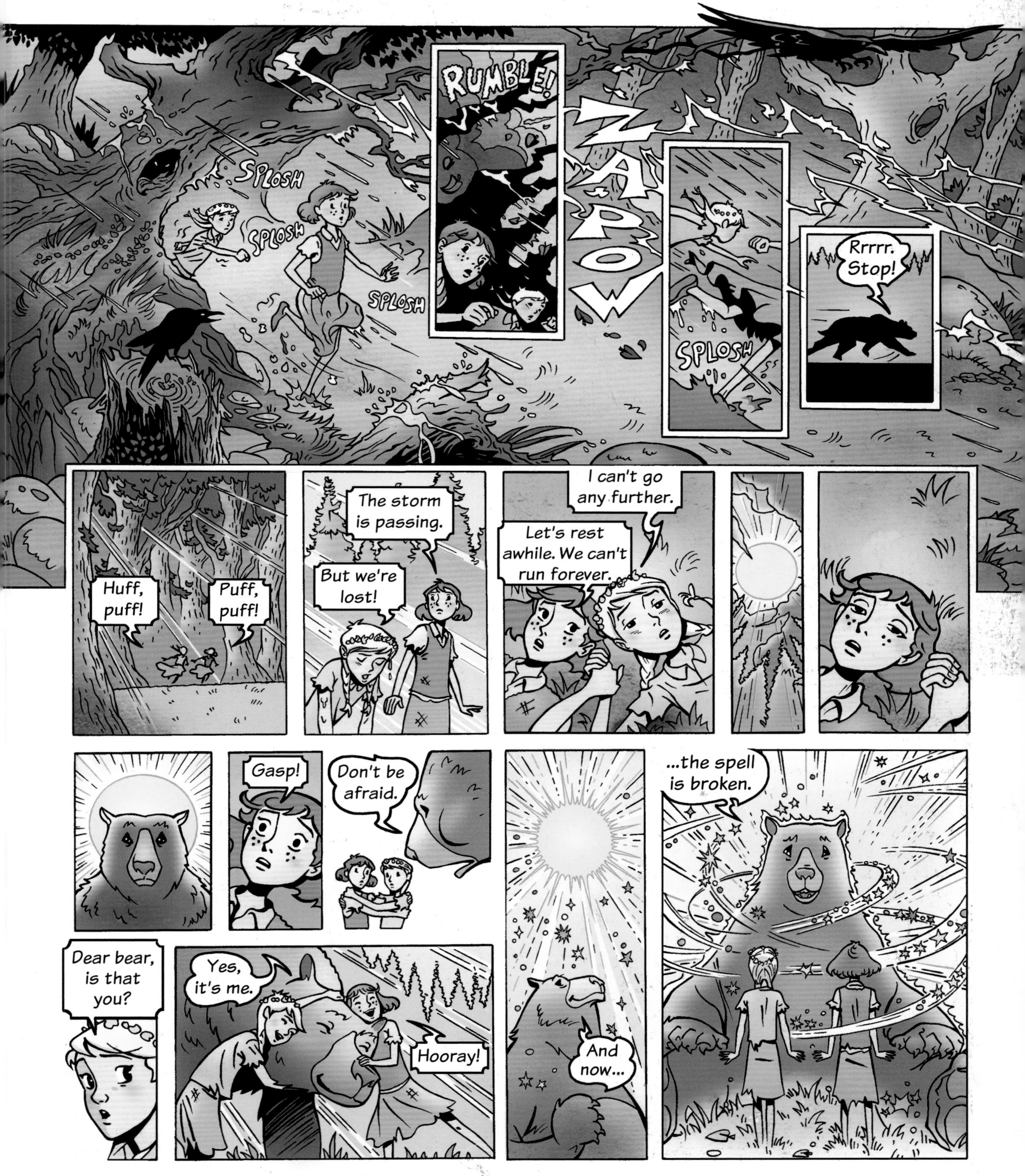
SPLOSH
SPLOSH
SPLOSH
RUMBLE!
ZAPOW
SPLOSH
Rrrrr. Stop!
Huff, puff!
Puff, puff!
The storm is passing.
But we're lost!
I can't go any further.
Let's rest awhile. We can't run forever.
Gasp!
Don't be afraid.
And now...
...the spell is broken.
Dear bear, is that you?
Yes, it's me.
Hooray!

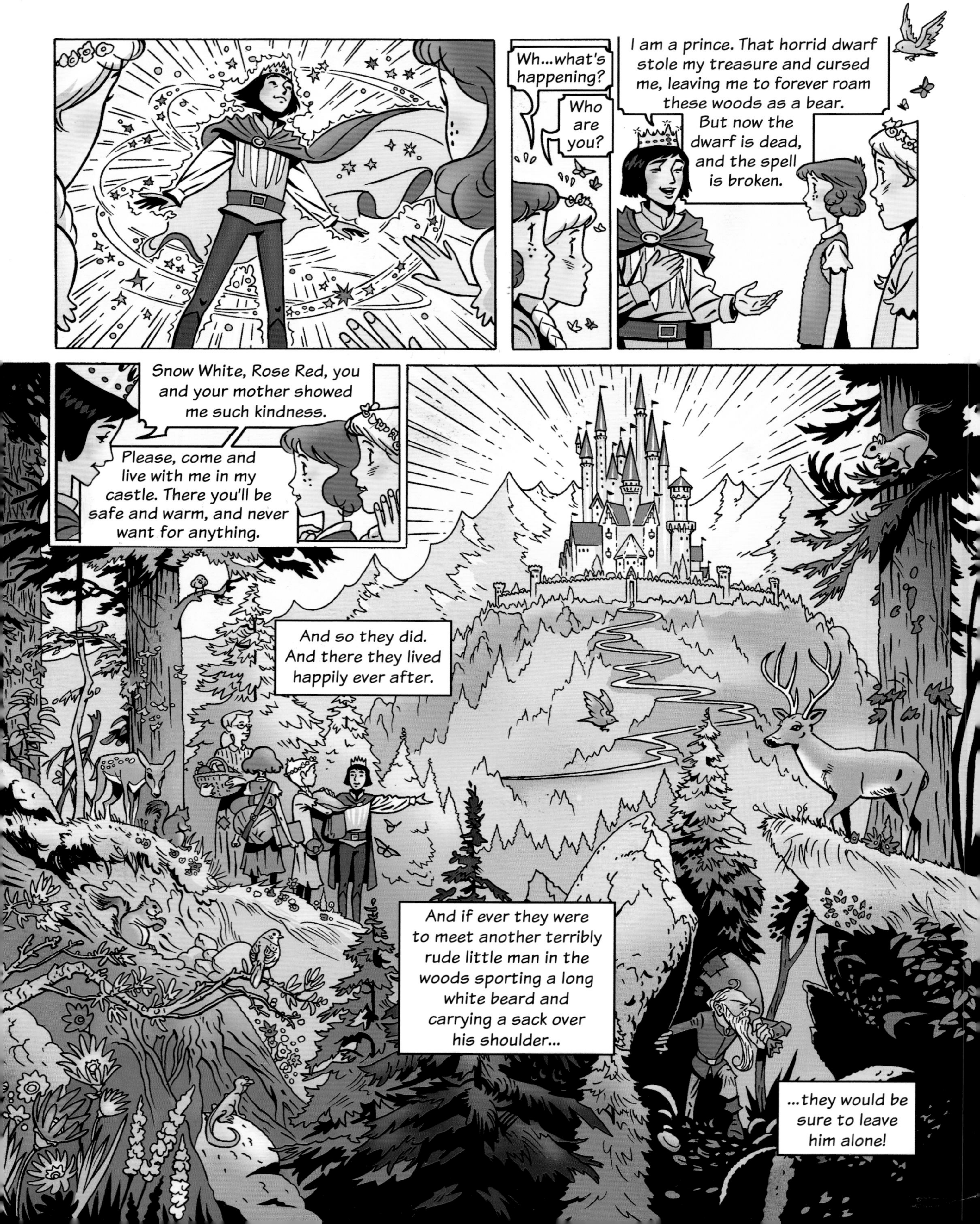
Wh...what's happening?
Who are you?
I am a prince. That horrid dwarf stole my treasure and cursed me, leaving me to forever roam these woods as a bear.
But now the dwarf is dead, and the spell is broken.
Snow White, Rose Red, you and your mother showed me such kindness.
Please, come and live with me in my castle. There you'll be safe and warm, and never want for anything.
And so they did. And there they lived happily ever after.
And if ever they were to meet another terribly rude little man in the woods sporting a long white beard and carrying a sack over his shoulder...
...they would be sure to leave him alone!

Momotaro

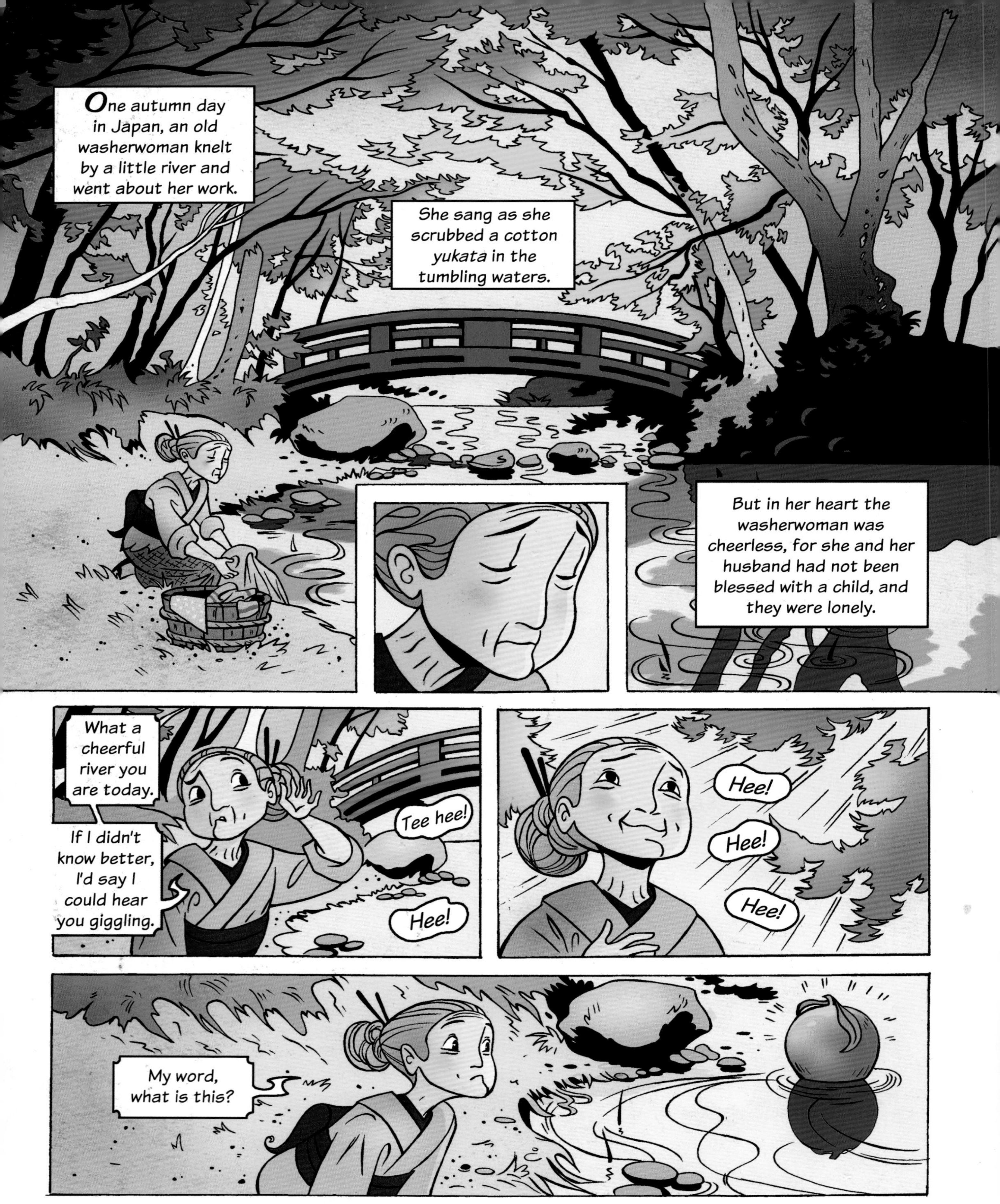
One autumn day in Japan, an old washerwoman knelt by a little river and went about her work.
She sang as she scrubbed a cotton *yukata* in the tumbling waters.
But in her heart the washerwoman was cheerless, for she and her husband had not been blessed with a child, and they were lonely.
What a cheerful river you are today.
If I didn't know better, I'd say I could hear you giggling.
Tee hee!
Hee!
Hee!
Hee!
Hee!
My word, what is this?

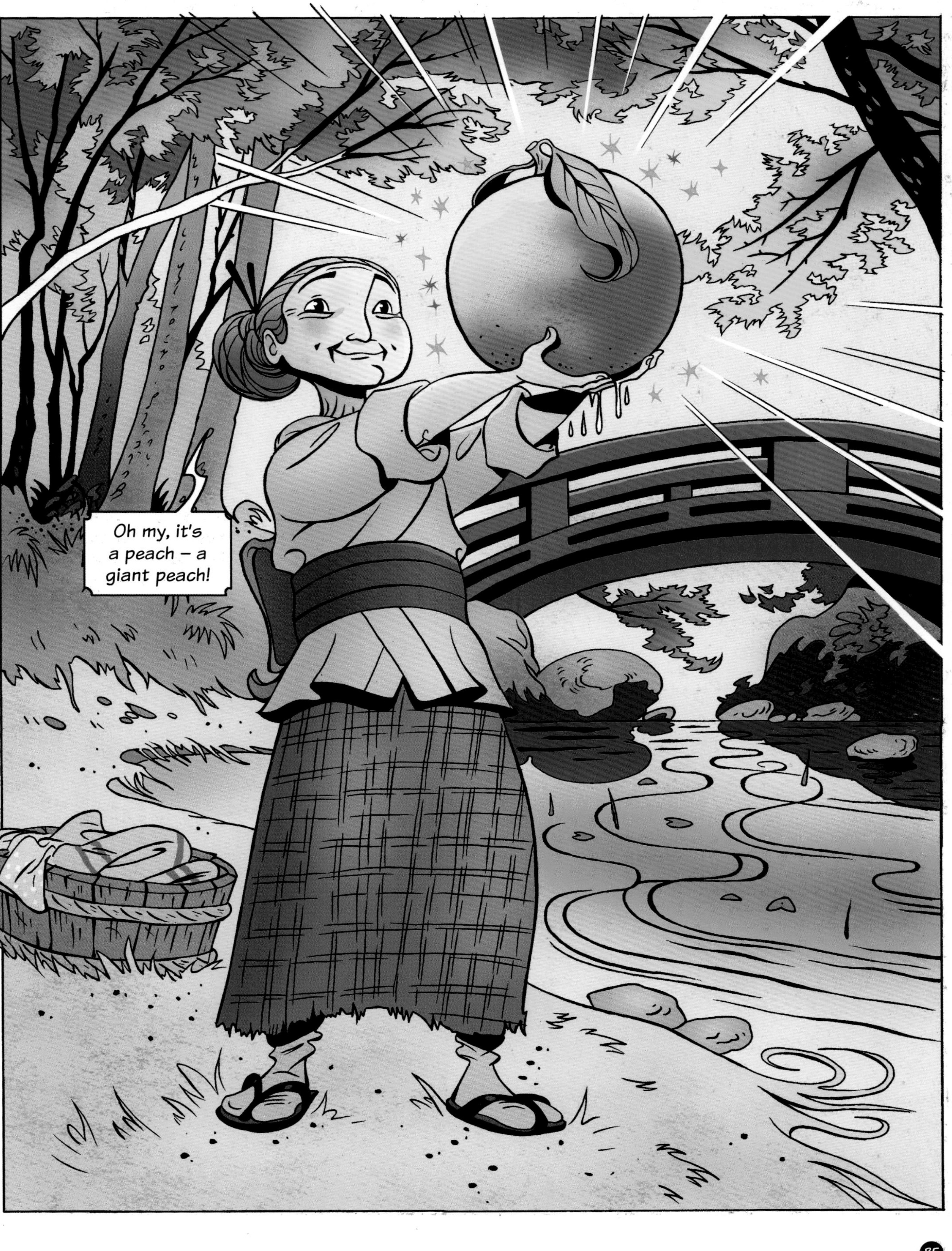
Oh my, it's a peach – a giant peach!

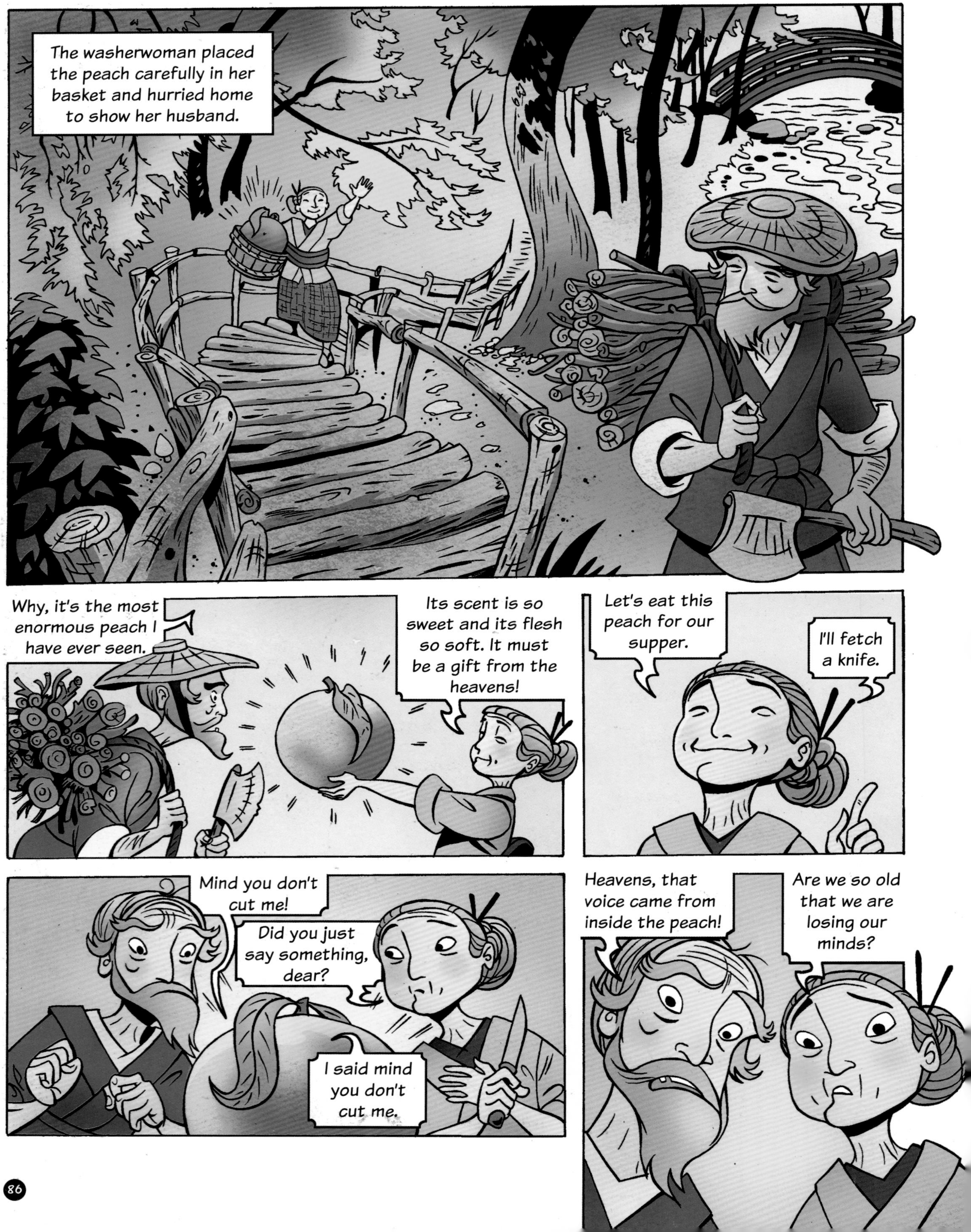
The washerwoman placed the peach carefully in her basket and hurried home to show her husband.
Why, it's the most enormous peach I have ever seen.
Its scent is so sweet and its flesh so soft. It must be a gift from the heavens!
Let's eat this peach for our supper.
I'll fetch a knife.
Mind you don't cut me!
Did you just say something, dear?
I said mind you don't cut me.
Heavens, that voice came from inside the peach!
Are we so old that we are losing our minds?

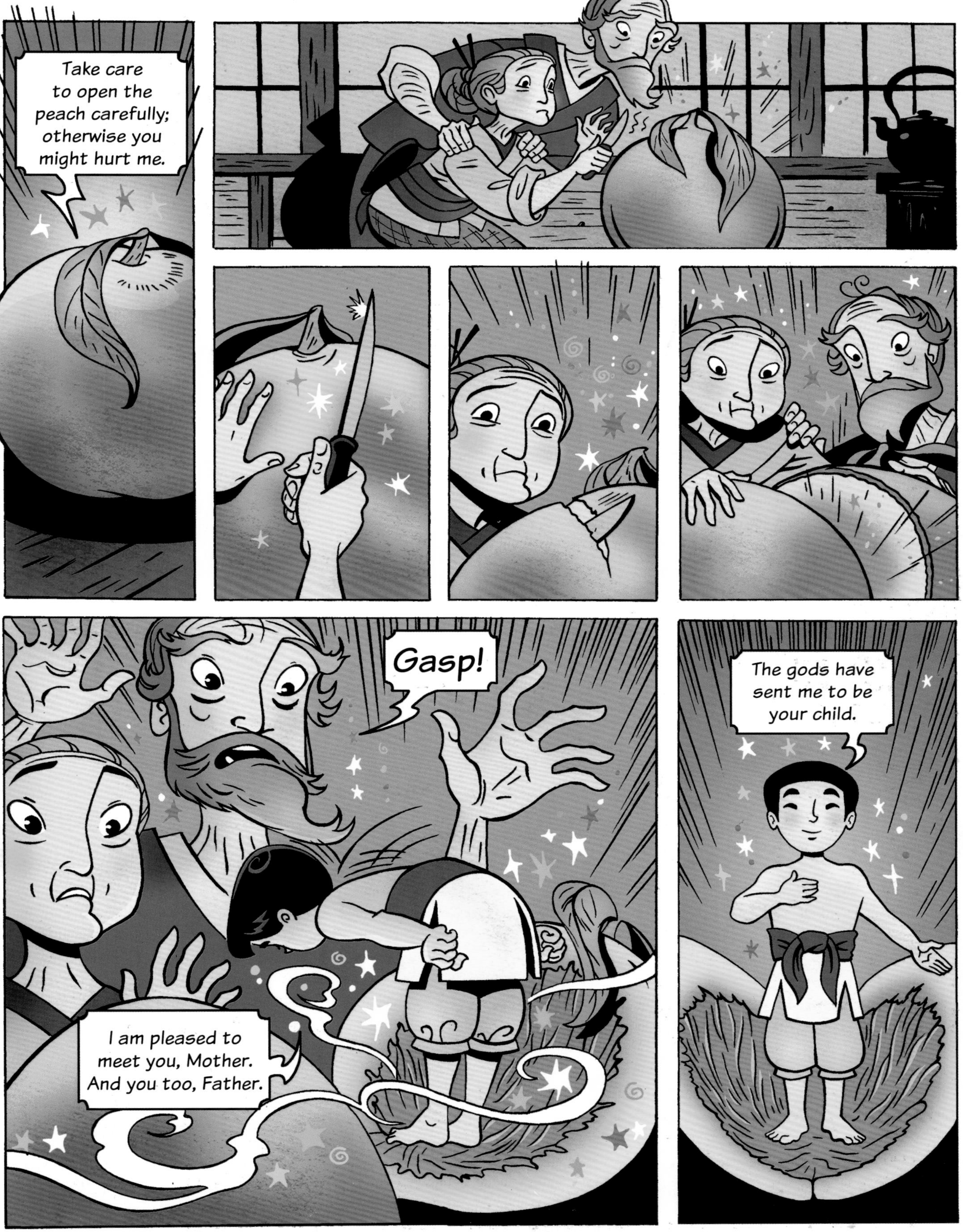
Take care to open the peach carefully; otherwise you might hurt me.
Gasp!
I am pleased to meet you, Mother. And you too, Father.
The gods have sent me to be your child.

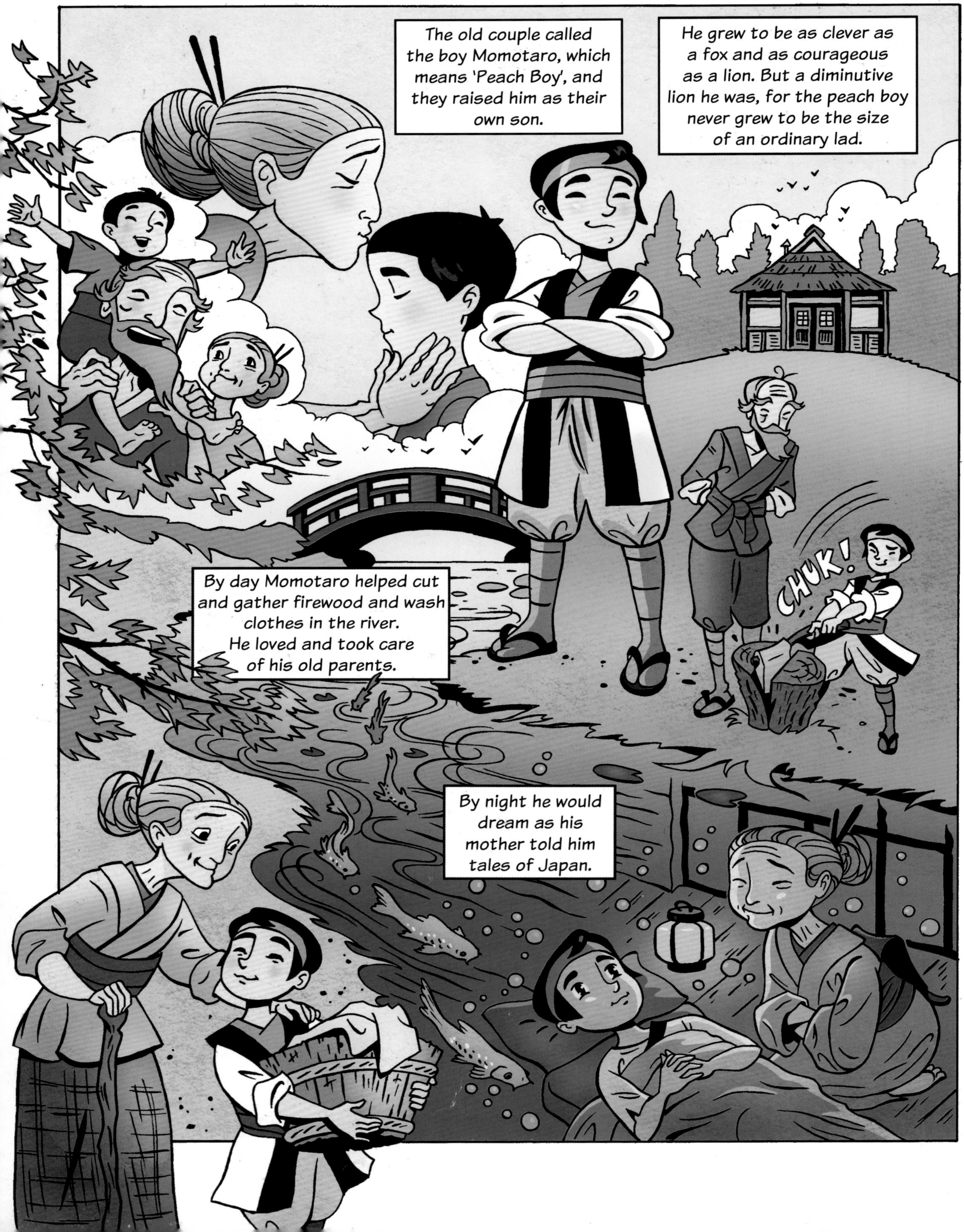
The old couple called the boy Momotaro, which means 'Peach Boy', and they raised him as their own son.
He grew to be as clever as a fox and as courageous as a lion. But a diminutive lion he was, for the peach boy never grew to be the size of an ordinary lad.
By day Momotaro helped cut and gather firewood and wash clothes in the river. He loved and took care of his old parents.
CHUK!
By night he would dream as his mother told him tales of Japan.

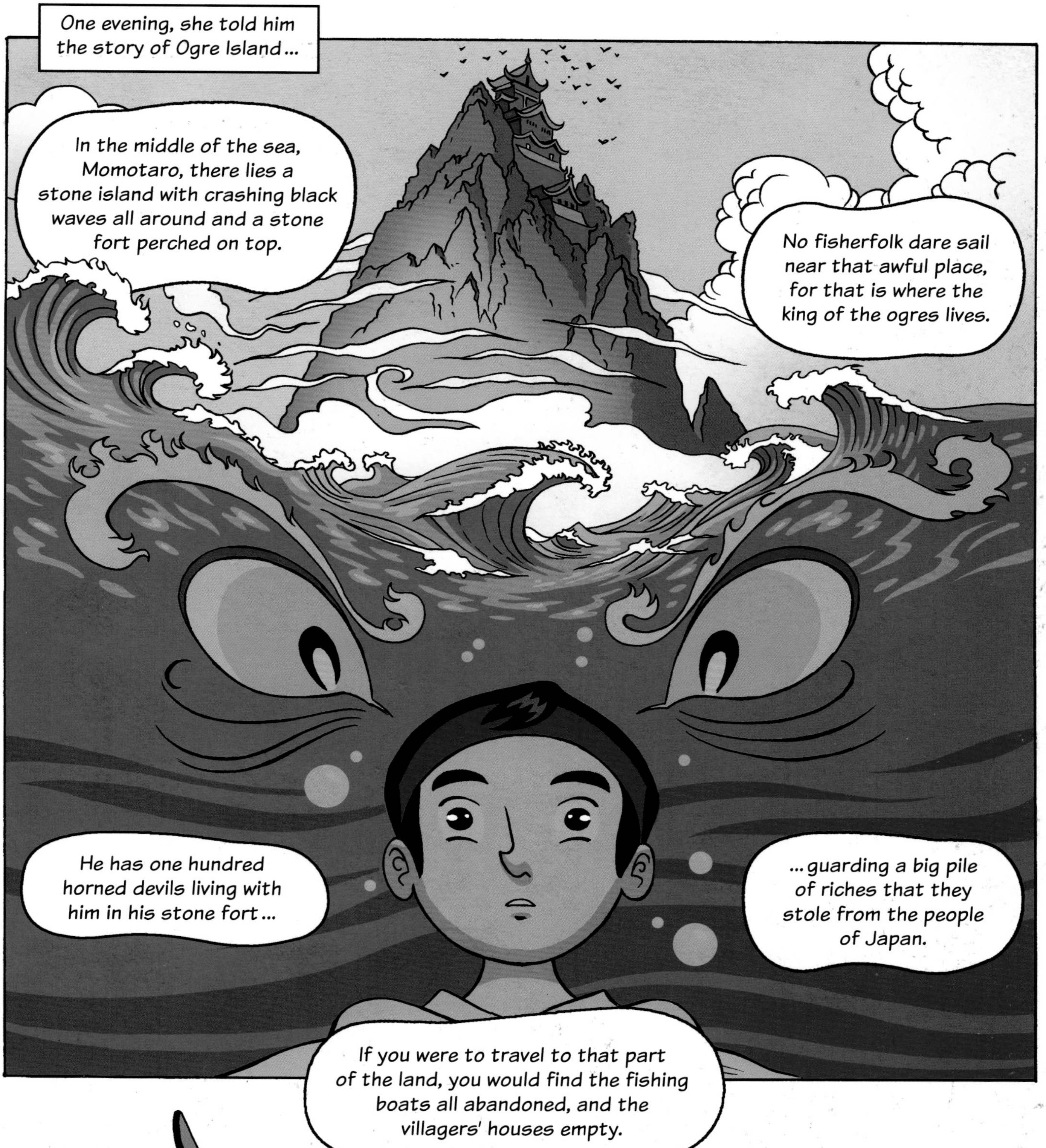
One evening, she told him the story of Ogre Island...
In the middle of the sea, Momotaro, there lies a stone island with crashing black waves all around and a stone fort perched on top.
No fisherfolk dare sail near that awful place, for that is where the king of the ogres lives.
He has one hundred horned devils living with him in his stone fort...
...guarding a big pile of riches that they stole from the people of Japan.
If you were to travel to that part of the land, you would find the fishing boats all abandoned, and the villagers' houses empty.

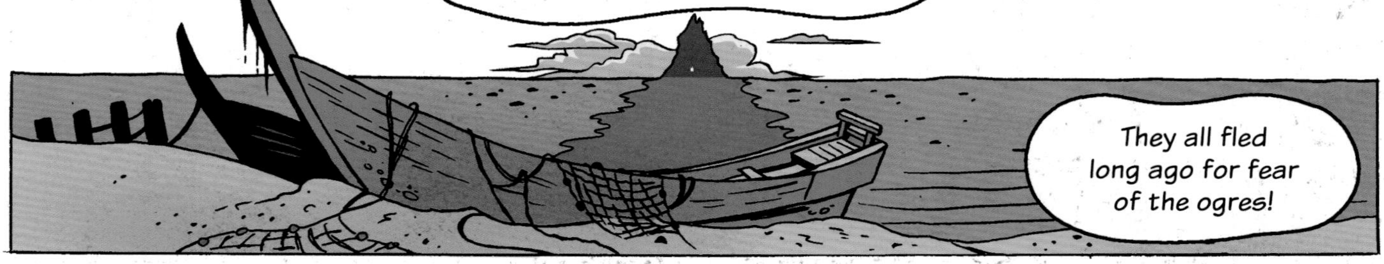
They all fled long ago for fear of the ogres!

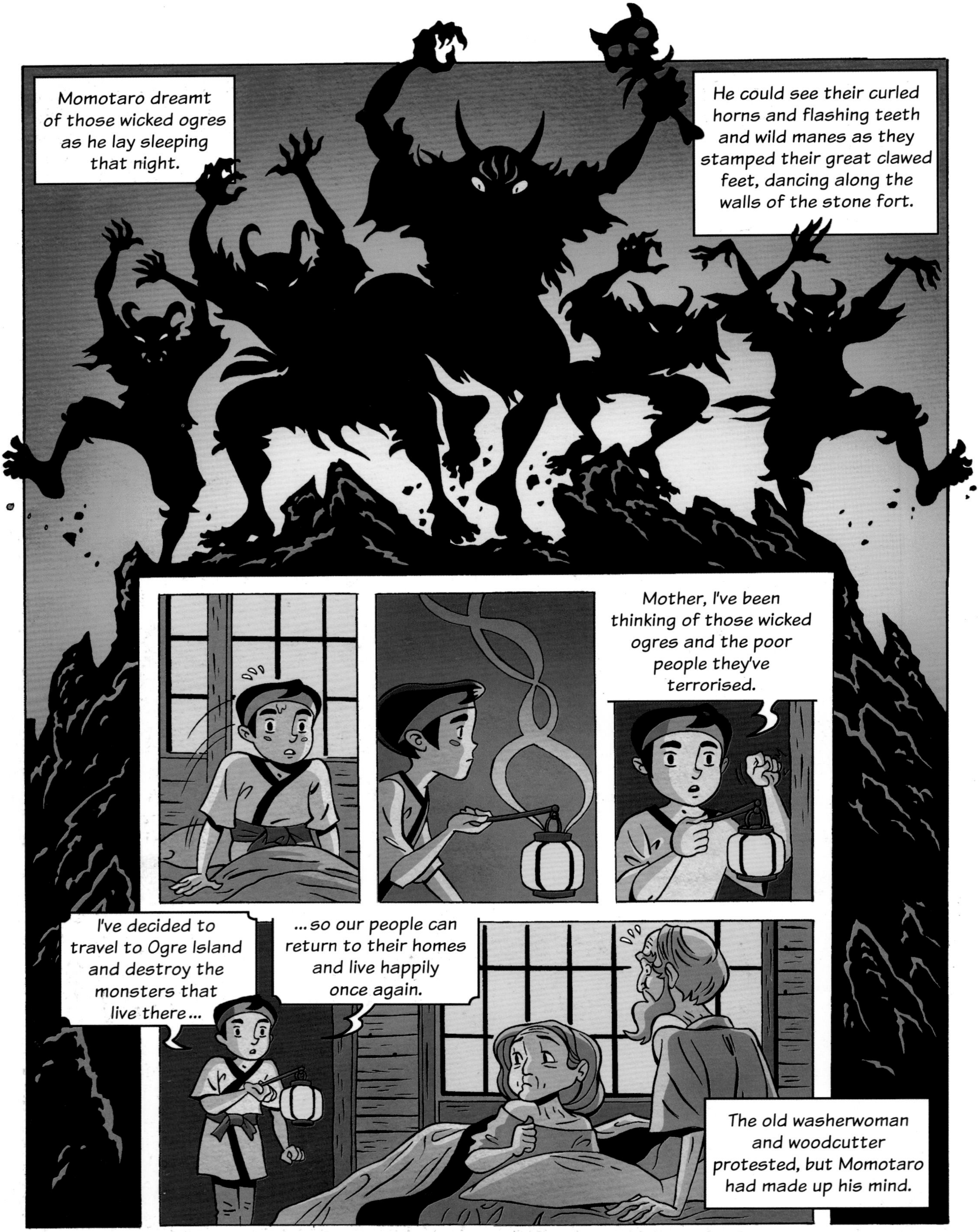
Momotaro dreamt of those wicked ogres as he lay sleeping that night.
He could see their curled horns and flashing teeth and wild manes as they stamped their great clawed feet, dancing along the walls of the stone fort.
Mother, I've been thinking of those wicked ogres and the poor people they've terrorised.
I've decided to travel to Ogre Island and destroy the monsters that live there...
...so our people can return to their homes and live happily once again.
The old washerwoman and woodcutter protested, but Momotaro had made up his mind.

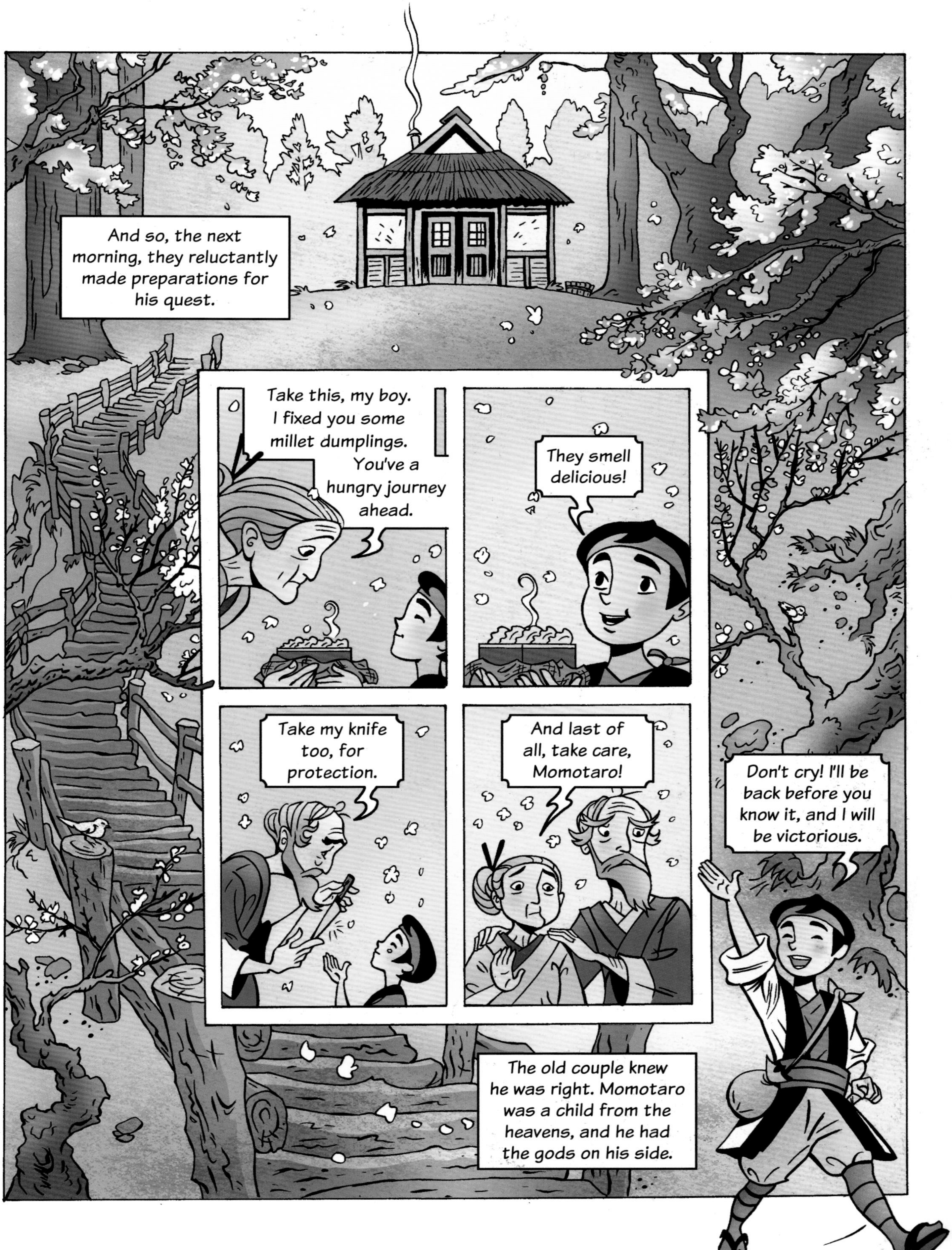
And so, the next morning, they reluctantly made preparations for his quest.
Take this, my boy. I fixed you some millet dumplings. You've a hungry journey ahead.
They smell delicious!
Take my knife too, for protection.
And last of all, take care, Momotaro!
Don't cry! I'll be back before you know it, and I will be victorious.
The old couple knew he was right. Momotaro was a child from the heavens, and he had the gods on his side.

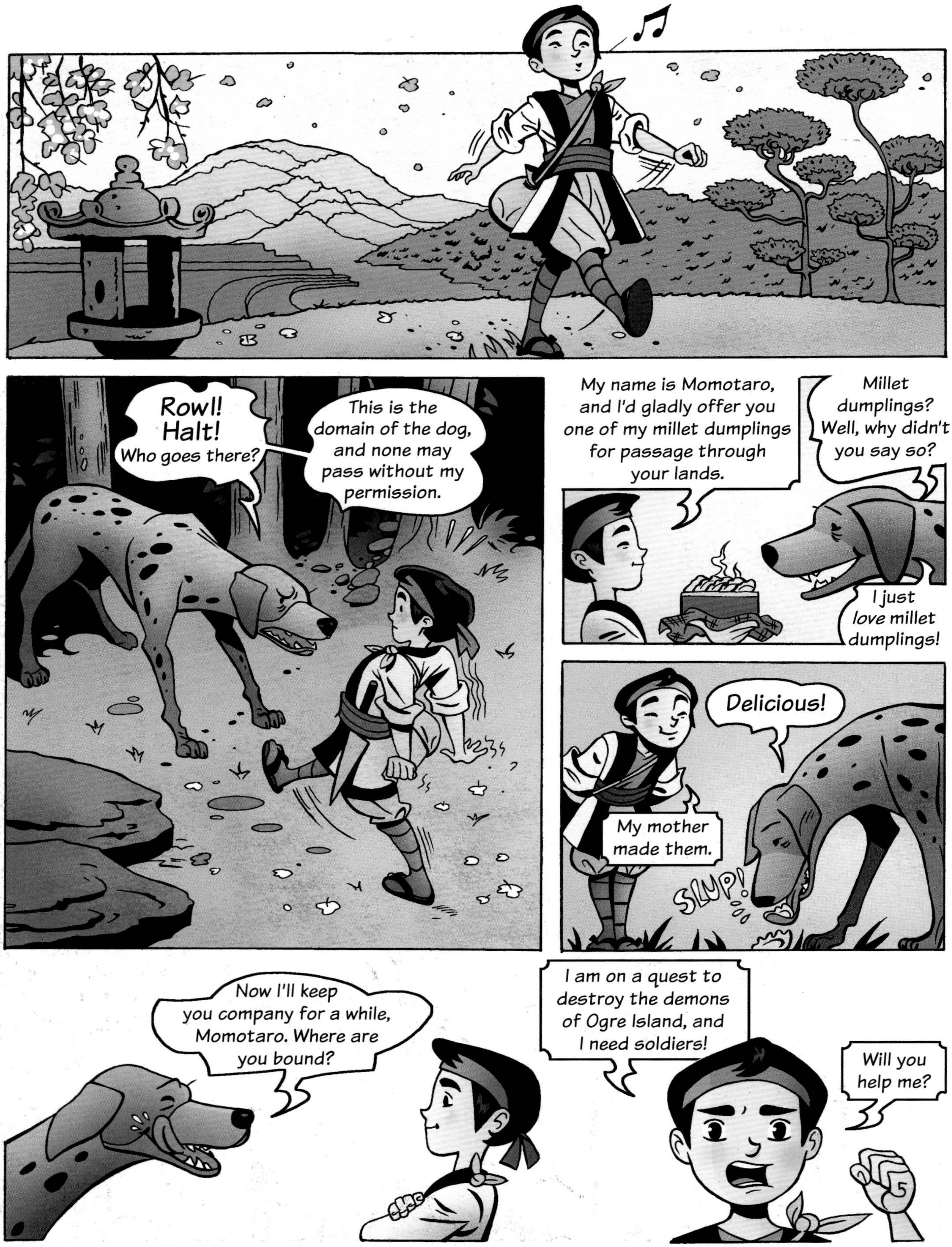
Rowl! Halt! Who goes there?
This is the domain of the dog, and none may pass without my permission.
My name is Momotaro, and I'd gladly offer you one of my millet dumplings for passage through your lands.
Millet dumplings? Well, why didn't you say so?
I just love millet dumplings!
Delicious!
My mother made them.
SLUP!
Now I'll keep you company for a while, Momotaro. Where are you bound?
I am on a quest to destroy the demons of Ogre Island, and I need soldiers!
Will you help me?

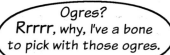

Ogres? Rrrrr, why, I've a bone to pick with those ogres.

Those horned hooligans have caused a lot of trouble for me and my ilk...

...pilfering and plundering and pillaging their way through my forest and scaring away all the good fellows who used to live here.

General Momotaro, I'd be honoured to serve you on your quest.

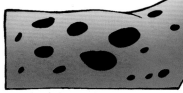

Sniff! Do you smell that? Hmmmm... sniff, sniff!

Aha – monkeys! We'd better be careful, Momotaro.

We have entered the land of the monkeys. I don't trust those curly-tailed tree-climbers one bit!

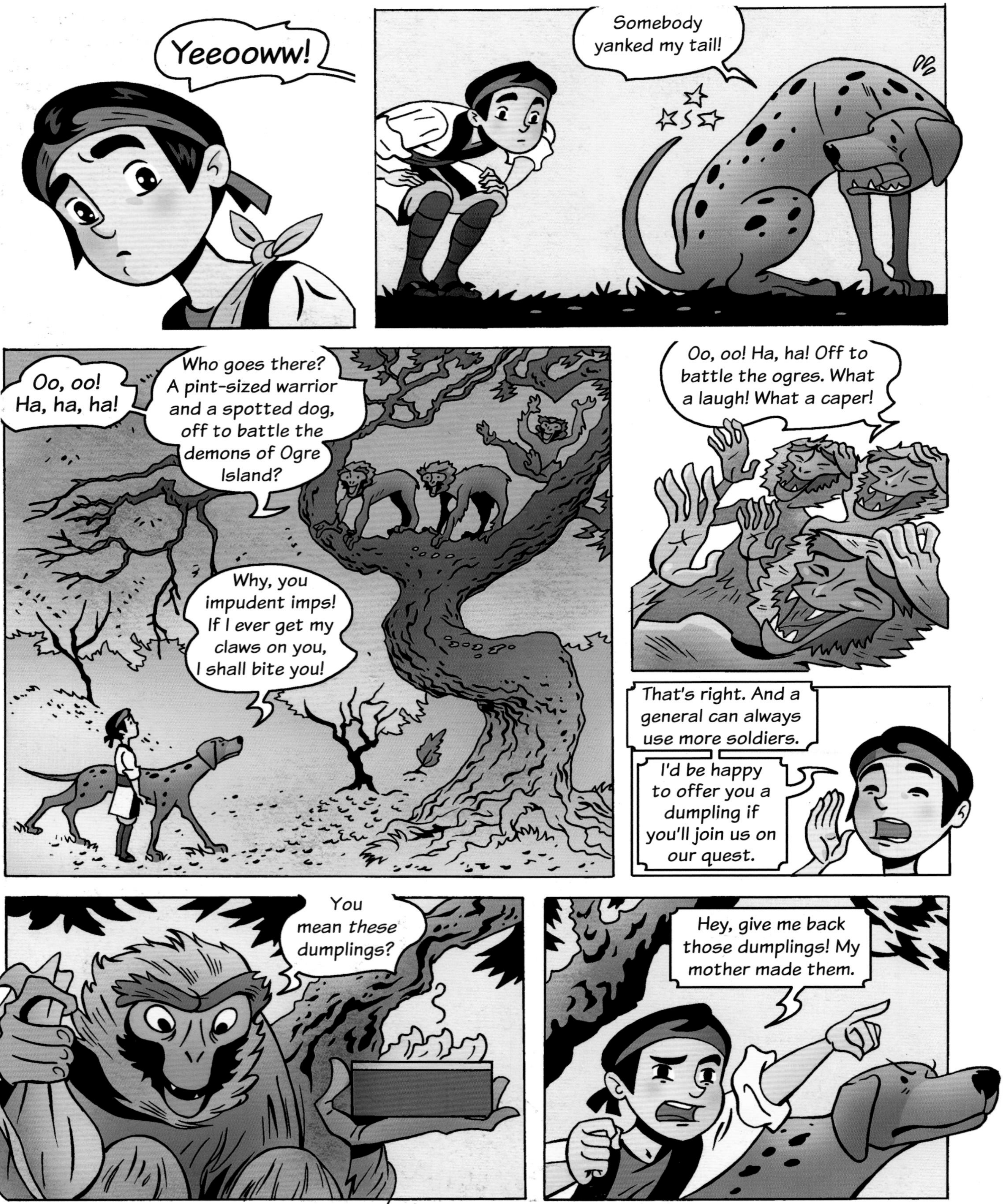
Yeeooww!
Somebody yanked my tail!
Oo, oo! Ha, ha, ha!
Who goes there? A pint-sized warrior and a spotted dog, off to battle the demons of Ogre Island?
Why, you impudent imps! If I ever get my claws on you, I shall bite you!
Oo, oo! Ha, ha! Off to battle the ogres. What a laugh! What a caper!
That's right. And a general can always use more soldiers.
I'd be happy to offer you a dumpling if you'll join us on our quest.
You mean *these* dumplings?
Hey, give me back those dumplings! My mother made them.

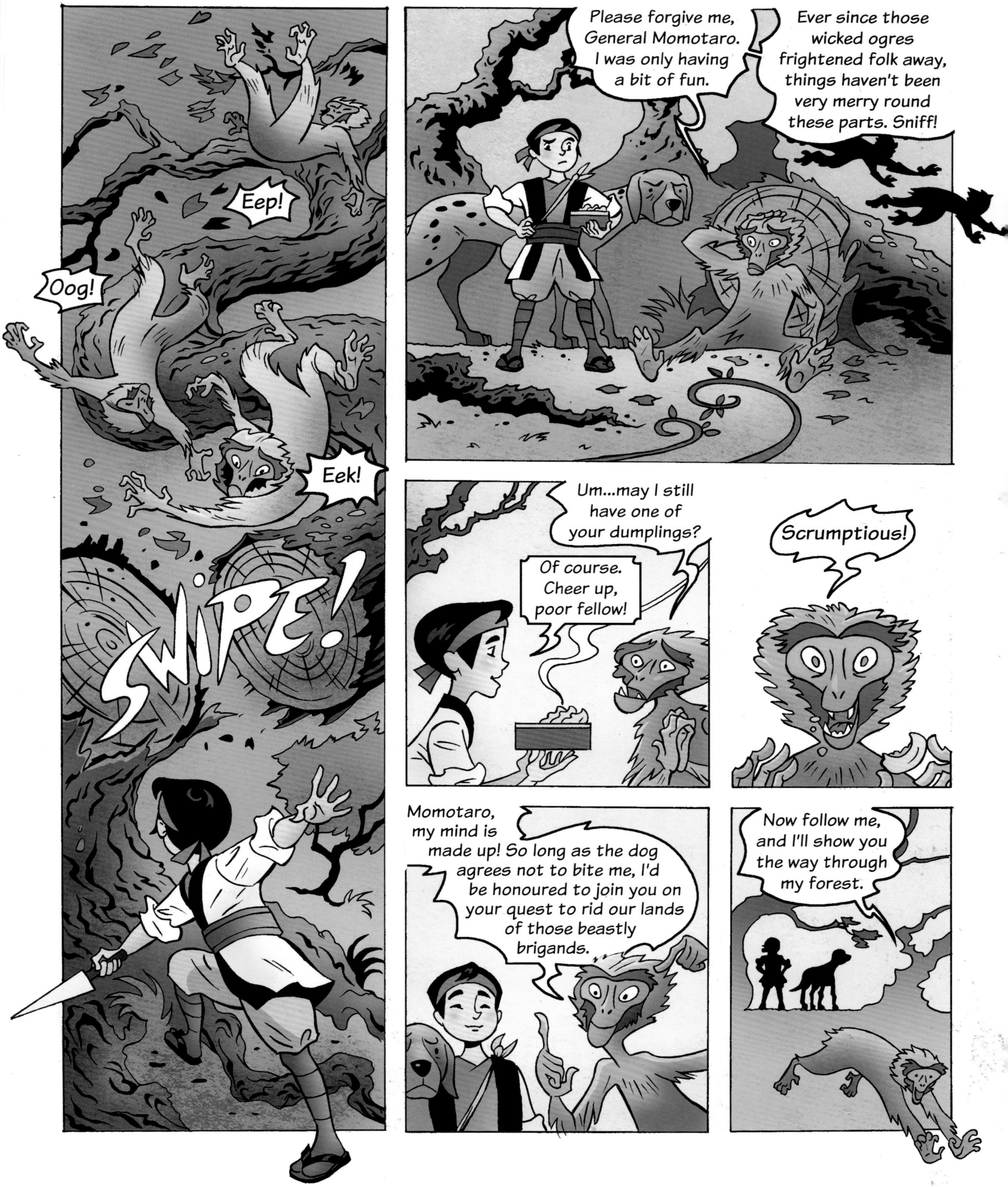
Eep!
Oog!
Eek!
SWIPE!
Please forgive me, General Momotaro. I was only having a bit of fun.
Ever since those wicked ogres frightened folk away, things haven't been very merry round these parts. Sniff!
Um...may I still have one of your dumplings?
Of course. Cheer up, poor fellow!
Scrumptious!
Momotaro, my mind is made up! So long as the dog agrees not to bite me, I'd be honoured to join you on your quest to rid our lands of those beastly brigands.
Now follow me, and I'll show you the way through my forest.

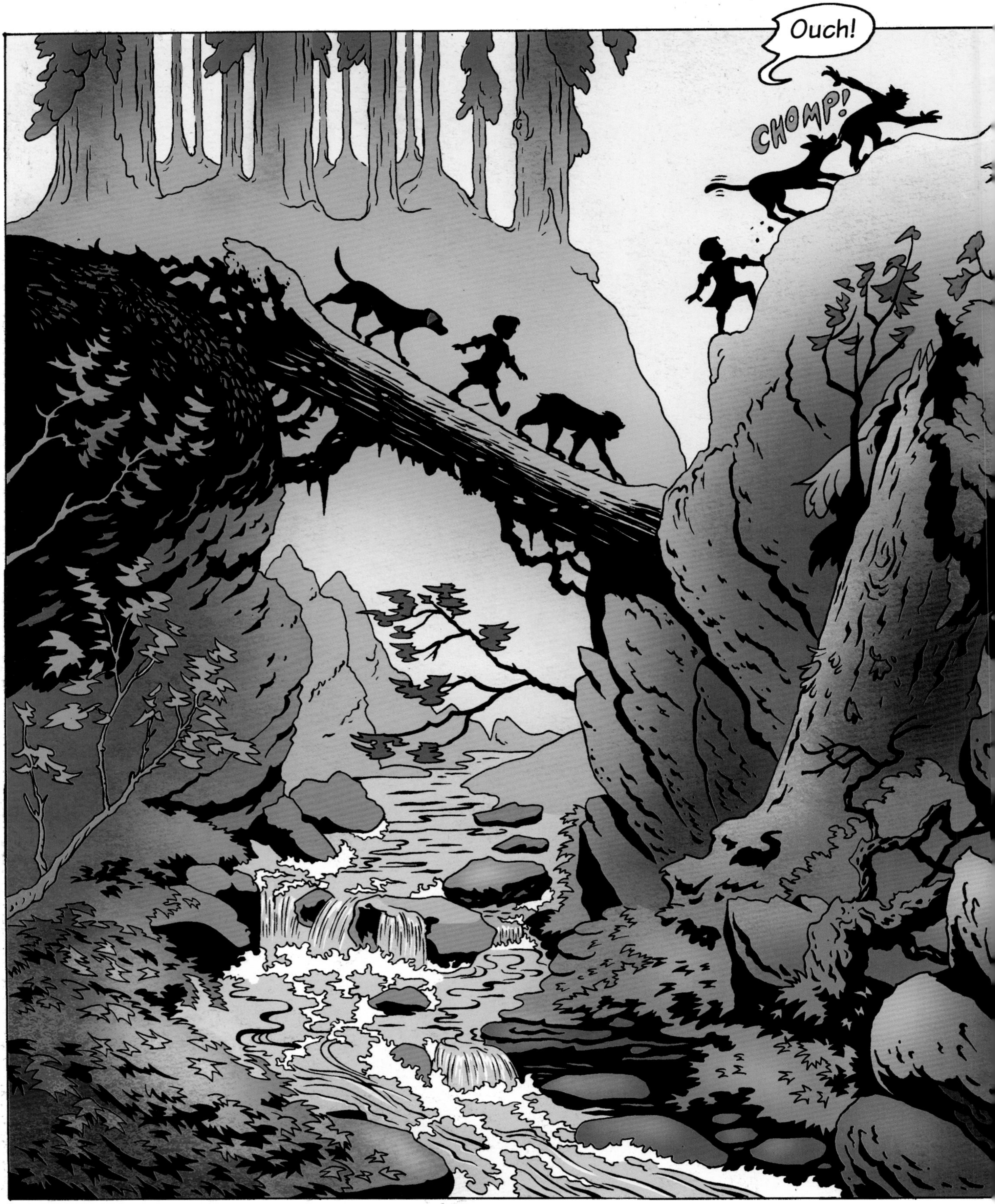
Ouch!
CHOMP!

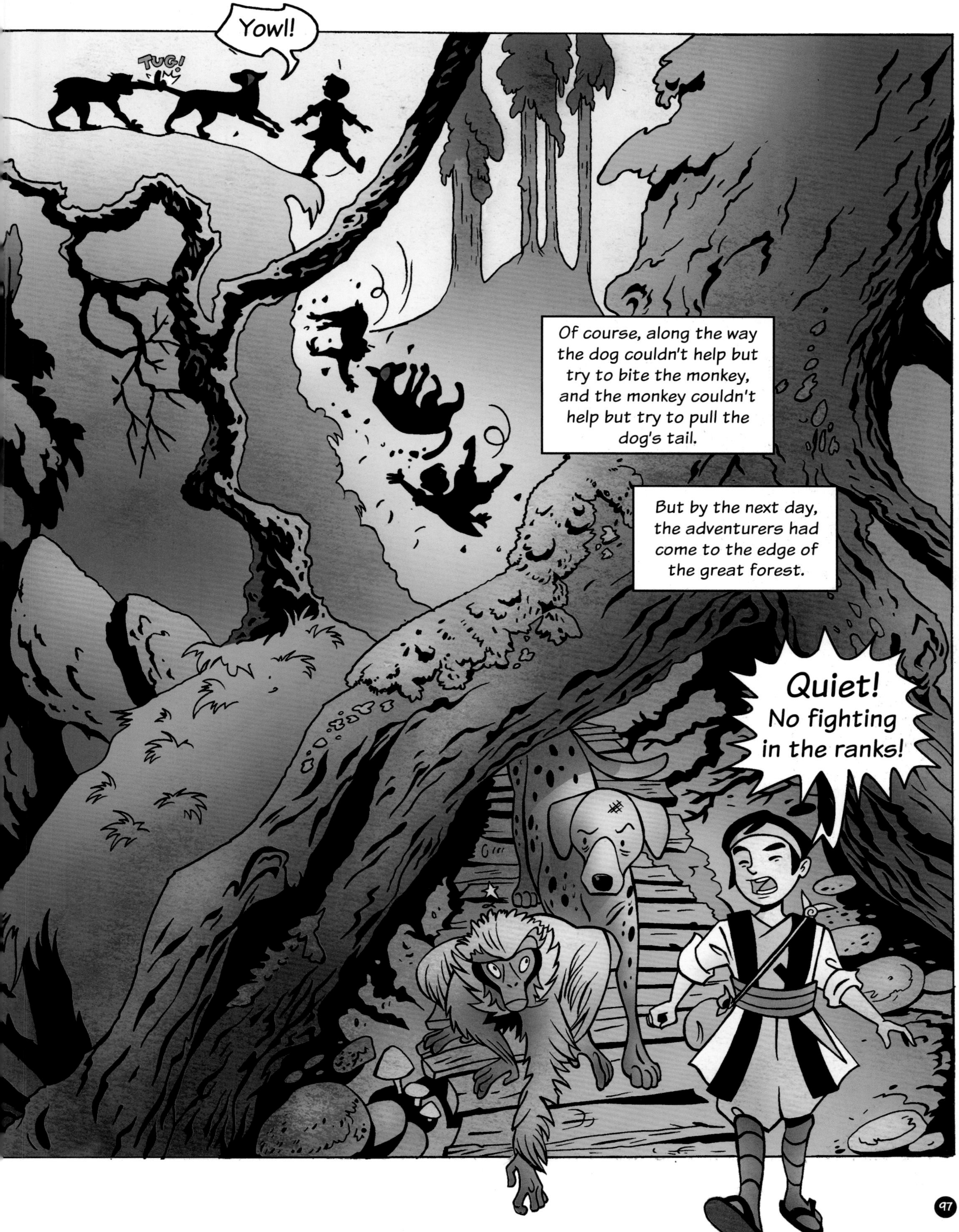
Yowl!
TUG!
Of course, along the way the dog couldn't help but try to bite the monkey, and the monkey couldn't help but try to pull the dog's tail.
But by the next day, the adventurers had come to the edge of the great forest.
Quiet! No fighting in the ranks!

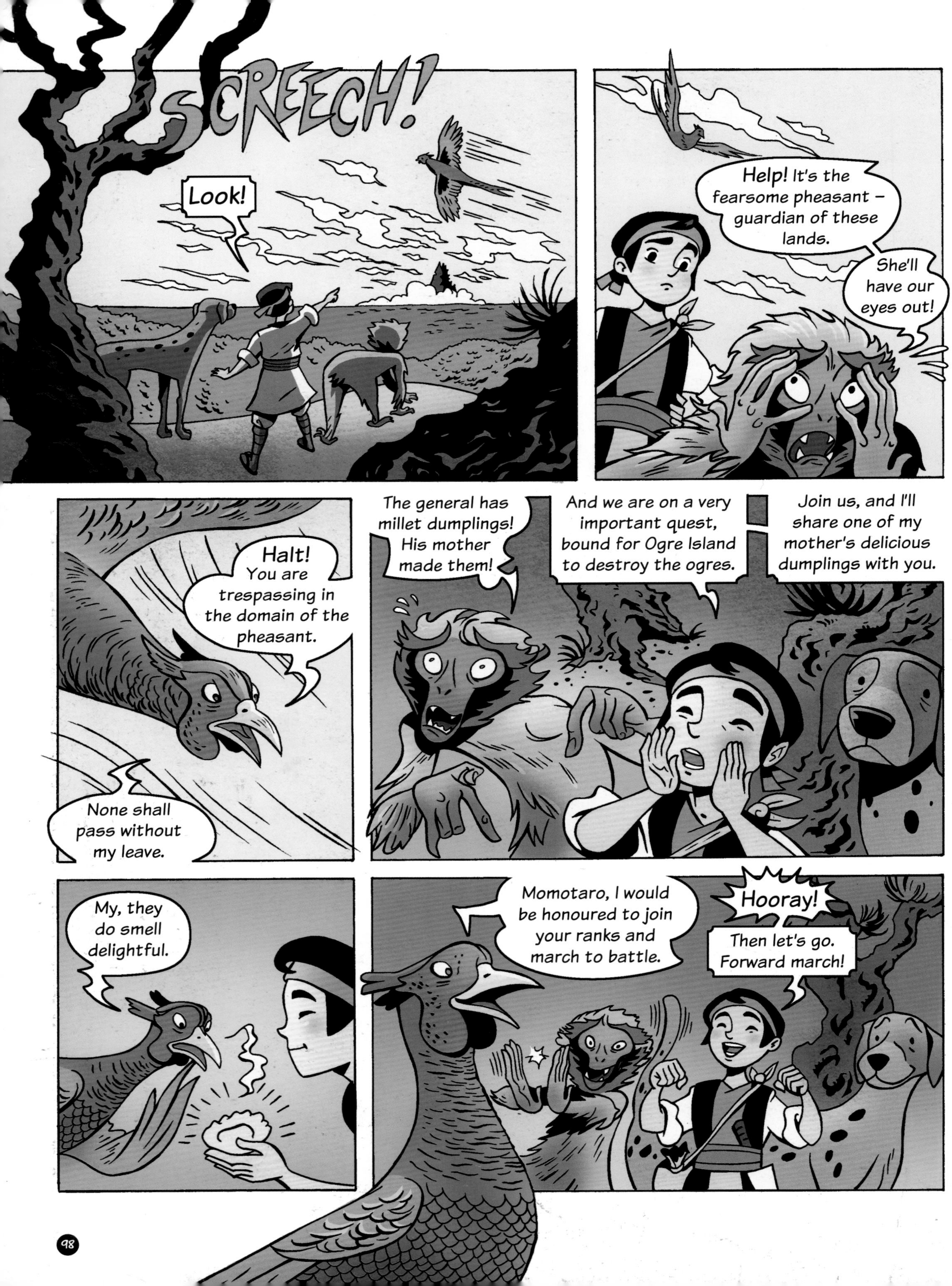
SCREECH!
Look!
Help! It's the fearsome pheasant – guardian of these lands.
She'll have our eyes out!
Halt! You are trespassing in the domain of the pheasant.
None shall pass without my leave.
The general has millet dumplings! His mother made them!
And we are on a very important quest, bound for Ogre Island to destroy the ogres.
Join us, and I'll share one of my mother's delicious dumplings with you.
My, they do smell delightful.
Momotaro, I would be honoured to join your ranks and march to battle.
Hooray!
Then let's go. Forward march!

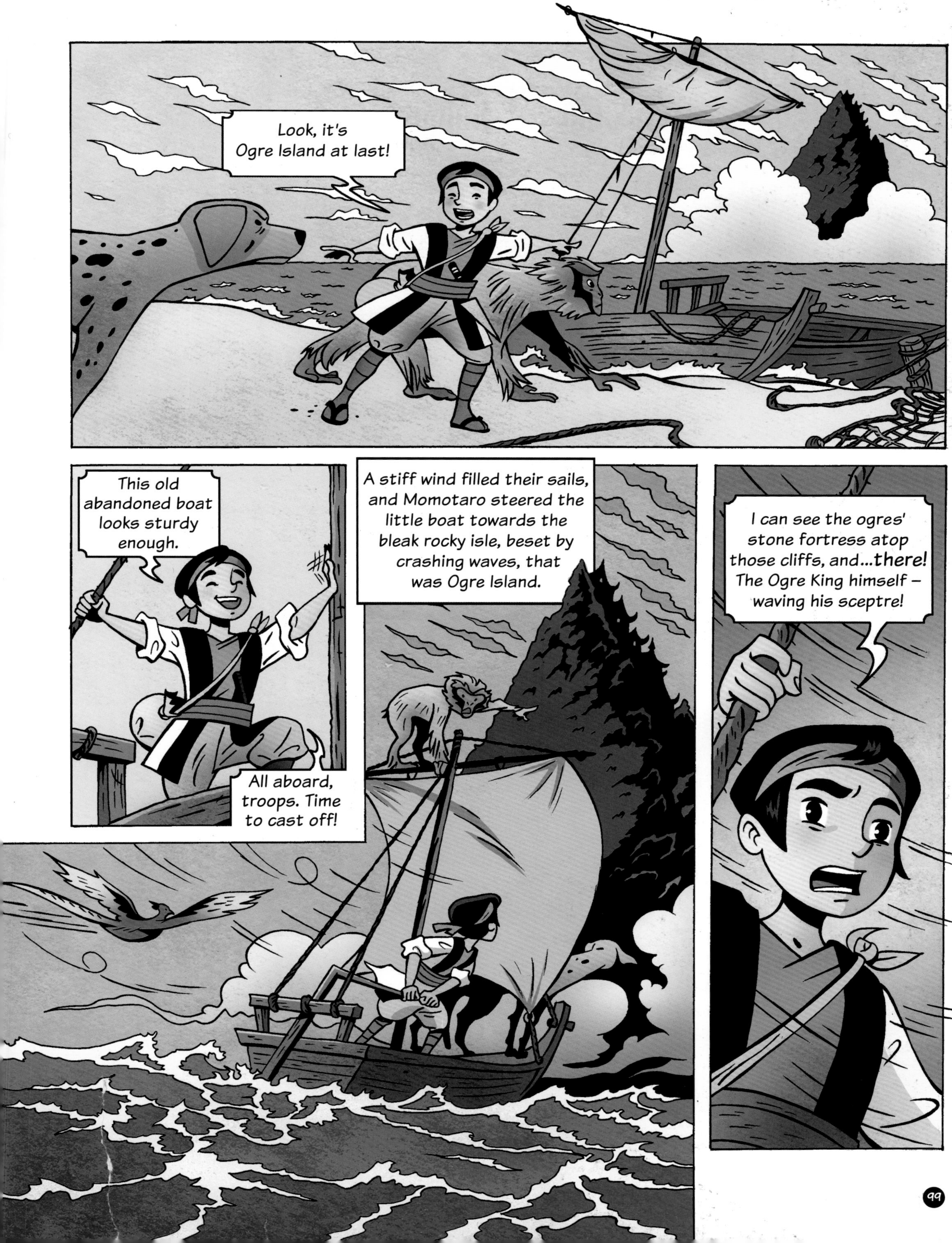
Look, it's Ogre Island at last!
This old abandoned boat looks sturdy enough.
All aboard, troops. Time to cast off!
A stiff wind filled their sails, and Momotaro steered the little boat towards the bleak rocky isle, beset by crashing waves, that was Ogre Island.
I can see the ogres' stone fortress atop those cliffs, and...there! The Ogre King himself – waving his sceptre!

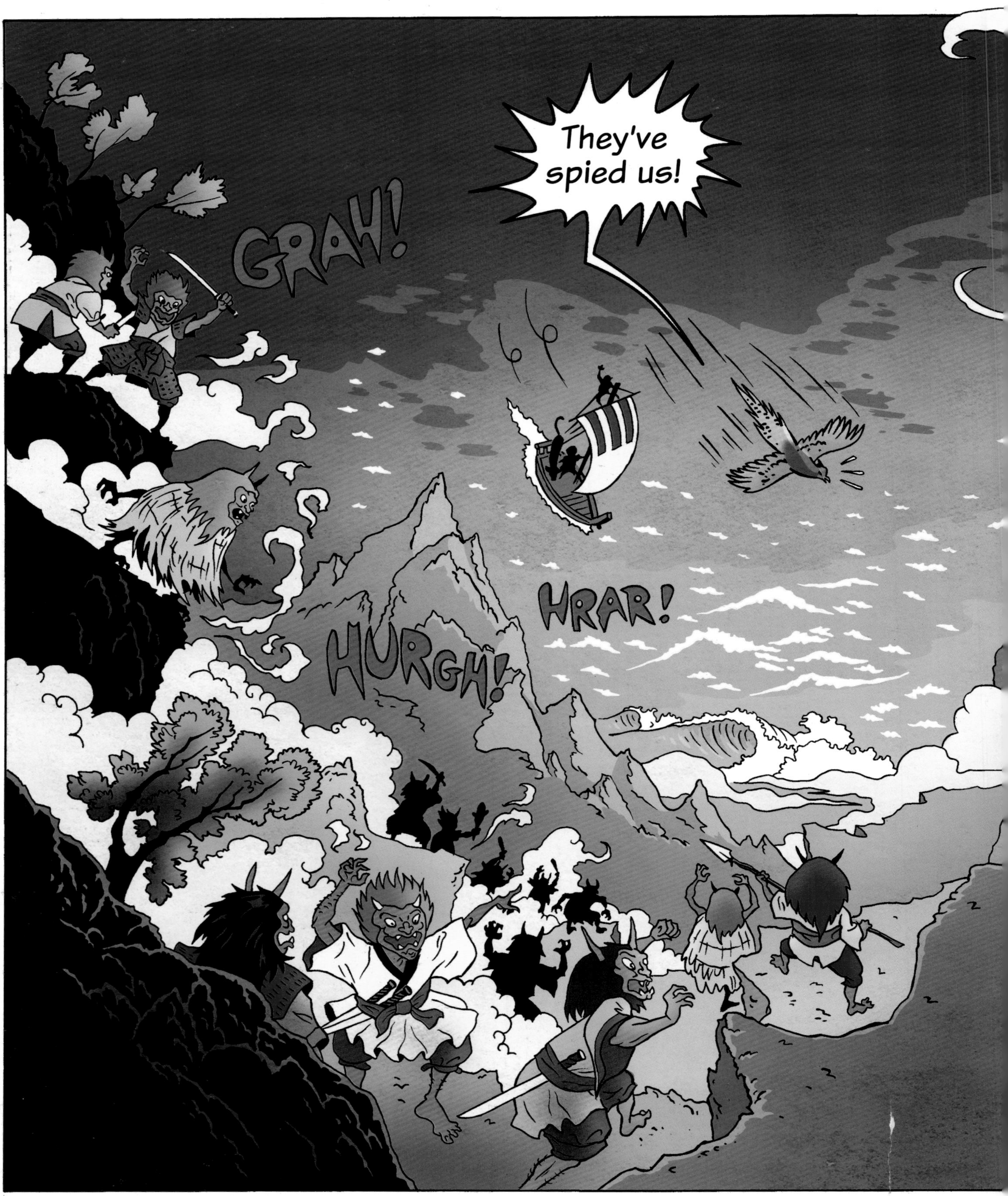
GRAH!
They've spied us!
HRAR!
HURGH!

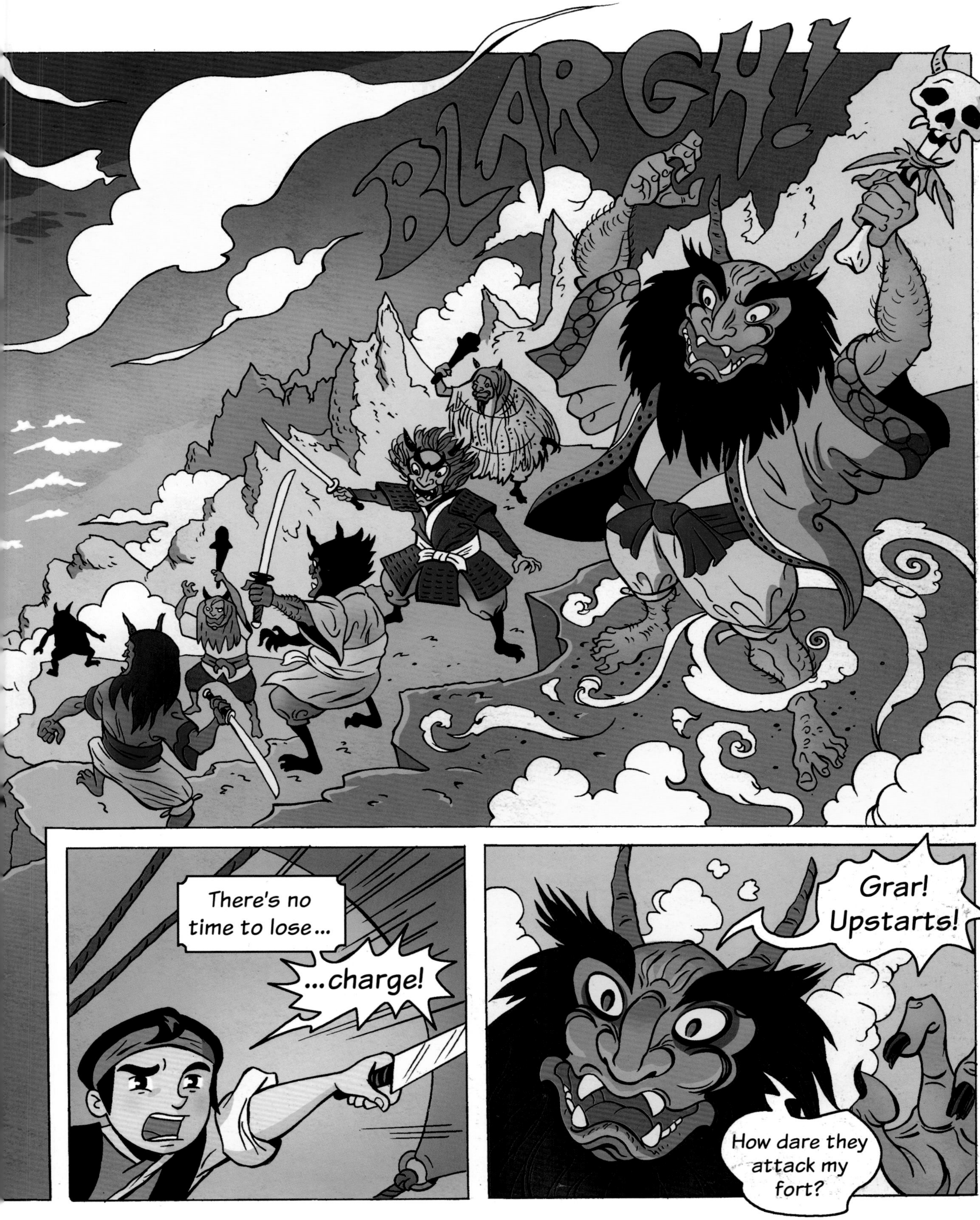
BLARGH!
There's no time to lose...
...charge!
Grar! Upstarts!
How dare they attack my fort?

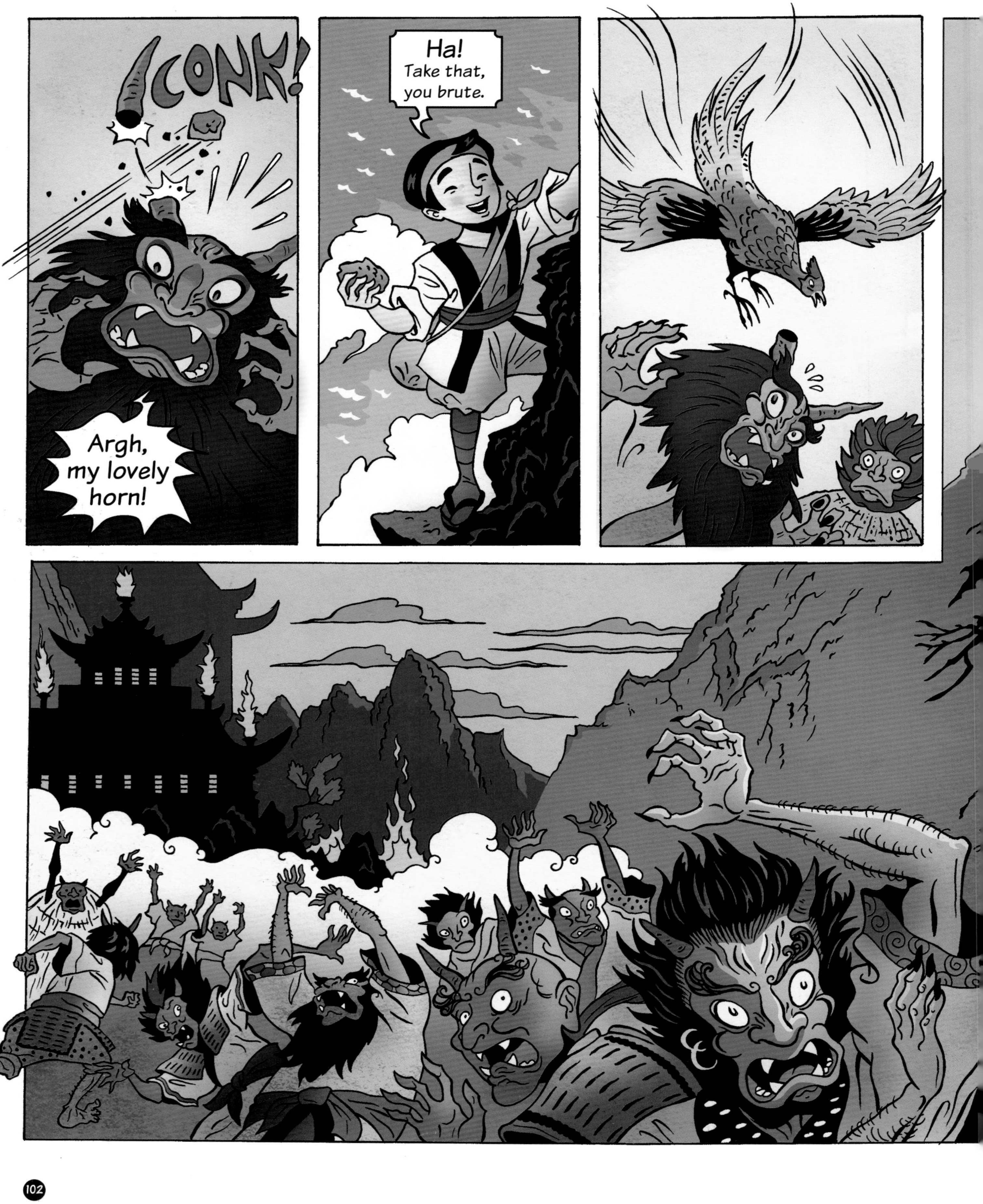
CONK!
Argh, my lovely horn!
Ha! Take that, you brute.

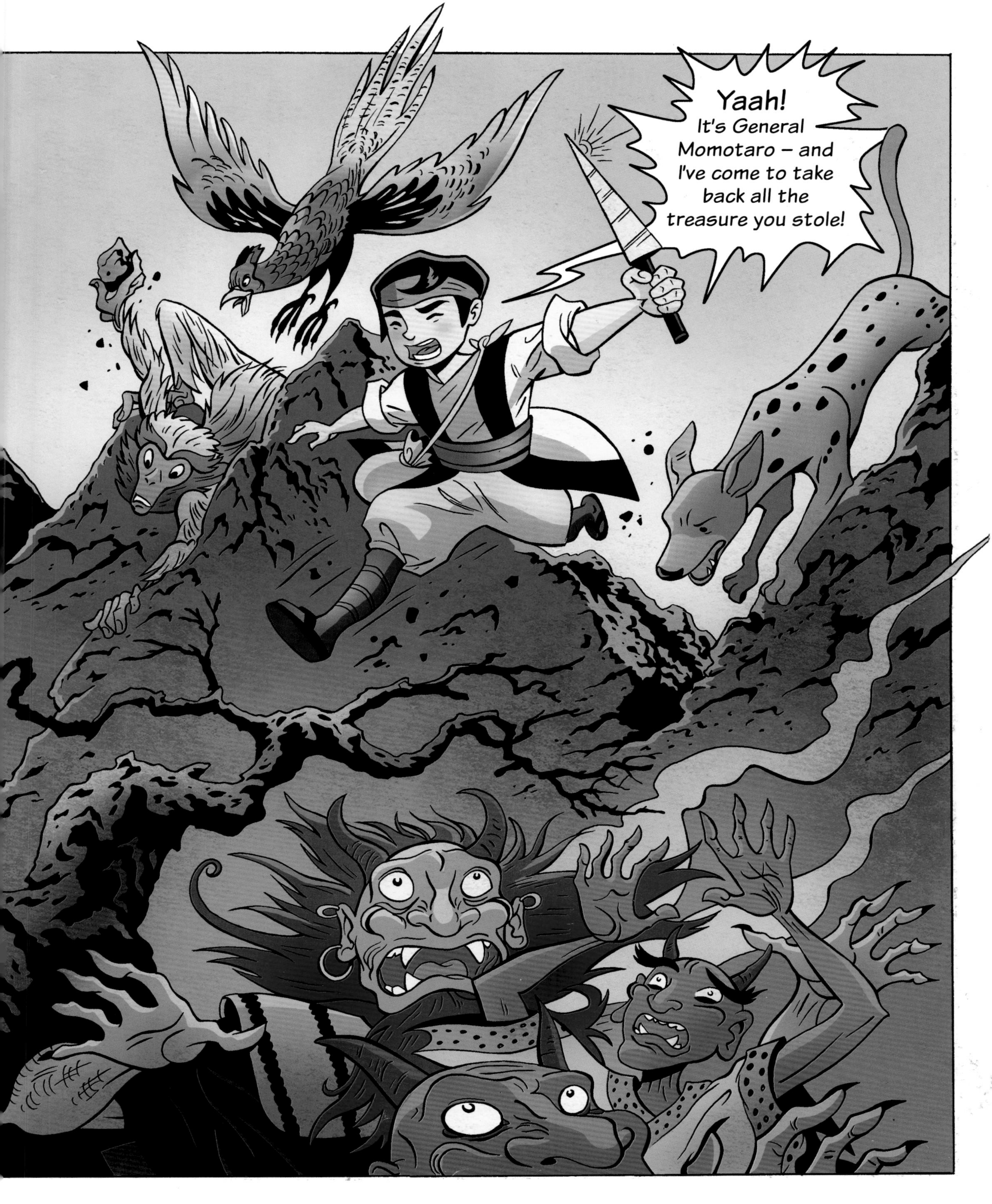
Yaah!
It's General Momotaro – and I've come to take back all the treasure you stole!

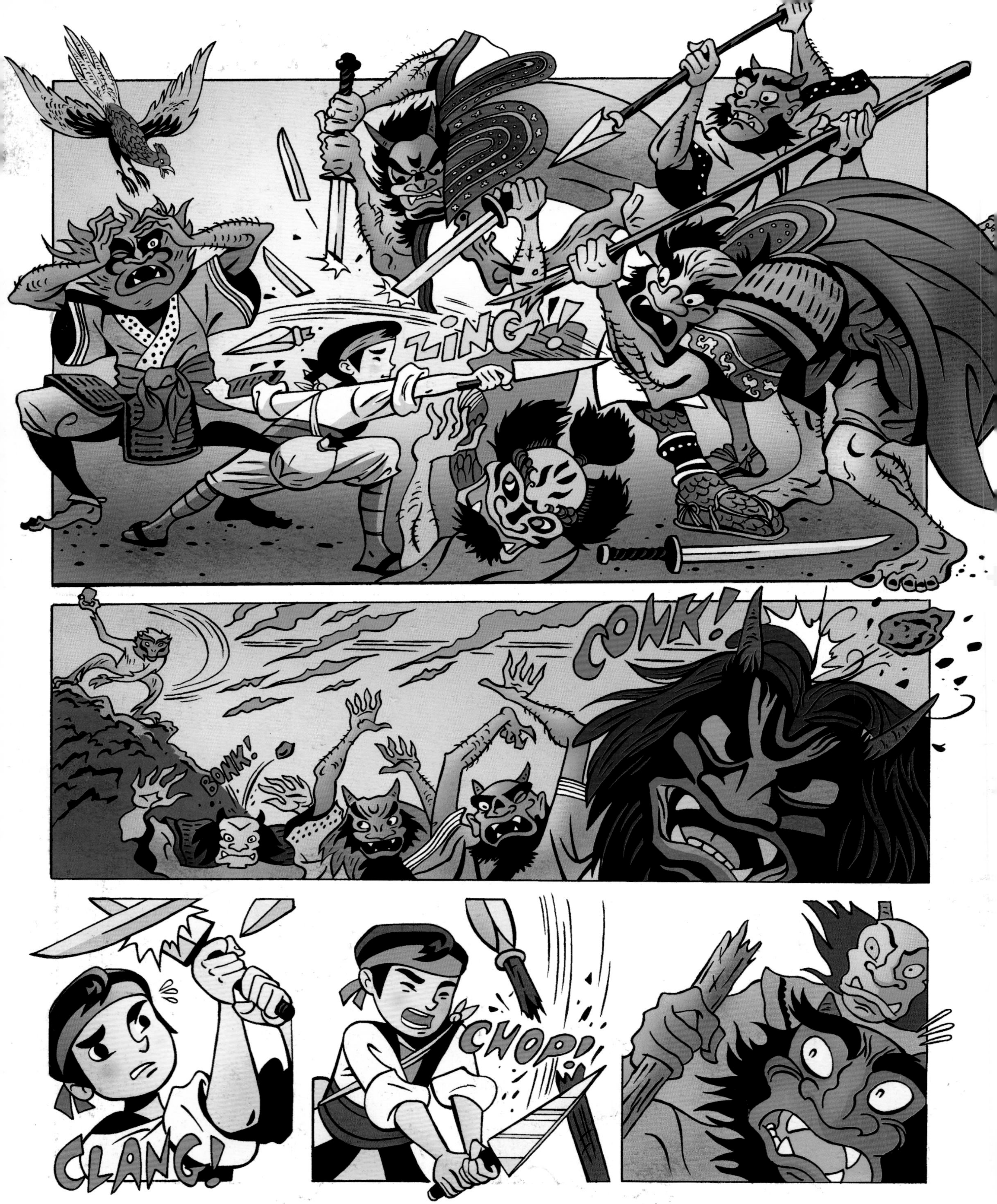
ZING!!
CONK!
BONK!
CLANG!
CHOP!!

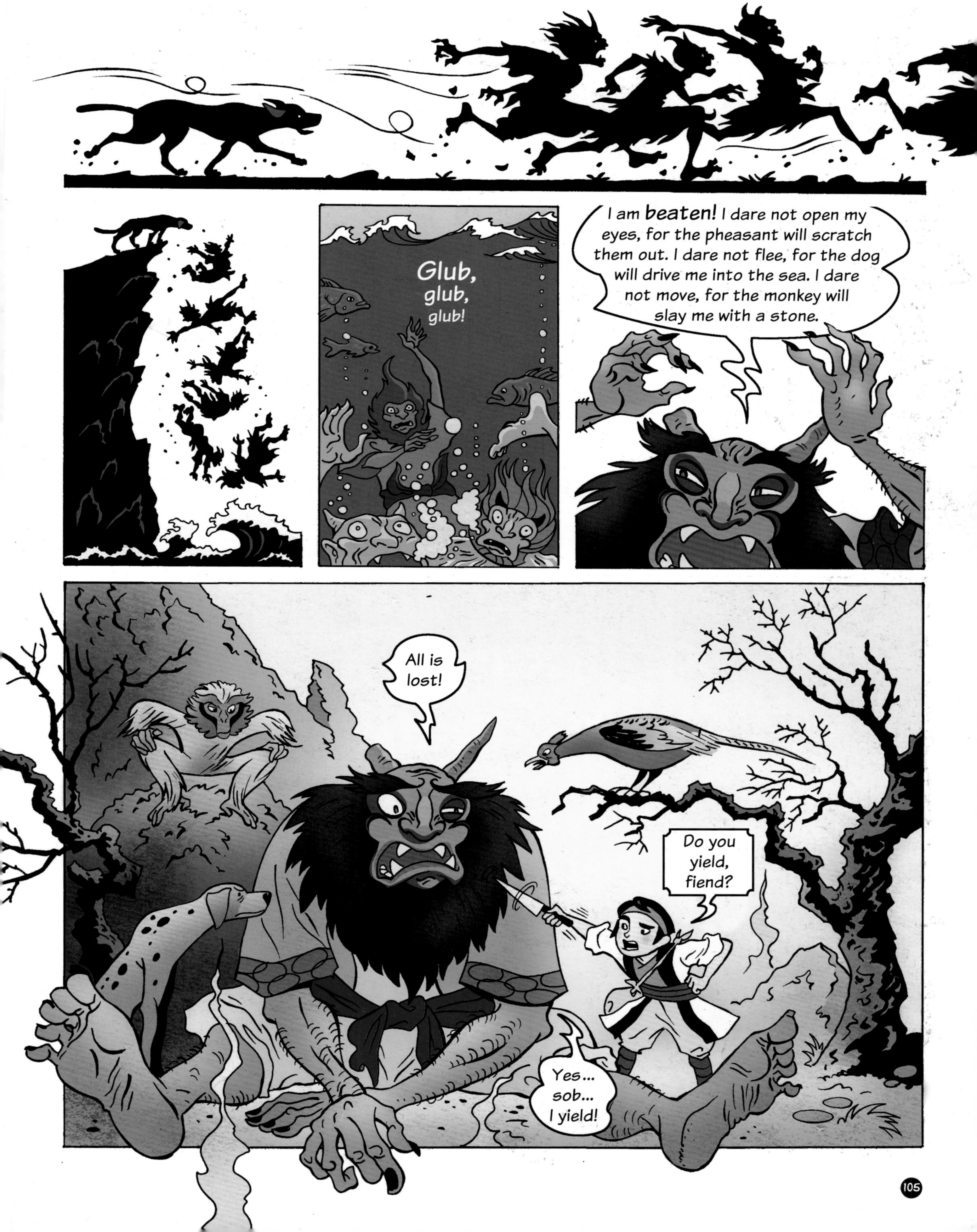
Glub,
glub,
glub!
I am beaten! I dare not open my eyes, for the pheasant will scratch them out. I dare not flee, for the dog will drive me into the sea. I dare not move, for the monkey will slay me with a stone.
All is lost!
Do you yield, fiend?
Yes... sob... I yield!

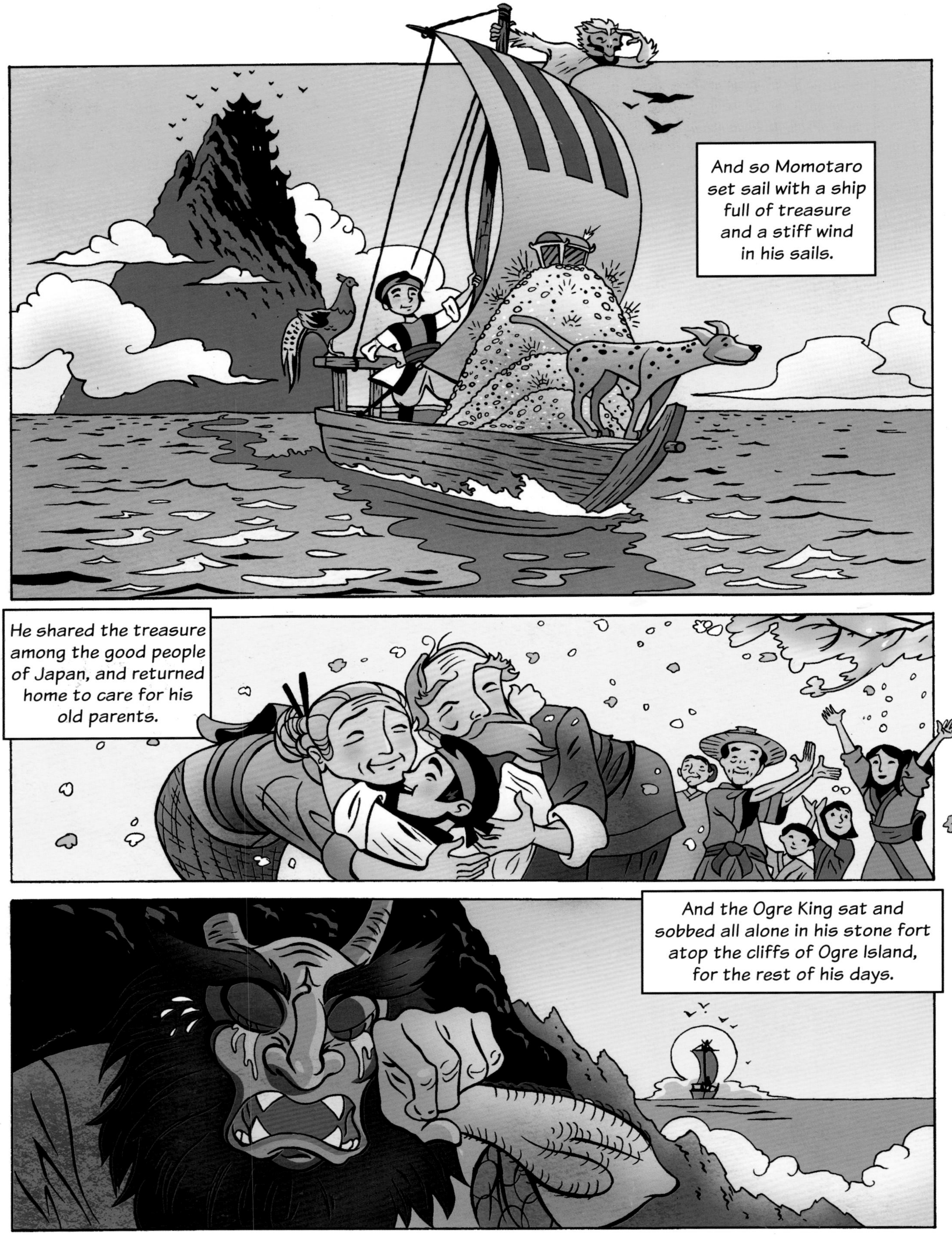
And so Momotaro set sail with a ship full of treasure and a stiff wind in his sails.
He shared the treasure among the good people of Japan, and returned home to care for his old parents.
And the Ogre King sat and sobbed all alone in his stone fort atop the cliffs of Ogre Island, for the rest of his days.

The King of the Polar Bears

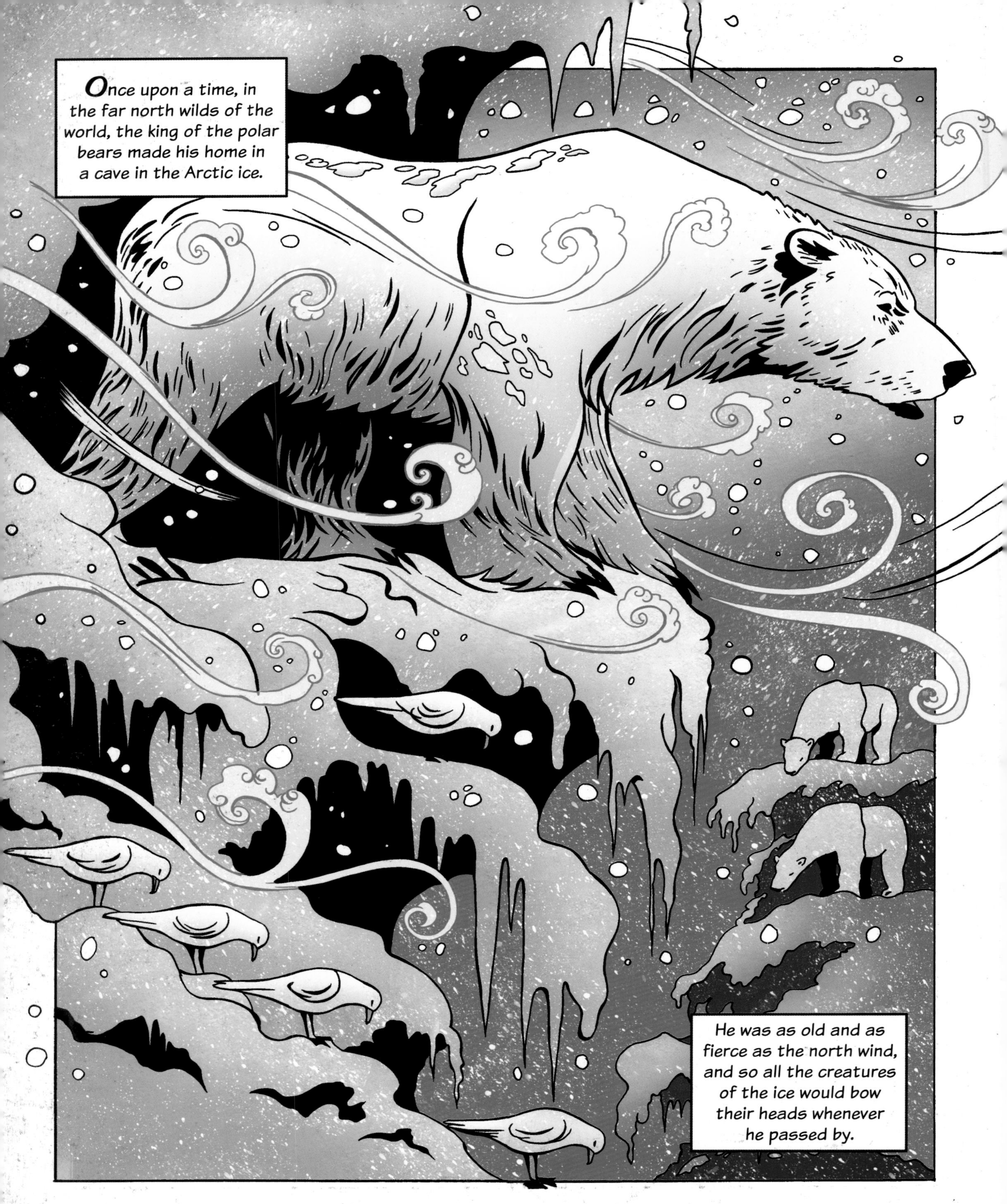
Once upon a time, in the far north wilds of the world, the king of the polar bears made his home in a cave in the Arctic ice.
He was as old and as fierce as the north wind, and so all the creatures of the ice would bow their heads whenever he passed by.

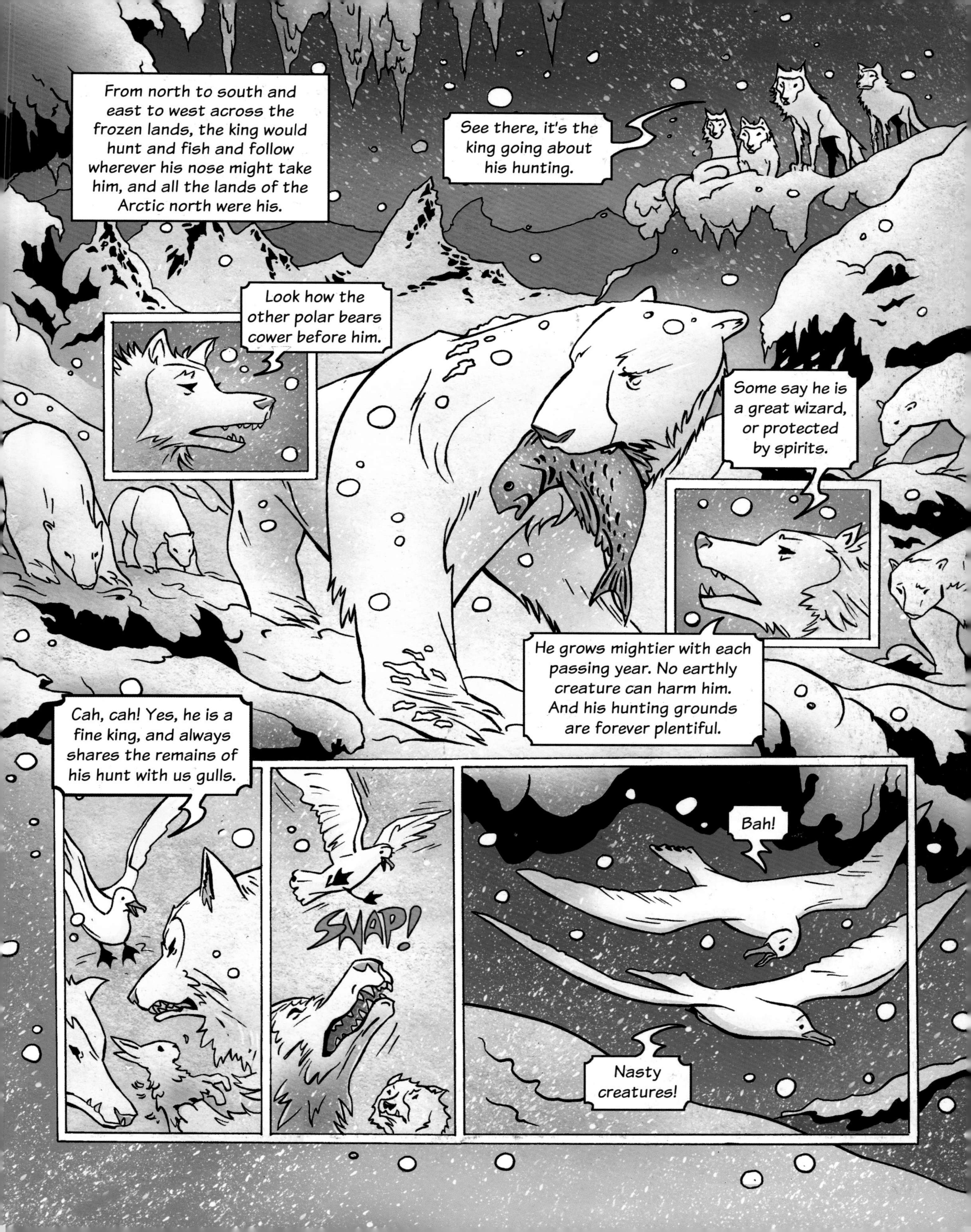
From north to south and east to west across the frozen lands, the king would hunt and fish and follow wherever his nose might take him, and all the lands of the Arctic north were his.
See there, it's the king going about his hunting.
Look how the other polar bears cower before him.
Some say he is a great wizard, or protected by spirits.
He grows mightier with each passing year. No earthly creature can harm him. And his hunting grounds are forever plentiful.
Cah, cah! Yes, he is a fine king, and always shares the remains of his hunt with us gulls.
SNAP!
Bah!
Nasty creatures!

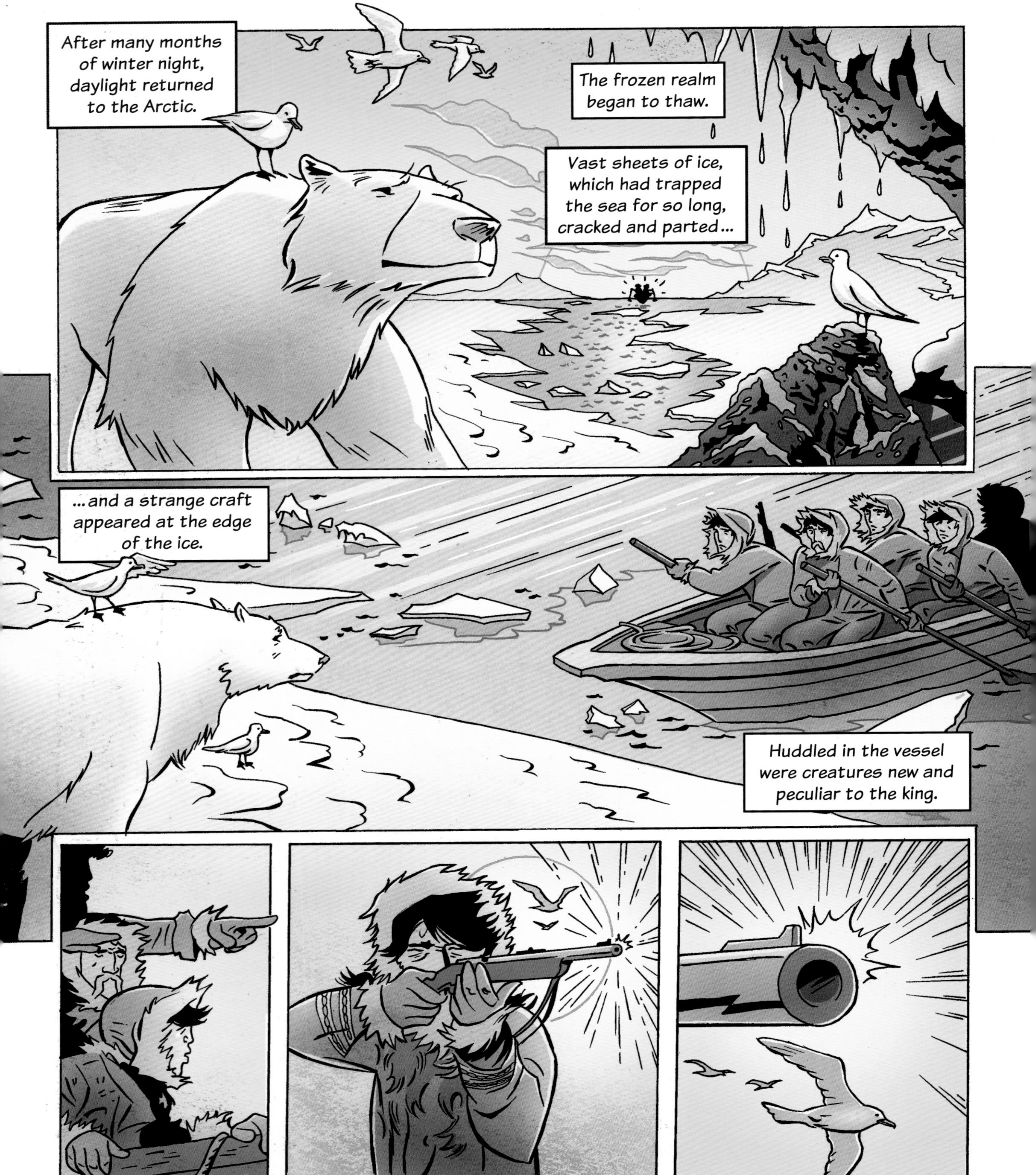
After many months of winter night, daylight returned to the Arctic.
The frozen realm began to thaw.
Vast sheets of ice, which had trapped the sea for so long, cracked and parted...
...and a strange craft appeared at the edge of the ice.
Huddled in the vessel were creatures new and peculiar to the king.

BANG

The mind
of the
Polar Bear King
went dark.

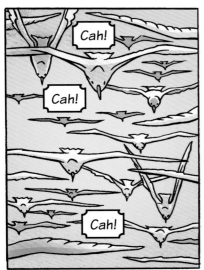

Cah!

Cah!

Cah!

Look! The king is dead.

Hunters stole his royal fur.

The gulls debated over whether it would be improper to eat their late king.

Until...

Grooaan!

Do you hear?

He's alive!

It is just as the wolves said – the king is a great wizard, unable to be killed!

But see how he suffers without his great fur. Quickly, spare as many feathers as you are able. Repay his kindness to us by giving him a new coat made of our finest plumage!

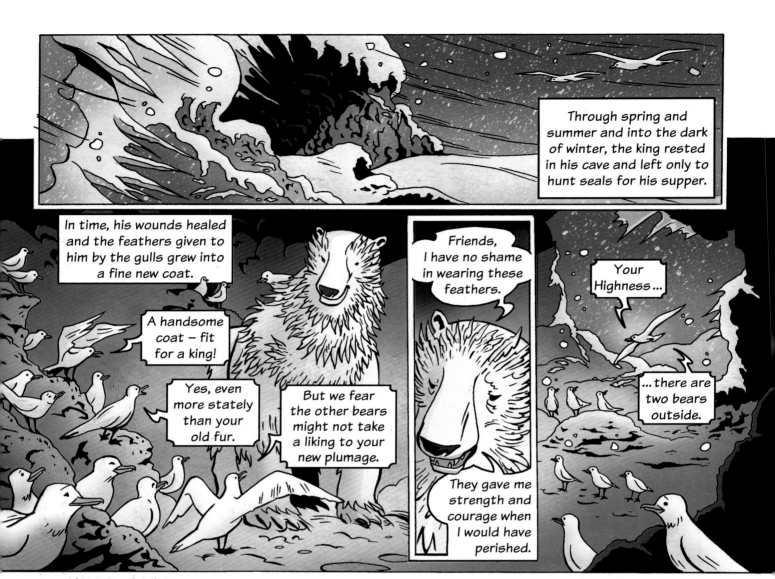

Through spring and summer and into the dark of winter, the king rested in his cave and left only to hunt seals for his supper.

In time, his wounds healed and the feathers given to him by the gulls grew into a fine new coat.

A handsome coat – fit for a king!

Yes, even more stately than your old fur.

But we fear the other bears might not take a liking to your new plumage.

Friends, I have no shame in wearing these feathers.

They gave me strength and courage when I would have perished.

Your Highness...

...there are two bears outside.

Greetings and salutations!

We wish to be granted an audience with the king.

We seek the great magician's wise counsel on the matter of this season's hunting.

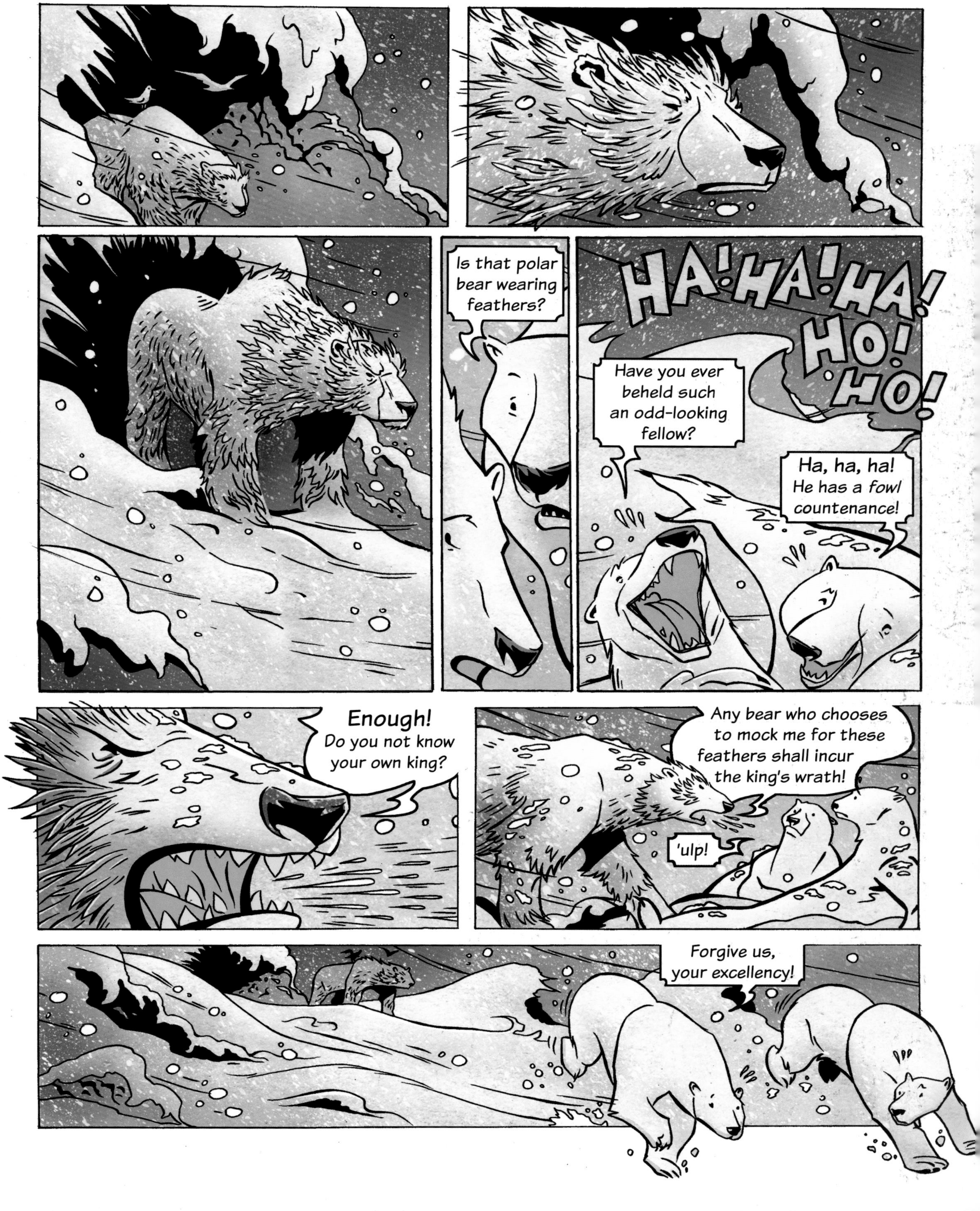

Is that polar bear wearing feathers?
HA! HA! HA! HO! HO! HO!
Have you ever beheld such an odd-looking fellow?
Ha, ha, ha! He has a *fowl* countenance!
Enough! Do you not know your own king?
Any bear who chooses to mock me for these feathers shall incur the king's wrath!
'ulp!
Forgive us, your excellency!

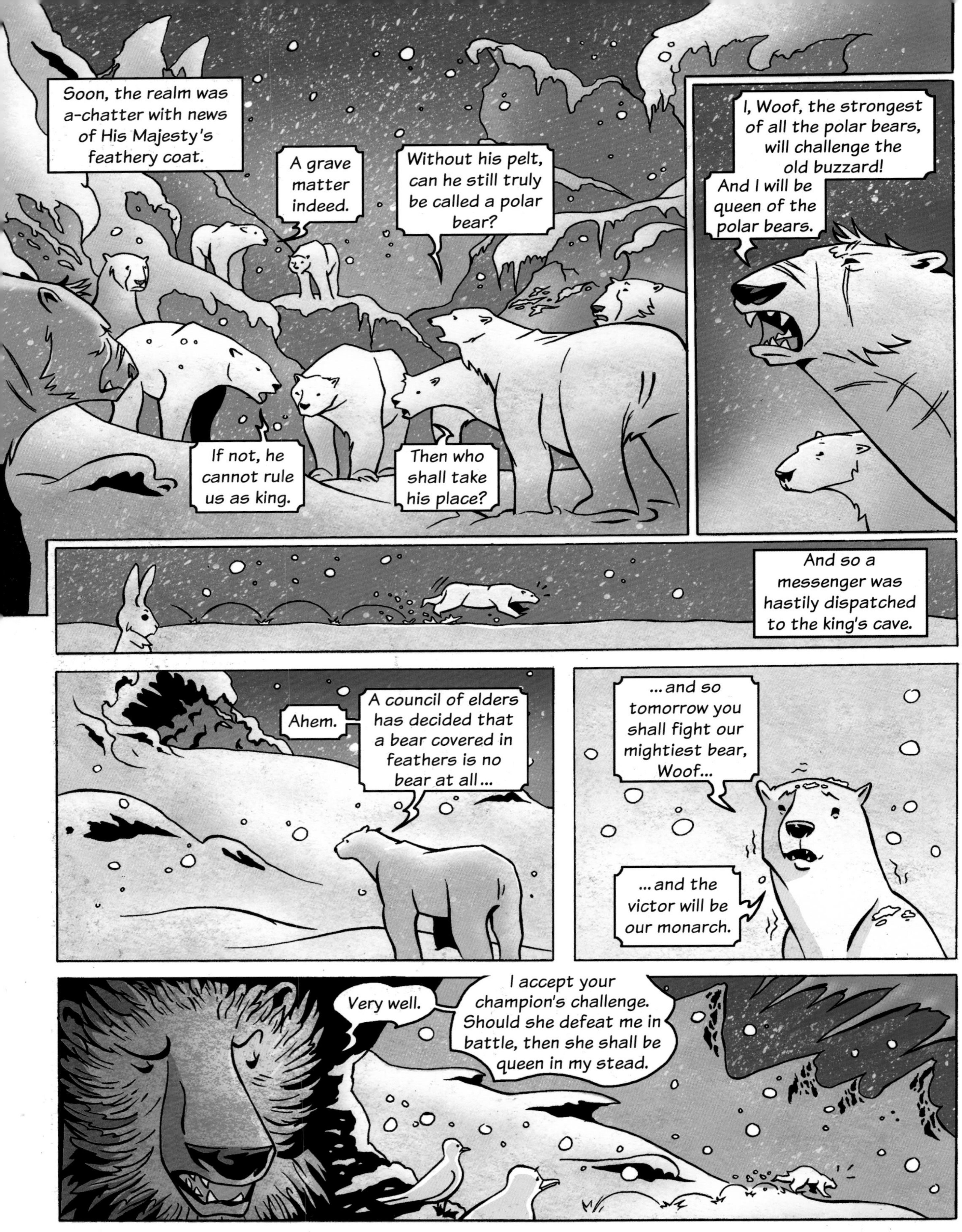
Soon, the realm was a-chatter with news of His Majesty's feathery coat.
A grave matter indeed.
Without his pelt, can he still truly be called a polar bear?
If not, he cannot rule us as king.
Then who shall take his place?
I, Woof, the strongest of all the polar bears, will challenge the old buzzard!
And I will be queen of the polar bears.
And so a messenger was hastily dispatched to the king's cave.
Ahem.
A council of elders has decided that a bear covered in feathers is no bear at all...
...and so tomorrow you shall fight our mightiest bear, Woof...
...and the victor will be our monarch.
Very well.
I accept your champion's challenge. Should she defeat me in battle, then she shall be queen in my stead.

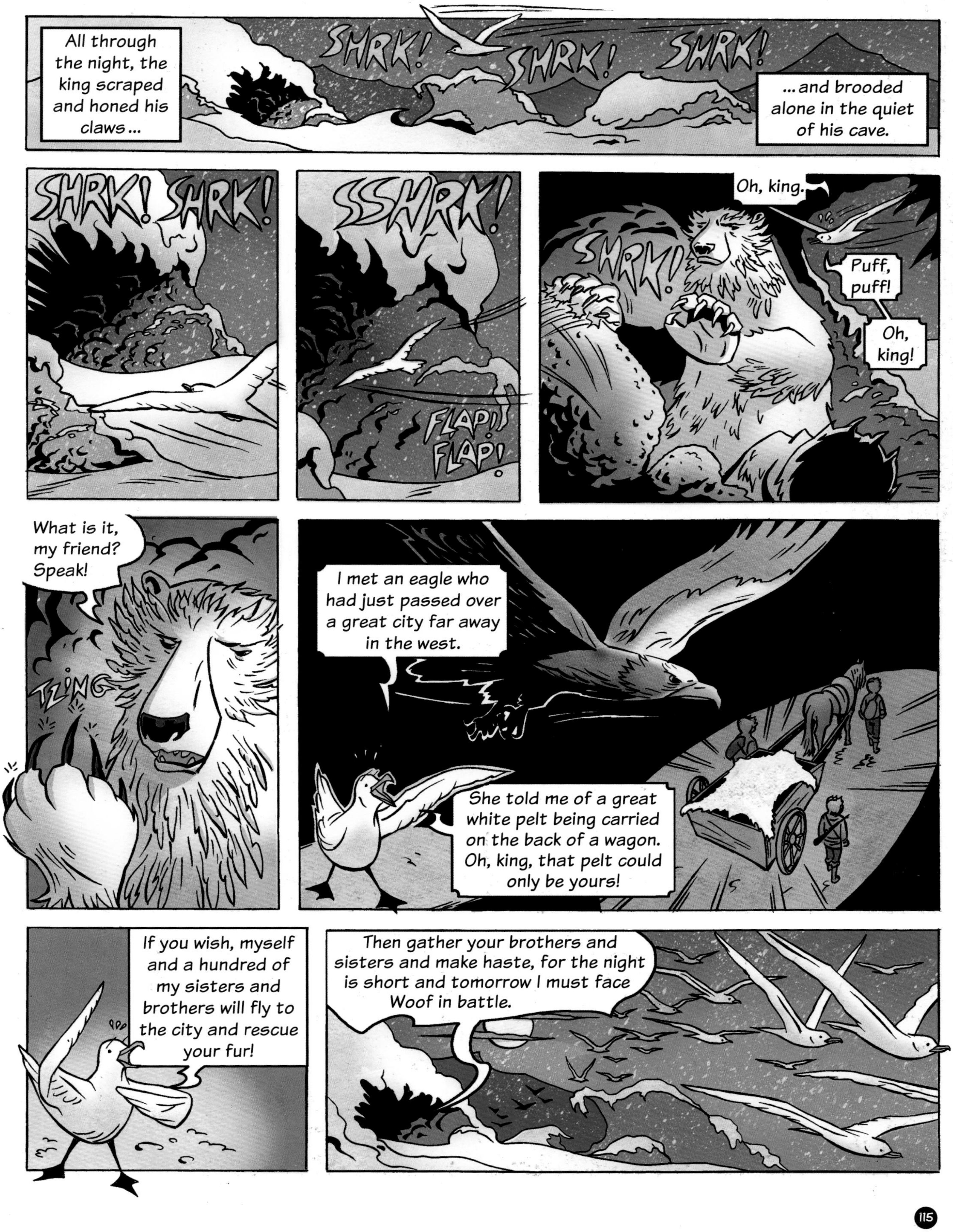
All through the night, the king scraped and honed his claws...
SHRK! SHRK! SHRK!
...and brooded alone in the quiet of his cave.
SHRK! SHRK!
SSHRK!
FLAP! FLAP!
Oh, king.
SHRK!
Puff, puff!
Oh, king!
What is it, my friend? Speak!
TZING
I met an eagle who had just passed over a great city far away in the west.
She told me of a great white pelt being carried on the back of a wagon. Oh, king, that pelt could only be yours!
If you wish, myself and a hundred of my sisters and brothers will fly to the city and rescue your fur!
Then gather your brothers and sisters and make haste, for the night is short and tomorrow I must face Woof in battle.

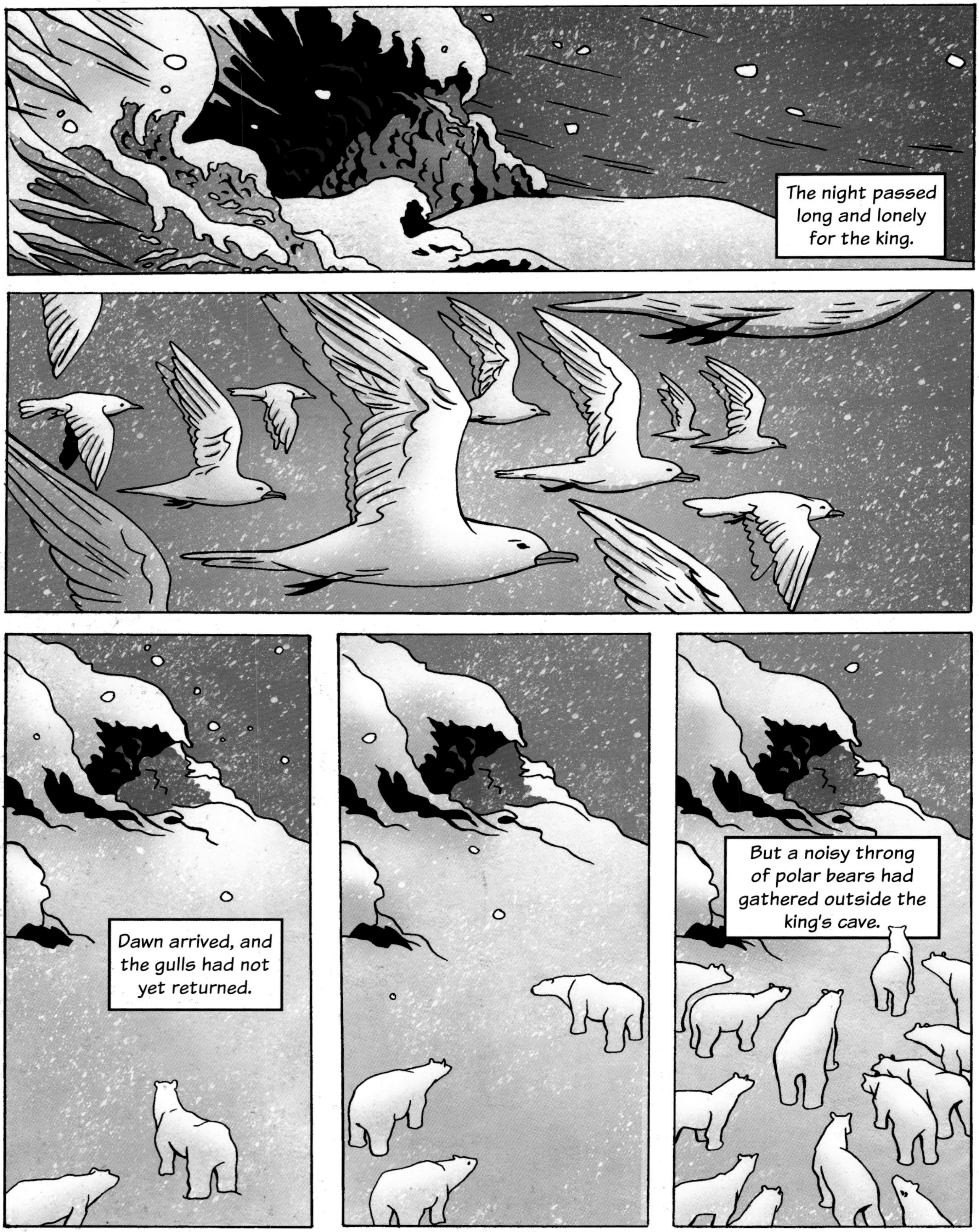
The night passed long and lonely for the king.
Dawn arrived, and the gulls had not yet returned.
But a noisy throng of polar bears had gathered outside the king's cave.

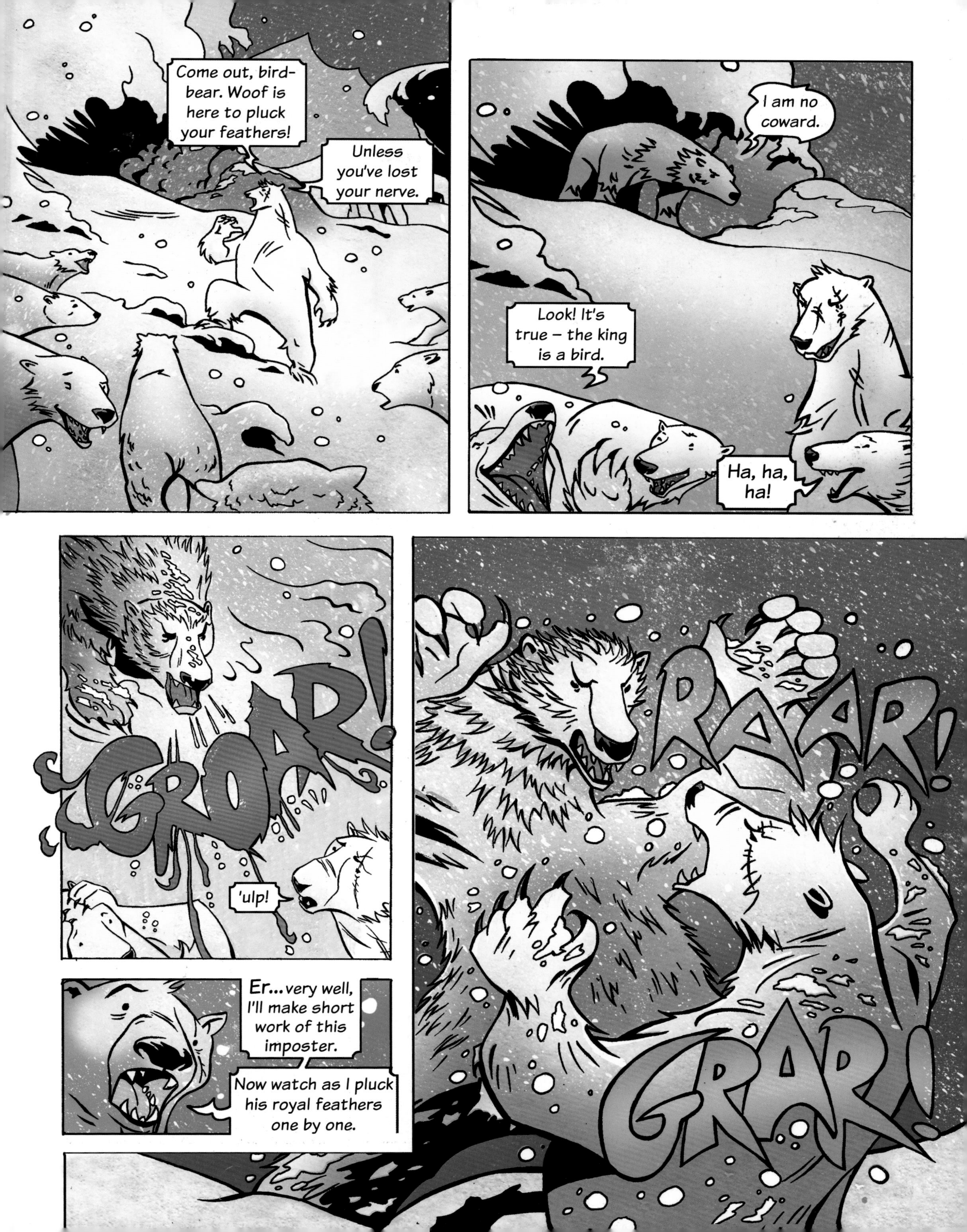
Come out, bird-bear. Woof is here to pluck your feathers!
Unless you've lost your nerve.
I am no coward.
Look! It's true – the king is a bird.
Ha, ha, ha!
GROAR!
'ulp!
Er... very well, I'll make short work of this imposter.
Now watch as I pluck his royal feathers one by one.
RAAAR!
GRAR!

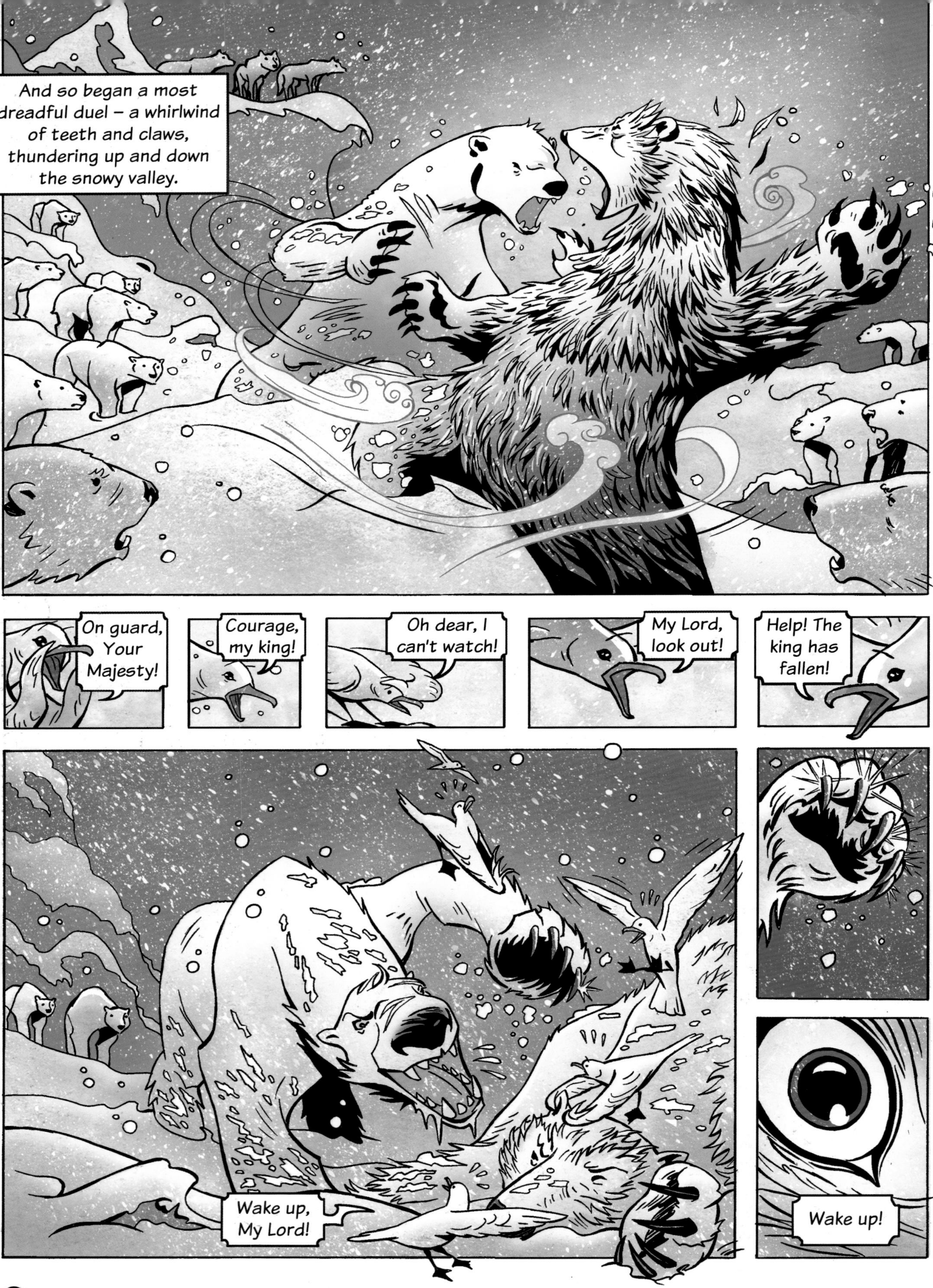
And so began a most dreadful duel – a whirlwind of teeth and claws, thundering up and down the snowy valley.
On guard, Your Majesty!
Courage, my king!
Oh dear, I can't watch!
My Lord, look out!
Help! The king has fallen!
Wake up, My Lord!
Wake up!

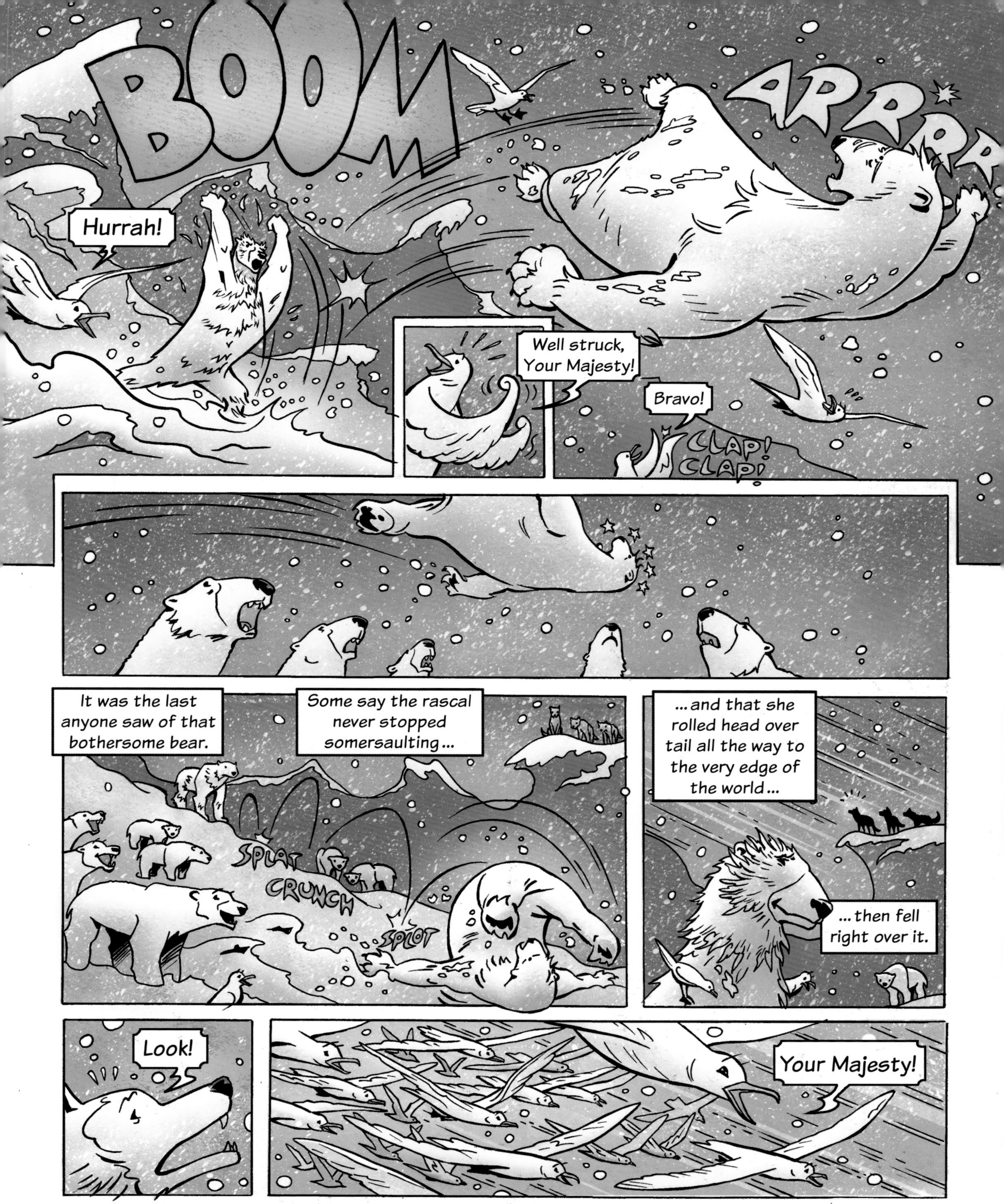
BOOM
ARRRR
Hurrah!
Well struck, Your Majesty!
Bravo!
CLAP! CLAP!
It was the last anyone saw of that bothersome bear.
Some say the rascal never stopped somersaulting...
SPLAT
CRUNCH
SPLOT
...and that she rolled head over tail all the way to the very edge of the world...
...then fell right over it.
Look!
Your Majesty!

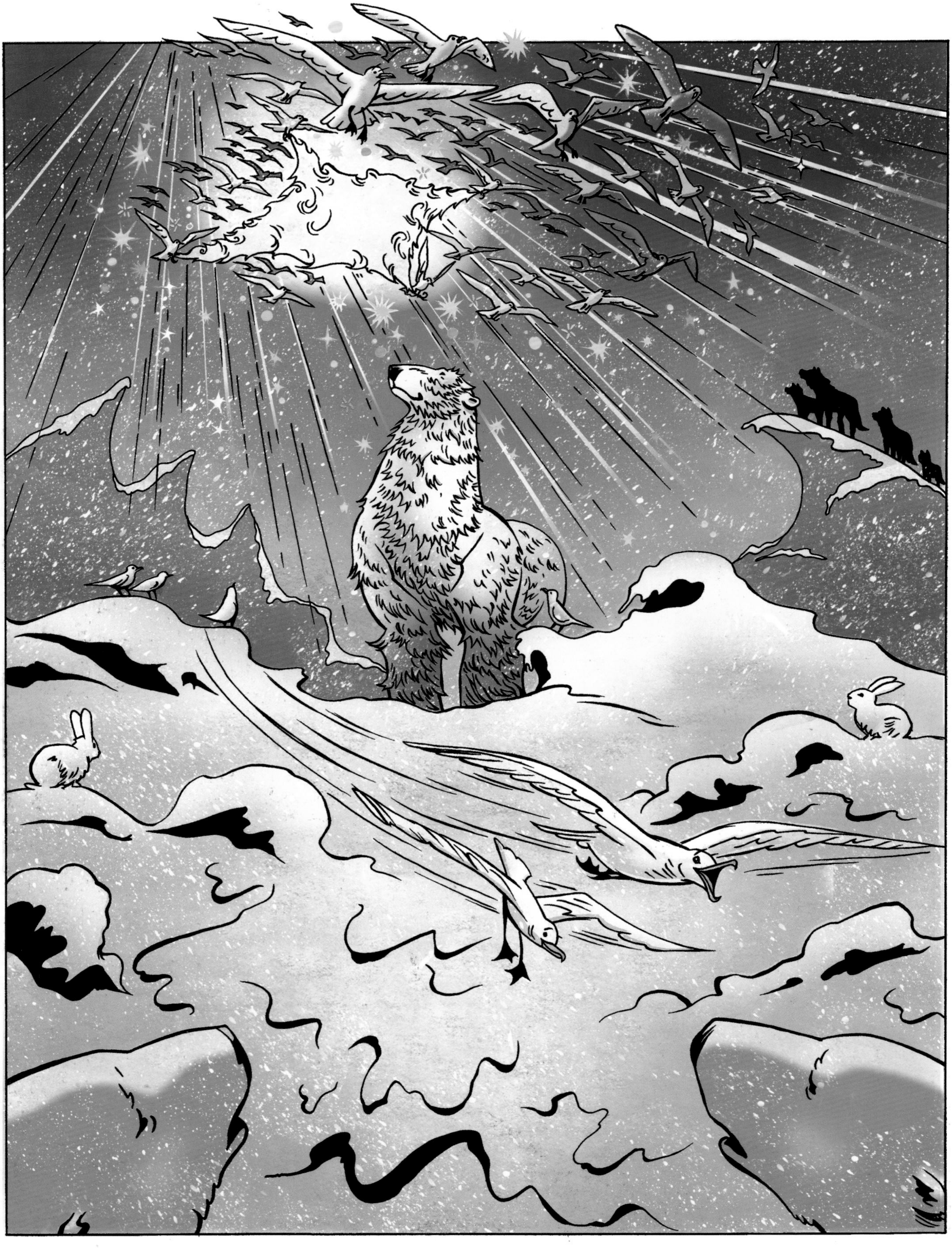

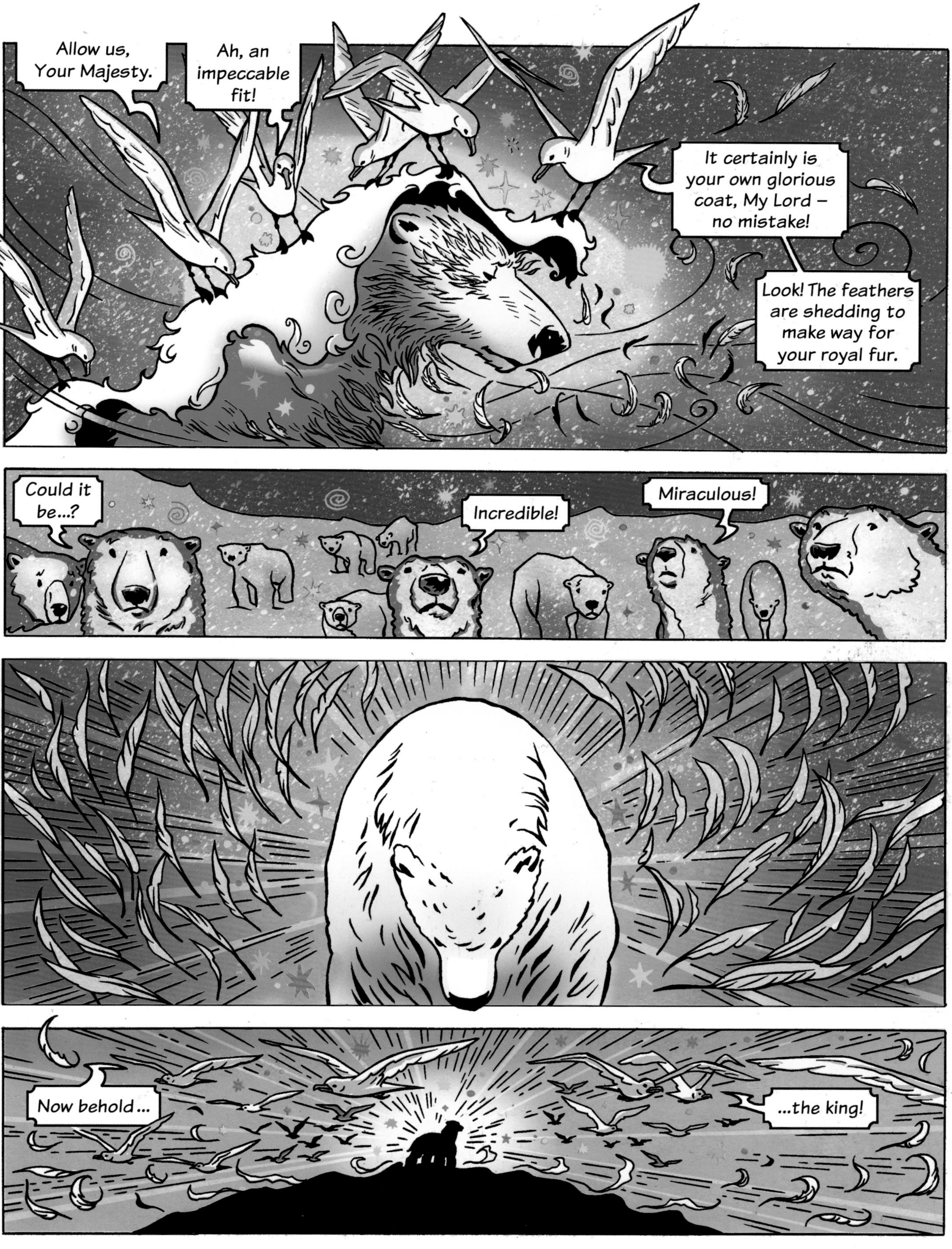
Allow us, Your Majesty.
Ah, an impeccable fit!
It certainly is your own glorious coat, My Lord – no mistake!
Look! The feathers are shedding to make way for your royal fur.
Could it be...?
Incredible!
Miraculous!
Now behold...
...the king!

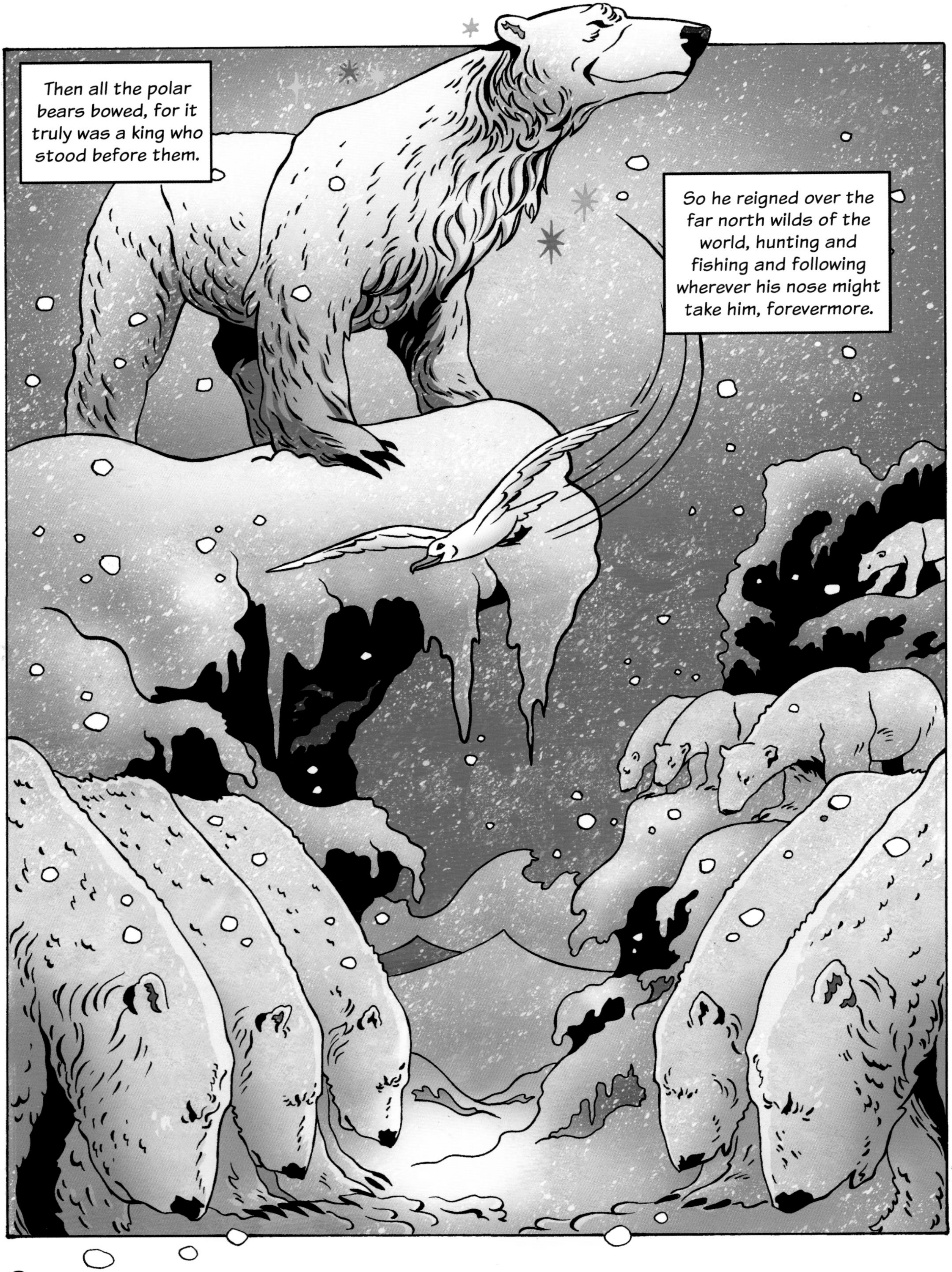
Then all the polar bears bowed, for it truly was a king who stood before them.
So he reigned over the far north wilds of the world, hunting and fishing and following wherever his nose might take him, forevermore.

The
Boy Who Was Never Afraid

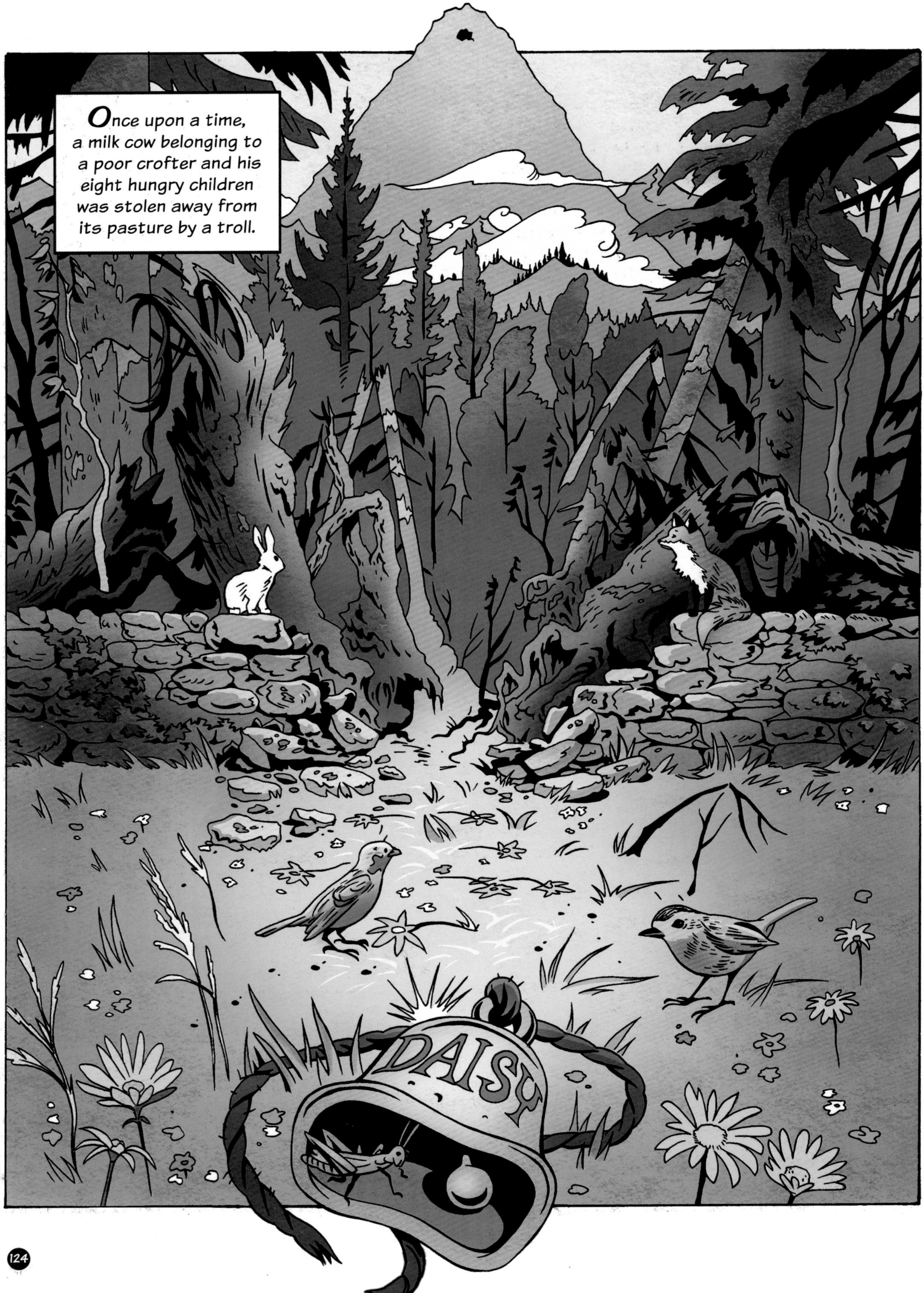
Once upon a time, a milk cow belonging to a poor crofter and his eight hungry children was stolen away from its pasture by a troll.
DAISY

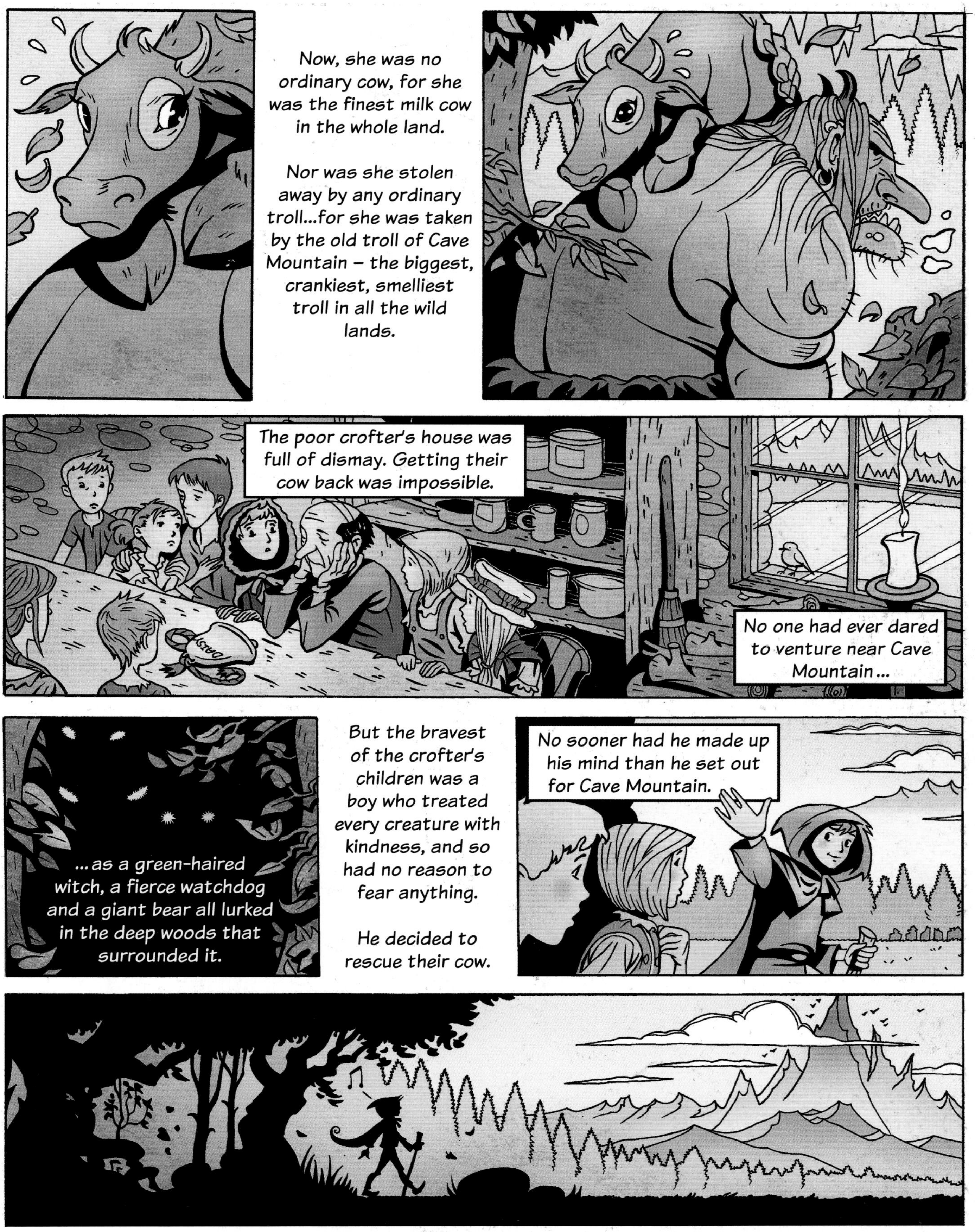
Now, she was no ordinary cow, for she was the finest milk cow in the whole land.
Nor was she stolen away by any ordinary troll...for she was taken by the old troll of Cave Mountain – the biggest, crankiest, smelliest troll in all the wild lands.
The poor crofter's house was full of dismay. Getting their cow back was impossible.
No one had ever dared to venture near Cave Mountain...
...as a green-haired witch, a fierce watchdog and a giant bear all lurked in the deep woods that surrounded it.
But the bravest of the crofter's children was a boy who treated every creature with kindness, and so had no reason to fear anything.
He decided to rescue their cow.
No sooner had he made up his mind than he set out for Cave Mountain.

Through the night and day, the boy who was never afraid journeyed into the deep woods...

...until he spied a peculiar creature perched atop a rocky ledge.

It was the old witch of the woods.

She sang as she combed her long green hair.

Who dares trespass in my woods?

Hello, kind mother!

I am searching for my cow, who was stolen away by the old troll of Cave Mountain.

Ha! Foolish boy, I don't care about you or your cow.

SNAP! RIP!

Waaaagh!

Help! My beautiful hair – it's caught.

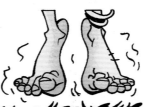

With her long green hair tangled in the branches, the old witch found herself completely stuck.

Oh, you poor thing. Let me help you down.

You're a strange one, to want to help me.

In return for your kindness, I will help you in your quest. Take this magical herb and place it in your ear.

It will allow you to communicate with all the creatures of the forest.

But beware! A fierce watchdog prowls nearby, and he does not take kindly to little strangers in his valley.

The green-haired witch of the woods led the boy who was never afraid through the gloom.

Cave Mountain lies beyond this valley. There you will find the old troll.

But that fierce watchdog likes green-haired witches even less than he likes little strangers...

...so here I will leave you.

Thank you, kind—

But the green-haired witch of the woods was gone.

Then the boy who was never afraid heard the scraping of claws and clicking of teeth and spied two great yellow eyes blinking at him.

Who dares trespass in my valley?

Hello, kind sir!

I am searching for my cow, who was stolen away by the old troll of Cave Mountain.

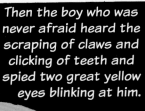

No one passes by this place without my saying so.

Not cows, nor trolls, and especially not little strangers.

Now begone, or I'll snap you up in my teeth and that will be the end of you.

Oh, my – a trap! Poor fellow.

Here, let me help you.

No wonder you're so cranky. There!

You're not like other humans, who only want to hurt me.

For your kindness, I'll carry you through my valley to the wild river, beyond which lies Cave Mountain. But beware! A giant bear makes his home on the riverbank ... and he does not take kindly to little strangers.

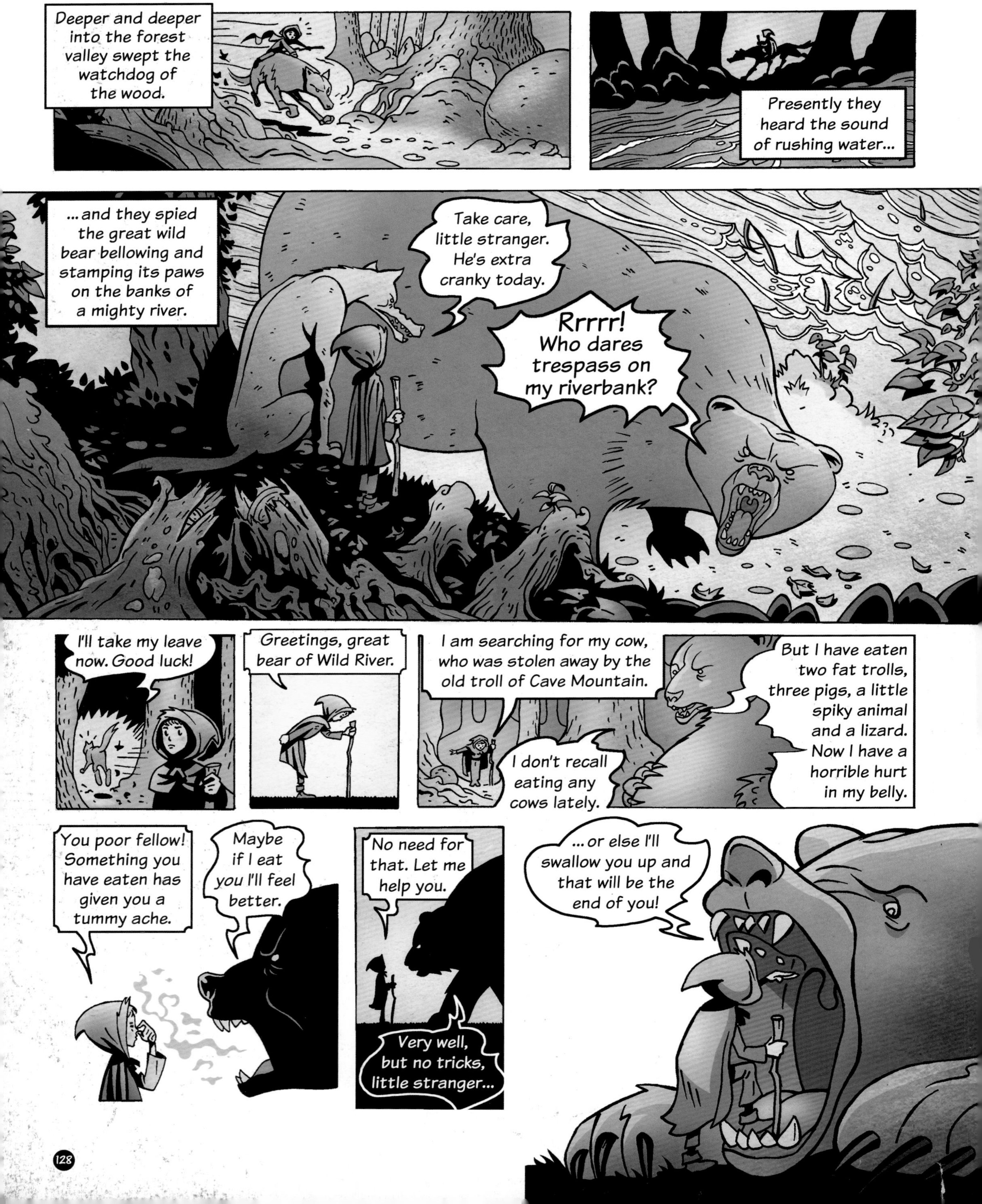
Deeper and deeper into the forest valley swept the watchdog of the wood.
Presently they heard the sound of rushing water...
...and they spied the great wild bear bellowing and stamping its paws on the banks of a mighty river.
Take care, little stranger. He's extra cranky today.
Rrrrr! Who dares trespass on my riverbank?
I'll take my leave now. Good luck!
Greetings, great bear of Wild River.
I am searching for my cow, who was stolen away by the old troll of Cave Mountain.
I don't recall eating any cows lately.
But I have eaten two fat trolls, three pigs, a little spiky animal and a lizard. Now I have a horrible hurt in my belly.
You poor fellow! Something you have eaten has given you a tummy ache.
Maybe if I eat you I'll feel better.
No need for that. Let me help you.
Very well, but no tricks, little stranger...
...or else I'll swallow you up and that will be the end of you!

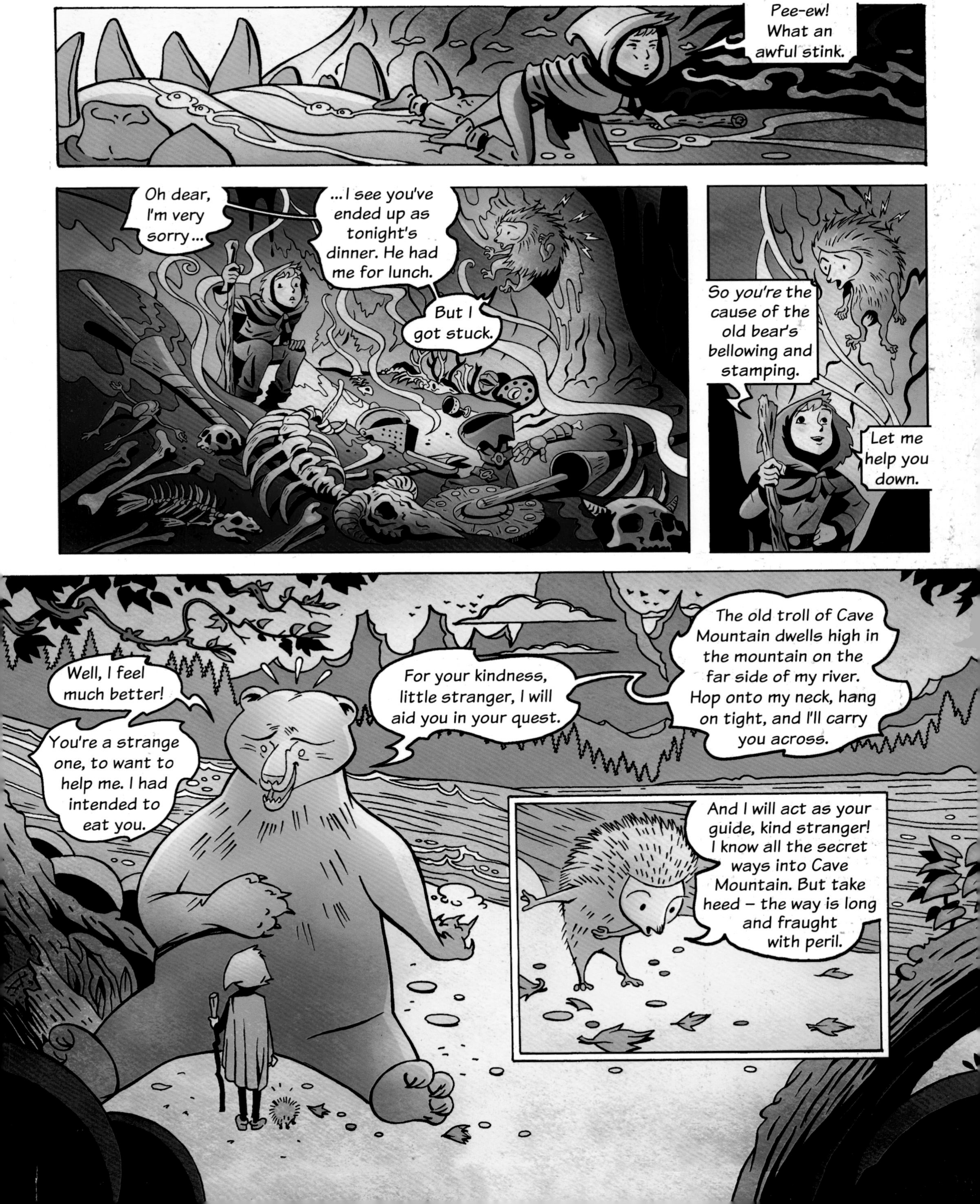
Pee-ew! What an awful stink.
Oh dear, I'm very sorry...
...I see you've ended up as tonight's dinner. He had me for lunch.
But I got stuck.
So you're the cause of the old bear's bellowing and stamping.
Let me help you down.
Well, I feel much better!
You're a strange one, to want to help me. I had intended to eat you.
For your kindness, little stranger, I will aid you in your quest.
The old troll of Cave Mountain dwells high in the mountain on the far side of my river. Hop onto my neck, hang on tight, and I'll carry you across.
And I will act as your guide, kind stranger! I know all the secret ways into Cave Mountain. But take heed – the way is long and fraught with peril.

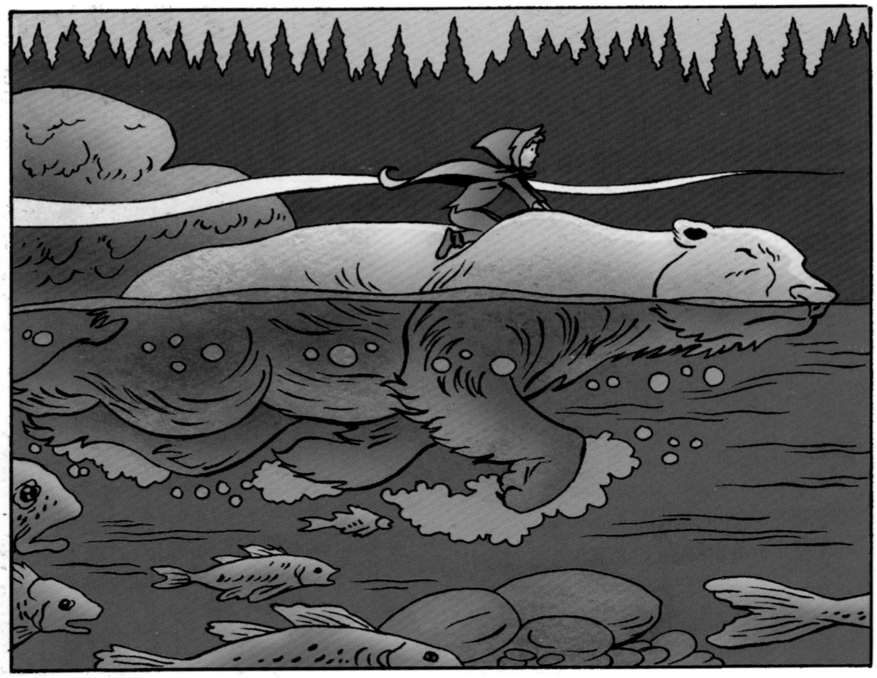

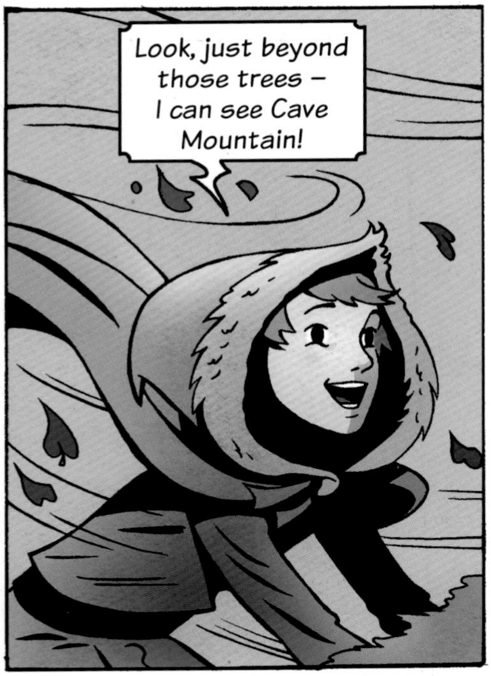
Look, just beyond those trees – I can see Cave Mountain!

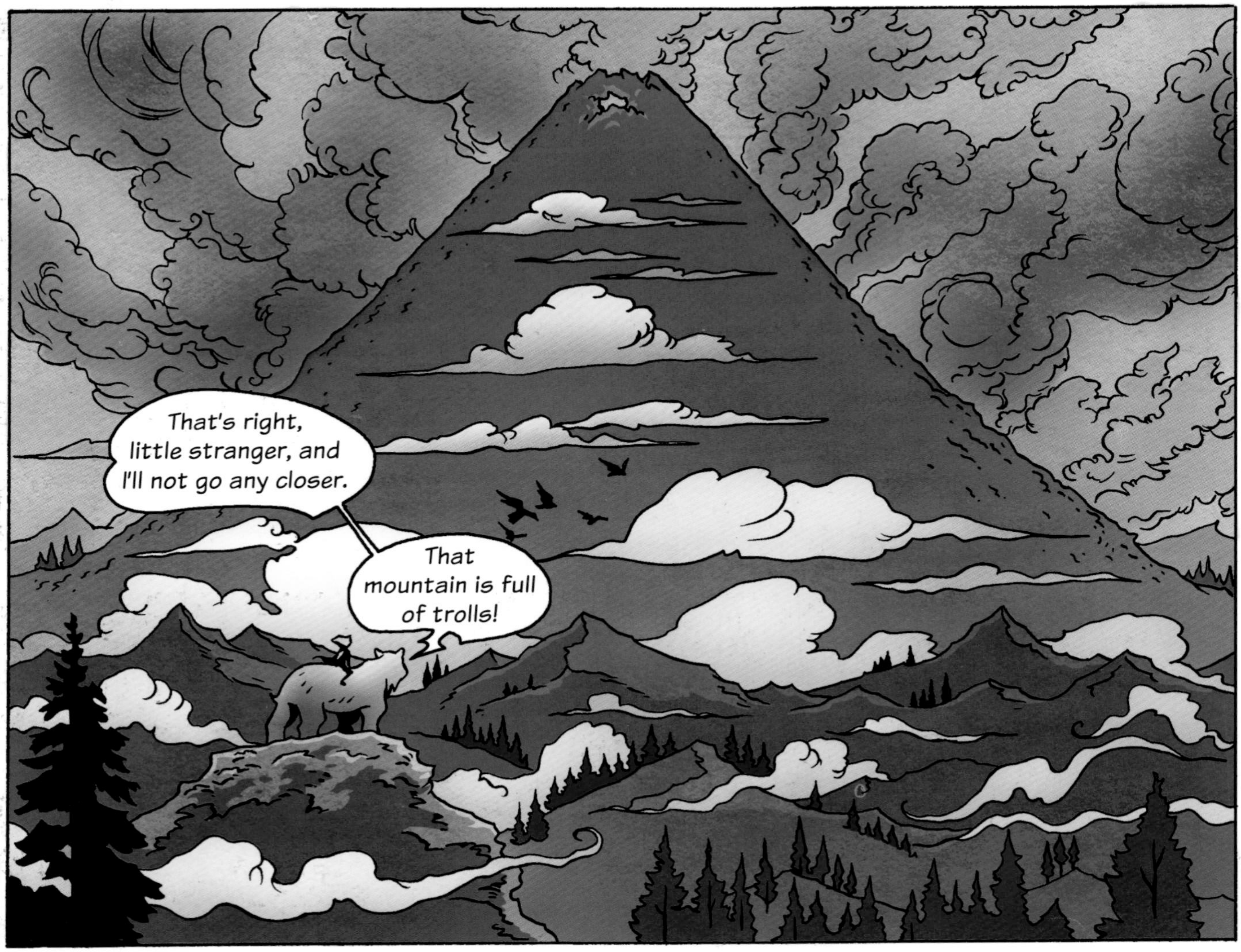
That's right, little stranger, and I'll not go any closer.
That mountain is full of trolls!

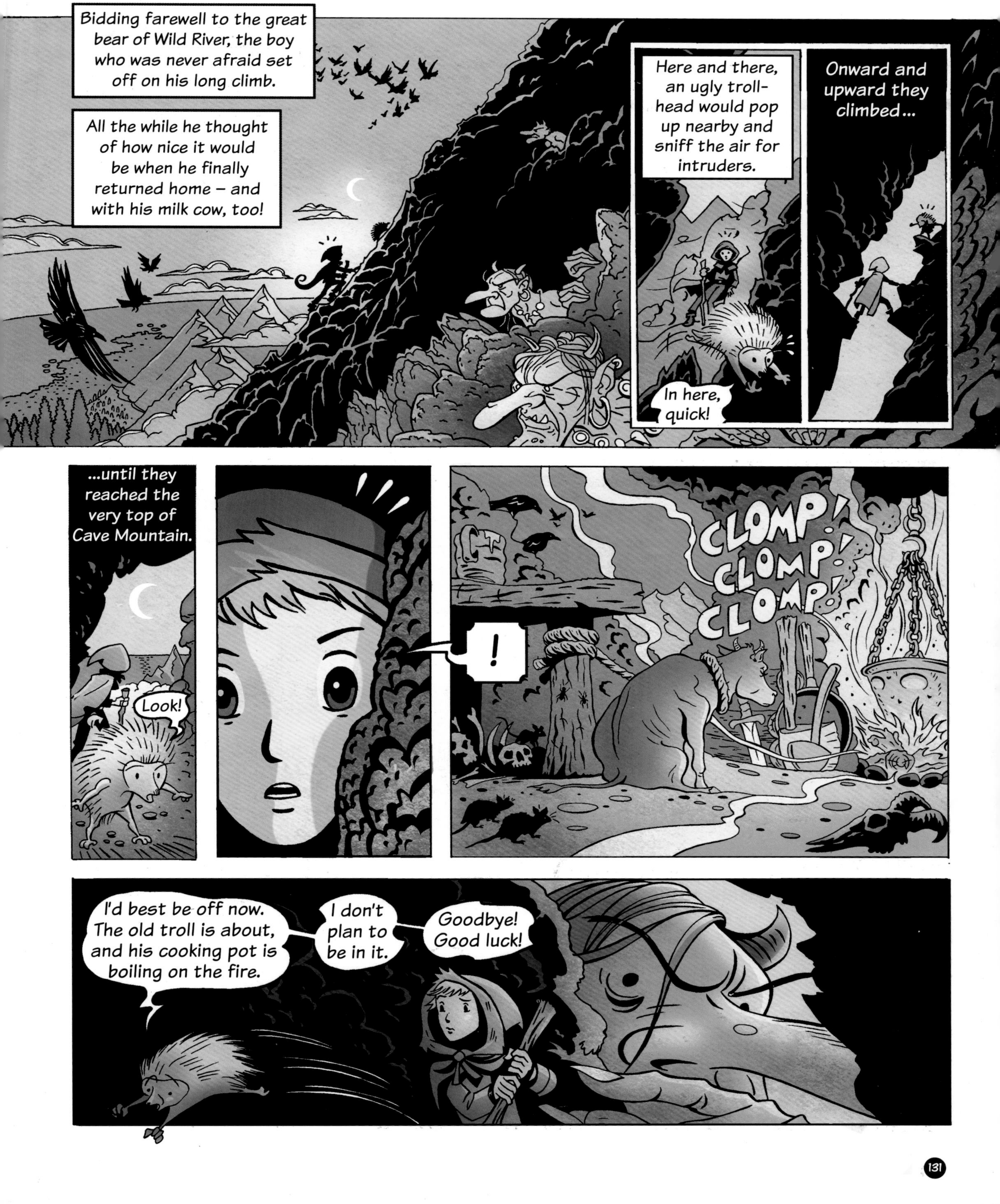
Bidding farewell to the great bear of Wild River, the boy who was never afraid set off on his long climb.
All the while he thought of how nice it would be when he finally returned home – and with his milk cow, too!
Here and there, an ugly troll-head would pop up nearby and sniff the air for intruders.
In here, quick!
Onward and upward they climbed...
...until they reached the very top of Cave Mountain.
Look!
!
CLOMP! CLOMP! CLOMP!
I'd best be off now. The old troll is about, and his cooking pot is boiling on the fire.
I don't plan to be in it.
Goodbye! Good luck!

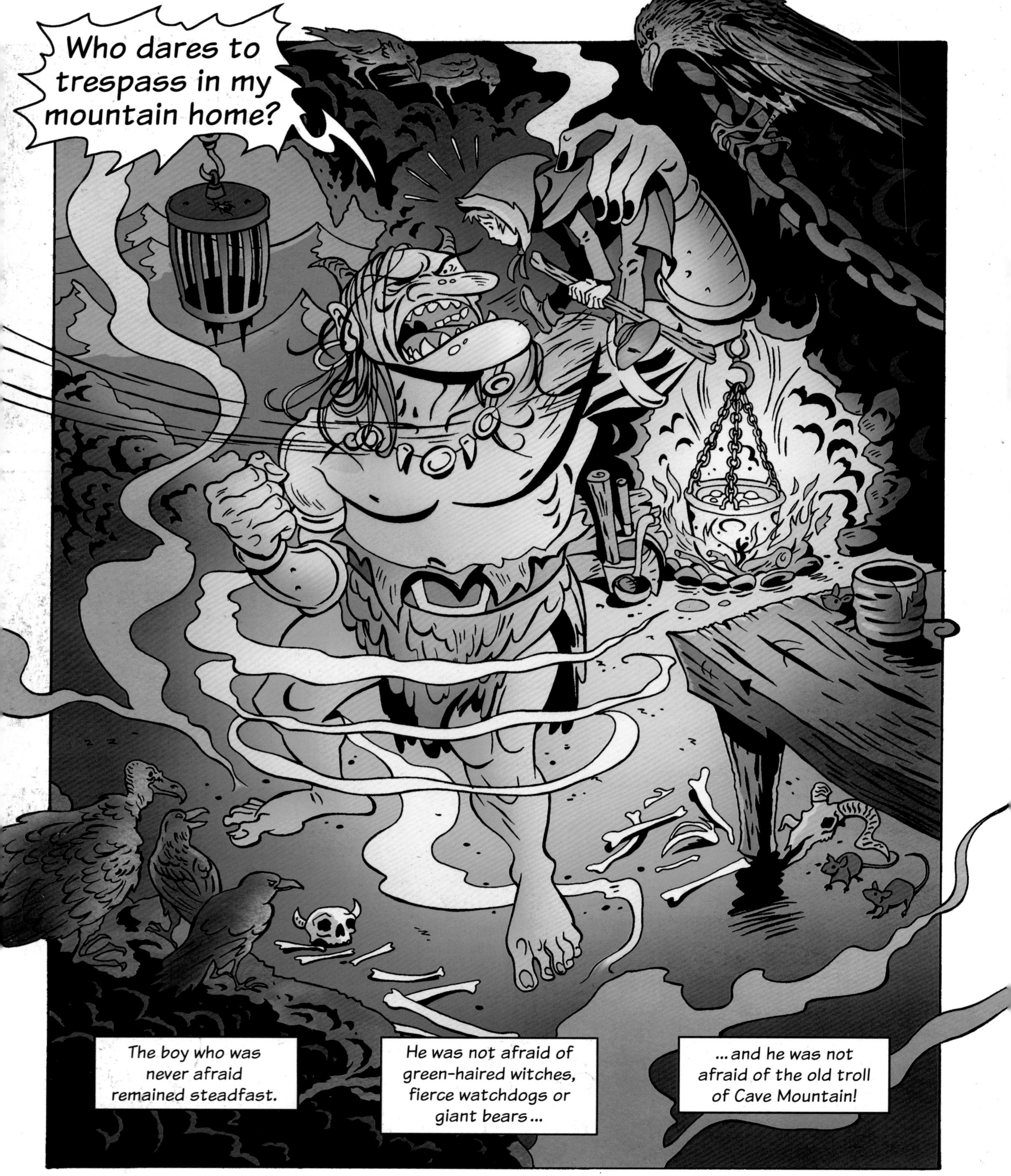
Who dares to trespass in my mountain home?
The boy who was never afraid remained steadfast.
He was not afraid of green-haired witches, fierce watchdogs or giant bears ...
... and he was not afraid of the old troll of Cave Mountain!

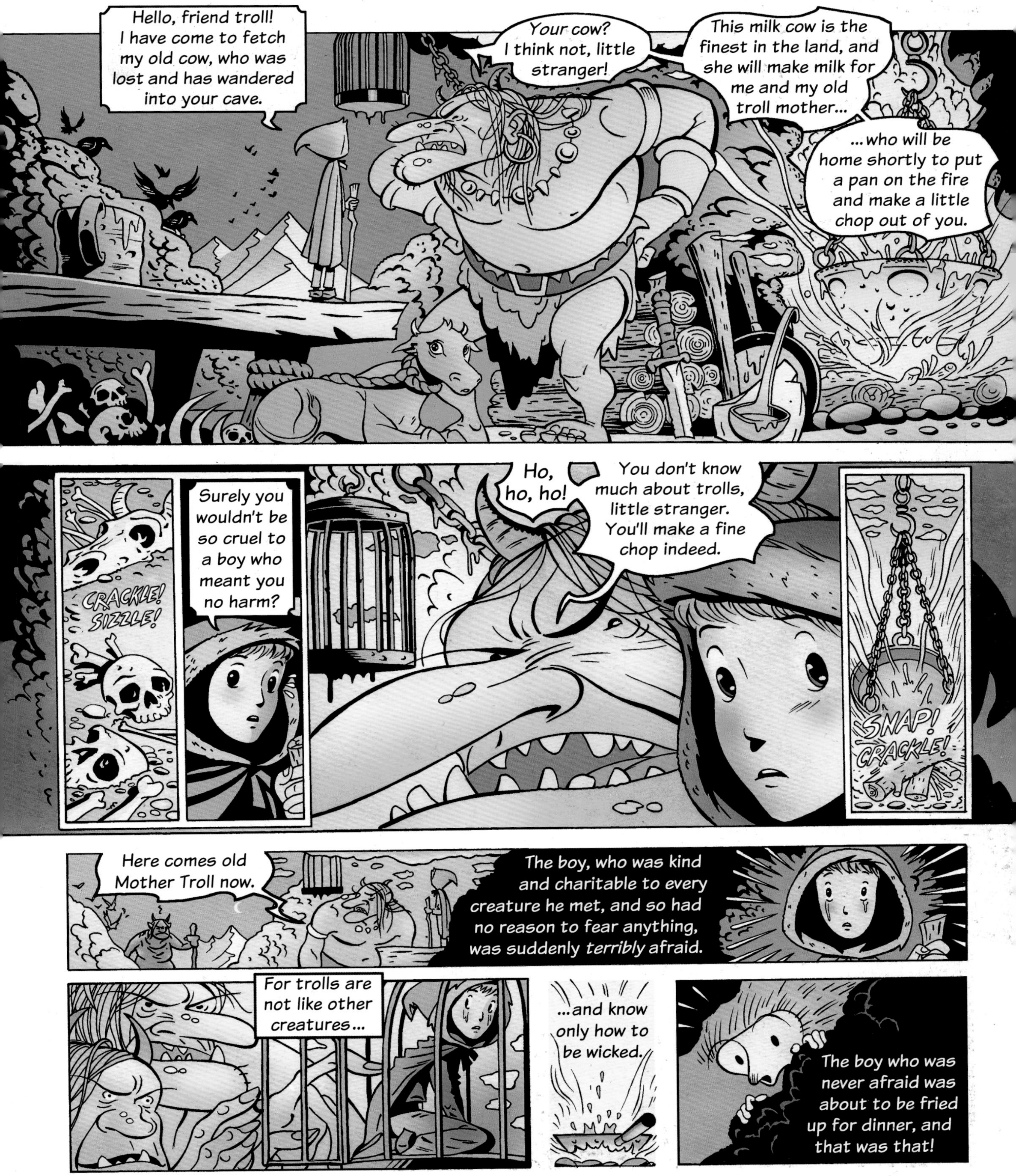
Hello, friend troll! I have come to fetch my old cow, who was lost and has wandered into your cave.
Your cow? I think not, little stranger!
This milk cow is the finest in the land, and she will make milk for me and my old troll mother...
...who will be home shortly to put a pan on the fire and make a little chop out of you.
CRACKLE! SIZZLE!
Surely you wouldn't be so cruel to a boy who meant you no harm?
Ho, ho, ho!
You don't know much about trolls, little stranger. You'll make a fine chop indeed.
SNAP! CRACKLE!
Here comes old Mother Troll now.
The boy, who was kind and charitable to every creature he met, and so had no reason to fear anything, was suddenly *terribly* afraid.
For trolls are not like other creatures...
...and know only how to be wicked.
The boy who was never afraid was about to be fried up for dinner, and that was that!

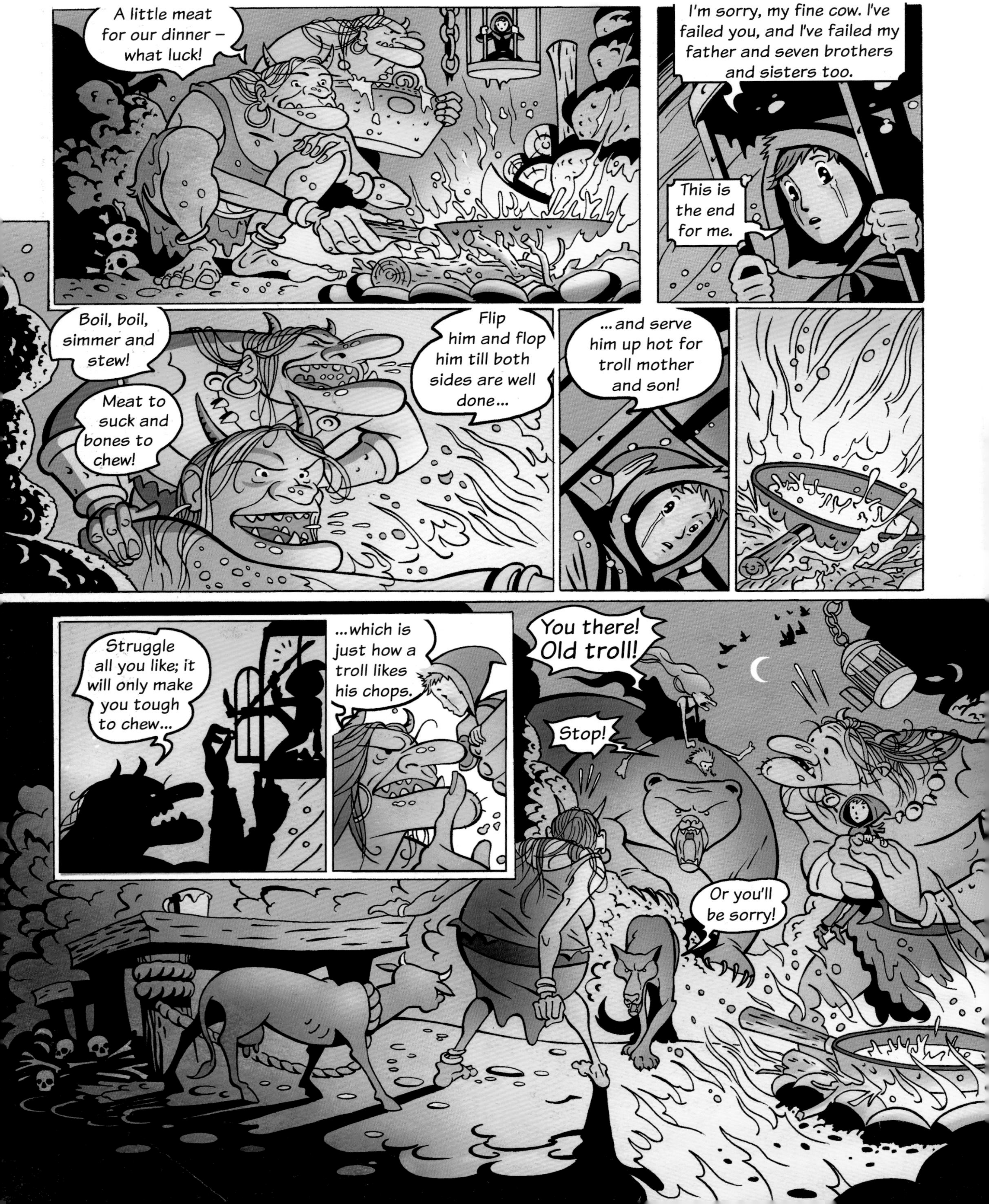
A little meat for our dinner – what luck!
I'm sorry, my fine cow. I've failed you, and I've failed my father and seven brothers and sisters too.
This is the end for me.
Boil, boil, simmer and stew!
Meat to suck and bones to chew!
Flip him and flop him till both sides are well done...
...and serve him up hot for troll mother and son!
Struggle all you like; it will only make you tough to chew...
...which is just how a troll likes his chops.
You there! Old troll!
Stop!
Or you'll be sorry!

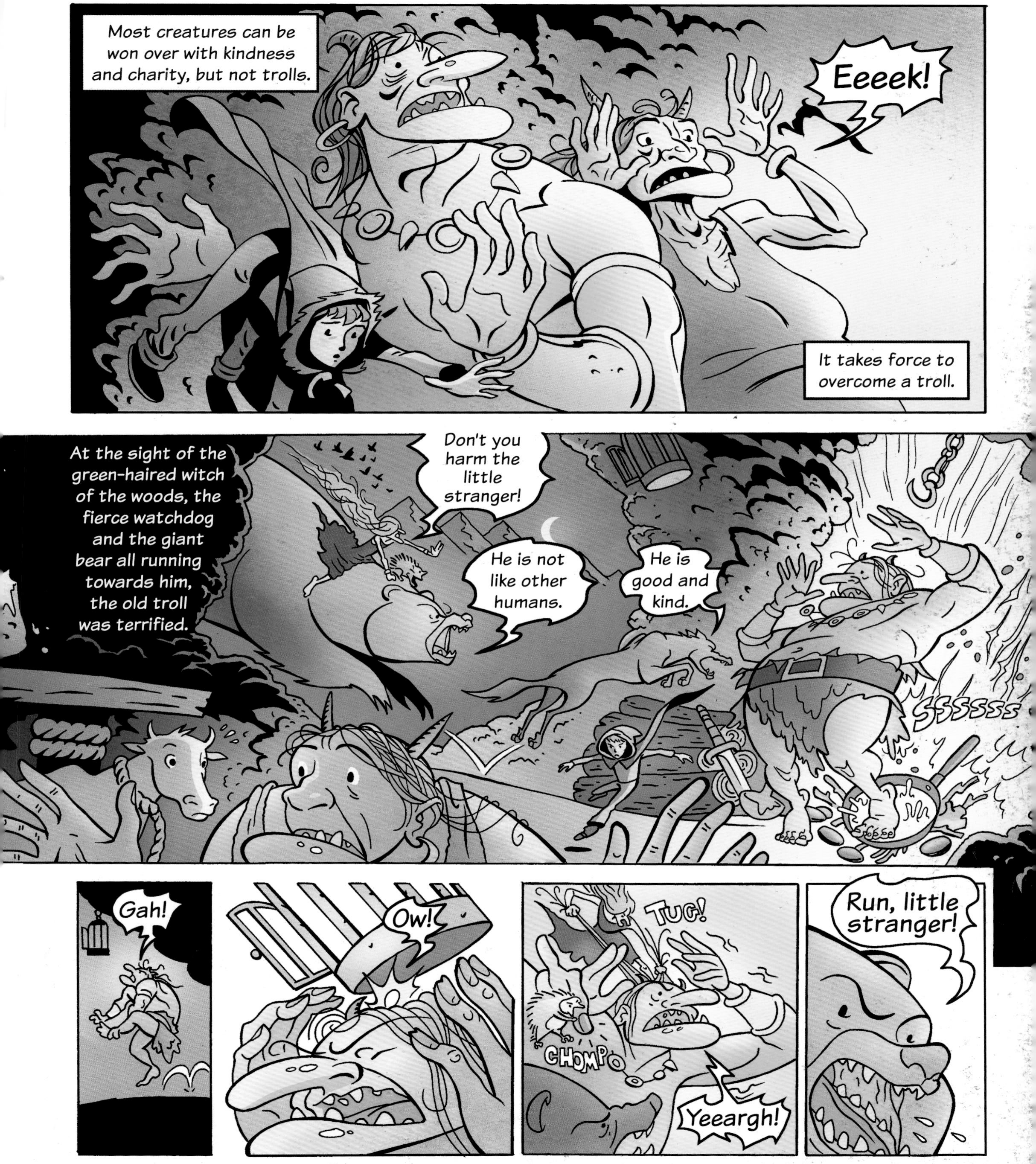
Most creatures can be won over with kindness and charity, but not trolls.
Eeeek!
It takes force to overcome a troll.
At the sight of the green-haired witch of the woods, the fierce watchdog and the giant bear all running towards him, the old troll was terrified.
Don't you harm the little stranger!
He is not like other humans.
He is good and kind.
SSSSSSS
Gah!
Ow!
TUG!
CHOMP
Yeeargh!
Run, little stranger!

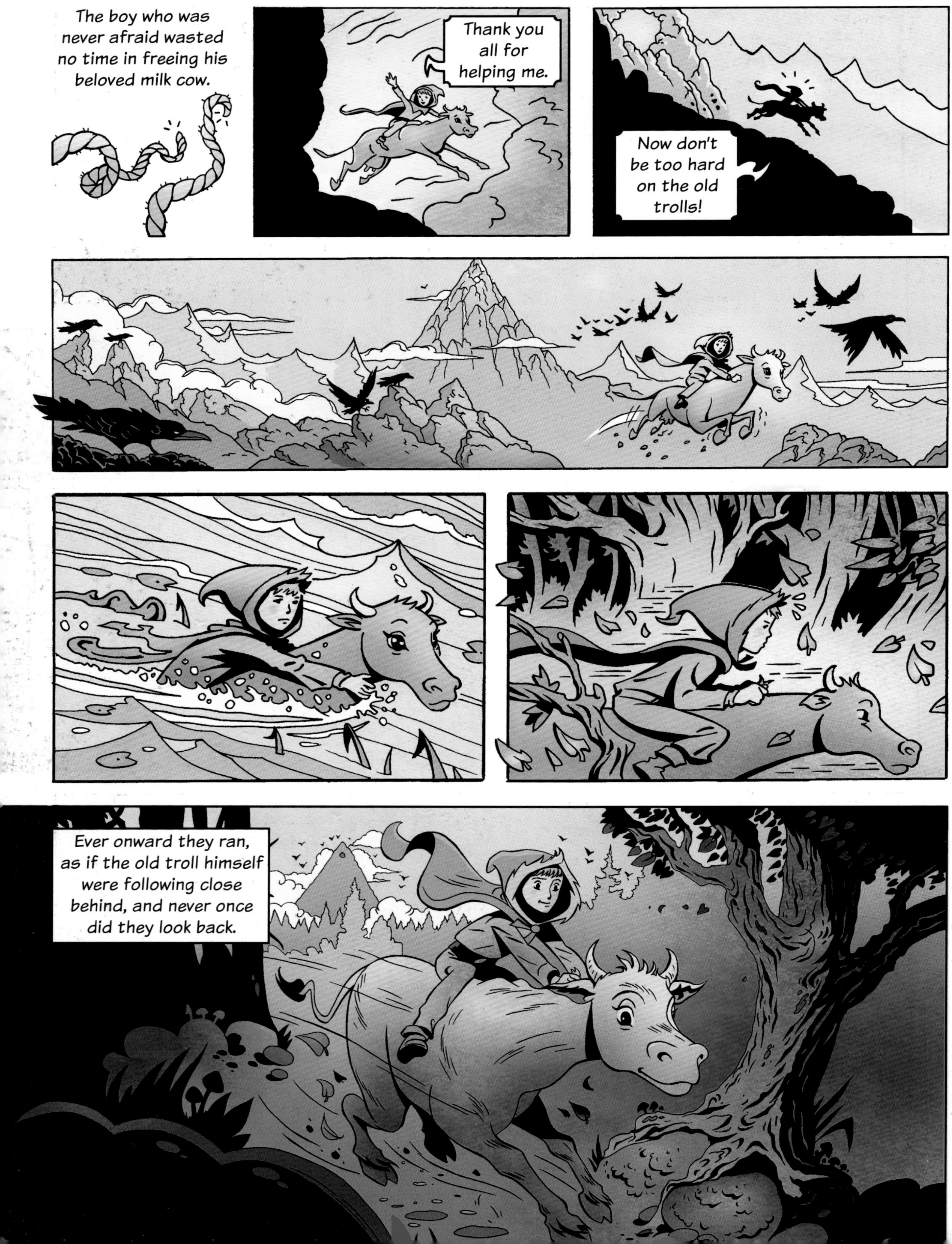
The boy who was never afraid wasted no time in freeing his beloved milk cow.
Thank you all for helping me.
Now don't be too hard on the old trolls!
Ever onward they ran, as if the old troll himself were following close behind, and never once did they look back.

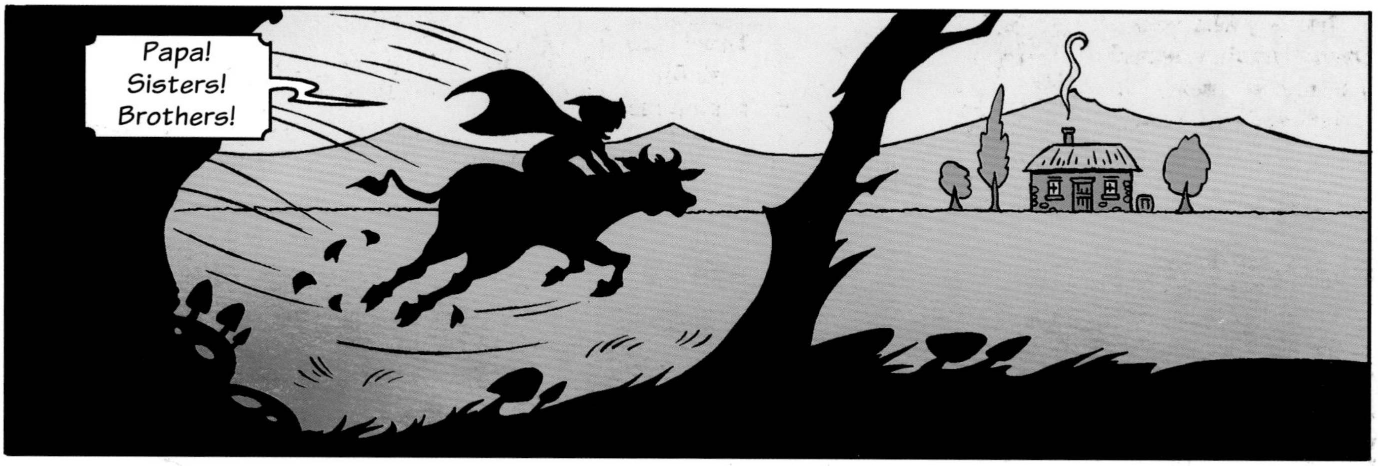
Papa!
Sisters!
Brothers!

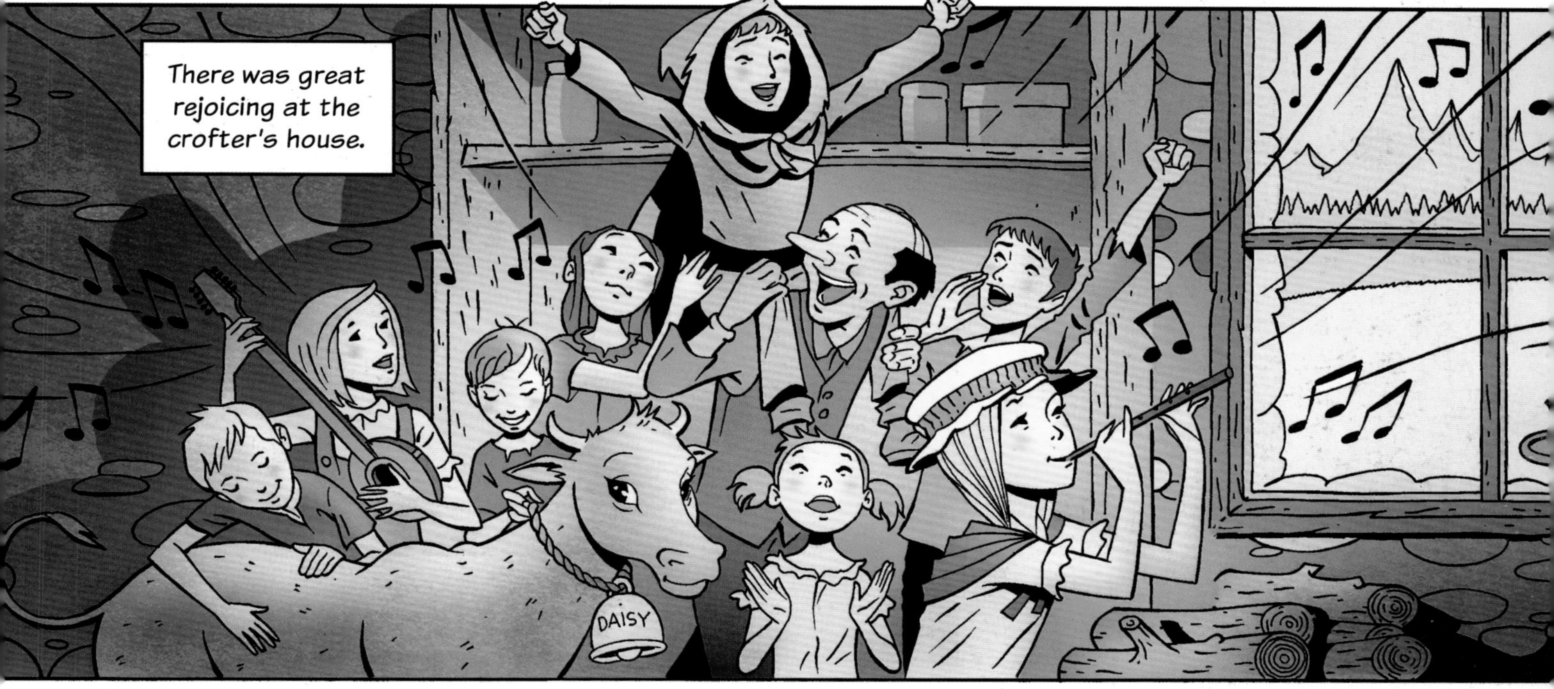
There was great rejoicing at the crofter's house.
DAISY

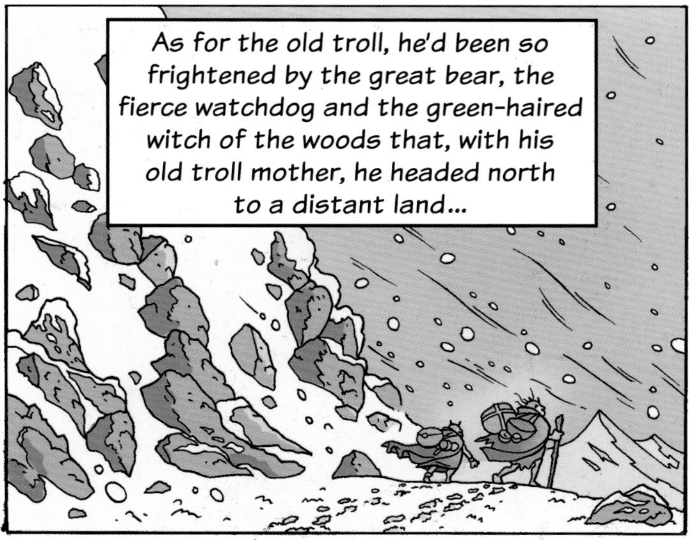
As for the old troll, he'd been so frightened by the great bear, the fierce watchdog and the green-haired witch of the woods that, with his old troll mother, he headed north to a distant land...

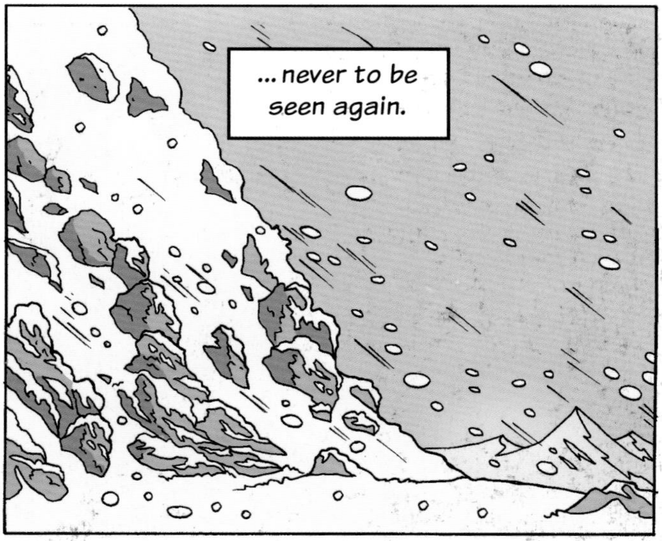
...never to be seen again.

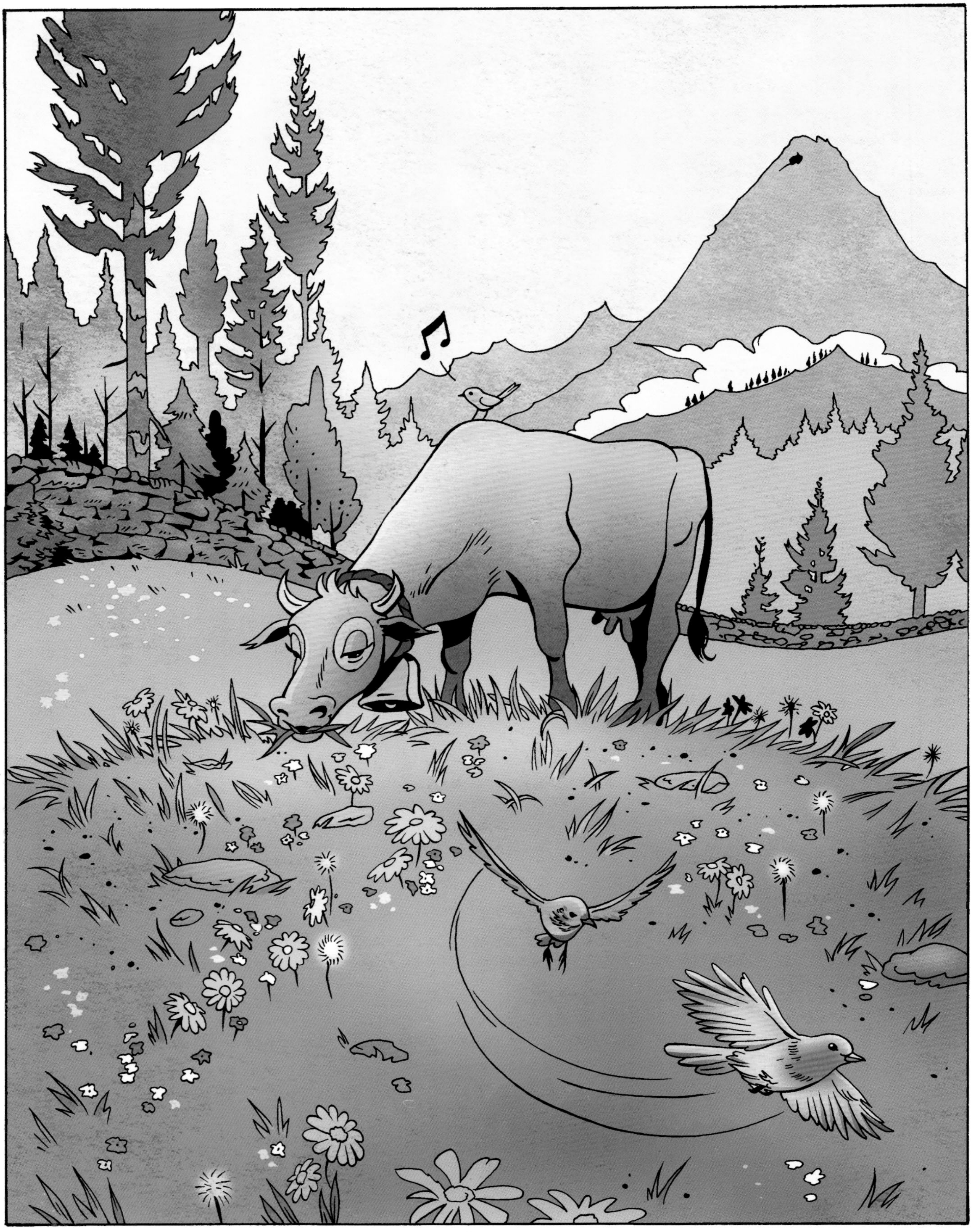

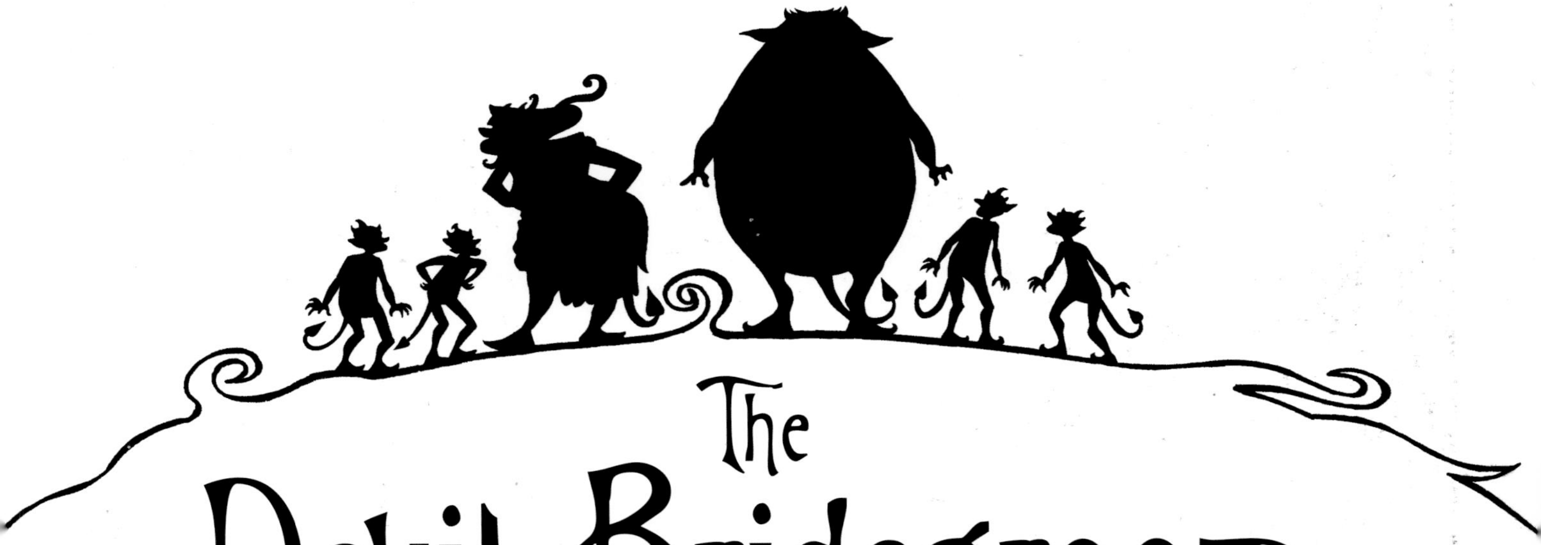

The Devil Bridegroom

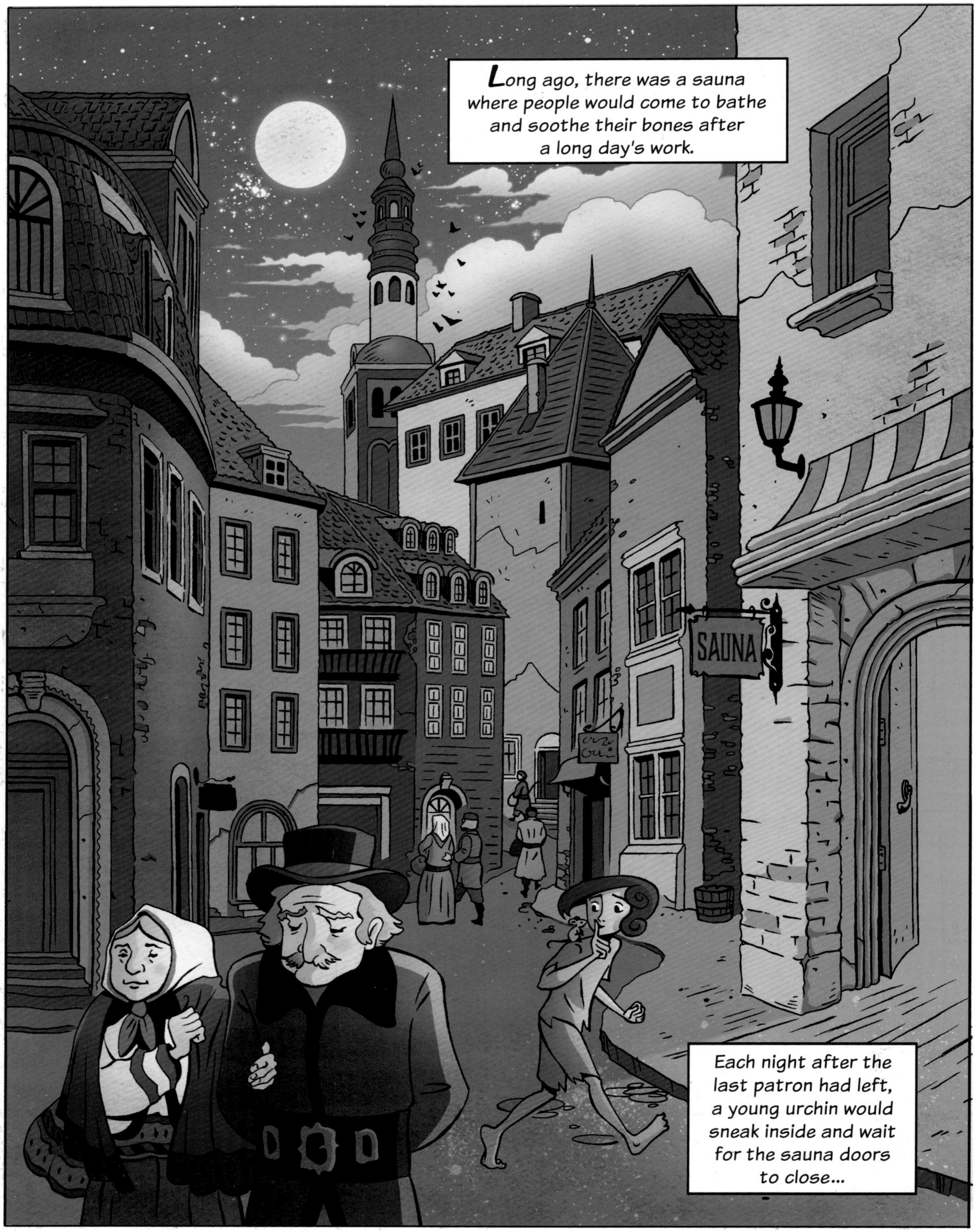
Long ago, there was a sauna where people would come to bathe and soothe their bones after a long day's work.
SAUNA
Each night after the last patron had left, a young urchin would sneak inside and wait for the sauna doors to close...

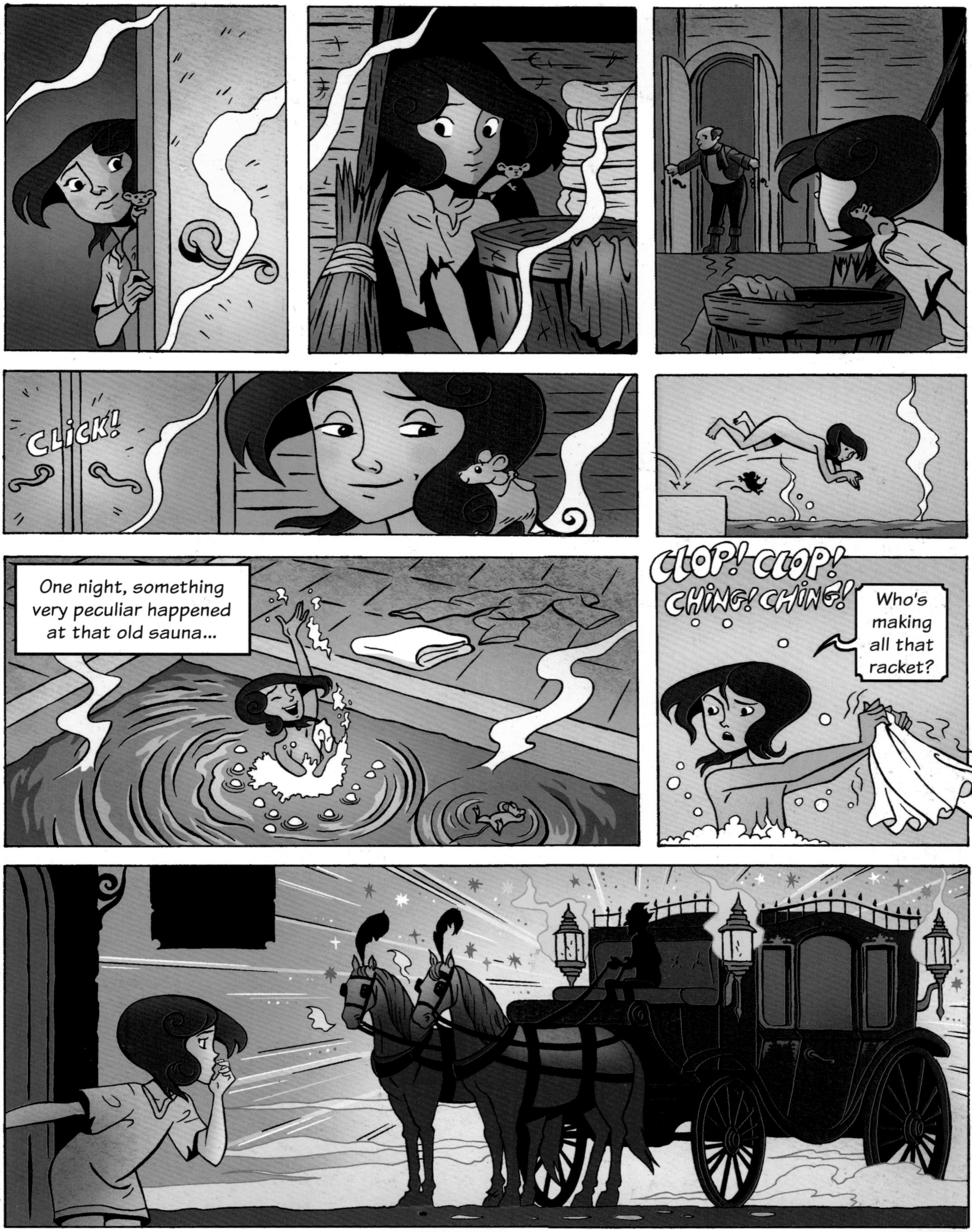
CLICK!
One night, something very peculiar happened at that old sauna...
CLOP! CLOP!
CHING! CHING!
Who's making all that racket?

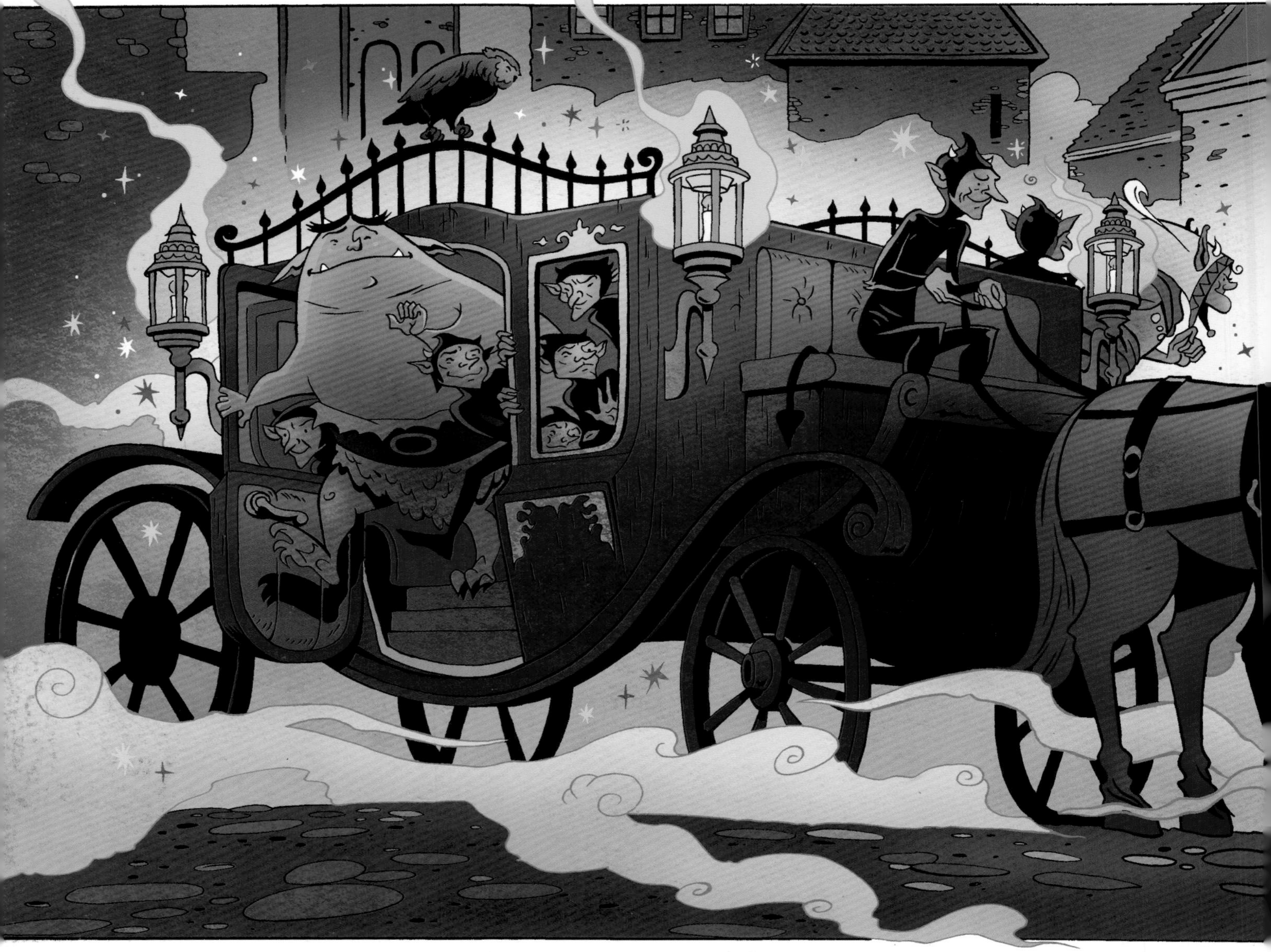

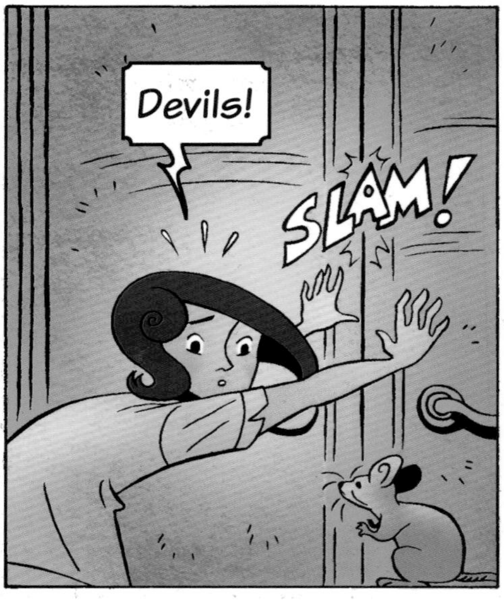
Devils!
SLAM!

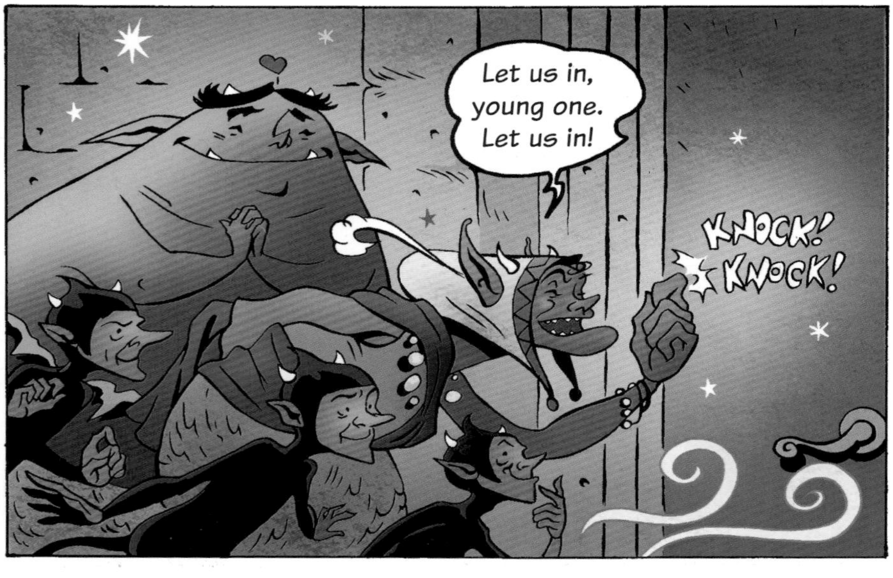
Let us in,
young one.
Let us in!
KNOCK!
KNOCK!

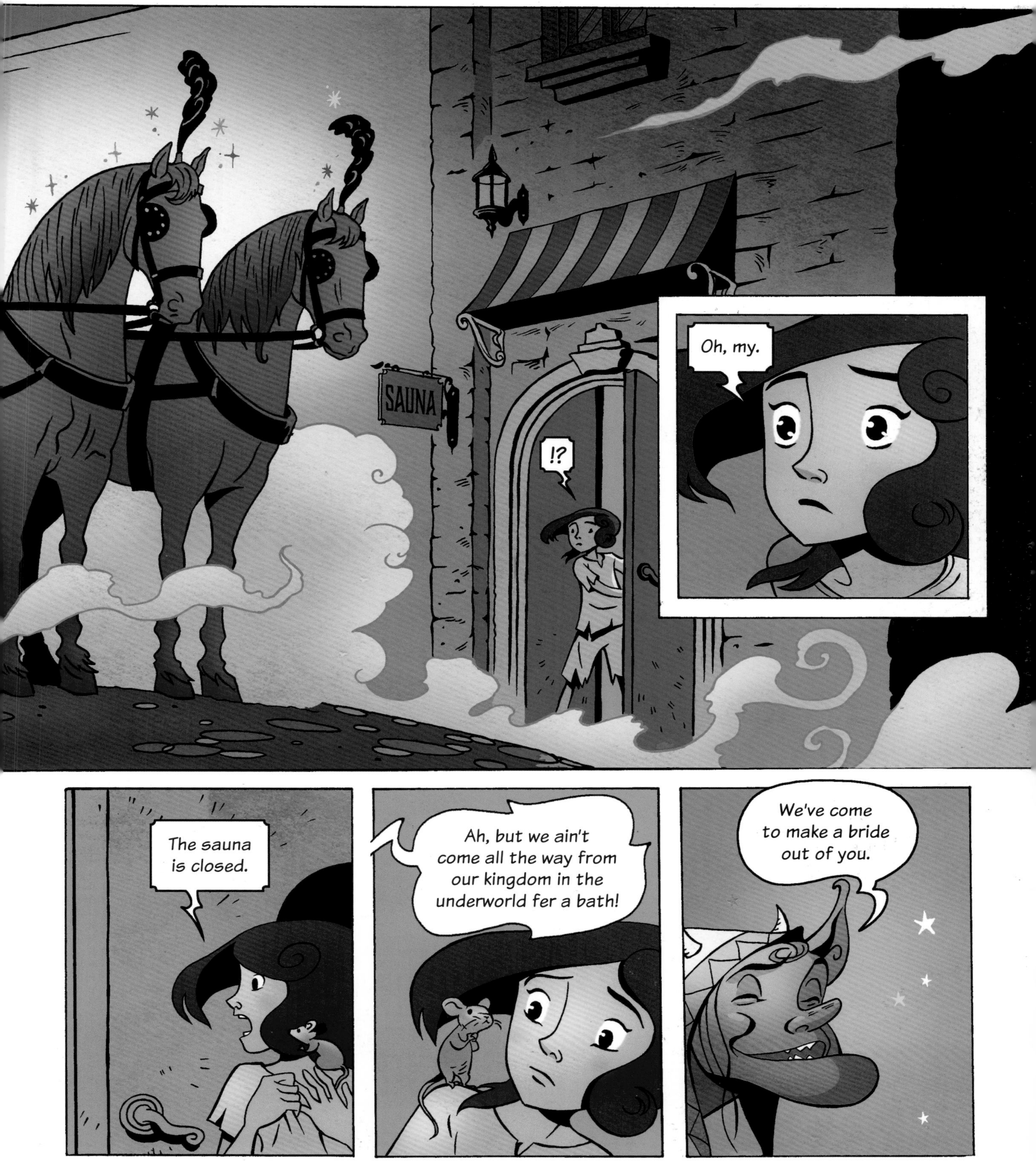
SAUNA
!?
Oh, my.
The sauna is closed.
Ah, but we ain't come all the way from our kingdom in the underworld fer a bath!
We've come to make a bride out of you.

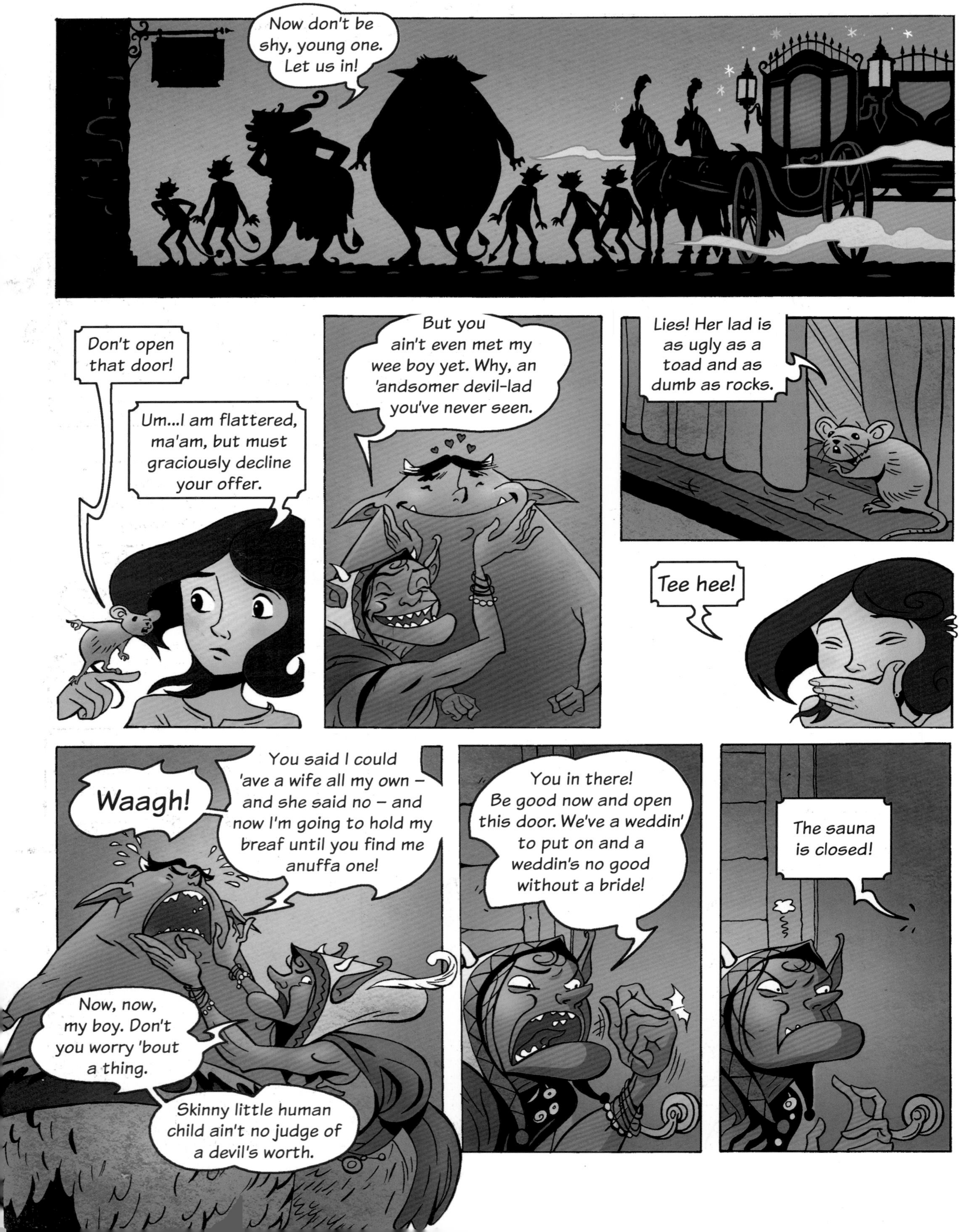

Now don't be shy, young one. Let us in!
Don't open that door!
Um...I am flattered, ma'am, but must graciously decline your offer.
But you ain't even met my wee boy yet. Why, an 'andsomer devil-lad you've never seen.
Lies! Her lad is as ugly as a toad and as dumb as rocks.
Tee hee!
Waagh!
You said I could 'ave a wife all my own – and she said no – and now I'm going to hold my breaf until you find me anuffa one!
Now, now, my boy. Don't you worry 'bout a thing.
Skinny little human child ain't no judge of a devil's worth.
You in there! Be good now and open this door. We've a weddin' to put on and a weddin's no good without a bride!
The sauna is closed!

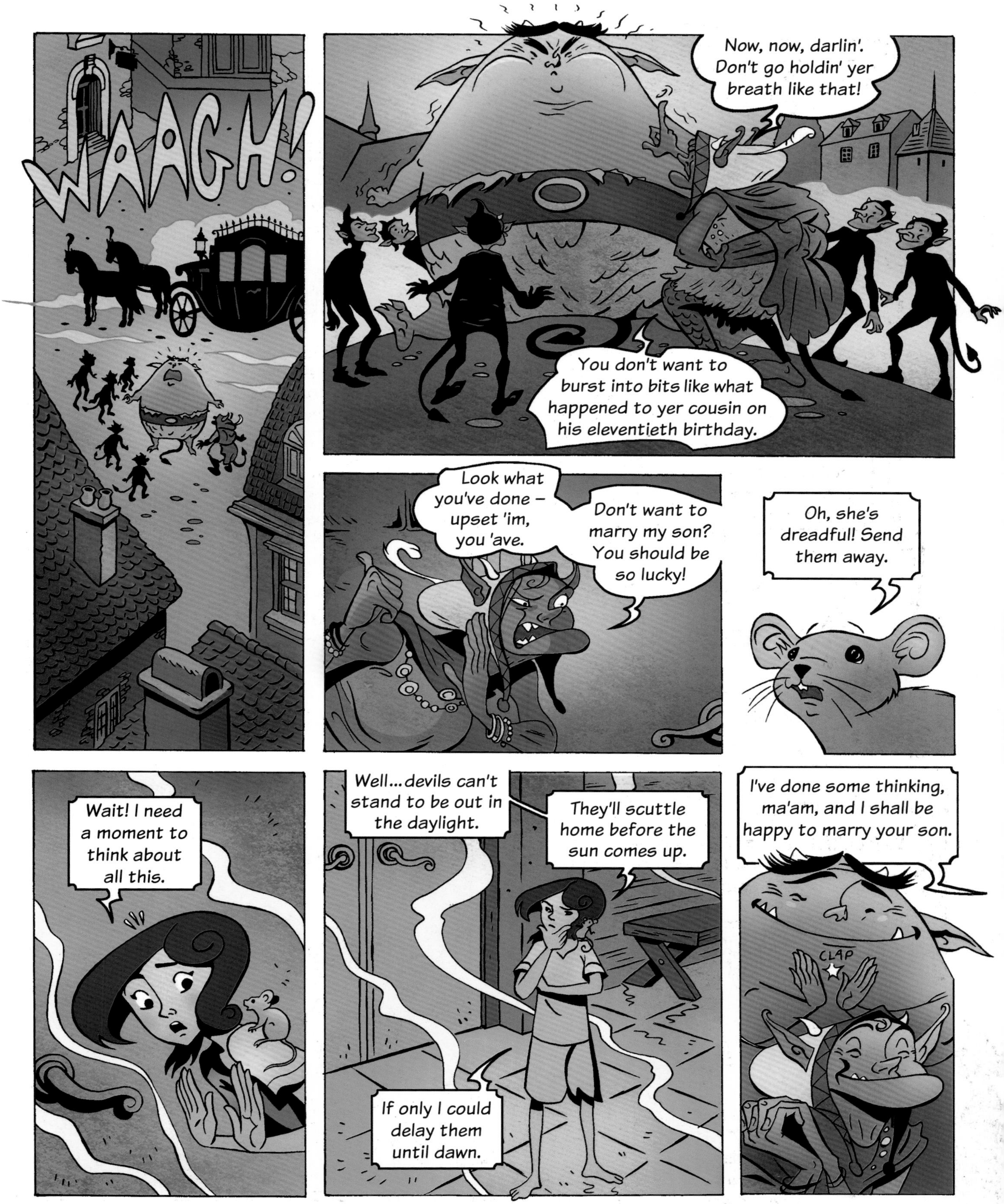
WAAGH!
Now, now, darlin'. Don't go holdin' yer breath like that!
You don't want to burst into bits like what happened to yer cousin on his eleventieth birthday.
Look what you've done – upset 'im, you 'ave.
Don't want to marry my son? You should be so lucky!
Oh, she's dreadful! Send them away.
Wait! I need a moment to think about all this.
Well... devils can't stand to be out in the daylight.
They'll scuttle home before the sun comes up.
If only I could delay them until dawn.
I've done some thinking, ma'am, and I shall be happy to marry your son.
CLAP

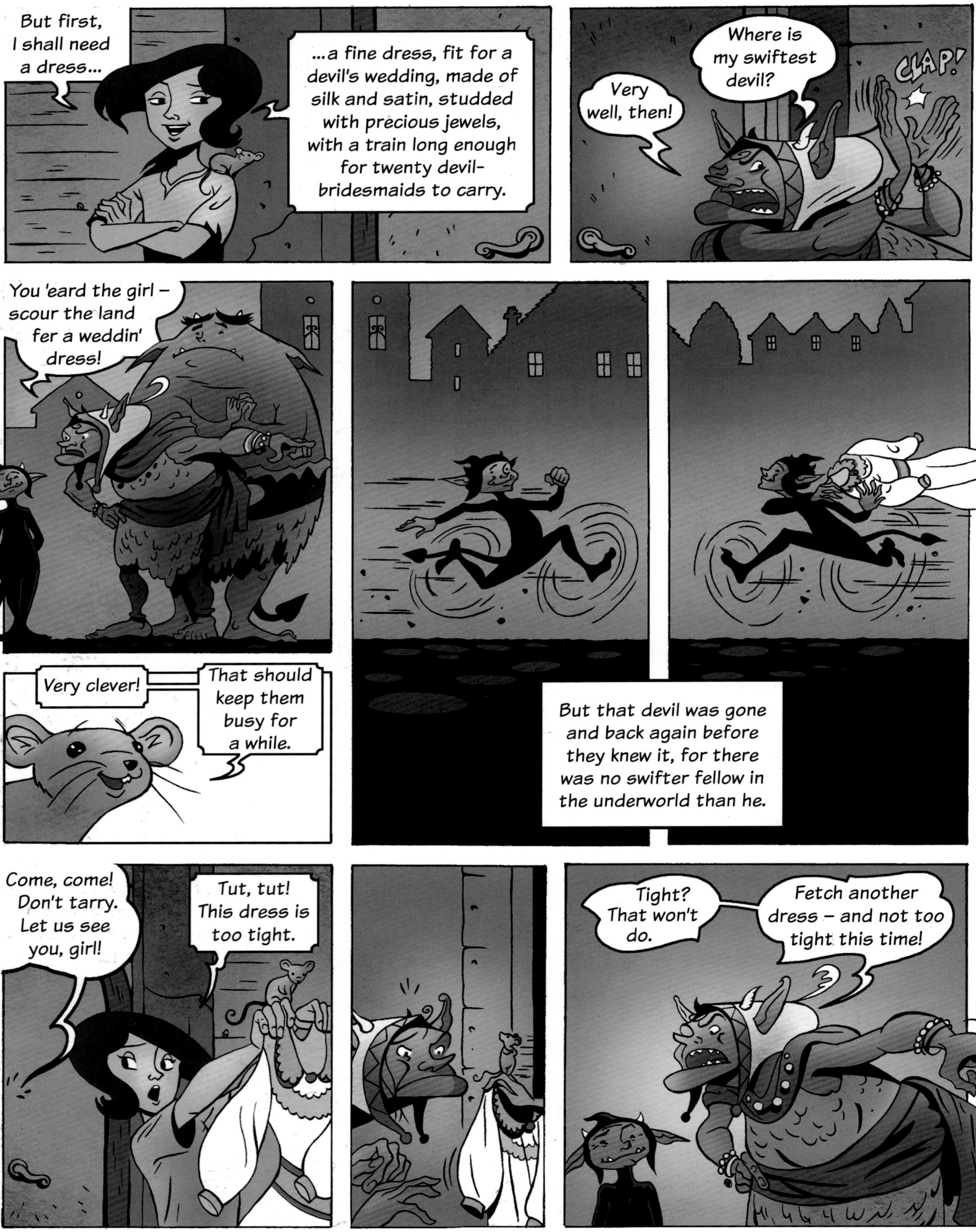
But first, I shall need a dress...
...a fine dress, fit for a devil's wedding, made of silk and satin, studded with precious jewels, with a train long enough for twenty devil-bridesmaids to carry.
Very well, then!
Where is my swiftest devil?
CLAP!
You 'eard the girl – scour the land fer a weddin' dress!
Very clever!
That should keep them busy for a while.
But that devil was gone and back again before they knew it, for there was no swifter fellow in the underworld than he.
Come, come! Don't tarry. Let us see you, girl!
Tut, tut! This dress is too tight.
Tight? That won't do.
Fetch another dress – and not too tight this time!

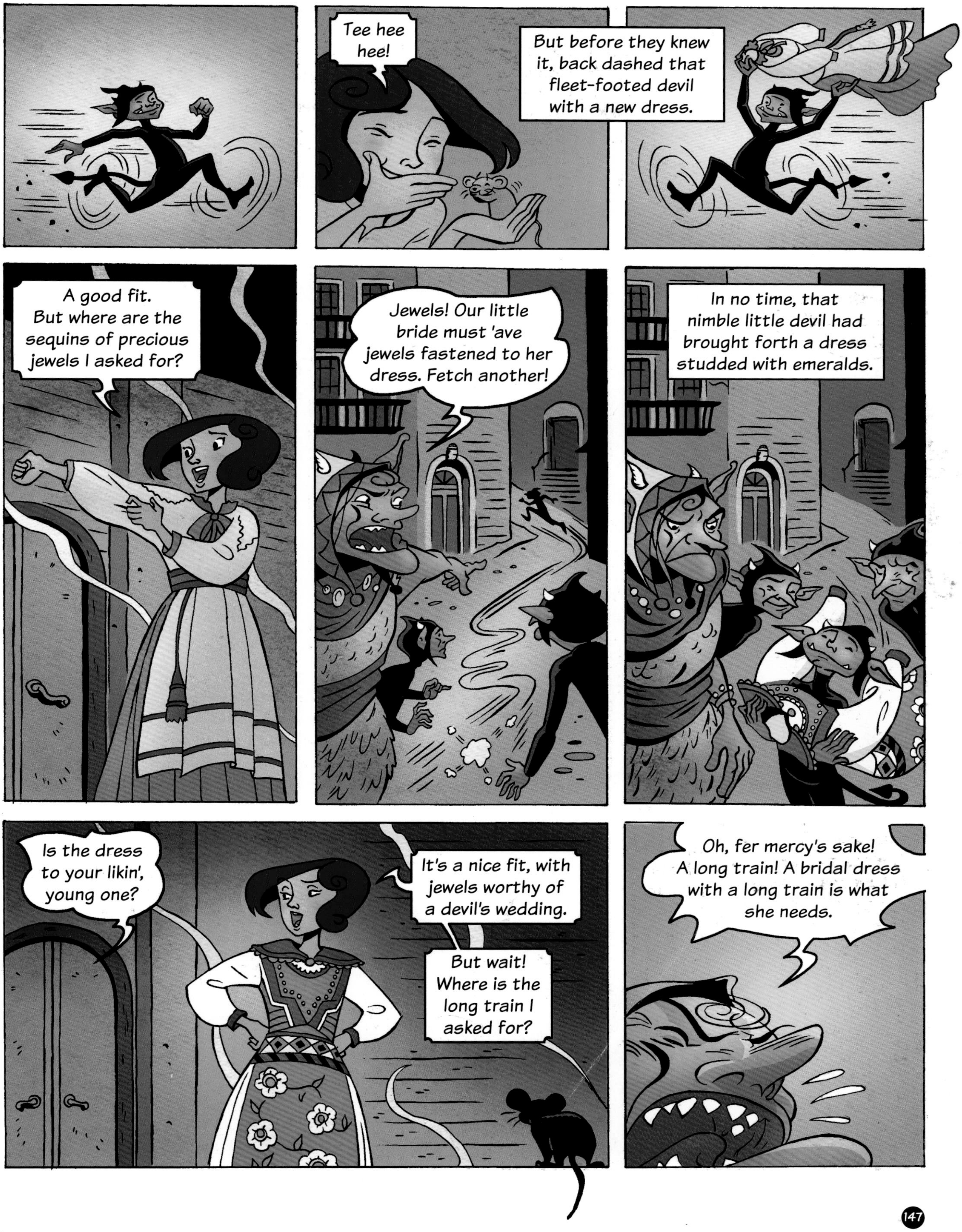
Tee hee
hee!
But before they knew it, back dashed that fleet-footed devil with a new dress.
A good fit. But where are the sequins of precious jewels I asked for?
Jewels! Our little bride must 'ave jewels fastened to her dress. Fetch another!
In no time, that nimble little devil had brought forth a dress studded with emeralds.
Is the dress to your likin', young one?
It's a nice fit, with jewels worthy of a devil's wedding.
But wait! Where is the long train I asked for?
Oh, fer mercy's sake! A long train! A bridal dress with a long train is what she needs.

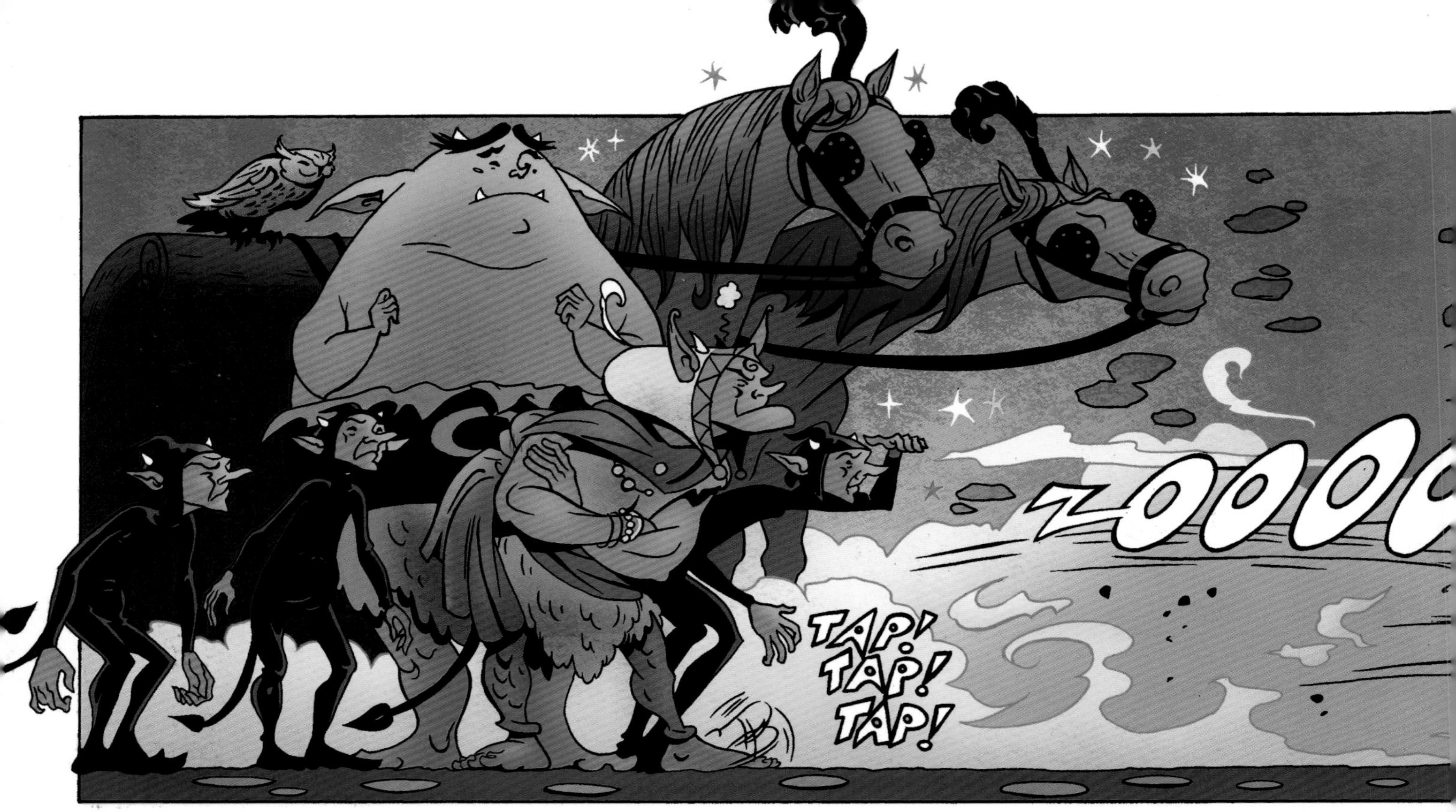
ZOOOO
TAP! TAP! TAP!

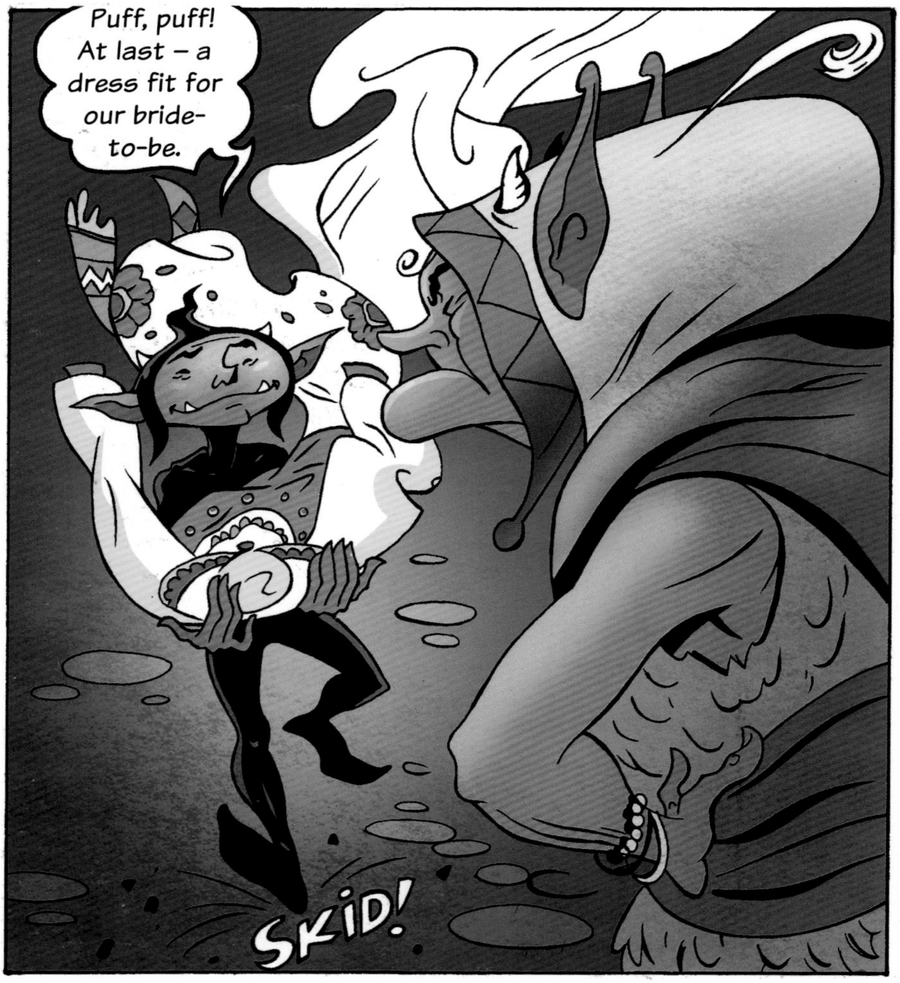
Puff, puff! At last – a dress fit for our bride-to-be.
SKID!

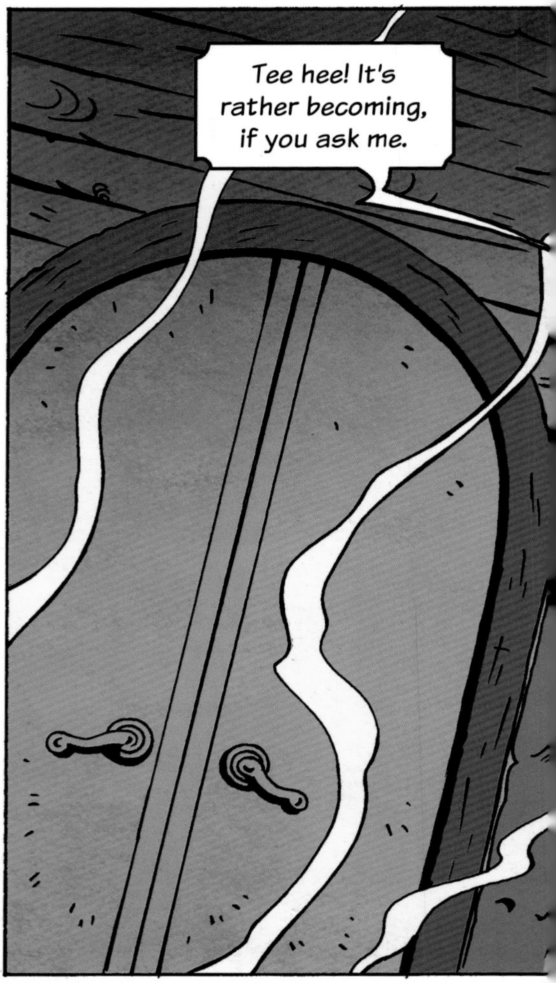
Tee hee! It's rather becoming, if you ask me.

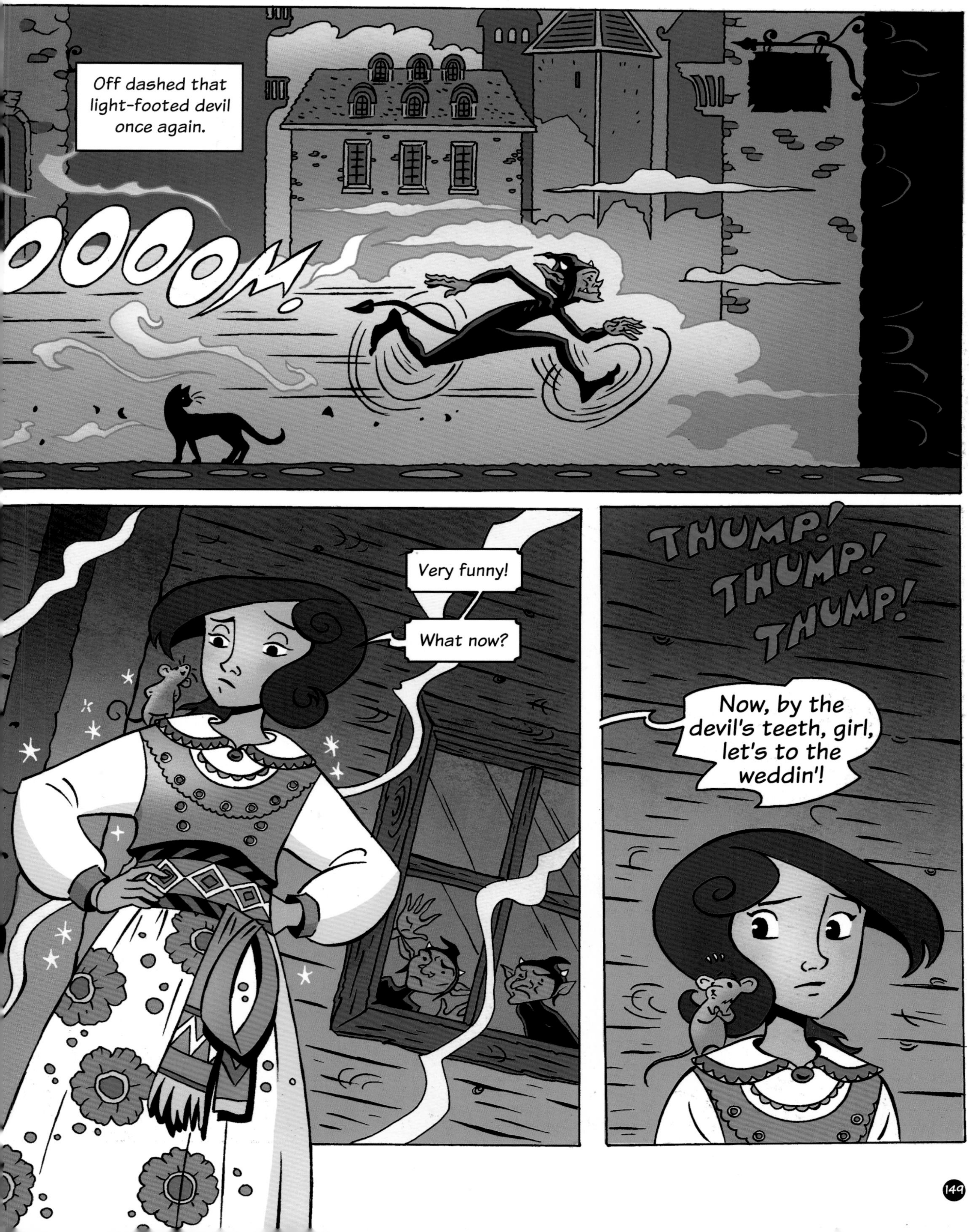
Off dashed that light-footed devil once again.
OOOOM!
Very funny!
What now?
THUMP! THUMP! THUMP!
Now, by the devil's teeth, girl, let's to the weddin'!

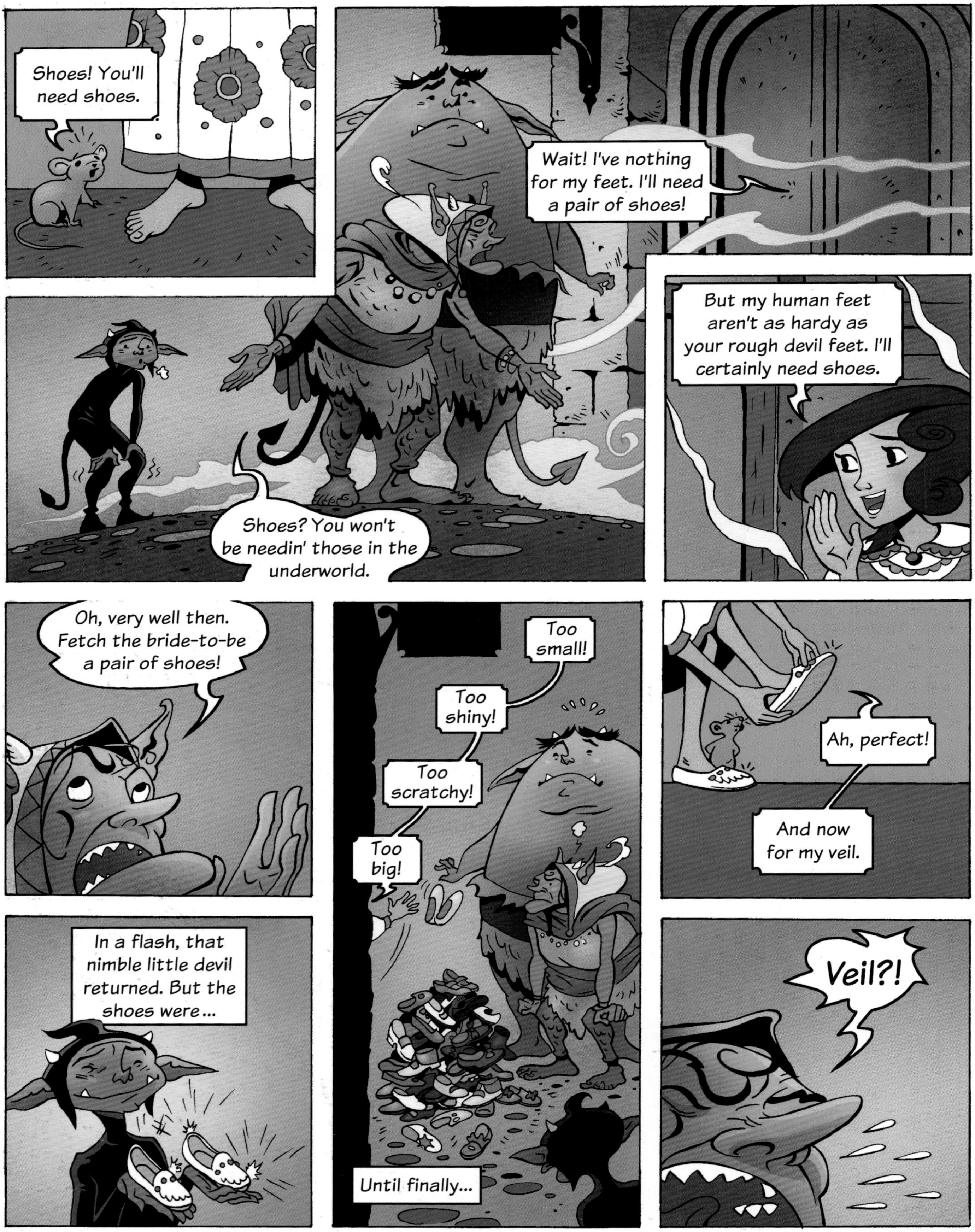
Shoes! You'll need shoes.
Wait! I've nothing for my feet. I'll need a pair of shoes!
Shoes? You won't be needin' those in the underworld.
But my human feet aren't as hardy as your rough devil feet. I'll certainly need shoes.
Oh, very well then. Fetch the bride-to-be a pair of shoes!
In a flash, that nimble little devil returned. But the shoes were...
Too small!
Too shiny!
Too scratchy!
Too big!
Until finally...
Ah, perfect!
And now for my veil.
Veil?!

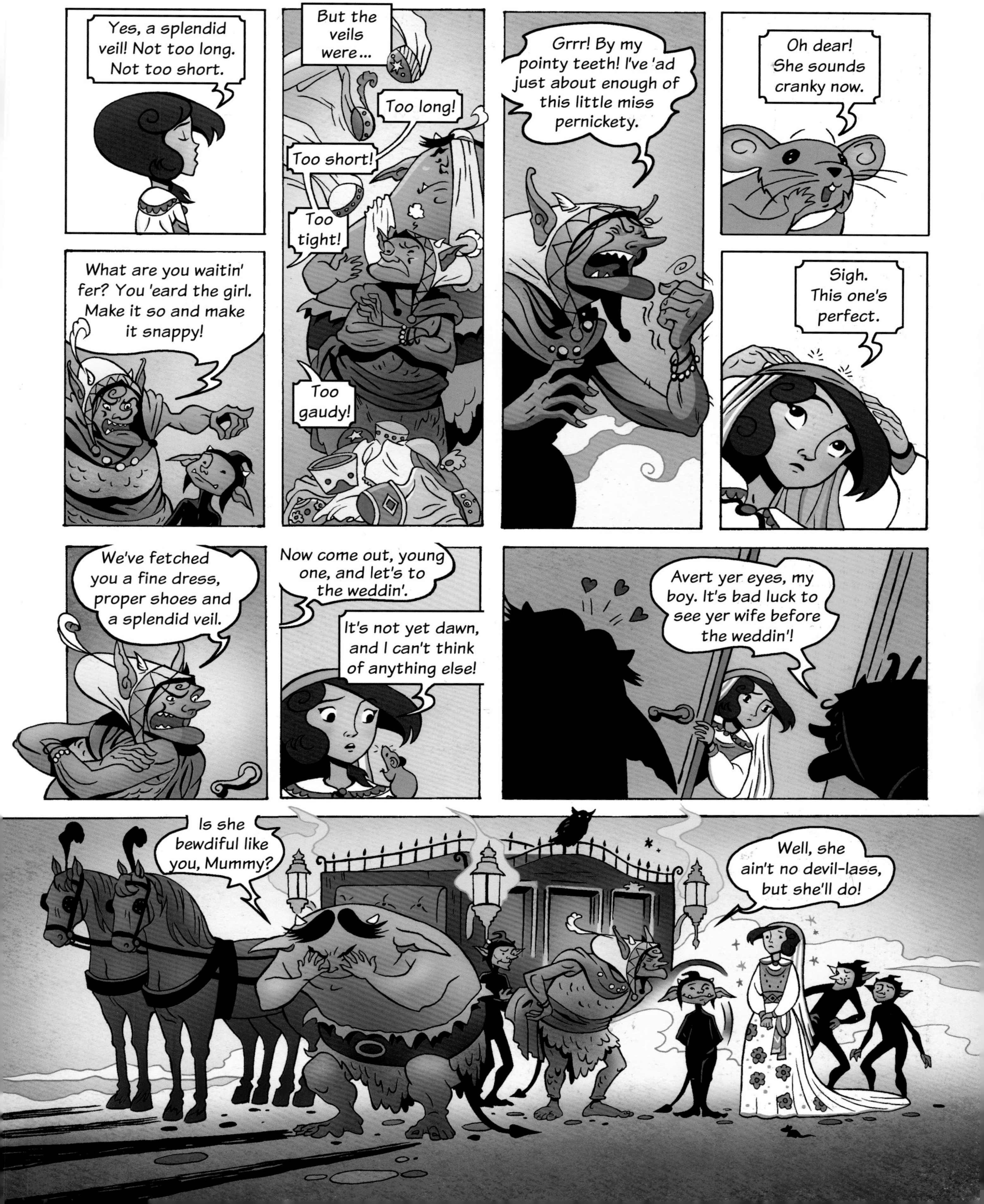
Yes, a splendid veil! Not too long. Not too short.
But the veils were...
Too long!
Too short!
Too tight!
Too gaudy!
Grrr! By my pointy teeth! I've 'ad just about enough of this little miss pernickety.
Oh dear! She sounds cranky now.
What are you waitin' fer? You 'eard the girl. Make it so and make it snappy!
Sigh. This one's perfect.
We've fetched you a fine dress, proper shoes and a splendid veil.
Now come out, young one, and let's to the weddin'.
It's not yet dawn, and I can't think of anything else!
Avert yer eyes, my boy. It's bad luck to see yer wife before the weddin'!
Is she bewdiful like you, Mummy?
Well, she ain't no devil-lass, but she'll do!

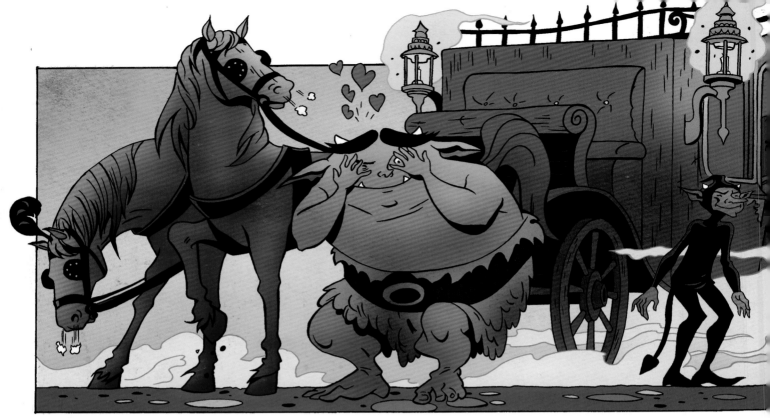

A gift?

Of course!

It's tradition for the groom to present his bride-to-be with a gift of fine jewels before the wedding.

Look, Mummy! The moon is almost gone.

By brimstone, he's right!

Fetch the bride a gift for her weddin' – immediately.

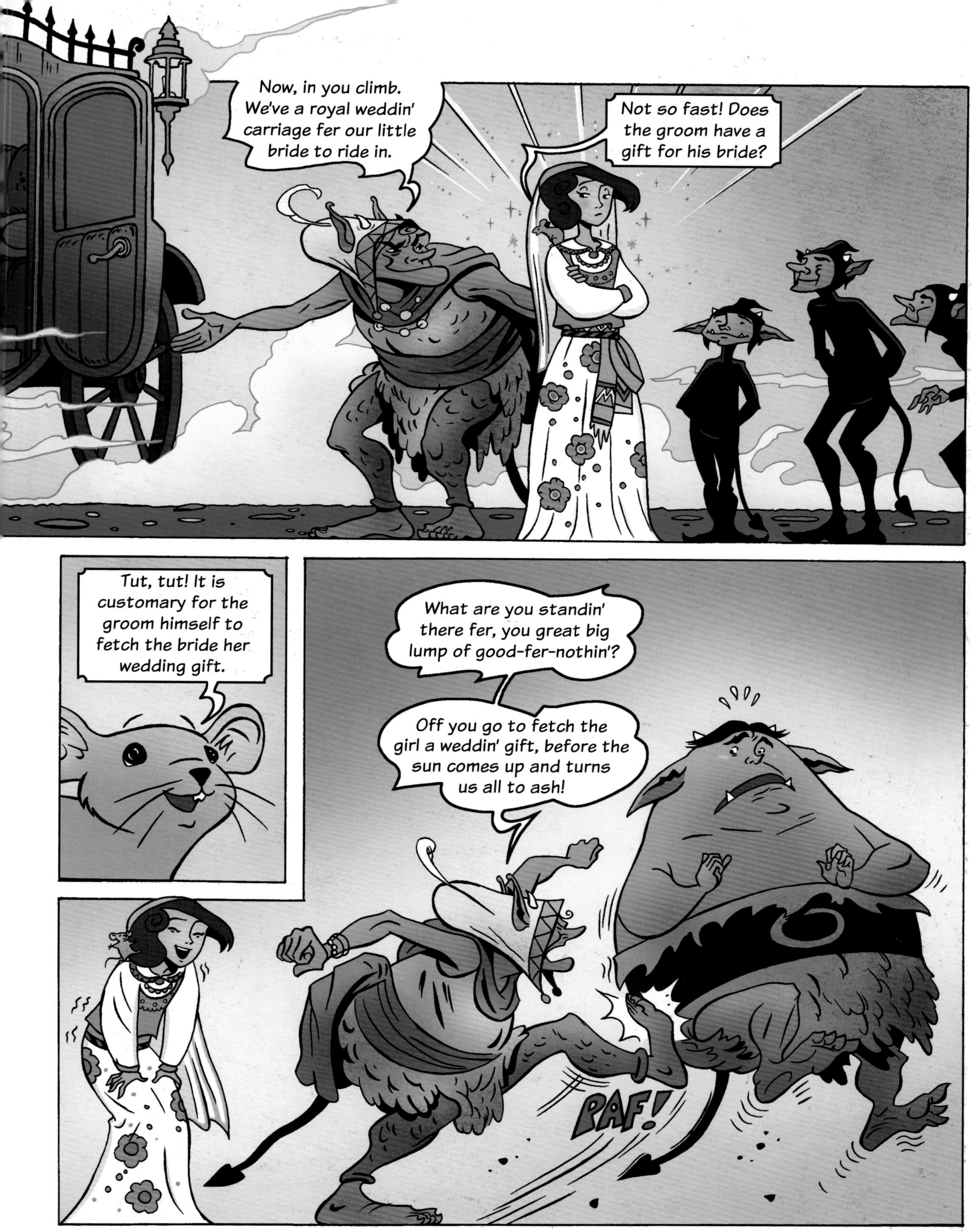
Now, in you climb. We've a royal weddin' carriage fer our little bride to ride in.
Not so fast! Does the groom have a gift for his bride?
Tut, tut! It is customary for the groom himself to fetch the bride her wedding gift.
What are you standin' there fer, you great big lump of good-fer-nothin'?
Off you go to fetch the girl a weddin' gift, before the sun comes up and turns us all to ash!
PAF!

Off lumbered the devil bridegroom, to fetch a wedding gift of fine jewels for his bride-to-be.

Where is 'e? Where is 'e? The sun will soon rise!

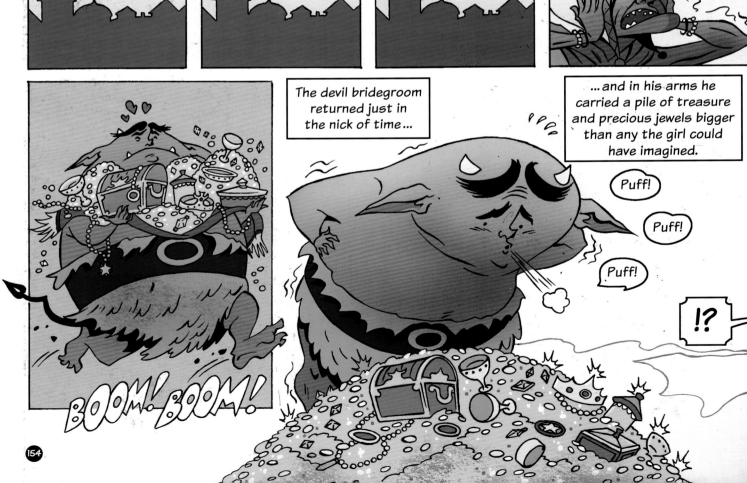

The devil bridegroom returned just in the nick of time...

...and in his arms he carried a pile of treasure and precious jewels bigger than any the girl could have imagined.

Puff!

Puff!

Puff!

!?

BOOM! BOOM!

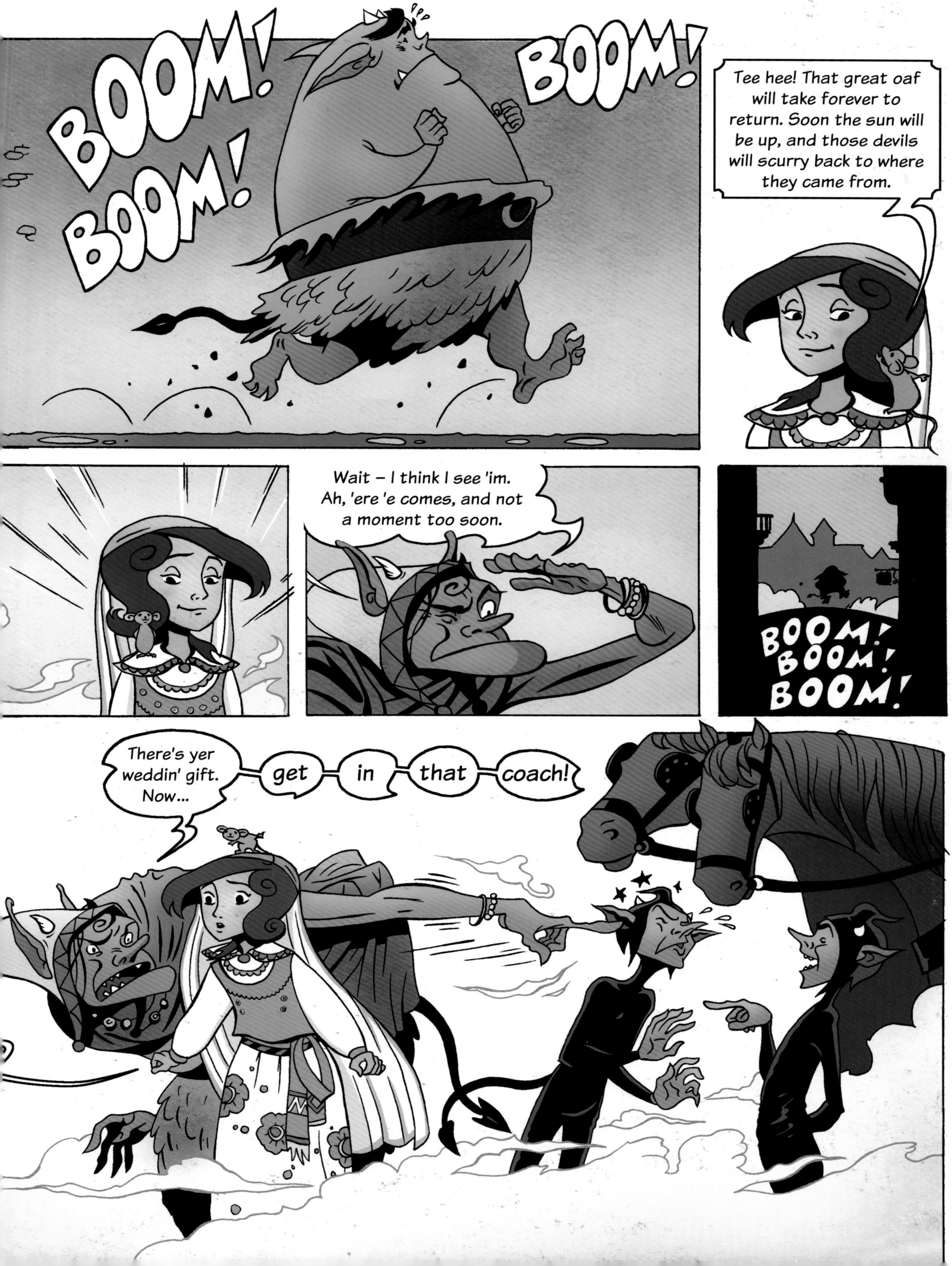
BOOM! BOOM! BOOM!
Tee hee! That great oaf will take forever to return. Soon the sun will be up, and those devils will scurry back to where they came from.
Wait – I think I see 'im. Ah, 'ere 'e comes, and not a moment too soon.
BOOM! BOOM! BOOM!
There's yer weddin' gift. Now...
get in that coach!

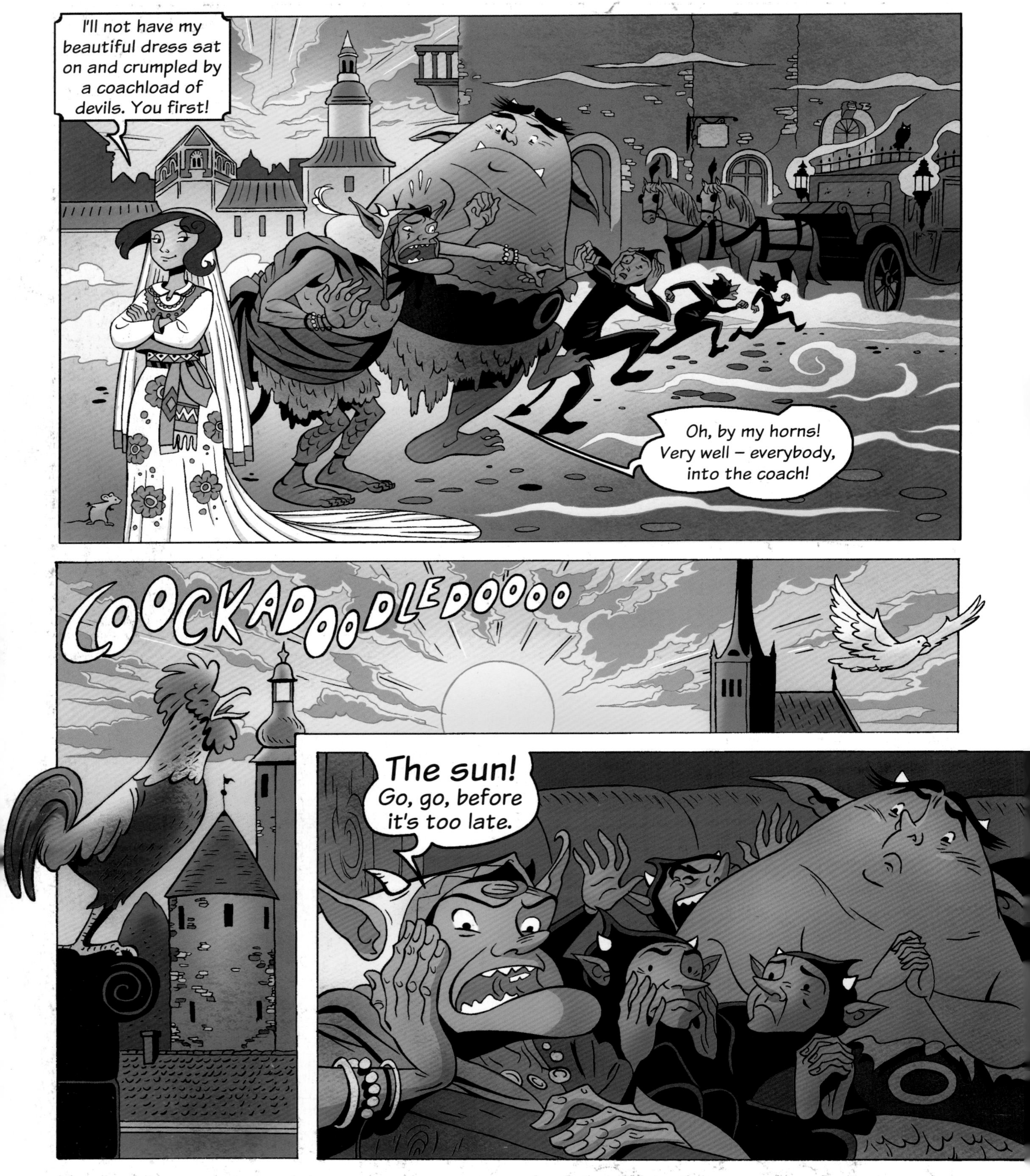
I'll not have my beautiful dress sat on and crumpled by a coachload of devils. You first!
Oh, by my horns! Very well – everybody, into the coach!
COOCKADOOODLEDOOOOO
The sun! Go, go, before it's too late.

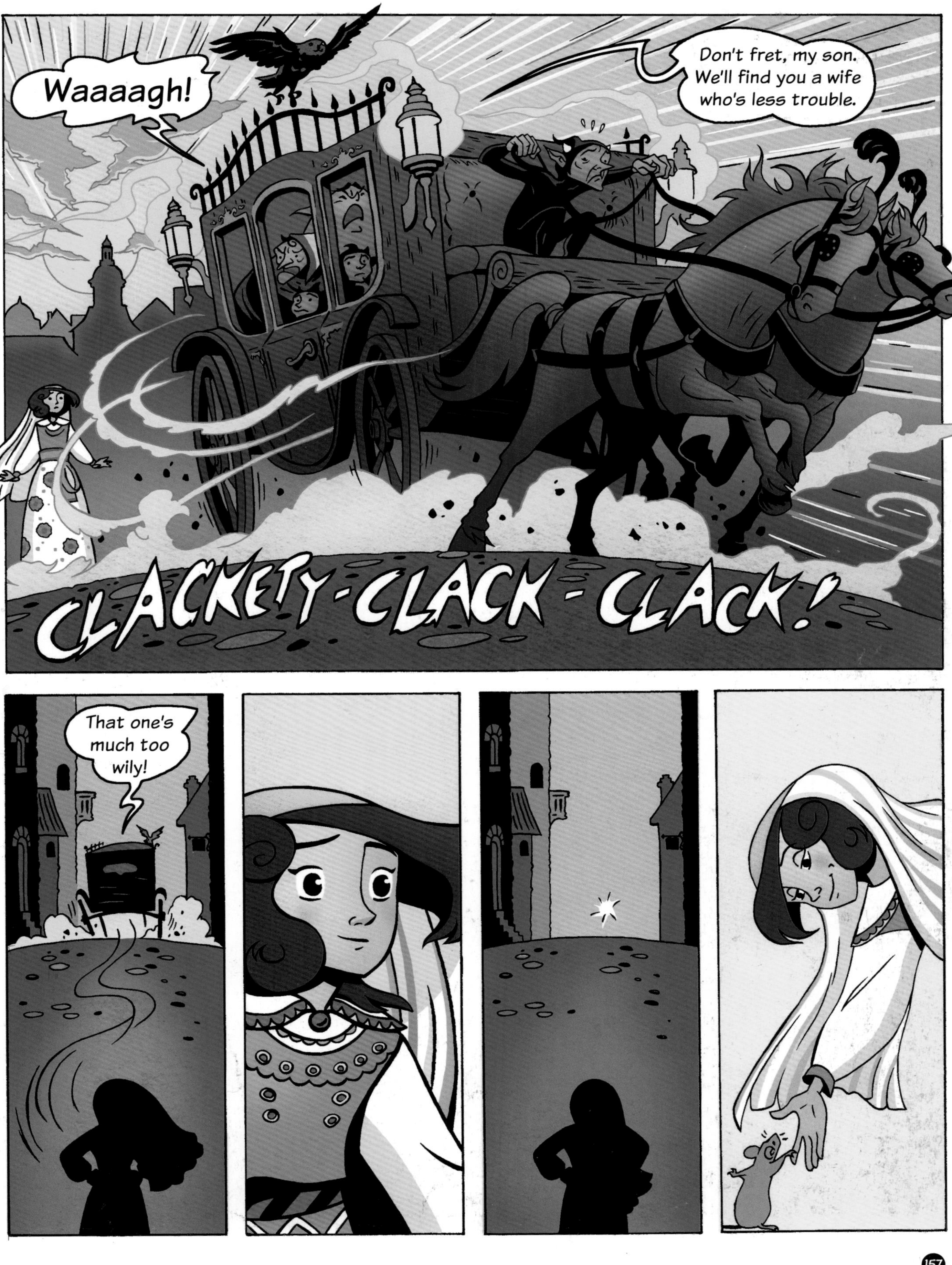
Waaaagh!
Don't fret, my son. We'll find you a wife who's less trouble.
CLACKETY-CLACK-CLACK!
That one's much too wily!

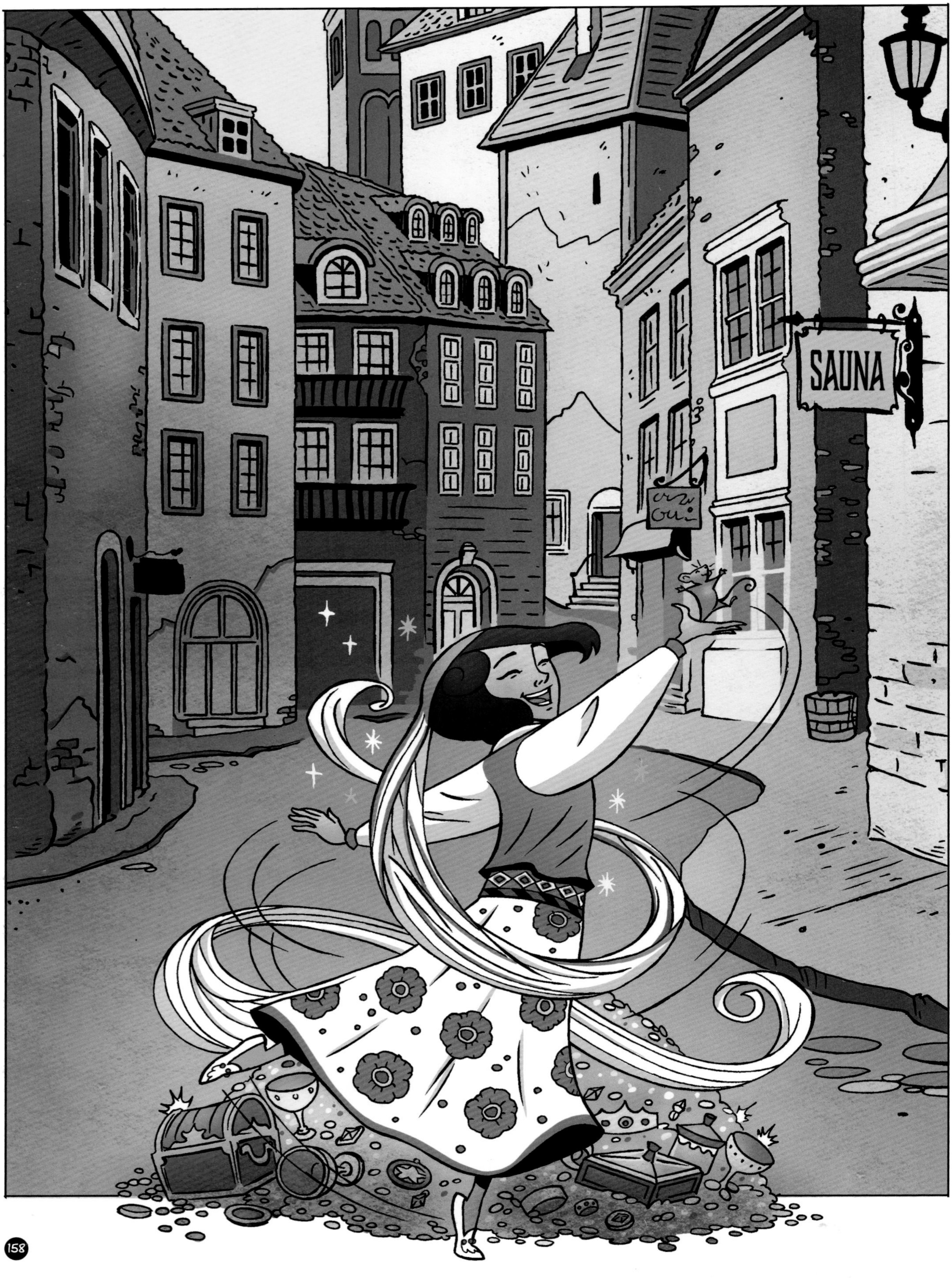
SAUNA

Finn McCool

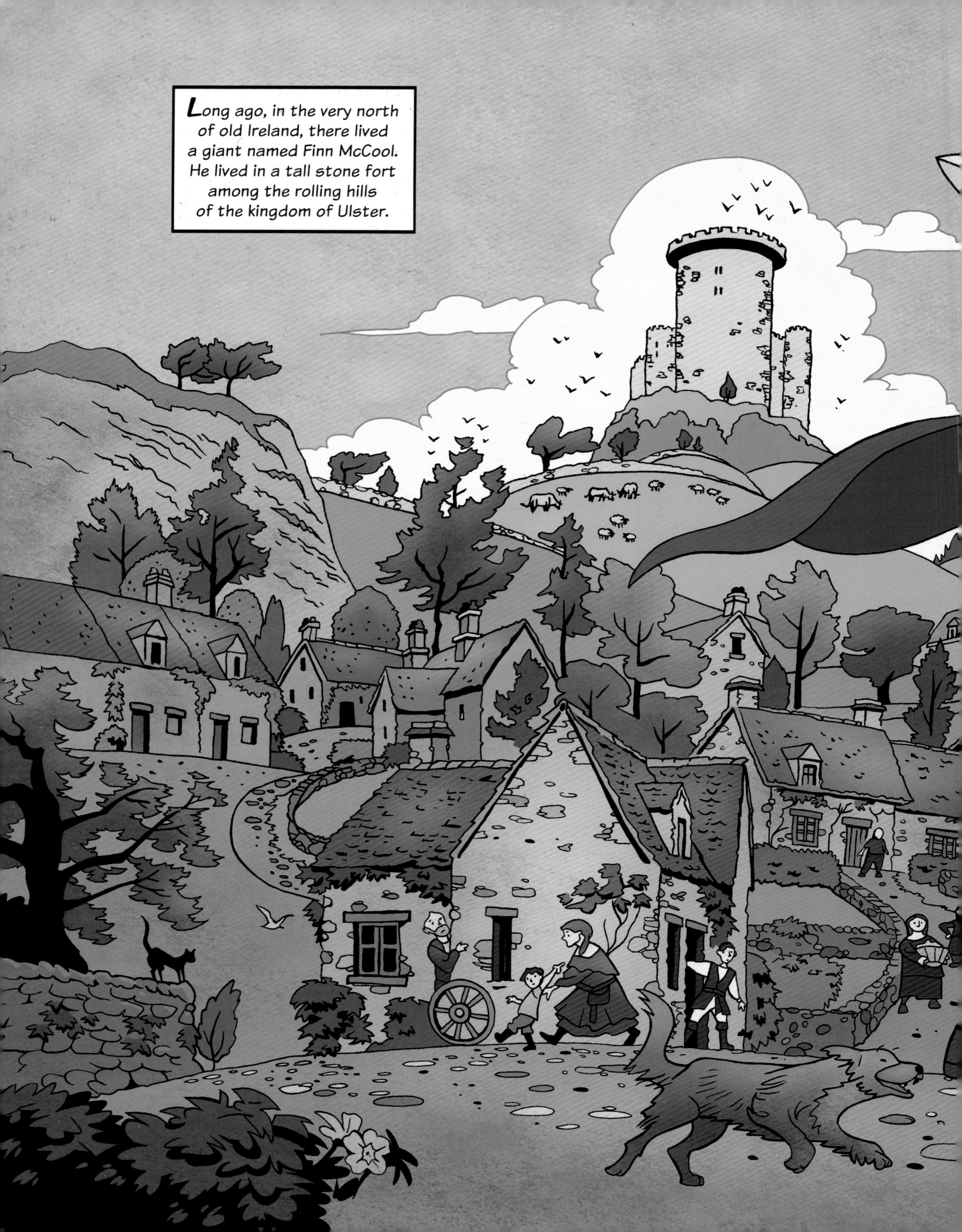
Long ago, in the very north of old Ireland, there lived a giant named Finn McCool. He lived in a tall stone fort among the rolling hills of the kingdom of Ulster.

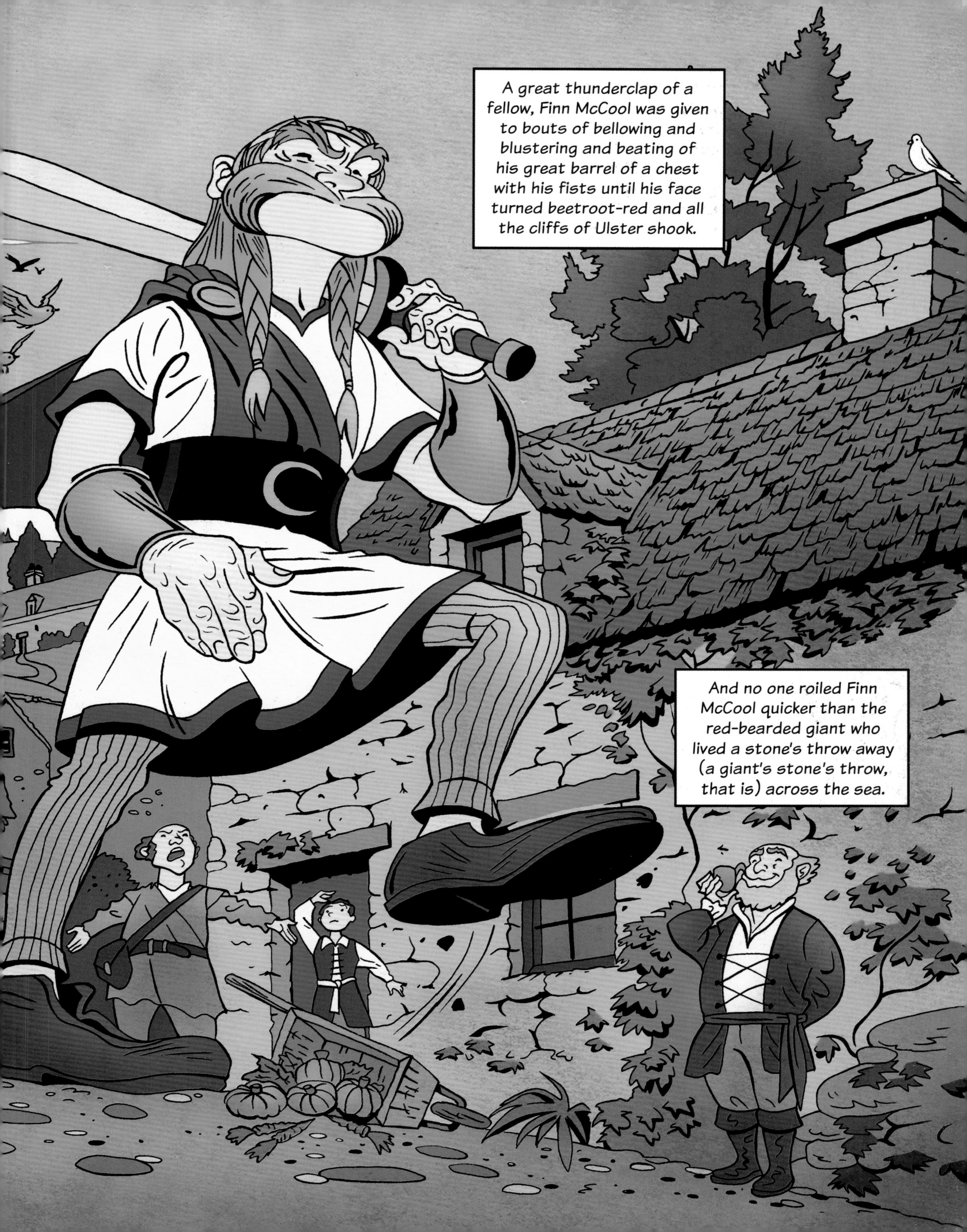
A great thunderclap of a fellow, Finn McCool was given to bouts of bellowing and blustering and beating of his great barrel of a chest with his fists until his face turned beetroot-red and all the cliffs of Ulster shook.
And no one roiled Finn McCool quicker than the red-bearded giant who lived a stone's throw away (a giant's stone's throw, that is) across the sea.

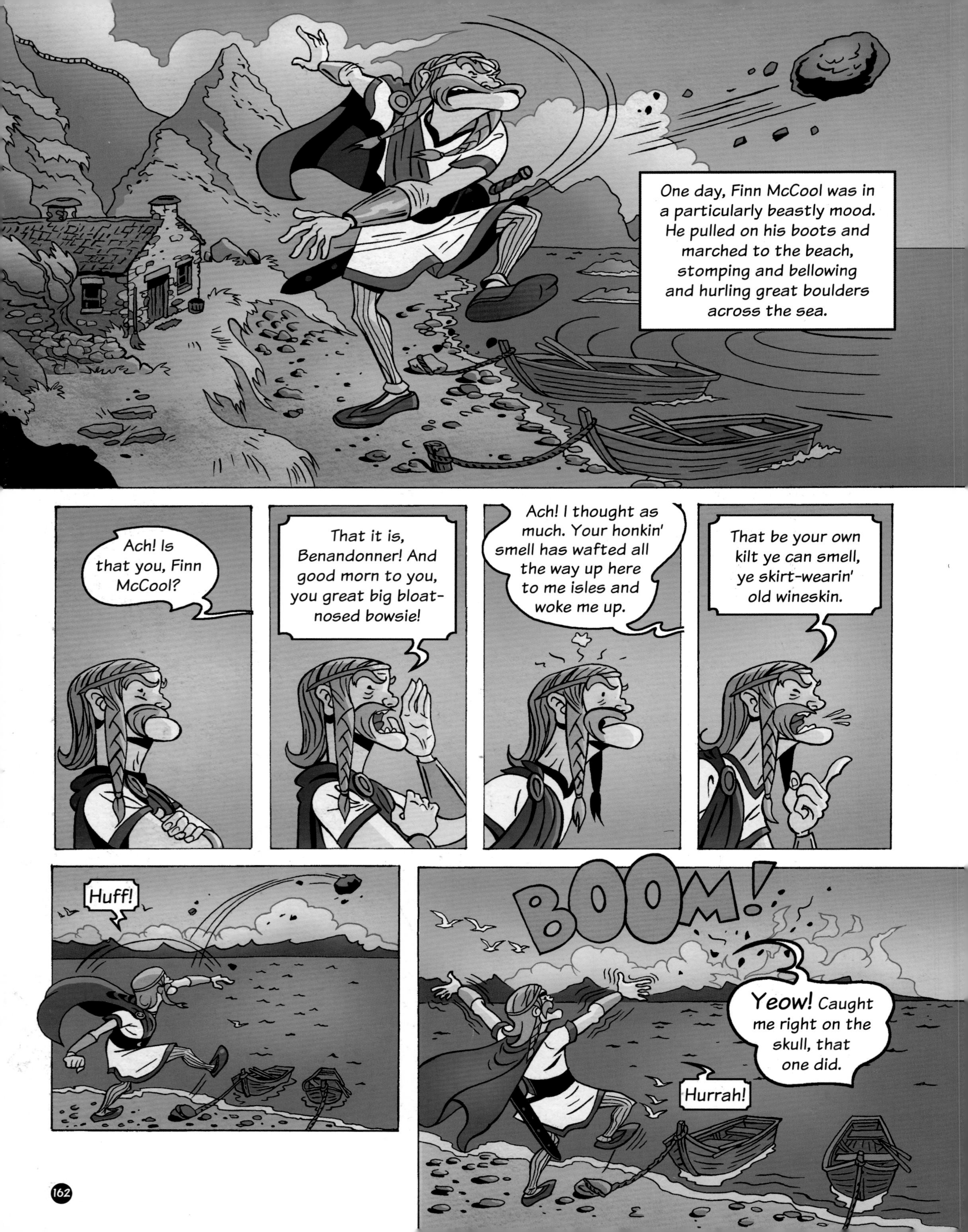
One day, Finn McCool was in a particularly beastly mood. He pulled on his boots and marched to the beach, stomping and bellowing and hurling great boulders across the sea.
Ach! Is that you, Finn McCool?
That it is, Benandonner! And good morn to you, you great big bloat-nosed bowsie!
Ach! I thought as much. Your honkin' smell has wafted all the way up here to me isles and woke me up.
That be your own kilt ye can smell, ye skirt-wearin' old wineskin.
Huff!
BOOM!
Yeow! Caught me right on the skull, that one did.
Hurrah!

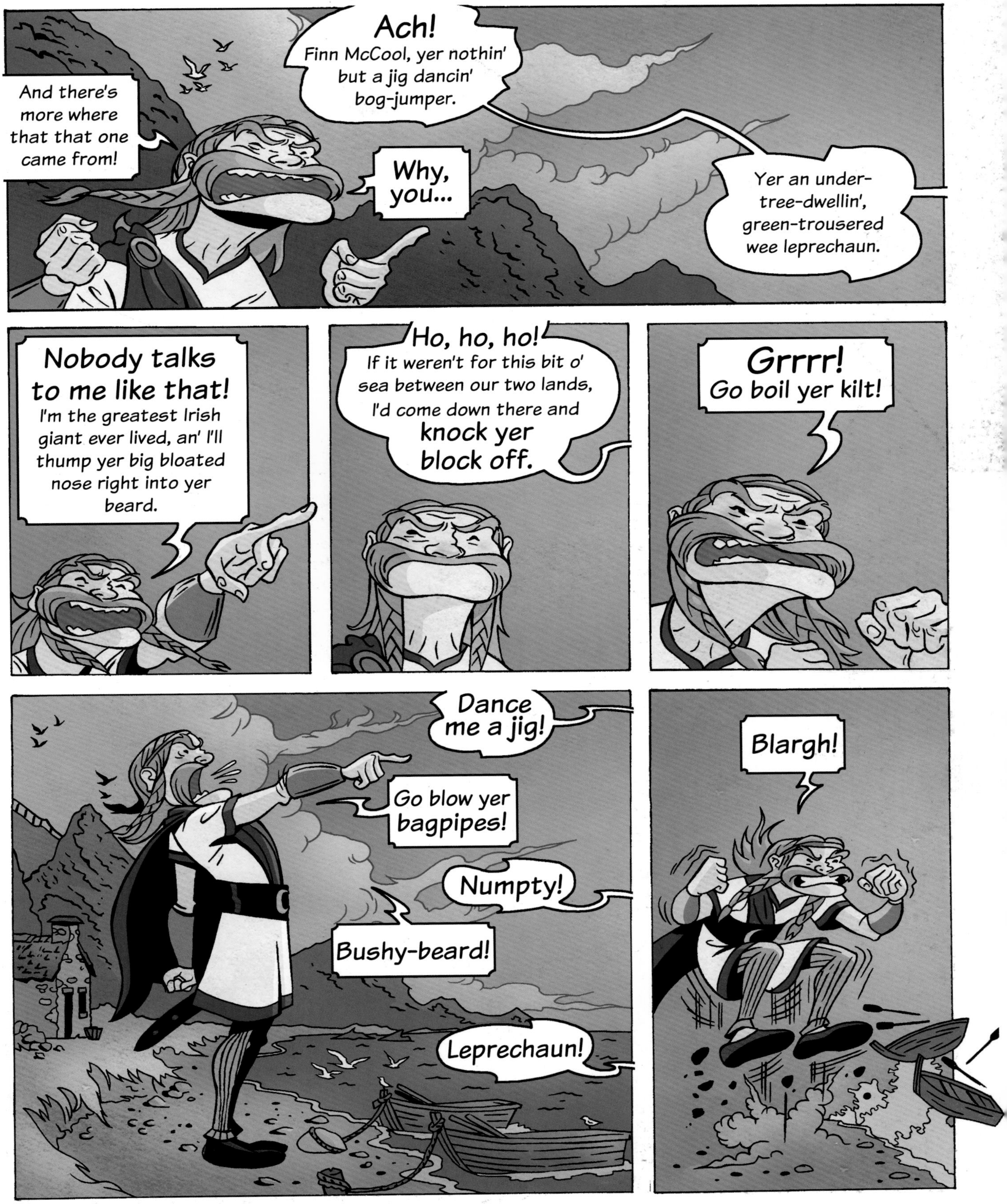
And there's more where that that one came from!
Ach! Finn McCool, yer nothin' but a jig dancin' bog-jumper.
Why, you...
Yer an under-tree-dwellin', green-trousered wee leprechaun.
Nobody talks to me like that! I'm the greatest Irish giant ever lived, an' I'll thump yer big bloated nose right into yer beard.
Ho, ho, ho! If it weren't for this bit o' sea between our two lands, I'd come down there and knock yer block off.
Grrrr! Go boil yer kilt!
Dance me a jig!
Go blow yer bagpipes!
Numpty!
Bushy-beard!
Leprechaun!
Blargh!

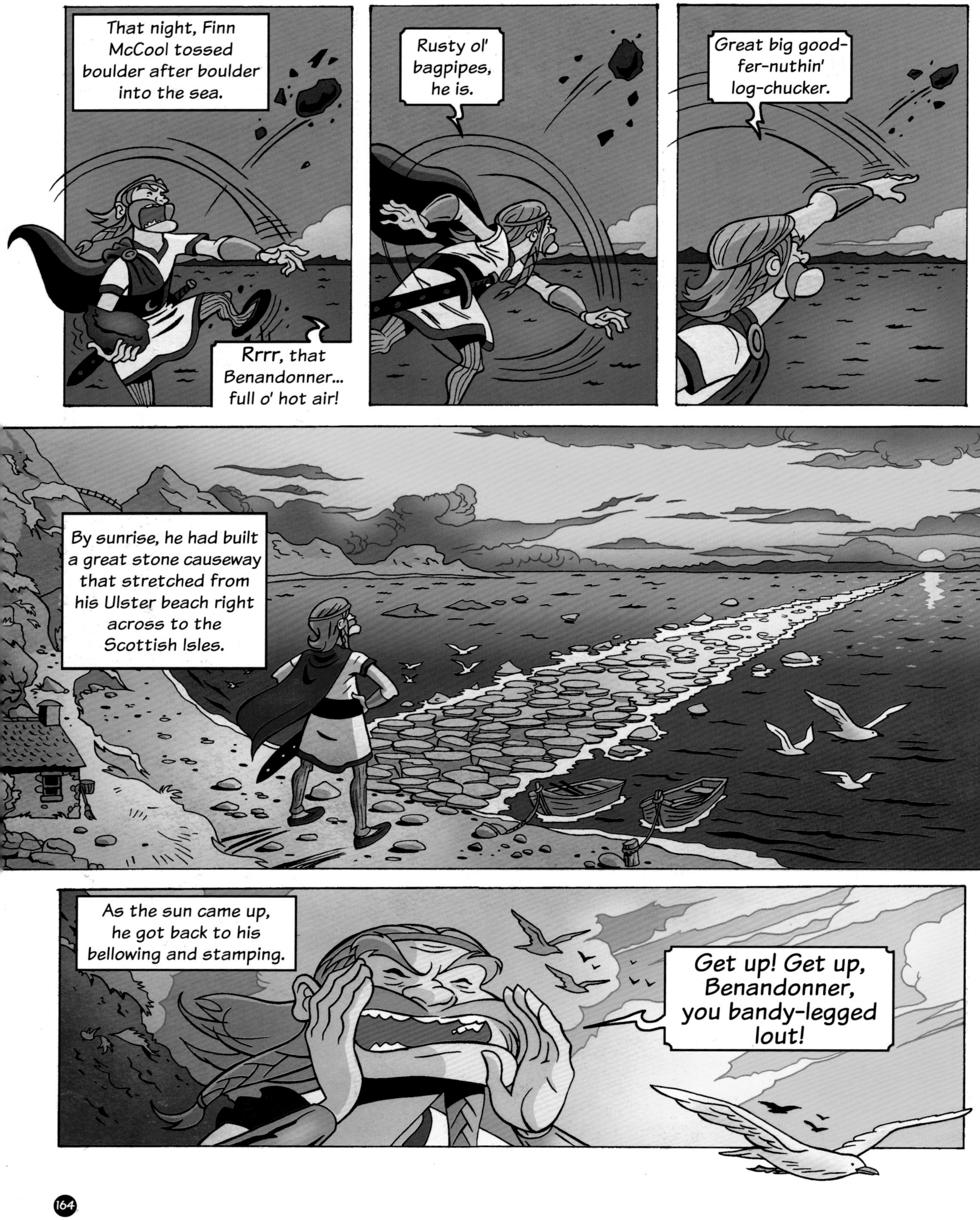
That night, Finn McCool tossed boulder after boulder into the sea.
Rrrr, that Benandonner... full o' hot air!
Rusty ol' bagpipes, he is.
Great big good-fer-nuthin' log-chucker.
By sunrise, he had built a great stone causeway that stretched from his Ulster beach right across to the Scottish Isles.
As the sun came up, he got back to his bellowing and stamping.
Get up! Get up, Benandonner, you bandy-legged lout!

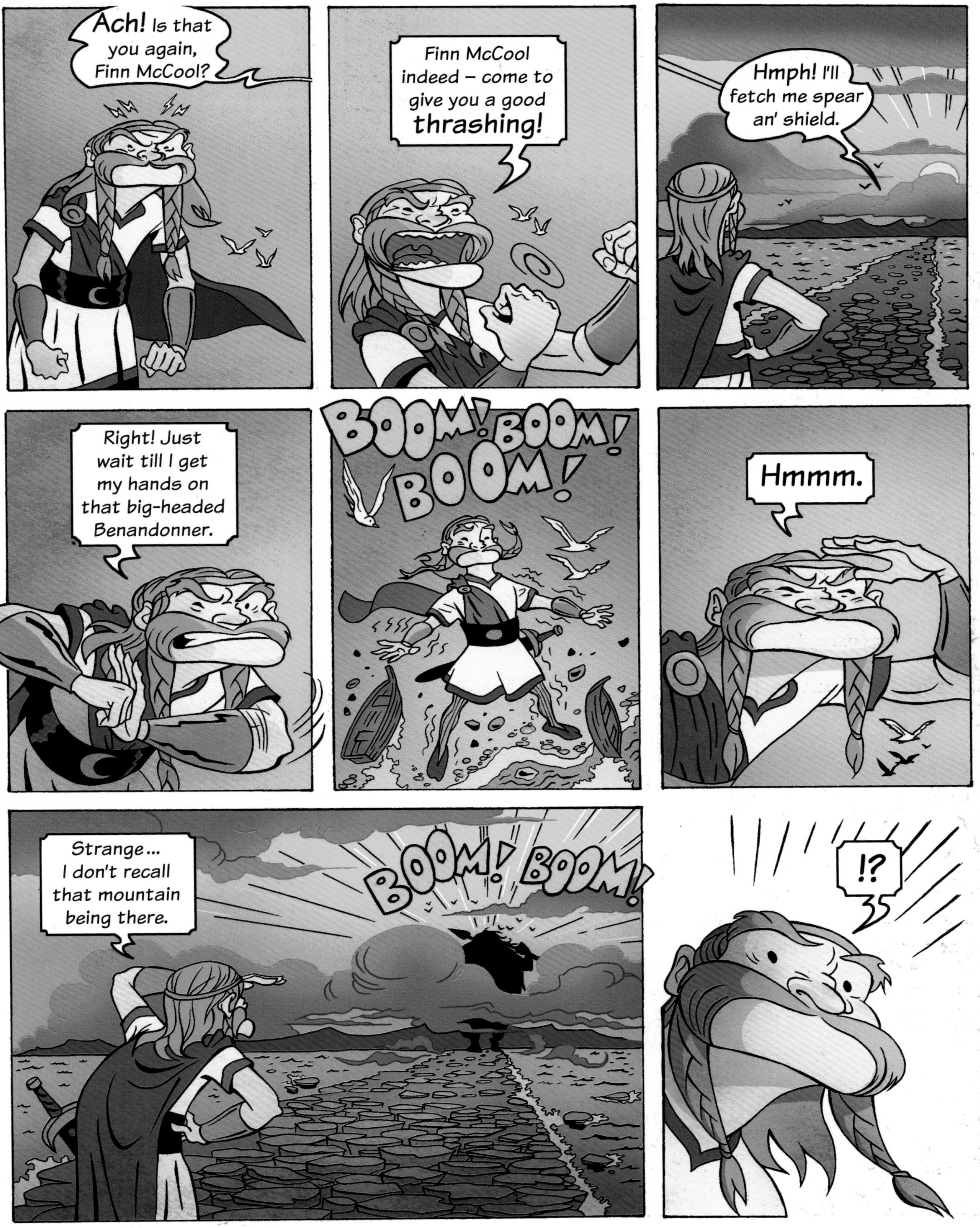
Ach! Is that you again, Finn McCool?
Finn McCool indeed – come to give you a good thrashing!
Hmph! I'll fetch me spear an' shield.
Right! Just wait till I get my hands on that big-headed Benandonner.
BOOM! BOOM! BOOM!
Hmmm.
Strange... I don't recall that mountain being there.
BOOM! BOOM!
!?

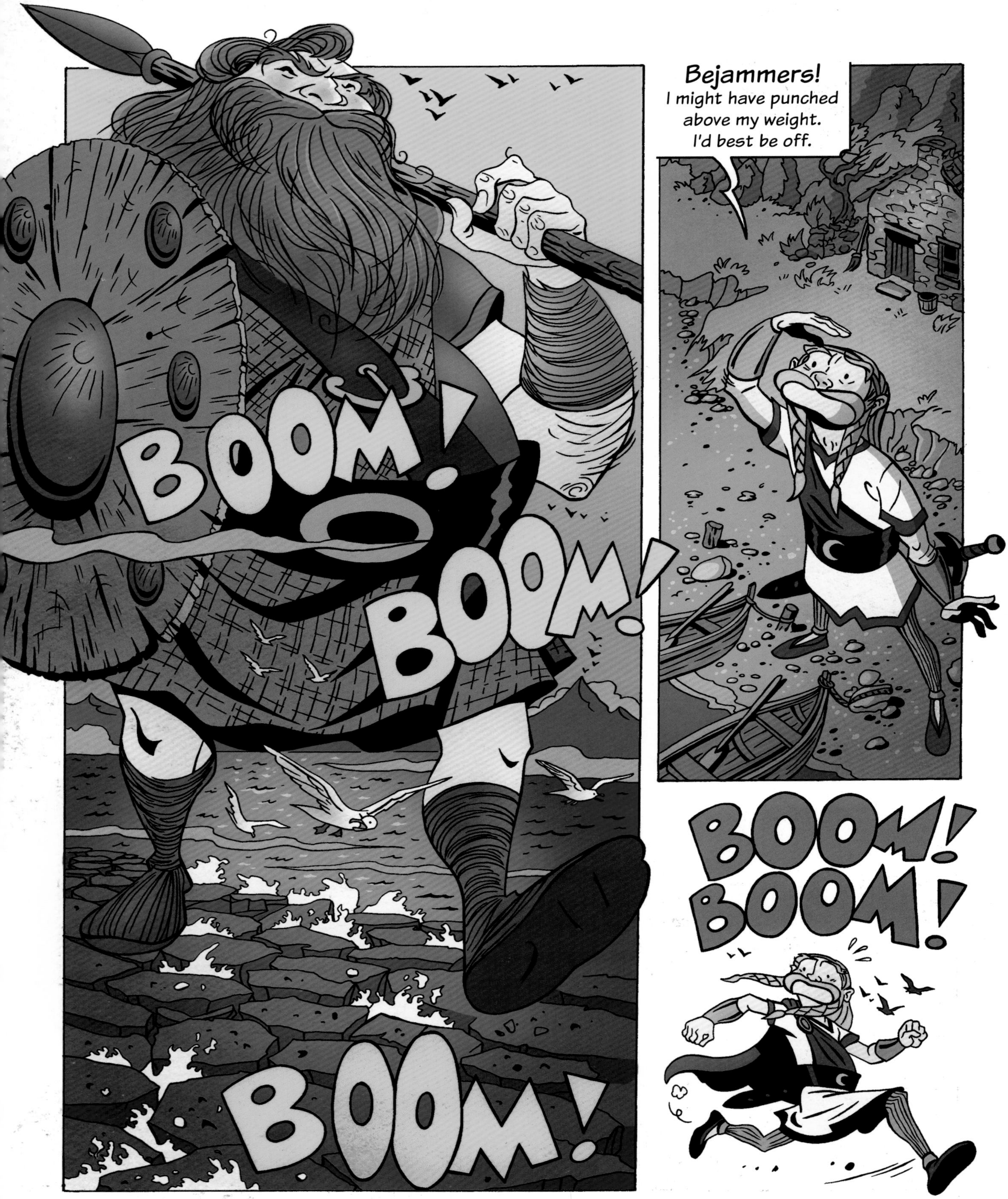
BOOM!
BOOM!
BOOM!
Bejammers! I might have punched above my weight. I'd best be off.
BOOM!
BOOM!

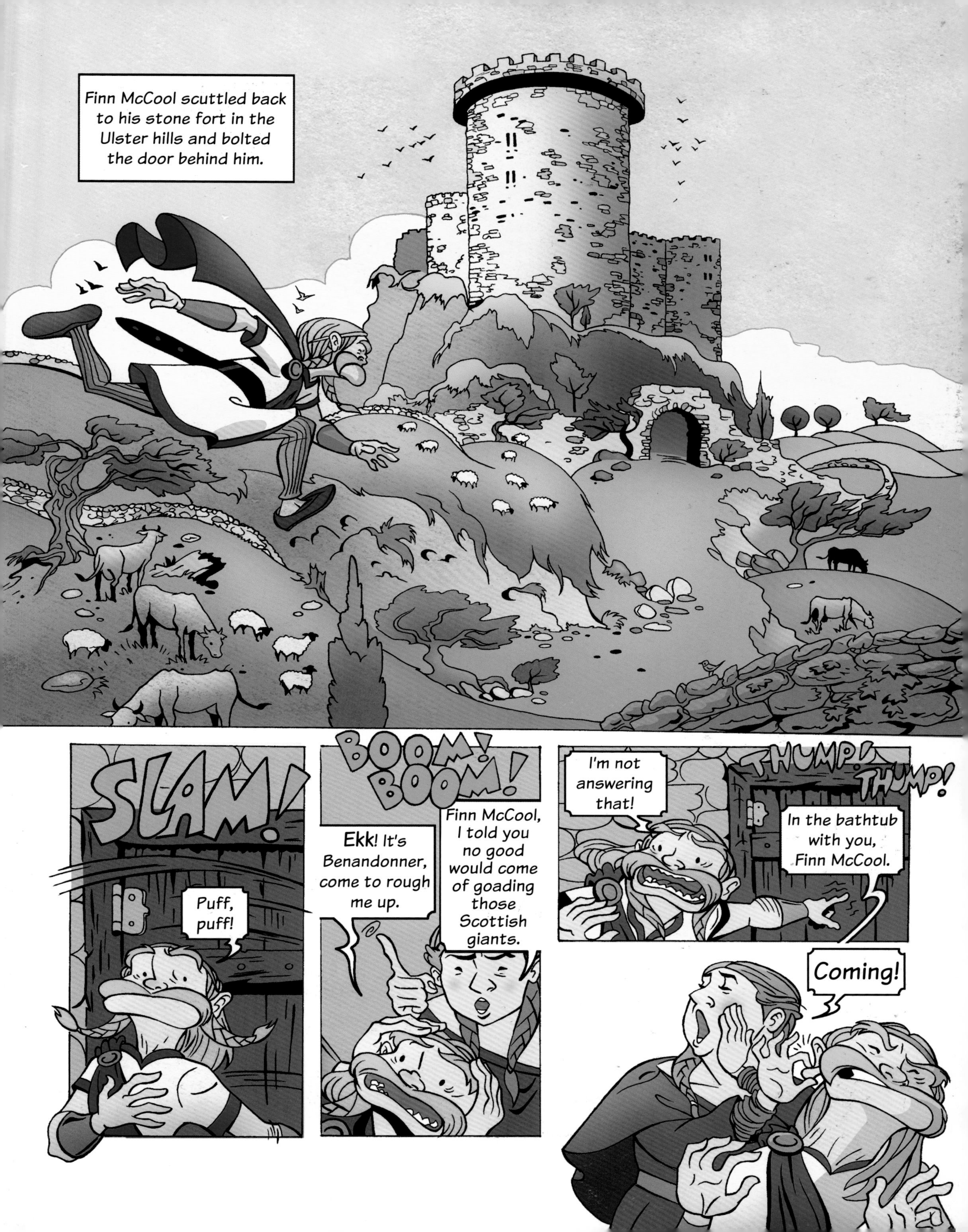
Finn McCool scuttled back to his stone fort in the Ulster hills and bolted the door behind him.
SLAM!
Puff, puff!
BOOM! BOOM!
Ekk! It's Benandonner, come to rough me up.
Finn McCool, I told you no good would come of goading those Scottish giants.
I'm not answering that!
THUMP! THUMP!
In the bathtub with you, Finn McCool.
Coming!

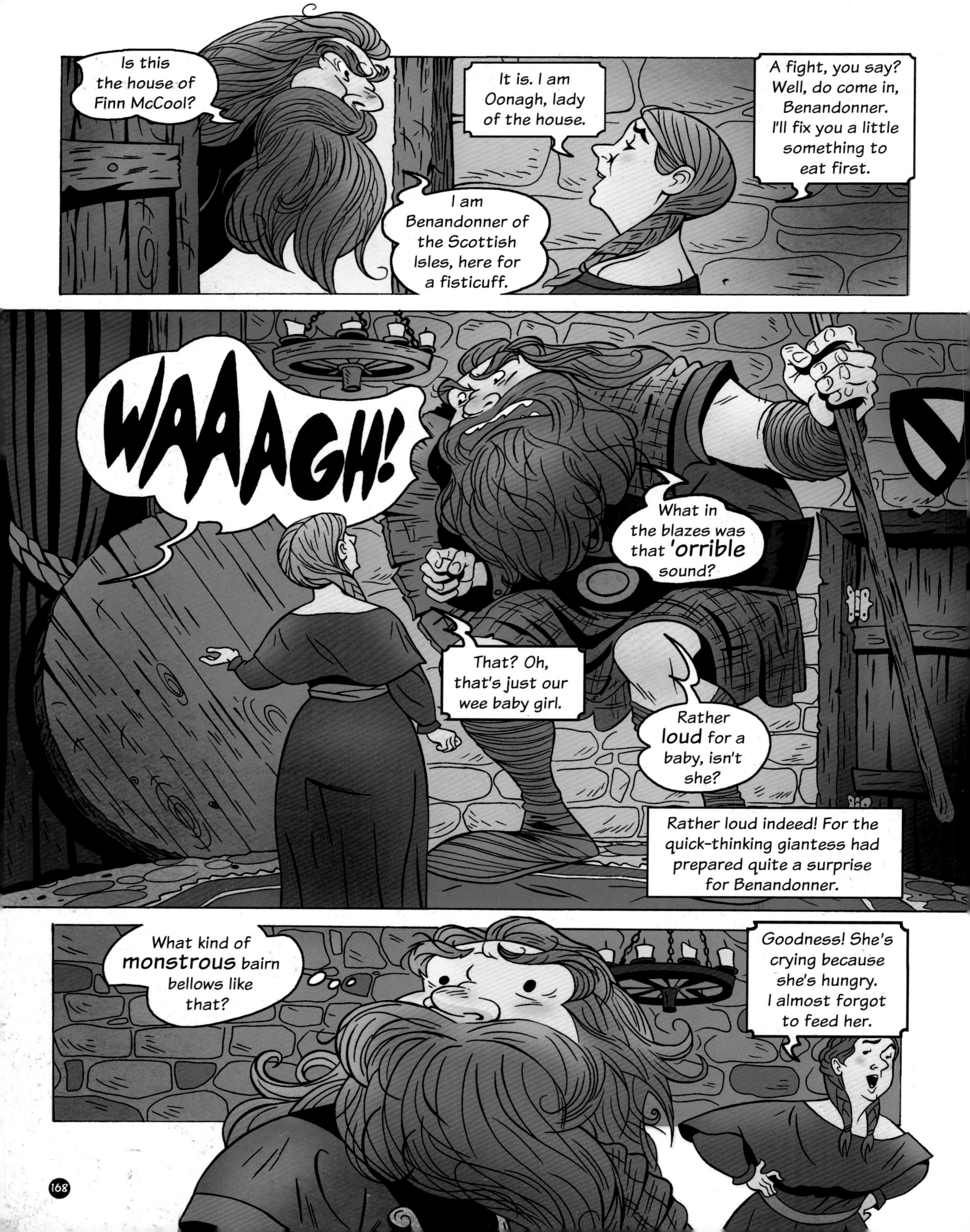
Is this the house of Finn McCool?
I am Benandonner of the Scottish Isles, here for a fisticuff.
It is. I am Oonagh, lady of the house.
A fight, you say? Well, do come in, Benandonner. I'll fix you a little something to eat first.
WAAAGH!
What in the blazes was that 'orrible sound?
That? Oh, that's just our wee baby girl.
Rather loud for a baby, isn't she?
Rather loud indeed! For the quick-thinking giantess had prepared quite a surprise for Benandonner.
What kind of monstrous bairn bellows like that?
Goodness! She's crying because she's hungry. I almost forgot to feed her.

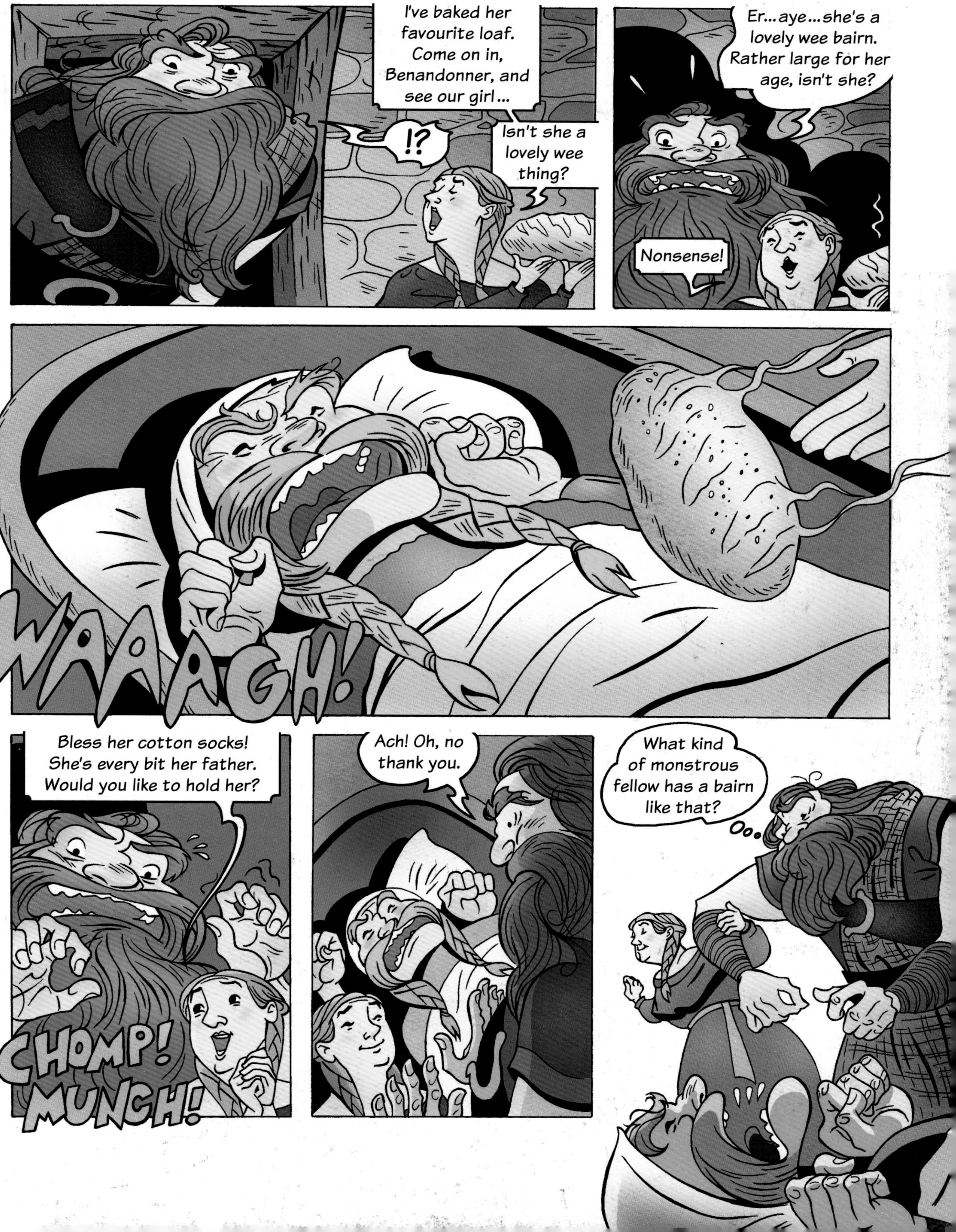
I've baked her favourite loaf. Come on in, Benandonner, and see our girl...
!?
Isn't she a lovely wee thing?
Er...aye...she's a lovely wee bairn. Rather large for her age, isn't she?
Nonsense!
WAAAGH!
Bless her cotton socks! She's every bit her father. Would you like to hold her?
CHOMP! MUNCH!
Ach! Oh, no thank you.
What kind of monstrous fellow has a bairn like that?
Ooo

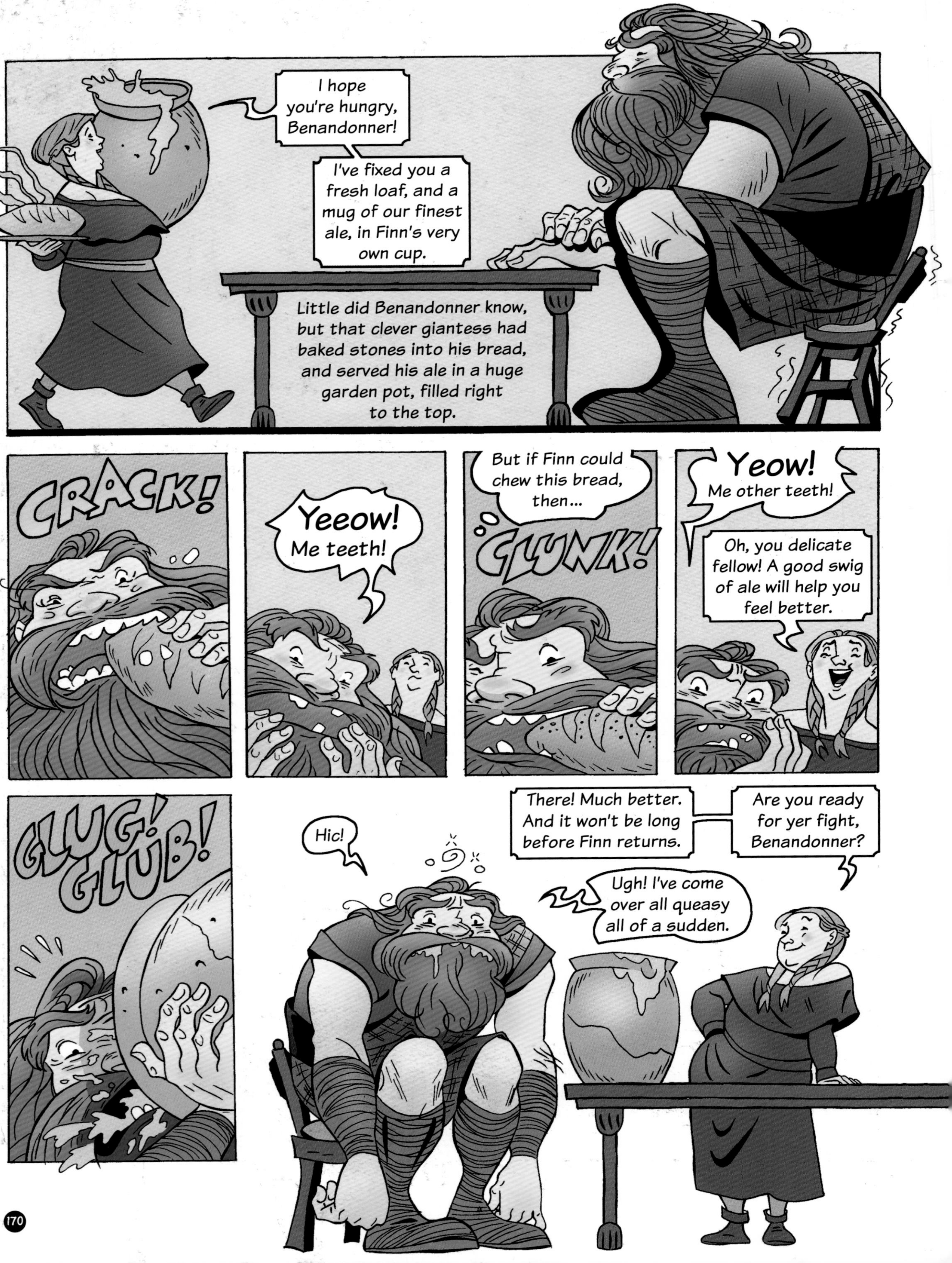
I hope you're hungry, Benandonner!
I've fixed you a fresh loaf, and a mug of our finest ale, in Finn's very own cup.
Little did Benandonner know, but that clever giantess had baked stones into his bread, and served his ale in a huge garden pot, filled right to the top.
CRACK!
Yeeow! Me teeth!
But if Finn could chew this bread, then...
CLUNK!
Yeow! Me other teeth!
Oh, you delicate fellow! A good swig of ale will help you feel better.
GLUG! GLUB!
Hic!
There! Much better. And it won't be long before Finn returns.
Are you ready for yer fight, Benandonner?
Ugh! I've come over all queasy all of a sudden.

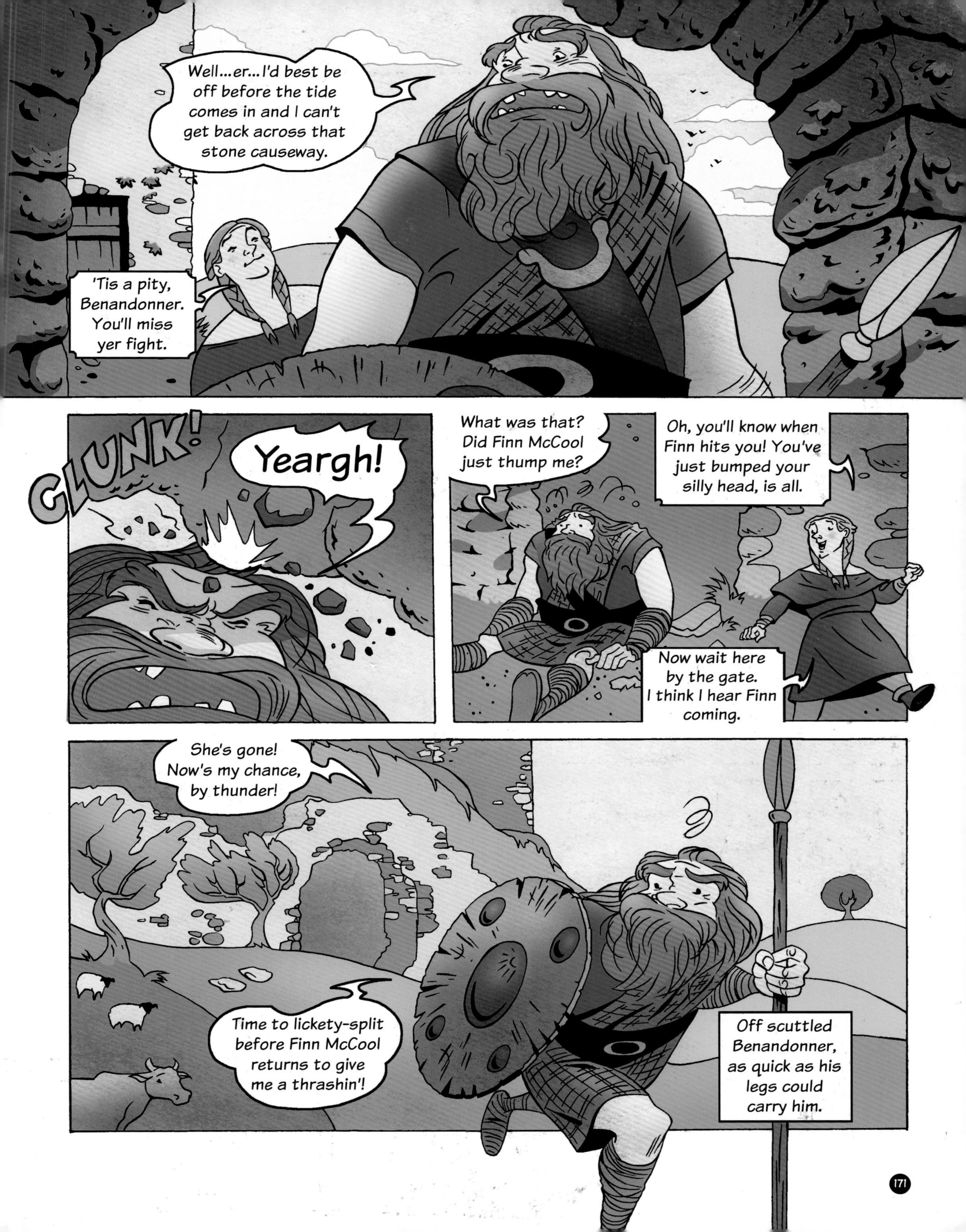
Well...er...I'd best be off before the tide comes in and I can't get back across that stone causeway.
'Tis a pity, Benandonner. You'll miss yer fight.
GLUNK!
Yeargh!
What was that? Did Finn McCool just thump me?
Oh, you'll know when Finn hits you! You've just bumped your silly head, is all.
Now wait here by the gate. I think I hear Finn coming.
She's gone! Now's my chance, by thunder!
Time to lickety-split before Finn McCool returns to give me a thrashin'!
Off scuttled Benandonner, as quick as his legs could carry him.

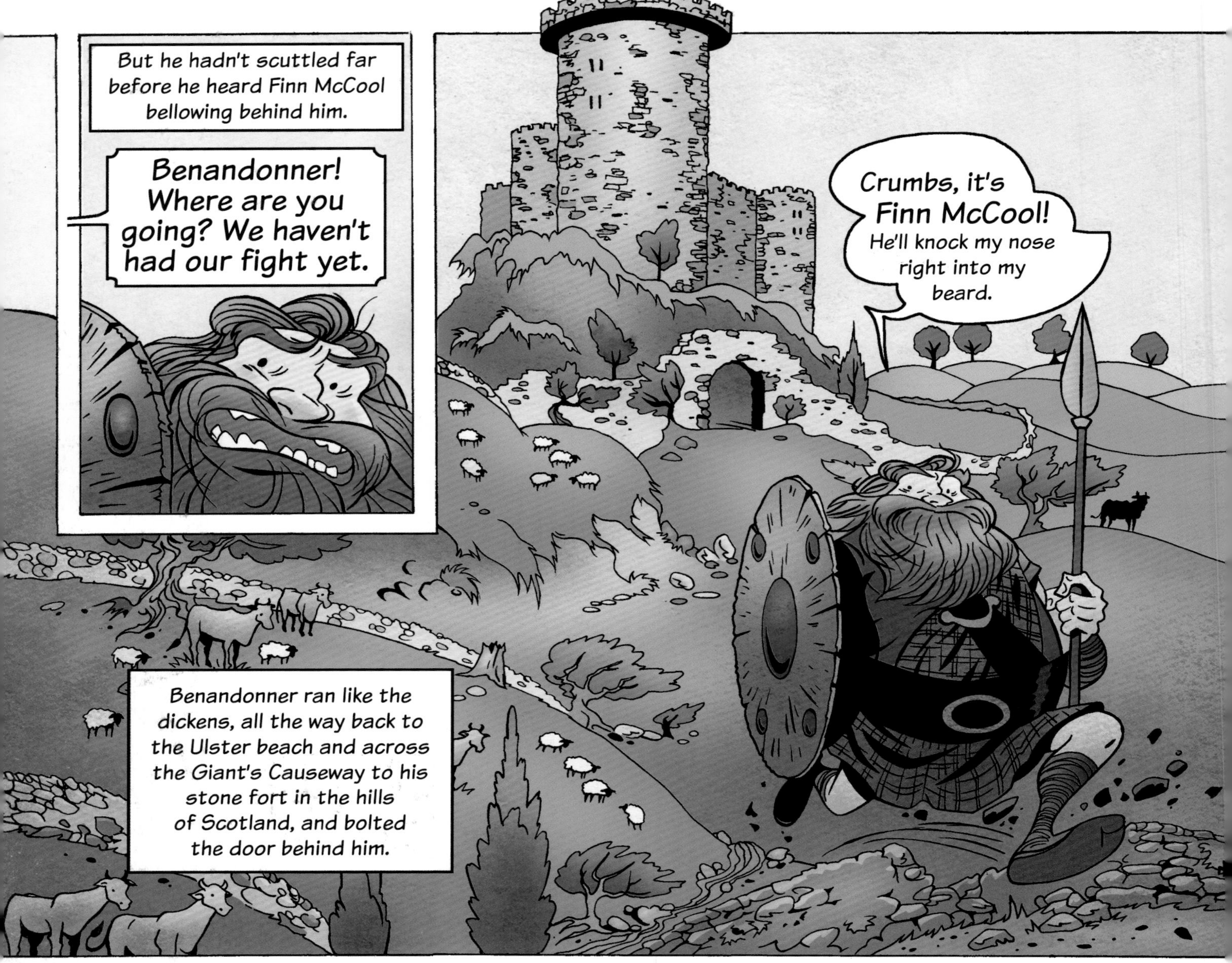
But he hadn't scuttled far before he heard Finn McCool bellowing behind him.
Benandonner! Where are you going? We haven't had our fight yet.
Crumbs, it's Finn McCool! He'll knock my nose right into my beard.
Benandonner ran like the dickens, all the way back to the Ulster beach and across the Giant's Causeway to his stone fort in the hills of Scotland, and bolted the door behind him.

And that is the tale of how Oonagh's quick wit saved Finn McCool's skin, and how the Giant's Causeway came to be.

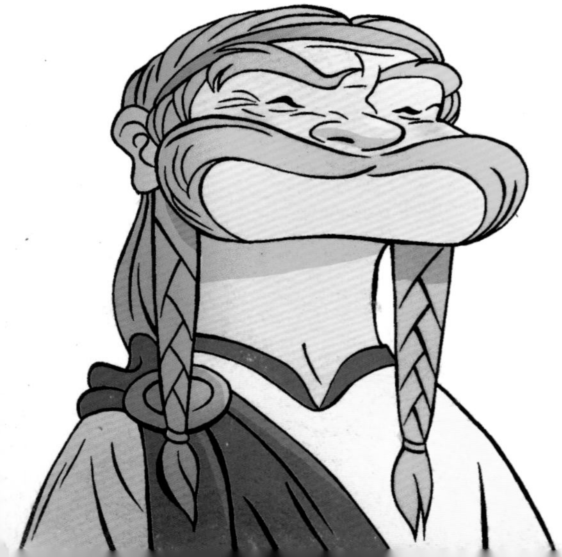

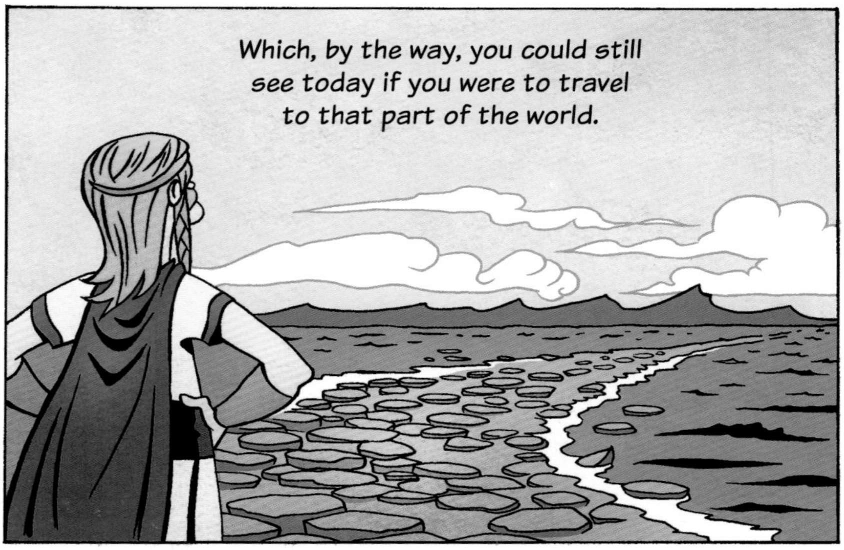
Which, by the way, you could still see today if you were to travel to that part of the world.

The Wawel Dragon

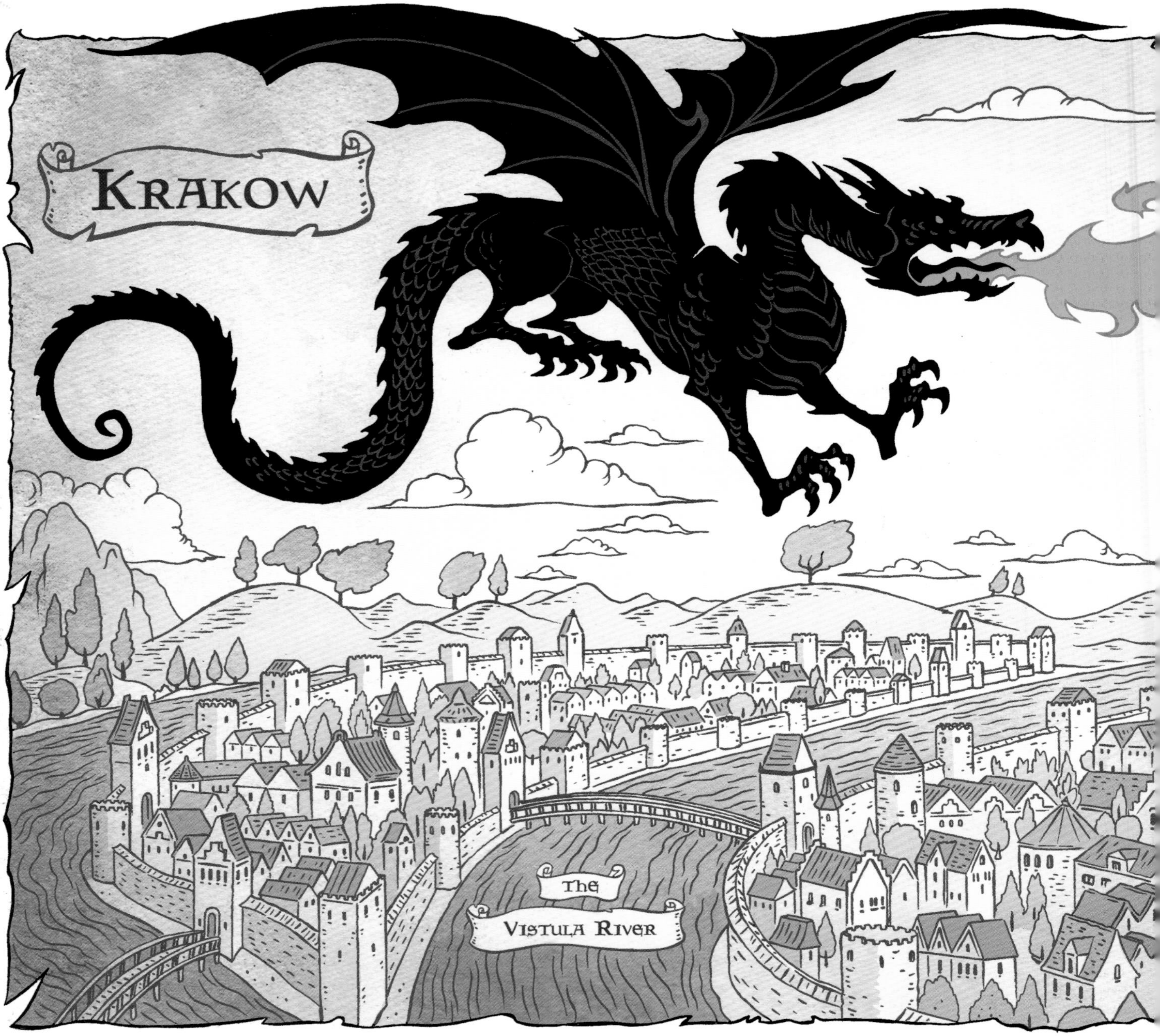
Krakow
The
Vistula River

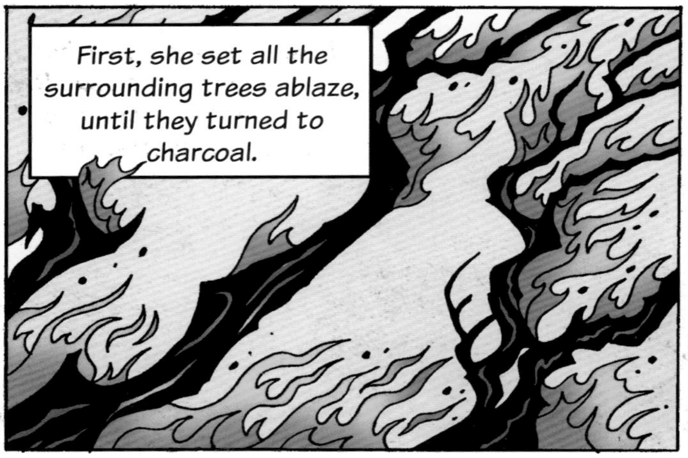
First, she set all the surrounding trees ablaze, until they turned to charcoal.

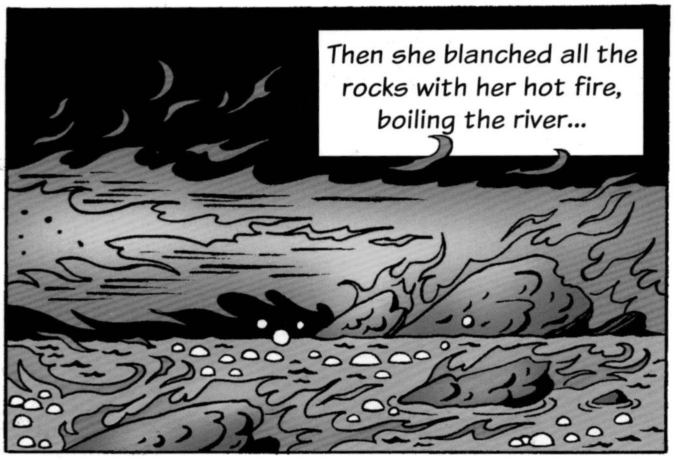
Then she blanched all the rocks with her hot fire, boiling the river...

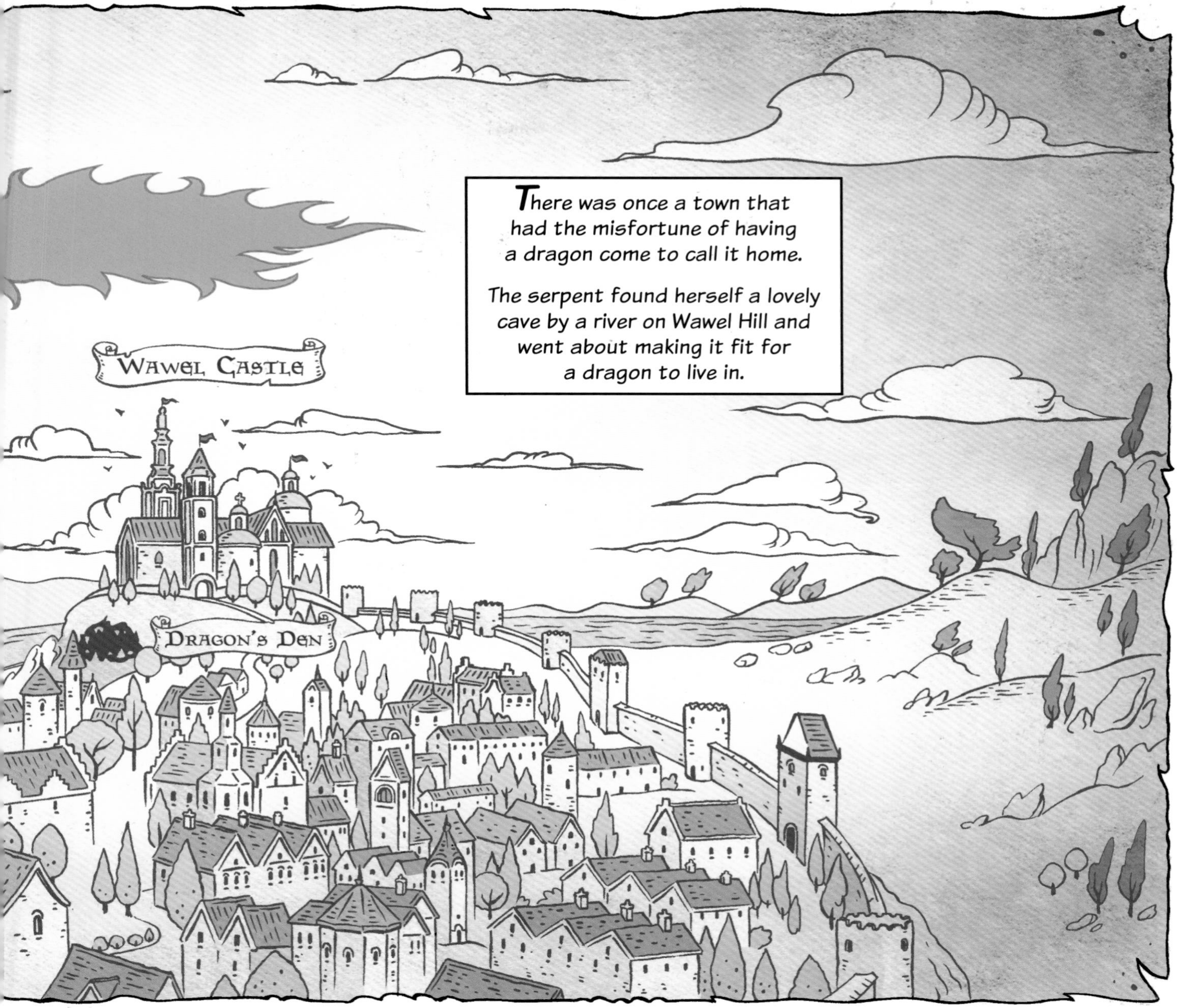
There was once a town that had the misfortune of having a dragon come to call it home.
The serpent found herself a lovely cave by a river on Wawel Hill and went about making it fit for a dragon to live in.
Wawel Castle
Dragon's Den

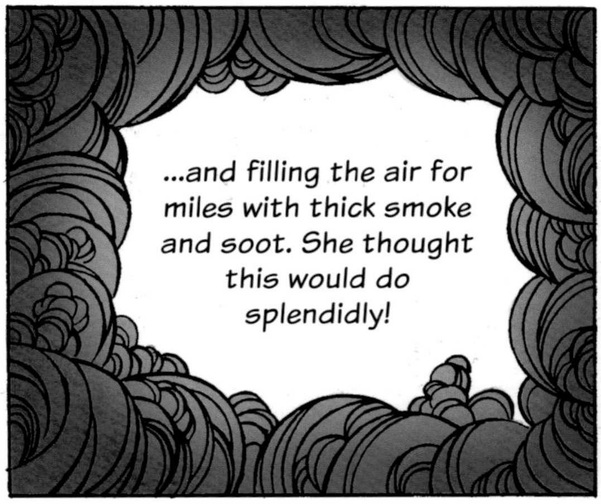
...and filling the air for miles with thick smoke and soot. She thought this would do splendidly!

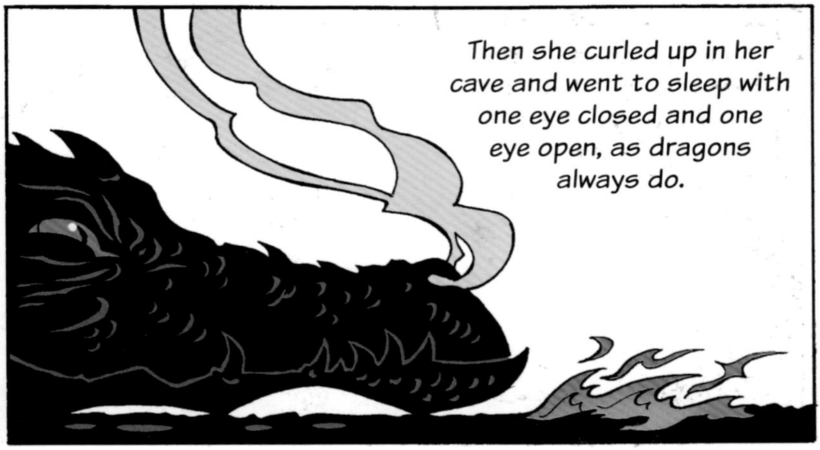
Then she curled up in her cave and went to sleep with one eye closed and one eye open, as dragons always do.

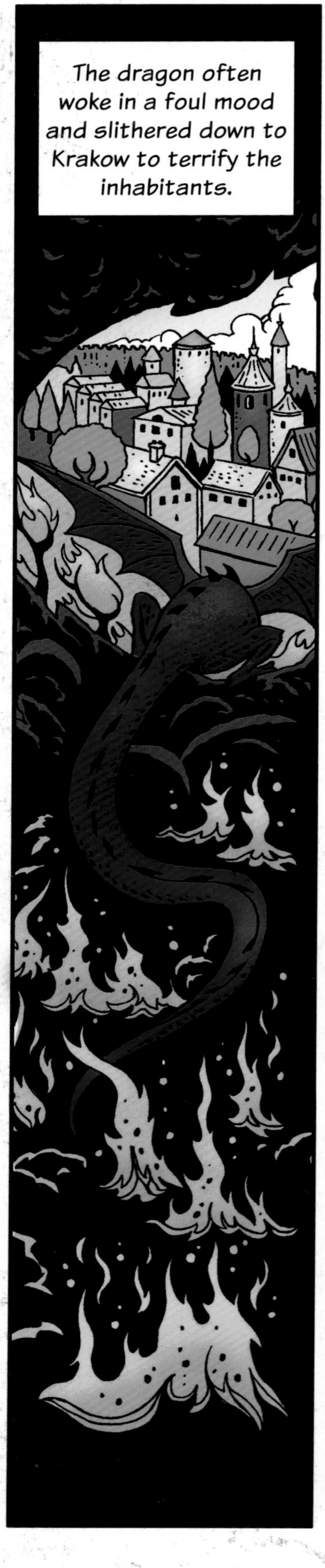
The dragon often woke in a foul mood and slithered down to Krakow to terrify the inhabitants.

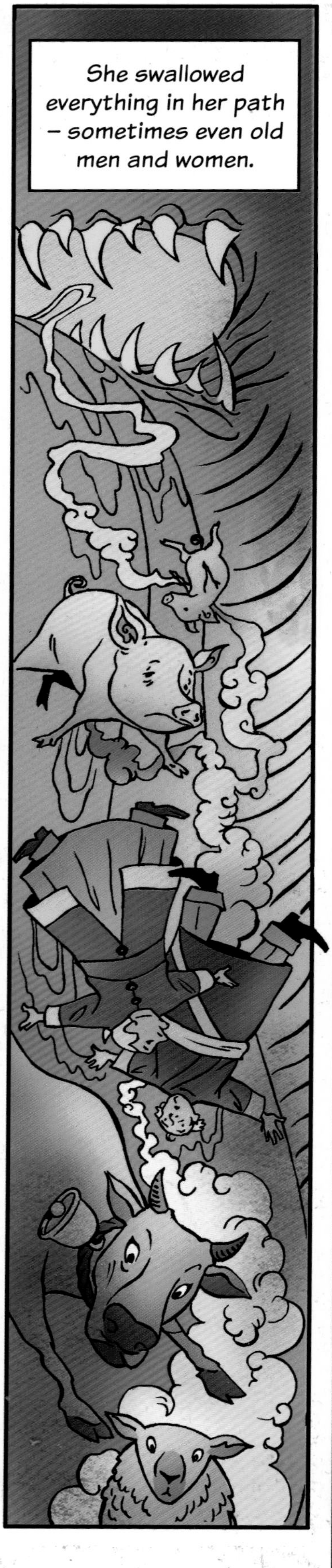
She swallowed everything in her path – sometimes even old men and women.

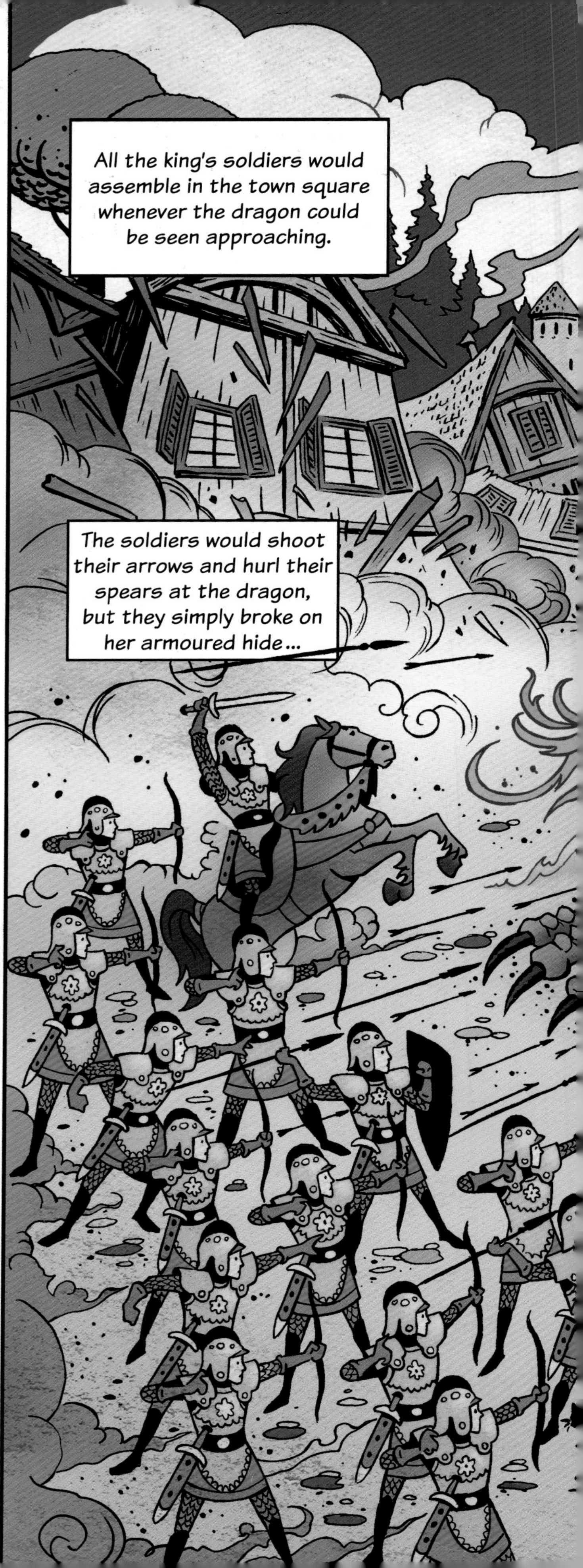
All the king's soldiers would assemble in the town square whenever the dragon could be seen approaching.
The soldiers would shoot their arrows and hurl their spears at the dragon, but they simply broke on her armoured hide...

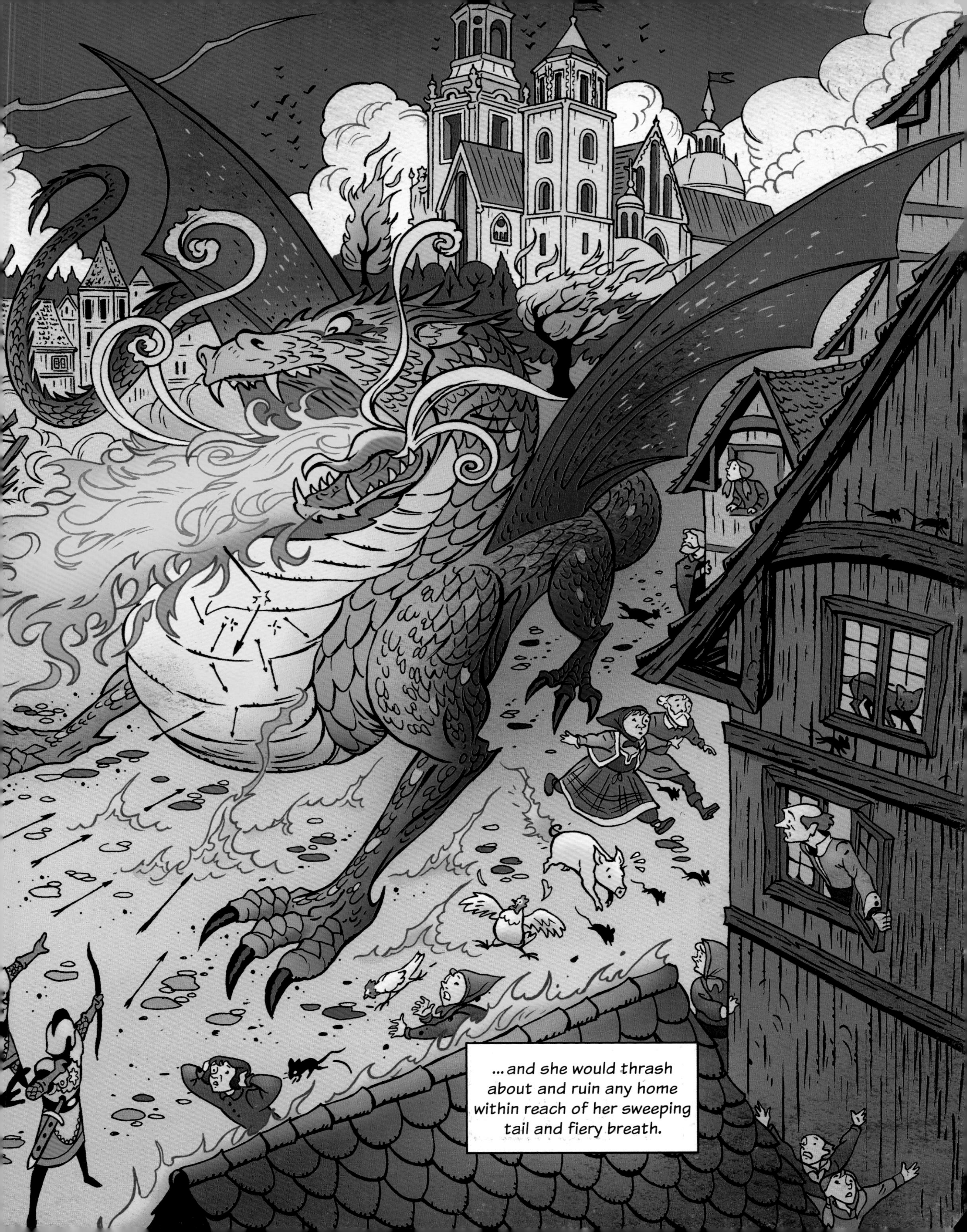
...and she would thrash
about and ruin any home
within reach of her sweeping
tail and fiery breath.

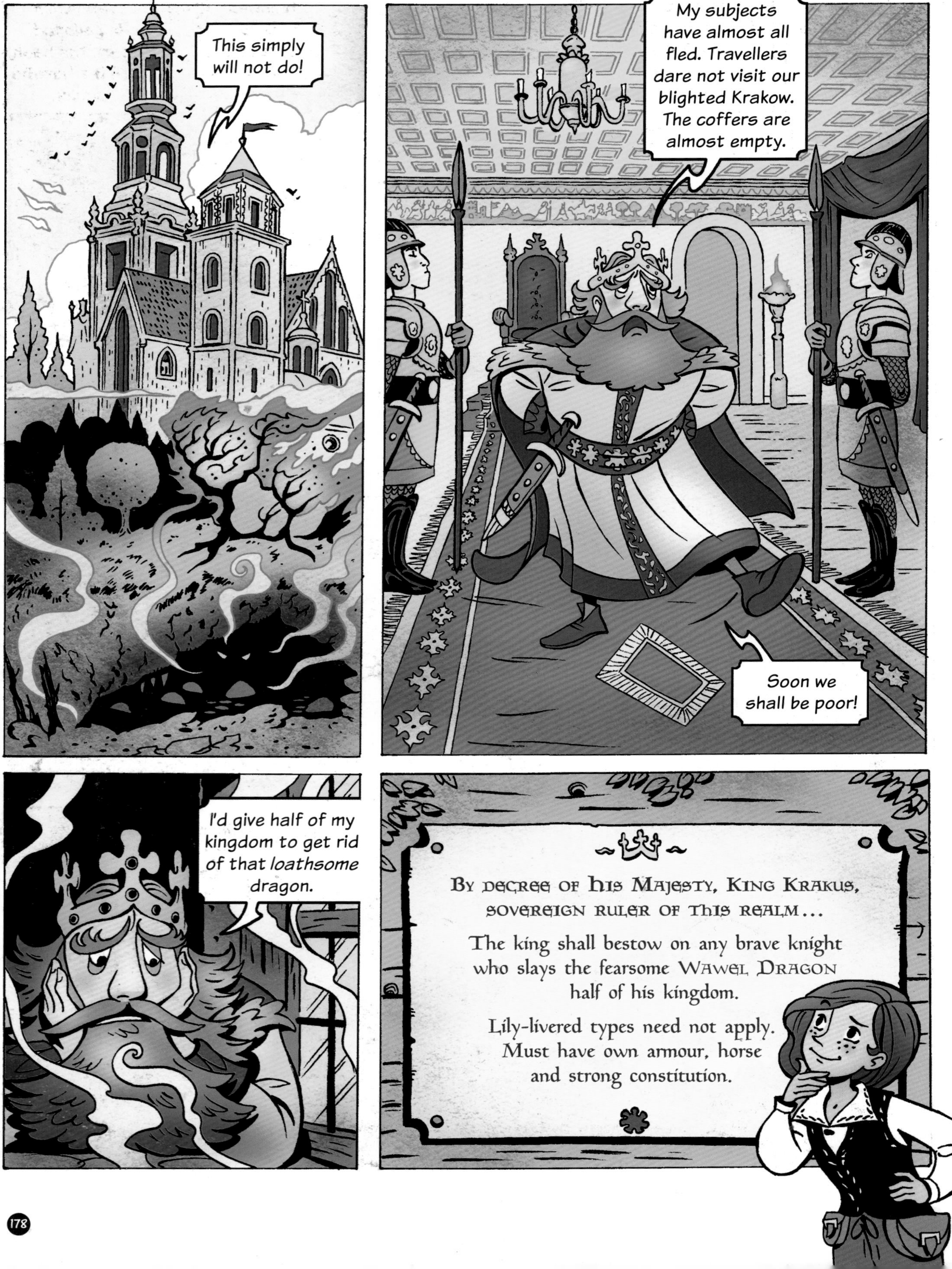
This simply will not do!
My subjects have almost all fled. Travellers dare not visit our blighted Krakow. The coffers are almost empty.
Soon we shall be poor!
I'd give half of my kingdom to get rid of that loathsome dragon.
By decree of his Majesty, King Krakus, sovereign ruler of this realm…
The king shall bestow on any brave knight who slays the fearsome Wawel Dragon half of his kingdom.
Lily-livered types need not apply. Must have own armour, horse and strong constitution.

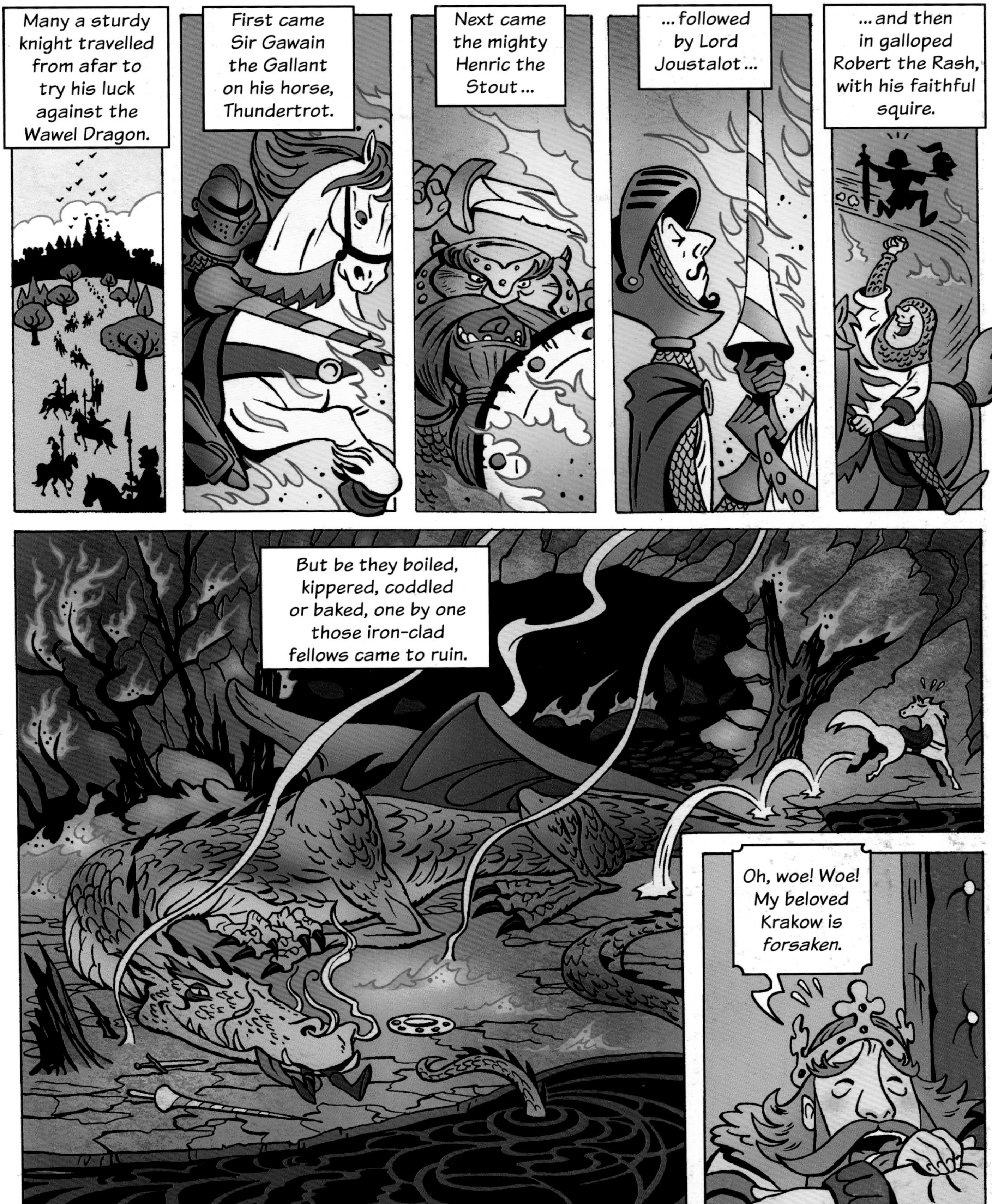
Many a sturdy knight travelled from afar to try his luck against the Wawel Dragon.
First came Sir Gawain the Gallant on his horse, Thundertrot.
Next came the mighty Henric the Stout ...
... followed by Lord Joustalot ...
... and then in galloped Robert the Rash, with his faithful squire.
But be they boiled, kippered, coddled or baked, one by one those iron-clad fellows came to ruin.
Oh, woe! Woe! My beloved Krakow is forsaken.

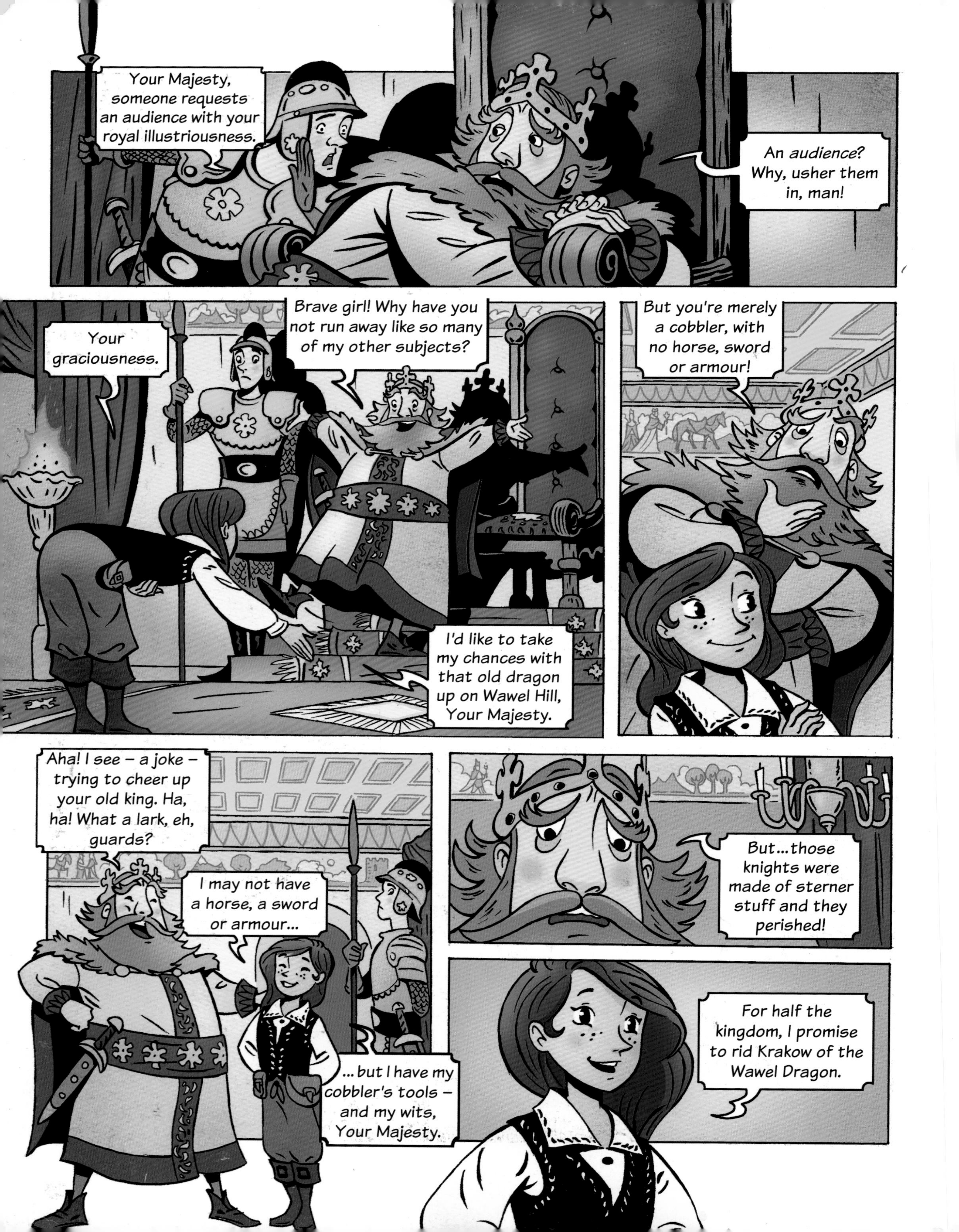

Your Majesty, someone requests an audience with your royal illustriousness.
An *audience*? Why, usher them in, man!
Your graciousness.
Brave girl! Why have you not run away like so many of my other subjects?
I'd like to take my chances with that old dragon up on Wawel Hill, Your Majesty.
But you're merely a cobbler, with no horse, sword or armour!
Aha! I see – a joke – trying to cheer up your old king. Ha, ha! What a lark, eh, guards?
I may not have a horse, a sword or armour...
...but I have my cobbler's tools – and my wits, Your Majesty.
But...those knights were made of sterner stuff and they perished!
For half the kingdom, I promise to rid Krakow of the Wawel Dragon.

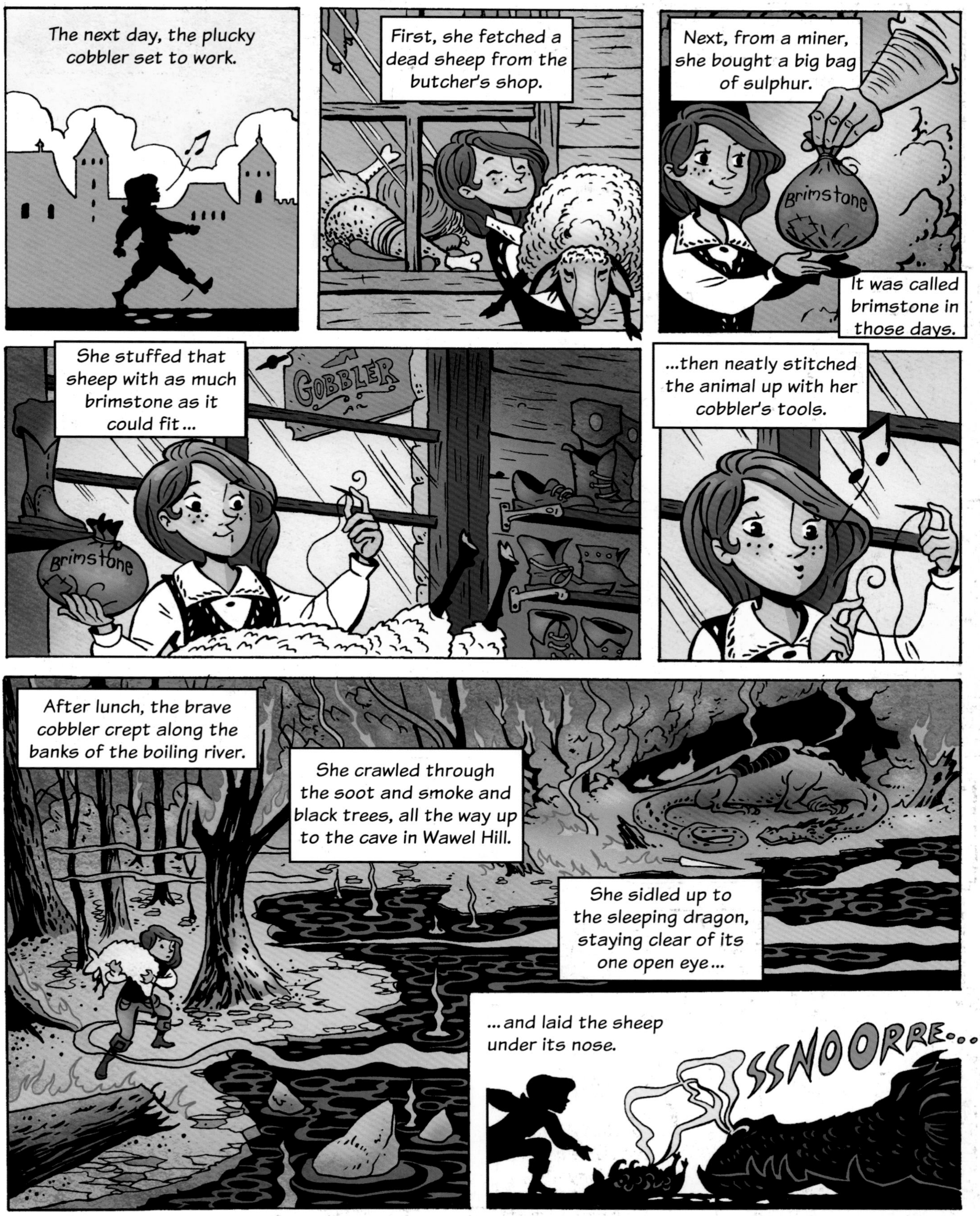
The next day, the plucky cobbler set to work.
First, she fetched a dead sheep from the butcher's shop.
Next, from a miner, she bought a big bag of sulphur.
Brimstone
It was called brimstone in those days.
She stuffed that sheep with as much brimstone as it could fit...
GOBBLER
Brimstone
...then neatly stitched the animal up with her cobbler's tools.
After lunch, the brave cobbler crept along the banks of the boiling river.
She crawled through the soot and smoke and black trees, all the way up to the cave in Wawel Hill.
She sidled up to the sleeping dragon, staying clear of its one open eye...
...and laid the sheep under its nose.
SSNOORRE...

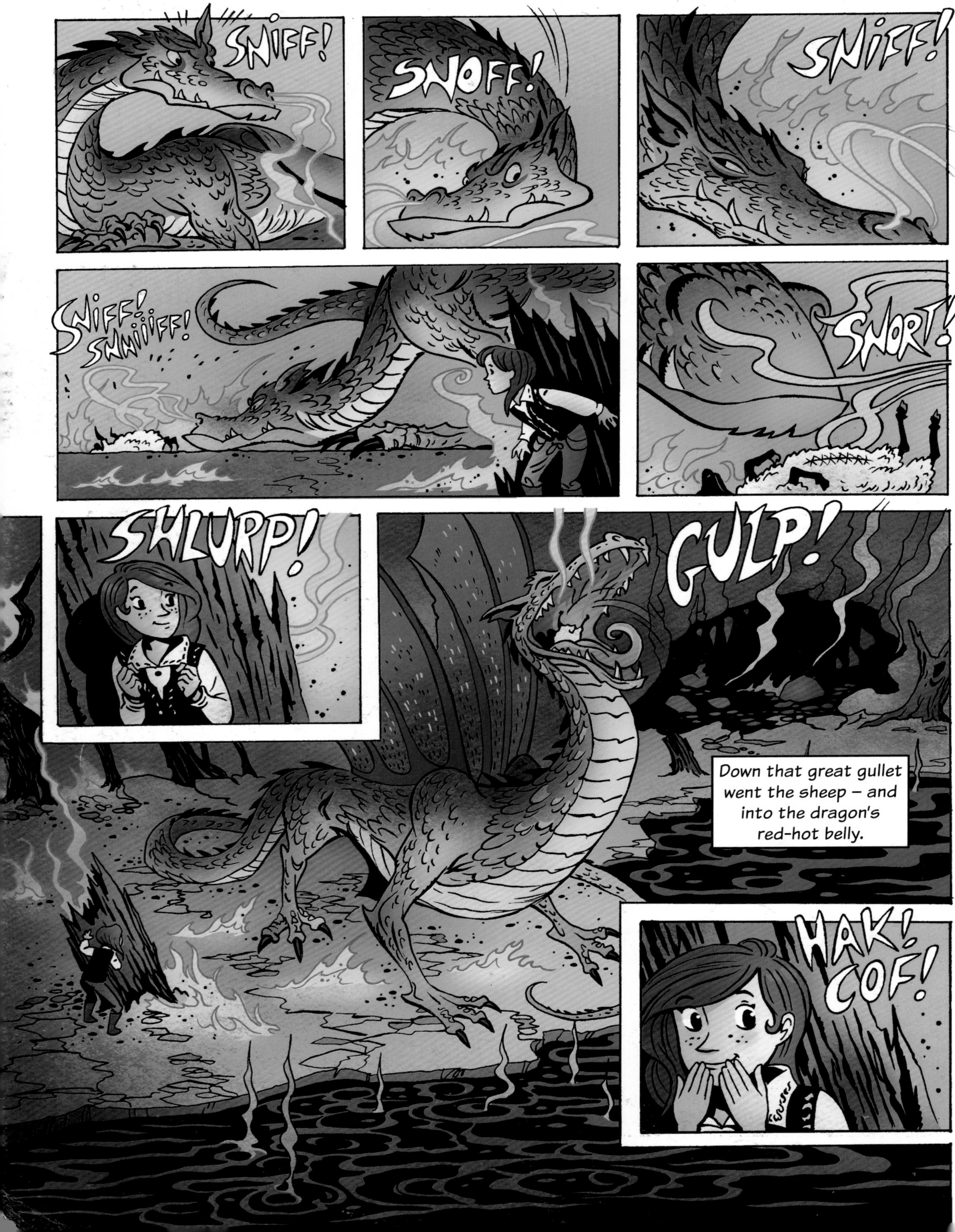
SNIFF!
SNOFF!
SNIFF!
SNIFF! SNNIIIFF!
SNORT!
SHLURP!
GULP!
Down that great gullet went the sheep – and into the dragon's red-hot belly.
HAK! COF!

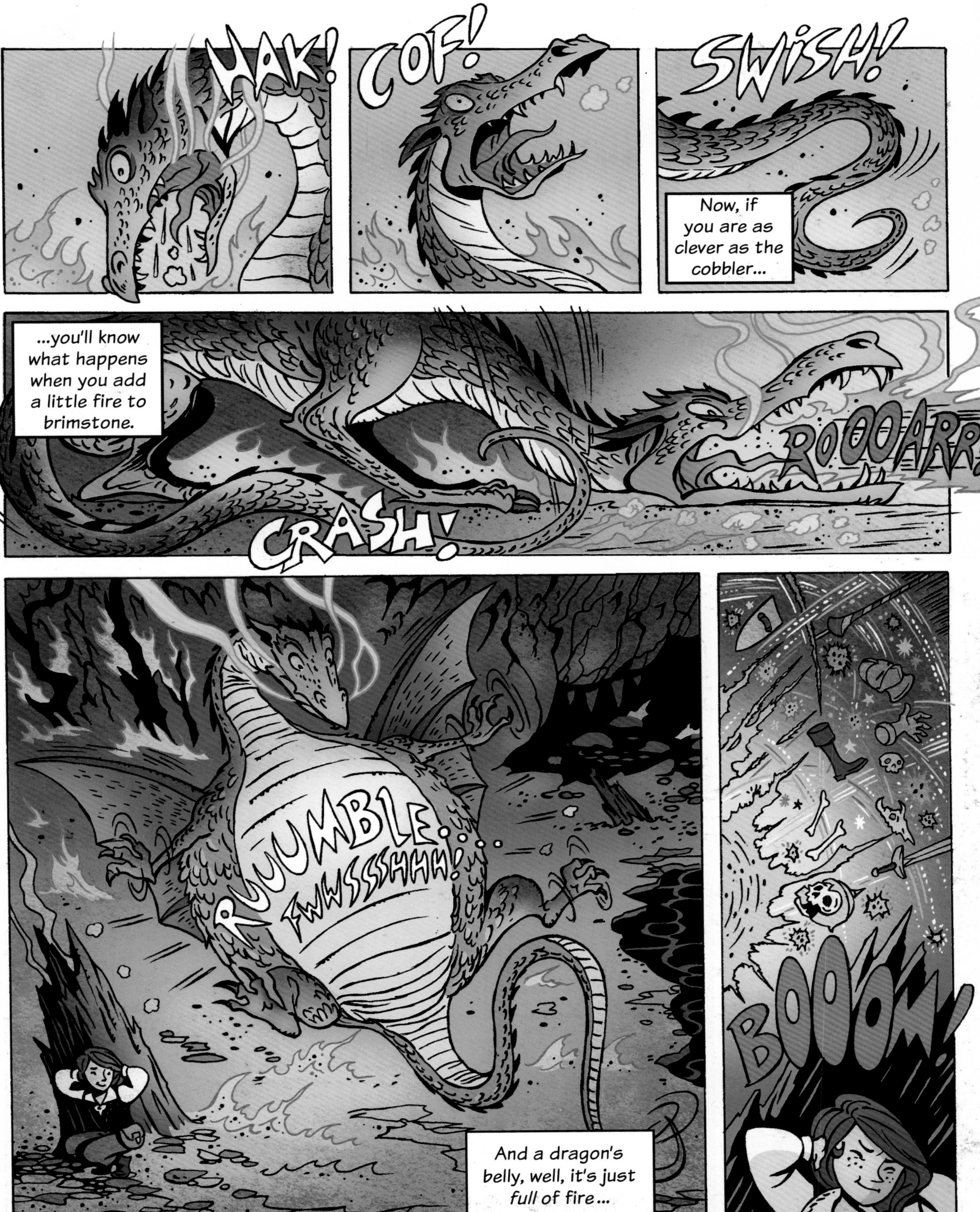
HAK!
COF!
SWISH!
Now, if you are as clever as the cobbler...
...you'll know what happens when you add a little fire to brimstone.
ROOOARR!
CRASH!
RUUUMBLE...
FWWSSSSHHH!
And a dragon's belly, well, it's just full of fire...
BOOOM!

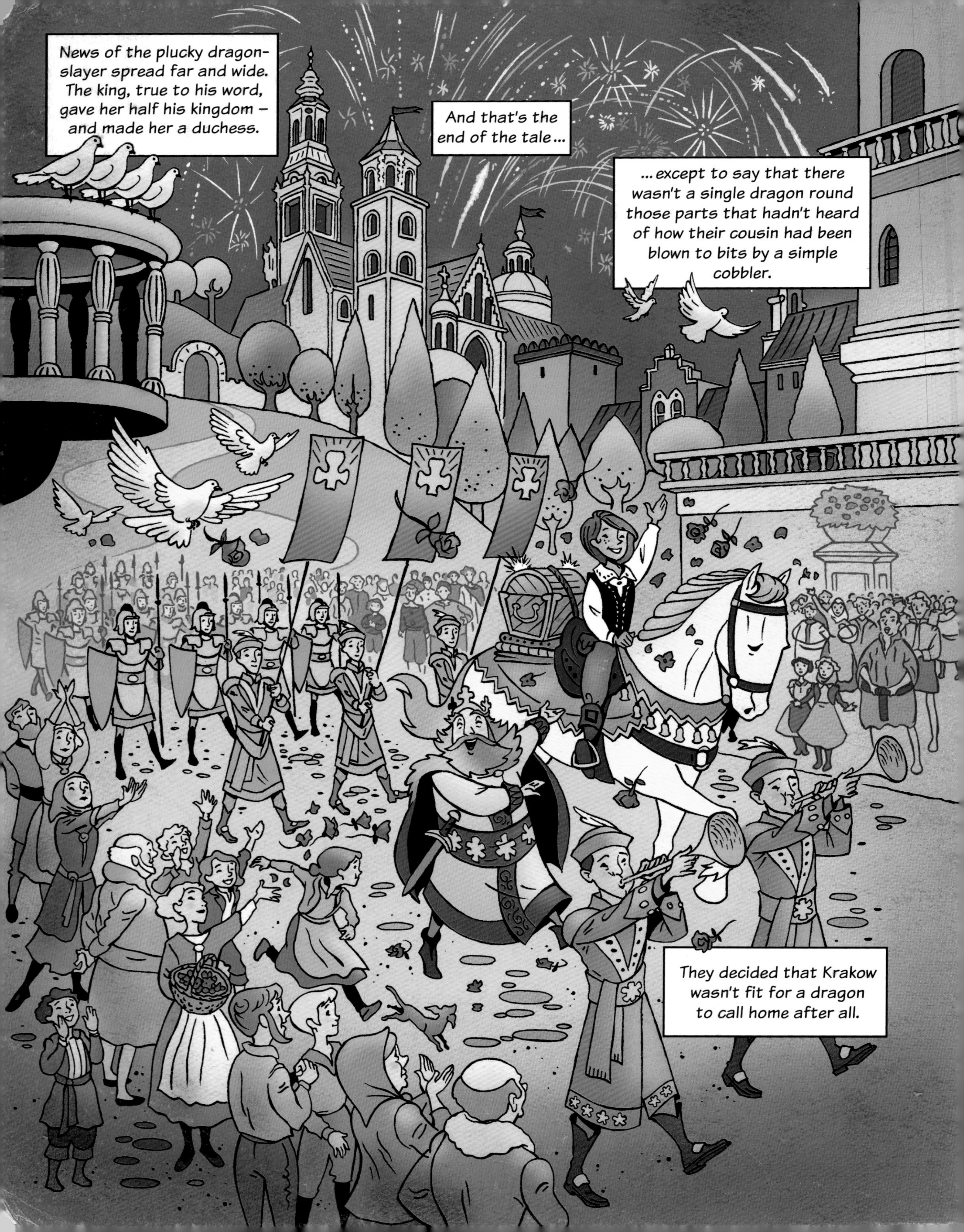
News of the plucky dragon-slayer spread far and wide. The king, true to his word, gave her half his kingdom – and made her a duchess.
And that's the end of the tale...
... except to say that there wasn't a single dragon round those parts that hadn't heard of how their cousin had been blown to bits by a simple cobbler.
They decided that Krakow wasn't fit for a dragon to call home after all.

Acknowledgements

Many hands went into the making of this book, and some thanks are in order...

Firstly, many thanks to Anna McFarlane for embracing these tales, and giving them a home at Allen & Unwin. Thanks also to Elise Jones for her guidance and expertise honing the words until they were just right, and to Sandra Nobes for her keen sense of design and eye for detail.

Many thanks to Latifah Cornelius, who worked long hours lending her sharp inks to 'Momotaro', 'The Devil Bridegroom' and 'Finn McCool'.

Thanks to Carole Wilkinson for generously lending her time and words in preparing the introduction to this book, and to Ted Naifeh for his wonderful endorsement.

Thanks to friend and fellow artist, Marcelo Baez, for creative input, valuable feedback and years of encouragement.

Thanks to Julie and Paul, and to Helena for generosity and support during the production of this work.

And thanks also to the Australian Society of Authors and the Australia Council for the Arts.

About the Author

Craig Phillips is a freelance illustrator, who works for publishers all around the world from his New Zealand studio. His first picture book was *Megumi and the Bear* (written by Irma Gold), inspired by travels to the snowy wonderland of Northern Japan. He has also created rock art posters for bands such as Queens of the Stone Age, DJ Shadow and the Foo Fighters. Craig has always had a great love for mythology and magic, and *Giants, Trolls, Witches, Beasts* is the book he has always wanted to make. On the rare occasions that he is not drawing, you might find him swimming in Lake Taupo or snowboarding down the majestic mountains of New Zealand.